Bogeyman

Jacki Bishop

Early Riser Publishing

Bogeyman

by Jacki Bishop ©2017 Jacki Bishop. All rights reserved.

ISBN: 978-0-9905315-1-7 (Paperback Version)
www.JackiBishop.com jaxstir@gmail.com

Cover Photo: Hank Bishop

Cover Design: Beverly Woods **www.beverlywoods.com**

—

Books by Jacki Bishop

The Seduction of Sarah

Death Sentence

Sarah's Gone Missing

—

This book is dedicated to

Lilia

Landon

Trey

Sophie

Tristan

Naomi

MaryJane

And all of the precious children in the next generation

Acknowledgements

I would like to thank my new editor/ facilitator, Beverly, for her expertise, patience, and willingness to take me through this difficult process.

Thanks to my good friend and mentor, Mary, for taking the time to read/ edit this third book. She and her husband, Lance, have supported all of my literary efforts.

Thank you, Lynn, for encouraging me and reminding me that my readers are *waiting* for my third book.

My husband, Hank, proofreader, tech advisor, and supporter deserves kudos for all he does.

My friends, readers, supporters have my sincere thanks for buying and reading my books.

Thank you, Rik, for helping to get me started on this journey and for all you taught me.

Prologue

The slender young man wearing an orange jumpsuit lay on the floor of the holding cell curled into a fetal position, his arms held protectively over his head. He was bruised and bloody. Mason Rowe was accused of sexually molesting his fiancée's daughter, Rachel.

The beating had happened so fast that by the time the sheriffs reached him, Rowe appeared unconscious. The two ran into the cell, pushing the other inmates aside, intent on checking his vital signs. They called 911 after they carried the injured prisoner out of the cell.

The larger of the two sheriffs directed his glare into the cell and addressed the four defendants.

"Somebody want to own this?" he asked. Silence.

"Okay, your choice," he began, "when you go before the judge today she will be advised that all of you were involved. You wanna' play that game, you can all go down together. You don't give a shit, I don't give a shit!" He turned away from the cell in disgust.

There was no response from inside the cell.

The EMT's arrived in short order and carried the injured prisoner out.

When they left, the other sheriff Jake, said, "No matter, we'll have a look at the security video, see how that shakes out. The camera doesn't lie."

The deputies reversed the disc on one of the cameras, the one with the best over-all view, and sat down to watch, their backs to the cell.

What they saw was disturbing, but not surprising. The two largest guys, white guys with shaved heads and swastika tattoos, were responsible for punching and kicking the prisoner. A smallish black guy appeared to be the lookout, and the fourth, an older black man, sat far from the fracas, head down, with his hands over his face.

The larger sheriff, Bud, spoke to the men in the cell. "You guys don't have to say a word. The judge will see this, come to her own conclusions and act accordingly. Hope you weren't planning on getting out any time soon."

Ignoring the muttered curses, he walked away and addressed the other sheriff, talking quietly, "Jake, I know suspected pedophiles aren't popular, I get that, but what ever happened to 'innocent until proven guilty'?" Bud continued, "As long as I've been here there are still things that shock and disgust me."

"I'm with you, Bud, but I doubt there's more than a handful of sheriffs who'd agree with us. Not to mention the prison guards who turn away when prisoners are beaten or even killed."

"True enough, and it's actually gotten much worse over the years I've been here. It's almost like prisoners, guilty or not, aren't treated as humans. I dunno, I gotta get out of here, I think," Bud said.

"Yeah," Jake replied, "I get it, but who will the new guys like me have to look up to? I know it's tough for you, but don't lose heart, man. Your opinion still matters around here, and people respect you."

"Thanks for that, Jake, I guess I can do something for this guy. I know a lawyer, Rory Chandler. She's smart and she cares; if anyone can help him, she can. I'll give her a call."

Chapter 1

Rory Chandler, private attorney and defender of "lost" causes, and her husband Marc, a forensic psychologist, were on vacation in Ireland, having a long delayed second honeymoon. It was, in fact, the first time they'd vacationed without their twin daughters since they'd been born, and now they were eighteen.

Marc and Rory had jumped at the chance when Marc's nephew, who'd gotten his PHD in History at Trinity College, had decided to stay in Ireland, and was getting married to a young Irish woman he'd met there.

The twins would've liked to go, but they were still in school and when it got out, they would be working as assistant coaches in summer softball camp. They were also rather pleased that their parents trusted them enough to leave them home alone for two weeks.

Actually, this vacation gave Rory and Marc an opportunity to take time to repair their relationship, which had been shaken when Marc revealed a one night stand he'd had in the recent past. They'd been in counseling, which was helping, but their therapist agreed that time for just the two of them could only help. Marc sensed that Rory did not fully trust him, and while he understood, he wondered how long he'd have to pay for his indiscretion.

They were resting in their hotel room after a morning of self-guided tours, when Rory's cell phone rang and she jumped. They'd had only a few calls from the girls, and Rory had made it clear that no one from the office contact her except in an emergency.

"Hello," Rory answered, a mix of annoyance and anxiety in her voice. "Yes, Blake, uh huh, and you think this is an emergency?" Now the annoyance had flared. "Well, there are three attorneys in the office, and if it's that important, assign it to one of them, or take it yourself." Rory listened to his answer and frowned. "So the real reason is that he's a friend of yours and of course you can't take it. How about Sam?" She listened again and her frown deepened.

Marc, who'd been lounging on the bed, sat up and appeared intrigued. A smile played about his mouth. He knew how tempted Rory would be to take this case, especially if it was a tough one.

"Look, Blake, I'm on vacation for another few days and I really don't want to think about any hard-luck case. So, find someone to do the bail hearing, and do not assume I will take the case. We'll talk when I get back. Goodbye."

"Dammit!" Rory exploded. "So Blake's got a friend who's in jail on the charge of child molestation, and I'm supposed to rush back and take over? I've never taken the case of a pedophile, and I don't know that I want to now."

Marc sat up straight, fully engaged now. He had a puzzled look on his face. "You've never defended an accused child molester?"

"No, I haven't." Rory said abruptly. "And I'm not sure I could. The whole idea is repugnant to me."

"I never knew…you've never mentioned it," Marc said, shaking his head. "It's just so out of character for you…"

"What, so now I should feel guilty because I don't deal with pedophiles? I do lots of other cases most attorneys wouldn't touch, and I do pro bono cases."

"Rory," Marc said quietly, "I know that, so it's hard for me to get my head around your refusal to take sex-offender cases."

"I've taken plenty of sex-offenders, just not child molesters!" Rory fired back.

"OK, I'm sure you have your reasons…" Marc began, a puzzled look on his face.

"Damn skippy I do!" Rory folded her arms across her chest, a sign to Marc that the discussion was closed, for now.

Marc got up and went to Rory, putting his arms around her. She stiffened, but Marc continued caressing her. He spoke in her ear. "I'm really sorry you got a call from the office, Blake shouldn't have done that. I hope you can tuck it away, so we can enjoy our last few days here. I love you, and I'm sorry I second-guessed you." Then he said, "What does 'damn skippy' even mean?"

Rory gave a belly laugh, "I have no idea," she said, smiling.

Chapter 2

Blake, Sam and Sarah sat in the office, with glum expressions. They'd all completed law school and obtained their Juris Doctorate. Of the three, Sam was the only one who'd taken and passed the bar in Pennsylvania. Sarah and Blake planned to spend the summer prepping for it. They were still able to practice law in the interim, but most of their time was spent studying.

Blake, who had been the office manager while he went to law school part time, spoke first.

"I guess it was a mistake to call Rory. I've never heard her so angry, well, at least not with me. But Mason's my friend, you guys met him, and he's no pedophile! I just want him to have the best defense, and I'm so accustomed to her taking cases no one else wants. I was so sure she'd take it."

"Has she ever taken the case of an accused child molester?" Sarah asked.

Blake sat, quietly thoughtful. "You know, I can't remember her taking one in the time I've worked for her. But I don't remember her turning one down, either."

"She may feel inexperienced, then," Sam said.

"But for Rory to refuse to take a tough case?" Sarah pondered aloud. "There's got to be something else. I would bet on it."

"We need to get down to business," Blake said. "The arraignment is tomorrow, and I think one of us, rather one of you two, should take it. You can do that without agreeing to take the case. By the way, Chad Forsythe, his boss, has offered to pay all legal fees for Mason."

"Forsythe, of Citadel, the company doing our reconstruction?" Sam asked.

Blake nodded. "He claims Mason's his best foreman. Hey, I'm not questioning it!'

"Ok," Sam said, "I'll be lead council for the bail hearing, and Sarah, if you don't mind helping out?" Sam said.

Sarah, who was engaged to Sam, said, "Well, I guess we need to start collaborating at the office, see how that works out for us." She smiled at Sam.

"But we have worked together, when we interned with Rory last year," Sam said, sounding defensive.

Sarah laughed, "You remember how that worked?"

"Well by the end of the summer, we were friends," Sam said.

"I'm sure we'll be fine, Sam, I'm just saying, we're engaged now, so it's a different situation."

Blake intervened, "OK, Sam, you'll be lead counsel and Sarah will accompany you. I assume you guys agree that I should recuse myself?"

"Absolutely!" Sam replied. "You have to, and also, please don't give us any more information about Mason."

"Oh, sure," Blake said, "I see your point. I'll do my best to avoid interference. And now I think we've talked enough. You need to go out to the prison and meet with Mason. He's in the infirmary wing, still recovering from the beating he took."

"Yeah, I forgot about that," Sarah replied, with a look of distaste on her face. "That's awful what they did to him. But I think pedophiles in general aren't treated well, including by professionals. We need to keep an open mind, so he gets a fair shake."

"Right," Sam agreed. "Let's go out to the prison."

"You should probably stop by the DA's office and get the discovery, what there is of it," Blake suggested.

"Good idea, Blake, how about you call the DA's office to tell them we're on the way," Sarah suggested.

"I'm on it," Blake replied, picking up the phone.

***

Having obtained the pertinent papers from the DA, Sam and Sarah discussed it as Sam drove to the prison.

"There's really not much here," Sarah told Sam as she scanned the paperwork. "It looks as though the DNA evidence was left in semen inside Rachel's vagina; apparently she wasn't fully penetrated," Sarah added, grimacing. "Oh, and the sperm were dead. Now that's a puzzle, I'm sure sperm can live up to two weeks, if I remember my Biology, and she was seen by the doctor the next day."

"I think you're right, Sarah, that's how I remember it, too. I wonder how they'll explain that," Sam mused.

"I doubt it will come up in the bail hearing, so we needn't get ahead of ourselves," Sarah weighed in. Then she said, "Sam, do you feel funny seeing Mason, since we already know him, at least a little, through Blake?"

"I'll be fine with it, Sarah, we've met him only once, but I think we should ask him how he feels."

The edifice of the grey stone prison, rolls of barbed wire topping all the walls, loomed into view. It looked especially unwelcoming with the dark clouds that had been gathering.

Sam killed the engine and went around and opened Sarah's door for her.

"You know we've never been here without Rory," Sarah spoke, with a catch in her voice.

Sam grabbed her hand. "But I'm here, so no worries."

Sarah was actually terrified of closed, locked, spaces since her abduction nearly a year ago. She was drawn into a replay of the events leading up to and including her abduction. Her cheeks were hot with shame as she recalled her affair with a man who turned out to be a drug lord, and her abductor.

Her thoughts were interrupted, as they approached the first gate. Sam still held her hand and gave it a squeeze.

They showed their ID, and were buzzed through three doors before arriving at the infirmary.

The guard posted outside Rowe's room also checked their ID and then knocked on the door, popping his head in to say, "Two attorneys here to see you," as he ushered Sam and Sarah in.

It was difficult for Sarah to look at Mason's injuries; his right eye was swollen shut, his face was bruised and bloodied. His scalp had been shaved to treat extensive cuts, and appeared to have been stitched in spots.

Sam said, "Mr. Rowe, I'm Sam and this is Sarah. I don't know if you remember us, but we work with Blake."

"Yes, of course I remember you," he said, his voice weak. "Blake said something about getting Rory Chandler to take the case. Are you here on her behalf?"

Their initial reaction was silence. Sarah looked at the floor, while Sam answered.

"Rory's in Ireland and won't be home for a few days, so we're taking over the bail hearing tomorrow. There's not much to that hearing, we just argue the case for why you should be released, and that's what we need to talk about."

"We need to ask you first if you feel comfortable with us representing you, since we know you through Blake," Sarah said.

"Hey, I'm happy to have you, I don't know what you charge, but I can't worry about that."

"Actually, your boss, Forsythe offered to pay," Sam said.

Mason did a double take. "Really? How come?" he asked, surprised.

"He claims you're his best foreman and he wants you back on the job," Sam informed him.

"Don't get me wrong, I'm pleased," Mason said, shaking his head. "But he's never told me that."

Chapter 3

Marc and Rory were just pulling up in front of their hotel in Dublin, where they would stay for two days before flying home. Marc hadn't mentioned the name of the hotel to Rory, and waited for a reaction from her.

When she looked away from Christ Church, across the street, she noticed the hotel and burst out laughing. "So you thought this would get me ready to go back to work? Is that your strategy? Jury's Inn, huh?" A small frown creased her brow and then she said, "Actually the jury is still out on this one."

"Hey, I booked this ages ago, thought you'd get a kick out of it."

"It's very funny, I have to admit," Rory smiled. "And I will try my best to put work at the back of my mind until we get home."

"I was also thinking you'd like to walk out the front door and see Christ Church right there."

"It's unbelievable, isn't it, just spectacular! We need to check in and get over to see it."

The doorman helped them to arrange their cases on the cart and they took the elevator to the fourth floor.

On the way up Rory's mind returned to the case that awaited her approval. She thought about the bail hearing, which she thought was today. She couldn't help wondering how it would go.

***

At the same time, five hours earlier in the U.S., Sam and Sarah were looking over the paperwork for Mason Rowe's arraignment. They didn't have much to go on, and it was unlikely that such a high-profile case would meet the burden for bail.

Sam ticked off the reasons that they had come up with: this was Rowe's first offense of any kind, he was employed, (ironically by Citadel Construction, the firm doing the reconstruction of Rory's office) and his employer, Chad Forsythe, had vouched for him as a valued employee, and would keep his job open.

Of course, on the down side, he'd been living with his fiancée, Dara Keene, whose daughter was the victim. He could certainly not return to her house, but he did have his own apartment, which he'd seldom used.

Sighing, Sam gathered up the papers, put them in his briefcase, and nodded to Sarah. "Time to go, we might as well get this over with."

Sarah, normally optimistic, looked glum. "I don't think there's much we can do, Sam."

"In all honesty, I think you're right, Sarah. But we have to give it our best shot."

As they prepared to leave for the short walk to the courthouse across the street, Chad Forsythe emerged from the plastic barrier between Rory's office and the new construction on the other side.

"Are you going to Rowe's hearing now?" he asked.

"Yes, we are," Sam answered briskly.

"Is it ok if I go, too?" he asked. "I could speak up for him…"

"That's good of you, but character witnesses are not put on the stand at this stage. The nature of the offense and the likelihood of the suspect absconding are the main issues to consider in an arraignment."

"But do you mind if I come?" he persisted.

"Yeah, you can come," Sam answered without enthusiasm, "but I need to warn you that it might be a long wait, and frankly, we're not too optimistic about the outcome."

Undeterred, Forsythe joined the couple as they walked the short distance to the impressive courthouse. It took up an entire block and had huge stone columns on either side of the entrance.

Passing through security, the three walked up two flights of marble stairs to the third floor, where the arraignment would take place. Sam indicated that Sarah and Forsythe take seats outside the courtroom, while he went in to find out who would be hearing the case.

Sam came out looking pale, and Sarah had to wonder who the judge was. She got up and motioned for Sam to follow her across the hallway, out of earshot of Forsythe.

"OK, spill it, you look like you ate worms!"

"I'll wish that was my only problem by the time we get out of court. Judge Dickenson is on the bench," Sam sounded beaten.

"I don't think I know that judge, what's the deal?" Sarah asked.

"Oh, jeez, of course you wouldn't know her," he said, his face darkening further. "She's pretty new to the bench and Rory went before her when you were…gone," Sam's voice had lowered almost to a whisper, as if he couldn't speak of it.

There was silence, as each of them recalled the horrific abduction. Sarah still had nightmares, but the therapy was helping. It was also difficult for her relationship with Sam, who'd become too protective of her. It was sweet and wonderful of him, but sometimes she felt like an invalid.

Sarah shook herself back to the present. "So what's this judge like?"

There was anger in his voice when he hissed, "She's a bitch, and our worst nightmare!"

"I think I get the picture." Sarah laughed at Sam's uncharacteristic portrayal. "At least she's not as crazy as Judge Keller!" Sarah reminded Sam of the case they'd worked as interns with Rory. "Or is she?"

"Crazy like a fox, maybe, but no she's just plain mean, and overly impressed with her status. Meanwhile, she wasn't elected to the bench, she was appointed to serve out the term of a judge who retired. We've got her for at least the next two years. She's a political hack is what she is!"

"Well Sam, we weren't really expecting a positive outcome…"

"So we won't be surprised when the wrecking ball drops," Sam finished her sentence.

As they walked back to join Forsythe, the bailiff opened the doors to the courtroom.

"Let's go in and sit in the back," Sarah suggested, leading the way.

They were about to take their seats, when Mason Rowe's case was called.

Surprised, Sam and Sarah walked to the defense table.

Peter Townsend, the DA, took his seat at the prosecution table, and nodded to them in a sort of smirking way, Sam thought.

Sam whispered to Sarah, "That's the same DA we had with her. They're like bookends, no, more like matching gargoyles."

Sarah lowered her head to stifle a giggle. As she raised her head, she saw Rowe stumbling into the courtroom in shackles, supported by two sheriffs, and wearing an orange jumpsuit. His bruises appeared as prominent as they'd been the day before. And now,

Sarah had to fight the tears that threatened.

Hearing some noise from the back of the courtroom, Sarah turned around. Several Citadel employees Sarah recognized from the office had entered and were sitting near Forsythe. He did not look happy.

The bailiff called the court to order and Judge Dickenson said, "The State may proceed."

The DA was on his feet and repeated the charges against Rowe. Then he said, "Your Honor, I can reach no conclusion other than to continue Mason Rowe in prison for the safety of the community and most especially the security of his young victim. His DNA was found inside the victim's vagina. That is perhaps the most powerful evidence available. He was living in the home of this child with her mother, Rowe's fiancée. I would request Your Honor to continue Mason Rowe in prison pending his trial. I would also request that a sex offender evaluation be conducted as soon as possible."

"Thank you, Mr. Townsend. Does defense have anything to add?"

Sam stood and answered the judge. "Yes Your Honor, Sam Logan for the defense. I wish to say that Mr. Rowe has no prior convictions of any sort, is gainfully employed, in fact his employer is present in the body of the court room, and willing to testify on his behalf. Mason Rowe has his own apartment, so would not be returning to his fiancée's home prior to his trial. And with regard to the DNA evidence…"

Without acknowledging Sam's testimony, or allowing him to finish his sentence, Judge Dickenson ordered, "Mason Rowe is to be returned to prison to await trial. A sex offender evaluation is ordered. Case closed." She banged the gavel.

Though not surprised, Sam's face registered shock at the speed with which this judge made her decisions. Most likely she'd made her decision before she entered the courtroom.

As Rowe was escorted from the courtroom, the men in the back, his co-workers, gave him words of encouragement.

Sarah understood why Sam had such a low opinion of this judge. No matter, she thought, Rory will take this case, she *has* to.

Chapter 4

Marc and Rory were embarking on their last day in Ireland. They'd seen Trinity College, with the Book of Kells, among other ancient artifacts. The campus had been bustling, even during summer term. It took Marc back to their college days, when he'd met Rory at Penn State. They'd bonded almost instantly, and had forged a long-term relationship. They had weathered troubles, as did any couple, but his affair, however brief, still hung over them like a dark cloud.

This vacation had been an effort to bring them closer, and it had. It had been very enjoyable. They'd been more intimate during this time than they'd been for a long while. He felt he'd broken through some of Rory's resistance. And if he was honest, things would never be what they once were. But it was better than it had been, and he had to live with that.

Rory emerged from the bathroom, freshly showered. "So, what's left to see in Dublin?" she asked brightly.

"Oh, we can do Dublin Castle, either before or after lunch. Then we can just stroll around, maybe take in the Temple area, even though it's for younger people." He smiled.

"You mean people who stay up later than 10pm?" Rory laughed. They'd certainly gone to bed early on this vacation, but not always straight to sleep. The thought pleased her. Maybe they could get back to the way it was before… In any case, she was ready to work for a better marriage. She was tired of the bitterness she felt.

"We have gotten to bed early," Marc said with a wink. "But we've packed a lot into every day and I think we've really seen Ireland. Don't you love it?"

"I do, and it's funny, but I've never really felt Irish before, and now I sort of do. The people are so welcoming!"

"Oh, I think I see your 'Irish' a lot," Marc joked. He was rewarded with a well-thrown pillow that found its mark on his face.

***

Blake got into the office early. He was feeling twitchy; he wanted everything to be just right when Rory came back. She was due back home tomorrow, but Blake knew she wouldn't come directly back to work. She might come back Friday, he thought. What could he possibly say to make her take Mason's case? Had he remembered to tell her that the sheriff, Bud, he thought was his name was, had called and asked for Rory to take the case? It might have made a difference. He couldn't understand her reaction; perhaps it was because he'd interrupted her vacation. But he felt it was something more.

He got up from his desk and went to look at the renovations, pushing through the heavy plastic curtain separating the two areas. Much had been accomplished since Rory had been gone, but it was still pretty dicey working there with the noise and dust.

And then there was Forsythe. Blake knew how much he wanted Rory to take the case, and he could be a real pain in the ass. He'd have to find a way to get Forsythe to back off.

Blake heard the front door open and hurried back to his desk.

"Hey, Blake, checking out the new offices? How does it look?" Sam asked.

"Morning, Sam, it looks much better, but I wish it had been completed before Rory came back."

"You're worried about her taking Rowe's case, aren't you?"

"Yeah, for sure, and I'm still a little surprised at how angry she was."

"Well, she did give strict instructions…"

"I know, I know, but I just thought she'd be her usual self and welcome a tough case. I think if she just met him…"

"Look, Blake, the last thing we should do is to try and force it on her. She'll push back hard. We just have to give it time…"

"Well, if I were the one sitting in jail, I doubt I'd feel that way!"

"Look, we did our best to get him released. The judge is a harpy!" Sam retorted heatedly.

"I'm not blaming you. I know you were up against it. I just feel bad for my friend, and since Katrina found out, she's been on my case. I think she's going over to see Rowe's fiancée, Dara, today.

She didn't even know why Dara was out of work until I told her. God, can you imagine how Dara feels?"

"Yeah, I get it, Blake, the whole situation sucks! And for the record, Sarah and I will take the case regardless. I know we're not Rory, but…"

"You will? You've talked about it?"

"Yes, we talked about it and we were impressed with Mason. We think he deserves a shot at acquittal," Sam said.

"Hey, thanks! I really appreciate that. At least I can give Trina some good news, and I think you guys can do it."

"One step at a time. I'm a newly minted attorney, and Sarah hasn't passed the bar…"

"But she will! You know that," Blake said

"She will, but taking this case will cut into her study time…"

"Yeah, but think of the experience she'll gain!" Blake enthused.

"Hey look, we've already agreed to take the case. Save the hard sell for Rory!"

***

Blake's fiancée, Katrina, had left a voice message for Dara the night before, and was at home on her day off hoping for a reply. Her heart ached for Dara, and she just didn't know what to think about Mason. She couldn't get her head around the whole thing. Katrina was hurt that Dara hadn't called her, because of their relationship, working together every day in the NICU. And she and Blake often went out with Mason and Dara. She guessed it was hard for Dara to talk about it, but she wanted to help.

She was on her hands and knees, scrubbing the kitchen floor with a vengeance, when her cell buzzed. She nearly knocked the bucket over in her haste to answer it.

Katrina grabbed the phone, heart racing, and saw that the call was from Dara. Sobbing on the other end made her wince.

"Dara, I'm so glad you called! I'm not trying to be nosey. I just want to help you if I can. Do you want me to come over? Do you want to come here?"

Dara finally spoke, "As much as I'd love to come over, Rachel's sleeping, and I haven't been able to leave the house all week. Can you come over?"

"I'll be there as soon as I can pick up lunch for us! Love you."

***

After picking up lunch for Dara and herself, Katrina drove down Front St., past the Courthouse and across from it, the office where Blake worked. She noticed that the construction crew was there, and the truck parked out front advertised Citadel Construction. Hmm, she thought, had Blake told her that the company where Mason worked as a foreman was renovating his office? She didn't remember.

Arriving at Dara's house on Monroe St., she glanced with envy at the big Victorian house Dara had inherited from her parents. One of many Victorians in Media, this one was distinctive for its paint. Katrina knew that Mason had painted the trim with gold, blue, and green paint. He'd seen a similarly painted house in Cape May, NJ, and tried to replicate it. The result was striking.

As much as she envied Dara's house, she didn't envy Dara's situation. It hardly seemed fair; Dara was one of the kindest people she knew. She did her job with compassion and skill, and Katrina had learned so much from her. Working at the neonatal intensive care unit took a special kind of person.

Realizing she was stalling, Katrina grabbed their lunches and exited the car. She was nervous, but had to keep in mind that this wasn't about her. Dara needed someone to listen to her.

When Dara opened the door, Katrina suppressed a gasp. She hardly recognized her friend Dara, whose beautiful, chiseled face was usually animated and radiant. Her normally shiny black hair hung limp and dull around her face. She'd also lost more weight than she could afford, which lent a haggard look to her overall appearance. Her eyes were red and swollen.

Katrina took Dara into her arms and just held her, as Dara began a new round of sobbing. She hugged her tightly, patting her back, as she would a baby. They stayed like this until Dara's sobs subsided.

"I'm sorry…" Dara began.

"Please don't apologize, no need. My God, I can't even imagine what torment you've been dealing with. Thank you for seeing me, I was worried!"

"Thank you for coming. It's been a nightmare and I haven't known which way to turn. But if you're willing to listen, I'll try to tell you what's been going on." Dara looked up with a combination of hope and fear playing across her face.

"That's why I'm here," Katrina said. "Just go ahead."

Dara took a deep breath and sat for a moment, as if collecting her thoughts. "Ok," she began. "Last week, Wednesday, I think, I was home from work and looking forward to a day with Rachel. Mason hadn't stayed over, and Rachel woke me up early. She got into bed with me and we just cuddled. But something about her was different. She was very clingy and much quieter than usual. I felt her head to see if she had a fever and asked her how she was feeling. She said, 'It hurts, down there.' When I asked her to show me where, she pointed to her vagina. When I pulled her panties down and looked, I almost threw up. But I stayed calm as I examined her vaginal area. It was bruised and swollen, I asked her what had happened, if she'd fallen off her tricycle, and she began to cry uncontrollably. Finally she said, 'No, the bogeyman did it. He woke me up and whispered in my ear, and said if I told anyone he visited me he'd hurt you. Please don't tell anyone.' She was terrified and asked me to *promise* not to tell anyone. He'd come before but she hadn't told me. This time he really hurt her. I asked if she recognized his voice and she said 'No,' but explained he always whispered. And it was always too dark for her to see him."

Dara sat back, exhausted. Katrina noticed, however, that some of the color had returned to her face and she looked more animated. "Jesus…what did you do?"

"Well, I became the *nurse*, not mommy, and that made it much easier. I did what I would do with any patient. I told her calmly that I wouldn't tell anyone about the bogeyman and that we had to take her to see the doctor. So, while she was out of earshot, I called the pediatrician and spoke with her, asked if she had access to a rape kit, and arranged for an appointment. Then I called Mason and asked him to meet me at the doctor's office. He seemed genuinely upset and left work to meet us."

"So what did the doctor find from her examination?" Katrina asked.

"She performed the rape kit and notified authorities, and then examined Rachel. She found that Rachel had been penetrated, but only partially. The bruising may have been caused by repeated attempts to penetrate, but after all, Rachel is a tiny girl, she's only three." The anguish of repeating this information prompted a fresh rush of tears, which Dara quickly controlled.

Katrina put her arm around the grieving mother.

Dara thanked Katrina, took out a tissue, wiped her eyes, and then continued. "I sent Rachel to the waiting room to sit with Mason while I spoke with the doctor. She told me that since Rachel is so young, she would probably forget this in time. But she stressed the need for therapy immediately so that this experience did not get suppressed, only to rise up and haunt her later in life. She referred me to a child psychologist, who's seeing her twice a week. She's doing play therapy with Rachel and expects that she will eventually be able to 'act out' with dolls what happened to her. I have to say that Rachel seems so much better already."

"Well, that's a relief!" Katrina said.

"Yes, it is, so on that front things are looking up, and I'm so grateful." Dara continued, "But the next bombshell hit two days ago. Of course, they did DNA testing, and the results came back. Mason had previously offered a sample of his DNA without being asked. Unfortunately, his matched the DNA from the semen in Rachel's vagina. So he was immediately arrested and was supposed to be arraigned yesterday, but he was beaten by other inmates…" Dara couldn't continue.

"Oh God!" Katrina said, as she stayed close to Dara.

When she settled herself, Dara continued, "Mason had stayed here that whole week, helped me talk it through. He played with Rachel, and we were all beginning to heal, and then he was arrested. I'll never forget the look on his face when they cuffed him and took him away. He looked like he'd been hit by a train. He was crying, but tried to be strong for me. He told me not to worry, they would straighten it out because it was a mistake."

"So," Katrina said, "all they have is DNA, right? Any other evidence?"

"None that points to him. The police found that the screen in Rachel's bedroom window was torn so the suspect could gain entry. It had evidently been torn for a while, but since I've had the AC on, the window was closed, but the lock on the window didn't work. I'd been meaning to have Mason fix it," she added, with a look of anguish.

"Anyway, they didn't find any viable prints. Mason didn't stay over the night it happened, because he was playing poker with the guys. He stayed at the host's house after they'd finished because he'd been drinking and was pressured to stay there," Dara said. "But the DNA's a match! That's the holy grail of evidence! What do I do with that? I haven't had the chance to talk with him yet. I don't know if he has a lawyer. I just don't know anything. My only solace is Rachel, and I'm trying to stay sane for her. I just can't think about what's going on with Mason because it's too upsetting."

"A detective came by to interview me," Dara continued. "I think he said his name was Herrera. Anyway, I told him that Mason hadn't stayed over the night of the poker game. I could tell he didn't believe me. He said the other men at the poker game would be interviewed, so maybe one of them could corroborate the fact that he stayed all night elsewhere." She shook her head, looking miserable.

A thought occurred to Katrina and she said, "Dara, it might help you to see a therapist to talk about what you're going through. I think you need to take care of yourself, for Rachel's sake and your own."

"You're right, I should. But I can't leave Rachel."

"I will come over and watch Rachel when you go to therapy. I think you need to go!" Katrina spoke more forcefully than intended, but she got Dara's attention.

"You'd do that for me?" Dara asked.

"In a heartbeat," Katrina answered. "I'll watch her any time you need me to, whenever you need to get away. Now, are you ready for lunch?"

"Do you know what? I suddenly seem to have an appetite! Thanks for listening and for lunch. I should've called you earlier. It helped so much to have someone listen."

Chapter 5

Rory and Marc had bid farewell to Dublin, and were in their seats waiting for takeoff. Rory was ready to go home; she'd grown tired of living from a suitcase. She missed her daughters and her cat, Peaches, who she knew, would punish Rory for leaving. And she really missed her home, and trusted that the girls had taken care of it in her absence.

She felt a twinge of anxiety, and realized that she was dreading going back to work. She would have to face that molester case, and she didn't want to. Unbidden, thoughts of her first cousin came back to her. She and Stella were the same age and more like sisters, since Rory had only a brother and Stella was an only child. The molester was Stella's stepfather, a man who was always disliked by the family, with good reason, as it turned out.

Stella was ten when the abuse began and twelve by the time she told her mother. It tore the family apart, and Rory and Stella lost their friendship for a while. To her aunt's credit, she believed Stella and promptly reported her husband, divorcing him as quickly as possible.

It had been too much for Rory to deal with, especially since her brother Sean, whom she adored, was going through his own hell of substance abuse. Though her parents tried to shield her from both situations, she knew what was going on. Rory's life was changed during this tumultuous time, and she could never forgive Stella's abuser.

Rory came to the present as the plane took off. She was on her way home, with mixed feelings.

Marc held her hand, something he always did at takeoff and landing. It was a touching gesture, and she squeezed his hand in return.

"Penny for your thoughts," Marc said. "Happy to be going home?"

"Yes," Rory said, knowing it wasn't completely true. "I'll be happy to be in our own bed tonight."

"Oh, thinking of bed already?" He grinned, and she smiled back.

"Yeah, I think we should keep going to bed early." She gave him the *look.*

It wasn't lost on Marc. He settled back in his seat, remembering how good the sex had been while on vacation, and fantasizing about the future.

***

Katrina and Dara had finished their lunches. Dara looked much better, Katrina thought. It was always better to talk things out, she believed. And just having someone listen to you was therapeutic. She noticed that Dara seemed pensive.

"Anything else going on?" Katrina asked.

"No, not really…well, I was wondering if you would feel comfortable staying with Rachel for a while today. Please feel free to decline," she added quickly. "But I need to see Mason. The look on his face as he was being hauled off was haunting. I see it in my nightmares. And now, he's been beaten..,"

"Of course I'll stay here with Rachel! I meant what I said, and I think it's important for you to see Mason. So, go get ready!"

Dara rushed to give Katrina a hug. "I can't find words to thank you enough!"

"Not necessary, that's what friends are for. Now, go on, get ready…"

Face flushed, Dara left the room.

Katrina sat thinking. She couldn't imagine what her friend must be going through emotionally. It was as if her whole world was being torn apart. *How does one recover from that, Katrina wondered.*

Her thoughts were interrupted a few minutes later when she heard crying. Realizing it must be Rachel, she hurried toward her room, calling to Dara, "I'll get Rachel, just get yourself together." She heard the whirr of the hair dryer, and doubted that Dara had heard anything.

Walking into the room, she saw Rachel sitting up in her bed, holding onto the side rail. "Hi Sweetie, remember me?"

"Aunt Trina!" Rachel said, smiling. "Out, please," she said.

"OK, you got it," Katrina said, picking her up. "My goodness, you're such a big girl!" she said, tickling her where she knew it would bring a response.

Rachel started giggling uncontrollably, then stopped suddenly, frowning.

"Did I hurt you?" Katrina asked, astonished.

"No," she said, not explaining her distress.

Katrina decided not to probe.

Just then, Dara joined them, dressed and ready.

"Mommy!" Rachel cried, brightening. "Aunt Trina got me out."

"That's wonderful, Honey, how was your nap?" Dara asked, her face relaxing into a smile.

"Yay! I like to see Aunt Trina," Rachel said.

"Well, Aunt Trina is going to stay with you while Mommy goes out."

"OK, Mommy, where are you going?" she asked.

"I'm going to see Mason, because he's sick," Dara answered.

"Can I go, too? I miss him!" Rachel said, frowning.

"I wish you could, Honey, but no kids are allowed. I'm sorry."

"Why not? I really, really want to go!"

"I know you want to go," Dara said sympathetically. "And I wish you could, but there are rules, just like we have at home and at daycare."

"Okay, tell him I love him and come home soon," the little girl said, her face crumpling.

"I will promise to do that, and I know he misses you very much, too. Now, how about a hug for me and one I can give to Mason," Dara said.

Rachel closed the distance between herself and her mother, opening her arms for a hug, and then giving her one for Mason. "See you soon, Baby, I love you. Now be the best girl for Aunt Trina."

"Yes, Mama," Rachel said, using her fondest name for her mother. "Bye, bye."

Dara gave Trina a hug before she left, whispering, "Wish me luck."

"You got it, my dear. Go on now."

Dara hurried across the street to where she'd parked her car. Looking around, as she always did now, she saw a man in a nearby alley turn abruptly and walk away down the alley. It gave her the creeps, but she thought it was probably nothing, just her imagination in overdrive.

***

The bogeyman hurried down the alley. This was the first he knew of Rowe's woman leaving the house without Rachel. Thoughts of Rachel and being with her were pushing out all other thoughts. Might she be taking a nap? Could he possibly get into her room without being noticed?

Before the voice of reason could take over, he found himself crossing the street and walking around to the back of the house. Stopping outside of Rachel's room, he saw with dismay that the torn screen had been removed, replaced by a storm window. There was a new lock on the inside window.

Face turning red, he balled up his fists in frustration.

***

Nearly a half-hour later, Dara pulled up in front of the prison. She'd been thinking obsessively about the man in the alley, and had gotten lost on the way. She'd never been to the prison and it certainly was not a welcome sight. The dull gray stone fortress was encircled by about a thirty-foot fence topped with barbed wire. There were watchtowers at each corner, armed apparently with sharpshooters. And this wasn't even a maximum-security prison.

Dara gave herself a mental shake and focused on the mission at hand. She needed to talk with Mason, to look him in the eye and to know for sure whether or not she could trust him.

She went through the main entrance and was buzzed through several doors. Before Dara reached her final destination, she was instructed by the guard, "Arms up," as she patted her down thoroughly. "Put your purse and any other belongings in the locker," she informed Dara, pointing to an open locker, which she closed and locked, the sound echoing off the walls.

Feeling somewhat anxious and stripped of her identity, she followed the guard down the hall. She could only imagine how much worse it must be for Mason.

The place reeked of disinfectant, but it could've been a worse smell, Dara thought, though her eyes smarted from the fumes.

Soon they arrived at the infirmary. There was an armed guard at Mason's door, probably for his protection, Dara reasoned. Her escort spoke to the guard, telling him that Dara could stay for ten minutes and then she would be back to get her.

The guard on duty at the door ushered her into the room, saying, "Rowe, you have a visitor."

Dara walked to the side of the bed as Mason turned over to see who it was.

Dara felt sick, when she saw his injuries. One eye was swollen shut and he had lacerations on his face, his arms, head and basically every part of him not covered by his hospital gown.

She reined in her emotion and spoke quietly to him. "Hi Mason, I've missed you. I didn't want you to think I'd deserted you."

"I wouldn't blame you if you did," he spoke with difficulty through swollen lips. "I keep wondering what you can possibly think, what with the evidence. I don't know what to think myself."

"I can't believe it," Dara said simply. "My whole world has been upside down since you left. And I can't even imagine how it's been for you."

Mason spoke again, "I didn't do it, Dara. I can't imagine how my DNA was on Rachel. It sickens me. And I don't know what to do about it."

After a few moments of silence, he said, "Oh, by the way, Sam and Sarah, Blake's friends, they're lawyers, and they took my bail hearing yesterday. Obviously I didn't make bail, I'm still here. But they said it wasn't unusual, with the charges."

"I'm sorry, I didn't know about the hearing…"

"It's just as well, nothing good happened. The judge was very nasty, but Sam said it was unlikely I'd get her again."

"Well, I'm glad you have attorneys, I hope it works out for you," Dara said. "Katrina came to see me today, and I did a lot of talking, too. I feel much better. She's staying with Rachel, who asked me to tell you she loves and misses you. And I have a hug from her, but I'm not sure I'm allowed to hug you."

Mason shook his head and his eyes filled with tears. "Tell her I love her, that's about all I can say for now," he added, swallowing hard. "And I hope you know how much I love you," he said looking at her.

There was a knock on the door and the matron said, “It’s time to go.”

Dara looked at Mason without blinking. Her emotions were in turmoil, and her thoughts were racing. She believed Mason; not to believe him would make a mockery of their almost two years together, and her world would spin totally out of control. But she knew in her heart it would take some time before the terrible doubt went away. She blew him a kiss, and left the room, tears streaming down her face.

Chapter 6

Rory was sleeping, something Marc envied, since he could never sleep on the plane. He was left with his thoughts. Marc was still stymied by Rory's reaction to representing a pedophile (alleged, he reminded himself). To his knowledge, she'd never refused a controversial or difficult case.

This guy was a friend of Blake's, and Blake vouched for him. Marc knew Rory, and he knew that she couldn't be pushed into doing something she didn't want to do. Nor would she voluntarily talk about her reason for the refusal. An idea began to emerge, and the more he thought about it, the more he liked it.

Marc decided that he would do a sex-offender evaluation on the guy, on his own, pro bono. If he were convinced of this guy's innocence, he would offer it to Blake or whoever ended up representing the defendant. Almost chuckling aloud, Marc thought about how curious Rory would be, and he guessed that she wouldn't be able to keep her hands off the case.

Of course, there were lots of 'ifs', and the first hurdle was that the evaluation would give a clear picture of 'innocence', to the degree that was possible. Sometimes he had a visceral reaction of repugnance before he even began the testing, and he thought he was good at assessing this group of sex offenders. If he had any suspicion of guilt, he wouldn't hesitate to recommend they not take the case.

Looking at his watch, he realized he was still on Ireland time. He mentally subtracted five hours and changed the time on his watch. They were due to land in less than an hour. Marc leaned against the little airplane pillow, and dozed off.

***

Sarah and Sam sat in Rory's office strategizing about Rowe's case. They realized that it was based on DNA evidence, and many prosecutors and defense attorneys believed that made the case.

Sarah had just reread the file from the DA's office. "I don't know a lot about DNA evidence, but as I've said before I have a feeling that the sperm should not have been dead. The report also mentions 'an unknown substance' that was found in the vaginal area. Why didn't they bother to find out what that substance was?"

"I'm guessing," Sam said, "because they believe the DNA sews up the case. So, we'll have to play on their weakness. It looked like a sloppy report to me."

"You know," Sarah replied, "if Marc is willing to work with us 'unofficially', that is, without Rory's knowledge, he could surely enlighten us on these issues."

"Good call, Sarah," Sam smiled. "Why don't you phone him, like tomorrow? I think they're getting in later today."

"I will," Sarah said. "I don't think he'll have a problem helping us out."

"In the meantime," Sam said, looking at the report, "We need to come up with some ideas on our own. I think the guys at the poker game the night of the molestation need to be interviewed. The report names the other men, and apparently they were questioned. But the report doesn't include those interviews. The guys who were there-- Jordan Kraft, the host, James Quinn, Gordon Howe, and Alistair Caldwell-- should be questioned by us. We can split them up, question them about the evening, their relationship with Rowe, and anything that could shed light on the situation."

"I'm all for that," Sarah answered, "I think we should start ASAP."

"Not quite so fast," Sam cautioned. "First, we might consider what specific questions we want to ask, and make sure we're on the same page."

"You're right, so let's get started. Maybe we should brainstorm, and just write down all the ideas, and then refine it. What do you think?"

"Good, idea, Sarah, let's have at it."

"I'll write the ideas down, so don't go too fast," Sarah said, getting a legal pad and a pen.

"How long have you known Mason Rowe? How did you meet? Do you play poker together regularly?" Sam dictated his questions.

"Ok, I got all that," Sarah said. "How about, 'Have you ever been to Rowe's home? Do you know Rachel and Dara?' "

"Good, good, here's another one, 'Why did Mason stay over after the game? Whose idea was it?' "

Sarah continued writing until they had a list of about twenty questions. "Enough!" she said. "Now let's go through and edit."

They spent another half-hour honing the list of questions they wanted to ask the four men who'd been at the poker game. When the list was complete, Sam suggested, "It's only ten thirty, we can take the first two on the list and interview them before lunch. We can ask Forsythe how to contact them. Didn't Blake say they all worked together?"

"Yeah, that was my impression," Sarah said. "So why don't you go ask where the first two are today?"

Sam grimaced, but pushed his way through the construction curtain to find Forsythe. Moments later he came back.

"So?" Sarah asked.

"So, he's always here when you don't want to see him, but now he's out. He did give me his card, so I guess I can call him." Sam fumbled in his pocket and came out with a card, then took out his cell and made the call.

Sarah watched as he scribbled the info from Forsythe. When he'd disconnected, Sarah went to look at the paper.

"OK, I'll go visit Kraft, I know the state park," she announced.

"Yeah, because God forbid you get lost!" Sam smiled as he thought about their first argument, which occurred when they'd gotten lost.

"Oh boy, that was fun! But you know I still have some issues about getting directions right. I do know where Jordan lives, though."

"See you back here before lunch, and call if anything comes up, ok? Are you ok going alone?"

"Yup, I'm fine." Sarah said with impatience in her voice. "Oh and let's leave our cards so they can call us if they think of anything, at least that's what the cops do."

"It's a good idea, Sarah." Sam bent down to give her a kiss. "See you back here later," he said, with a look of concern on his face.

***

Jordan Kraft was off this particular day, so Sarah went to his home in the state park. It wasn't as easy to find as she'd expected. She thought she knew the trail well, having walked it every day for several months. She was a bit unnerved about going to his home alone, no doubt another vestige from her kidnapping. But at the same time, she was relieved that Sam hadn't insisted on going with her, and it surprised her. He'd been dogging her almost constantly since the kidnapping. He did it out of love of course, but it could be stifling. She had to get her moxie back, and this was a good start. She found the place, set far back from the bike trail at the top of a long winding driveway.

Parking the car and walking up to the front door, she squared her shoulders and rang the doorbell.

The sound was still echoing when the door swung open.

"Hi, I'm Jordan Kraft." He held his hand out and Sarah shook it. "The boss told me to expect someone, but he didn't mention it was a beauty queen." He flashed a smile revealing bright white teeth, his smile lighting up his face. He was tan, lean and extremely handsome, with dark curly hair and bright blue eyes. Sarah was pretty sure he knew it and used it.

She tried her best to ignore her embarrassment, but she felt her cheeks grow hot. "Thank you for seeing me on your day off," she said briskly, attempting to set a business- like demeanor.

"No problem," he said easily, ushering her to a comfortable chair, and taking a seat across from her.

He seemed very relaxed, but she would have to watch and see how he reacted to her questions.

"I'll try not to take up too much of your time," Sarah said. "I'm sure you know this is about Mason Rowe's arrest, and I understand he was at your home, and in fact stayed overnight, the night of the assault."

"That's true," Kraft said, looking appropriately somber.

Sarah asked several of the questions she and Sam had discussed. Then she asked what she thought of as the most important question. "Can you tell me why he stayed the night, and who decided it should happen?"

"Hmm," Jordan looked thoughtful. "It appeared he'd had too much to drink, which was unusual for Mason. I made the final decision, but I don't recall who suggested it first."

"Do you know that he stayed all night, or is it possible that he left some time during the night?"

"I can't answer that with any certainty. I stayed up for about a half hour when the guys left, to clean up. He didn't move during that time. And the next morning, Mason was difficult to rouse, and hadn't appeared to have moved. His car was parked right out front in the same spot, I'm pretty sure. But I should mention that I'm a heavy sleeper, so if he'd left during the night, I probably wouldn't have heard it." He gave a whistle, and a large Great Dane trotted into the room and sat at his feet. "And apparently, according to my neighbor, I don't even hear Riley if he barks when I'm asleep." He scratched the dog's ears and said, "Go see Ms. Sarah."

Riley trotted over to Sarah obediently, offering his paw.

"Well, Hello, Riley," she said, patting his head, as he thumped his tail. "He's a real sweet dog," she said to Kraft.

"He is a love, but make no mistake, if I sic him on someone, he does the job. He's smart and was easy to train," Kraft added.

Referring to her list of questions, she asked Kraft a few more. His responses were adequate, but he'd already answered the most important question. Unfortunately this was not the alibi witness she'd hoped for.

Sarah looked at her watch, and said, "Much as I'd love to stay and play with Riley, I need to get going. Here's my card, in case you think of anything else. And thank you for seeing me."

"My pleasure," Kraft said, accepting her card, with another winning smile.

Chapter 7

It was noisy at the Seven Stones Café when Sarah and Sam arrived for lunch. Normally most of the patrons would be eating outside, but because of the uncomfortable heat and humidity, they were all inside.

Sarah had her heart set on one of their delicious wraps, or they'd have left to seek out another eatery. There were many from which to choose in Media. It had become 'the place to be', with real estate values rising, and businesses doing a brisk trade, Rory had told her. Sarah was glad she and Sam were sharing the rent in a charming apartment, on the second floor of an old Victorian house.

Now she said to Sam, "Let's get this to go so we can actually talk over lunch."

"Good idea." Sam smiled.

As soon as their sandwiches were ready, the two left for the office. Unwilling to begin the conversation about their interviews, they walked quickly and in silence.

At the office, the front door was unlocked and they greeted Blake as they entered, surprised to see him there.

"Thought you were working from home today, we could've gotten you lunch if we'd expected you to be here." Sam said."

"I had lunch at home. It's Katrina's day off and I couldn't get any studying done. It felt like I was being questioned by the Gestapo! She just has to have her hand in everything, and wants to give me 'advice' on Mason's case. She doesn't grasp the concept that I have recused myself from the case. So *please* don't give me any information about the case; I might crack under pressure!"

Sam and Sarah were chuckling at Blake's dramatic speech.

"Hey, you think I'm kidding? Promise me you won't tell her anything if she tries to pump you!"

"I promise!" Sarah said as she put her hand over her heart.

Sam said, "No worries! We'll be working in Rory's office, so don't let me find you skulking around outside of it. And don't put through any calls from Katrina!"

"You guys still think it's funny," Blake grumbled as they closed the door to Rory's office.

At that moment, Forsythe came through the curtain from the construction area.

"Did I just hear Sam and Sarah come in? I wanted to ask them how the interviews went. I forgot who they interviewed…"

Blake tried to hide his annoyance as he answered, "They did just come back, and they went into Rory's office, asking not to be disturbed. And I don't know who they interviewed. I'll give them your message."

"Oh, ok," Forsythe said, still standing there.

"And, I've recused myself from the case because Mason's my friend, so I know nothing," Blake said, hoping Forsythe would take the hint.

"OK, do you have any idea what time they'll be done?" Forsythe persisted.

Blake shrugged his shoulders, feeling the annoyance bloom. "Couldn't say, but I will give them your message," Blake said, with more emphasis than was necessary.

"Thanks," Forsythe said as he ambled towards the construction site.

Blake scribbled a note to Sam and Sarah, "When you come out of Rory's office, go stealth, Forsythe's waiting to pounce." And he slipped it under their door.

Sam heard the whoosh of paper, and picked up the note. Scanning it, he laughed and handed it to Sarah.

"Oh Jeez! Not that bore-ass again! What's up with that?'

"You've heard of 'micro-managing'? Imagine what it must be like working for him!"

"I can't, we're really lucky to be working for Rory. And I can't wait for her to come back."

"Ditto," Sam replied. "Now we need to get back to work."

"Well, I've told you generally about Kraft. He was a little cagey, especially when I asked him how they knew each other, and he said it was at Citadel. But he also said he'd known him for eight years, and Mason's only been at Citadel for four."

"That's funny," Sam said, referring to his notes, "Gordon Howe said he'd known him for about eight years, too. Coincidence?"

"It will be interesting to see what the others say. Maybe we should see the other two tomorrow?" Sarah queried.

"That's probably a good idea. That way they won't have much time to get their stories straight, if that's what they're doing," Sam added.

"Well, I could understand if they were. Who'd want to be implicated in a case this serious?"

"But, if they're innocent, why worry?" Sam wondered aloud.

***

The bogeyman was in a state. So far, the arrest and incarceration of Rowe had gone as planned. But now, he thought maybe it had gone awry. He'd assumed that Rowe would be out on bail, but that hadn't happened, so any new cases involving children couldn't be blamed on him. The bogeyman hadn't counted on that.

He would just have to improvise, and be cautious. With a tug of regret, he'd realized, after yesterday's futile visit, he couldn't go back to Rachel, and she'd been such a tasty morsel! People just didn't understand how seductive little girls were. And they invited the attention he gave them.

Finding another little girl, she would have to be nine or under, young, but not too young, might be difficult, but not impossible. He had groomed many a young girl, and they'd grown attached to him. Foster children were particularly vulnerable, as were children whose parents didn't keep close tabs on them.

He would find someone, and soon.

***

Sam and Sarah were still in Rory's office discussing the interviews when Blake put a call through.

"I think you'll want to take this one," Blake said mysteriously.

Sarah picked up, "Hello?" She listened, her face working its way into a smile. "Marc, welcome home! I think you just made our day!"

Chapter 8

On their first day home Marc woke up early, filled with a sense of urgency. He wanted to leave the house before Rory awoke, so he didn't have to prevaricate. He hated lying to Rory, and besides she usually got the truth out of him anyway.

Dressing quietly after his shower, he glanced at Rory. She appeared to be in a deep sleep, which was good. He was soon dressed and headed downstairs to quiet the girls as they rattled around in the kitchen.

He kissed the twins, Alex and Kate when he entered the kitchen. "Your mom is still sleeping, so let's not wake her. In fact, why don't we go out for breakfast? Can you spare the time?"

The girls looked at each other, smiling. "Sure, why not?" Kate said. "The kids have been straggling in later every day, so let's do it!"

It being late June, the girls had begun their jobs as assistant coaches at softball camp.

"Good," Marc said. "We can leave the car home for your mom, and one of us can pick you up later."

"Or we can get a ride home," Alex added.

"Then, off we go!"

"Dad, aren't you forgetting something?" Alex asked.

"Oh, yeah, a note for your mom…"

"You're looking a little guilty today, Dad," Kate pointed out.

"I'll explain over breakfast, now can we go?"

***

Over an hour later Rory began to show signs of waking. She was dreaming, and in the dream she heard a lawn mower. It seemed close by. Marc must be mowing the lawn. The persistent sound finally brought her close to consciousness. Turning in the direction of the noise, she found herself looking at a furry mass. Her cat, Peaches, had been purring up a storm next to her ear.

"Oh you sweet thing, I missed you too!" she cooed, hugging the cat to her chest.

She reached over to find Marc and found an empty, cold bed. She sniffed the air for coffee, and detecting none, Rory rolled over, still sleepy. But soon the silence got to her and she had to get up and investigate.

Marc had left the room, and hadn't closed the door, thus the appearance of Peaches. She was normally left outside the room because of her penchant for close purring.

"I'm sure no one fed you, Sweetie, but I will." Sitting up in bed, she felt nauseous. It was hot in here, had no one thought to turn on the air? She flopped back onto her pillow, but it was too hot to go back to sleep. Right now she wished she were back in Ireland, where it had been cool all the time. She could put up with the rain, because it wasn't hot and humid. The Irish complained about having no summer, and she told them to come to Philadelphia one summer and then they could appreciate their weather.

Rory made another attempt at sitting up, but she still felt groggy and dizzy. A shower was what she needed. Stumbling into the bathroom, she almost tripped over the mound of wet towels Marc had left on the floor. So, he must've gone out if he showered. She didn't remember him saying anything about it last night. But she'd been so tired she'd fallen into bed and gone to sleep instantly.

The warm spray felt good, and it was nice to be back in their own bathroom, where she knew how to operate the faucets and she didn't have to wait forever to get hot water. She had found the plumbing in Ireland inadequate. God knew, they had plenty of water, but the toilets rarely flushed on the first try, and the showers took an age to get warm.

Rory stepped out of the shower feeling better, but her stomach wasn't right. Maybe it had been those "full Irish breakfasts", featuring three kinds of meat, and baked beans, of all things! She'd settled for fruit and yogurt after a few of those breakfast marathons. But she'd had one before they left yesterday, since she wasn't fond of airplane food.

Dressing in shorts and a tank top, Rory headed downstairs, Peaches close enough to lick her legs. "Ok, now I'll feed you, I promise!" Peaches chirped her reply.

The first thing she did was to switch on the air. The temperature in the house read 78. Jeez no wonder she felt sick! She punched in 70, and went to look for cat food. There was one can left, and it looked as though the girls had done no shopping in the two weeks they'd been gone.

She opened the can and fed Peaches, who practically inhaled the food.

Seeing a note on the table, Rory picked it up and read. "Didn't want to wake you, so I took the girls out for breakfast. I'll be working in the 'burbs today, something came up. I should be home for lunch. I left the Prius so you can go shopping. Love, M."

"Well, that tells me nothing," she muttered, suddenly feeling abandoned. She'd spent so much time with Marc over the past few weeks, so she wasn't really accustomed to beginning her day without him. They had fallen into the habit of discussing the days' plans over coffee. Speaking of which, where was it?

The cabinets appeared empty of anything other than soup, pasta, and some other canned goods. The girls had scarfed anything worth eating and hadn't replaced a thing. There was no coffee to be found! That did it, she was pissed! And now she would have to go shopping without any coffee. She'd go to Trader Joe's where they gave samples of coffee. She wouldn't need a list, they needed everything, she thought angrily.

***

Marc had spent nearly two hours evaluating Mason Rowe. He'd interviewed hundreds of alleged pedophiles, probably half of them innocent. He trusted his gut by now, and often had strong feelings one way or the other about their guilt or innocence. Very few of the people he'd evaluated had been particularly forthcoming, nor did they welcome the evaluation.

Mason Rowe was the exception. He welcomed the opportunity to speak and he thanked Marc several times for seeing him. He appeared to be authentic. His answers were quick and to the point. He passed all the tests with flying colors, even answering the built in 'lie detectors' correctly.

Marc found that this was a guy who was suffering because of the allegations and was seeking an explanation. Rowe was also very smart. Marc had sensed as much, so employed a short-version IQ test. Mason tested close to the 'Genius' range, which didn't surprise Marc. Rowe's education included two years at MIT, after which he was forced to leave because both parents were killed in a car crash.

Of course his high intelligence meant that Rowe could've easily manipulated the evaluation and the evaluator. Somehow it didn't feel that way, but Marc had to consider it was a possibility.

Rowe deserved and needed a top-notch attorney. The case against him was based solely on DNA evidence, and the report was sloppy. The dead sperm in the sample was a red flag, which had been ignored. Marc had encountered many such cases and knew there were ways to leave bogus DNA evidence. Rory *had* to take this case, and Marc would be right by her side. But he couldn't overplay his hand.

***

Rory arrived home with the groceries a few minutes before Marc. She was struggling with three bags, when he pulled up behind her and jumped out to help.

"Let me get that," he urged, grabbing at a bag. She pulled away and the bag dropped, sending the groceries in all directions. She stormed into the house without a backward glance, leaving him to clean up the mess.

Oh boy, he thought, I'm in for it now. She either found out what I did this morning or, who knew what? He'd be paying for this for a while.

There were three fully packed bags of groceries left in the car, and he grabbed them all, ready to begin his penance.

He helped Rory put away the groceries, and endured a scowl when he put something in the wrong place. But he soldiered on, watching carefully and taking Rory's lead.

When everything was in place, she said, "You can help yourself to whatever you want for lunch; there's food in the house again!" And she flounced off.

He shrugged, thinking, *Hell if I know what's pissed her off*, and got himself some lunch. He toyed with the idea of making her lunch, but decided against it. He had work to do.

As soon as he'd finished lunch, leaving dirty dishes in the sink, he went into his office to type the evaluation, closing the door a tad harder than usual. He knew he was being petty, but two could play at this game.

Rory had gone to her bedroom. She was furious, she felt nauseous, and she just wanted to cry. Was anything going her way? Or was she being overly emotional? She wondered. She hadn't felt this way since… oh God, since she was pregnant with the twins.

***

Dara had just gotten Rachel up from her nap, when a loud knock echoed down the front hall. Since she wasn't expecting anyone, she felt anxious. Looking through the peephole, her anxiety rose. It was her ex-husband, whom she hadn't seen for several months. The last she knew he was in another halfway house upstate.

She slowly opened the door. "Hello, Paul, how are you?"

"How am I? You have to ask? My daughter's been molested by your live-in boyfriend, and you wonder how I am? Did you think about letting me know? I had to get a call from a stranger to find out!"

Chapter 9

It was suppertime, and all the kids whose parents cared had been called in. One lone girl remained on the playground. She was on a swing, which she moved side to side, in an apparent attempt to twist and twirl.

The bogeyman stepped out from under a tree and looked around. Seeing no one, he put a pleasant smile on his face and approached the girl.

"HI," he said, "do you need some help twirling?"

"Yes, I do," she said shyly, looking up at him.

"OK, get ready!" he enthused.

After several twirls, he slowed down the swing. "You'll get dizzy, you need a rest. What's your name?"

"I'm Carly," she said quietly, turning her eyes up to look at him.

"Why that's very close to my name, you can call me 'Charlie'," he said. "Why don't you come and sit on the bench with me?" He sat and patted the spot next to him. She came over and sat beside him.

"That's better, Sweetie," he said, putting his arm around her. He started stroking her face and playing with her hair. "Does that make you feel sleepy?" he asked.

"A little bit," she said, putting her head on his shoulder.

His excitement began to build; she was so responsive! He had to forcibly control himself, despite his growing erection. "Maybe you'd like to sit on my lap?"

She nodded, so he shifted her over to sit directly on top of his erect penis. If that troubled her, she didn't show it. The thought occurred to him that she'd done this before. She seemed to know the ropes. He began to bounce her on his lap, feeling elated and almost out of control.

The bogeyman felt, rather than saw, someone watching. He froze, losing his erection. When he turned around he saw a man he knew, someone he worked with, across the street, staring at him.

Putting the little girl down, he said, "I think you should go home for supper, but I'll meet you here the same time tomorrow." He got up and left, crossing the street.

***

Rory had ordered take-out for dinner, because she just didn't feel like cooking. She was pretty pissed at everyone. When she heard Marc leave to pick up the girls, she went out to get the food.

As planned, they returned before she did, and when she came into the kitchen with the food, the three were standing around looking lost.

"Hi, Mom," Alex said, giving her a kiss. "Is that dinner?"

Rory nodded.

Kate took the bait, and said, "Gee, we were all hoping for one of your great home cooked meals!"

"I'm not sure why, because there was not a smidgen of food in the house! It might've been nice…" She left the sentence dangling and stormed off.

Marc shrugged. "She was pissed at me when I got home and offered to help her carry the groceries, go figure…"

"It's not tough to figure, if you think about it," Alex said. "We used up all the food while you were away and didn't think to replace it. Then we left for breakfast, and she got up to an empty house with no food or coffee. I think she feels we take advantage of her."

"I guess, but I don't know why she was pissed with me," Marc said. "I left her a note."

"Well, you took us out for breakfast without asking her, and when she got up, well, you can imagine…" Kate said.

"Whatever," Marc said, "since she got the food, let's eat!"

They got their drinks and took the food to the nook. There were two pizzas in the bag.

"She didn't get herself a salad," Alex noticed. "Maybe she's sick. I feel bad," she said.

Silence fell as the three of them began to eat the pizza.

To break the monotony, Kate said, "How did the eval with that guy go? The one you went to see at the prison?"

"It went really well, and I'm glad I saw him. I have a gut feeling that he's ok. I think he needs a good attorney…"

Marc turned in the direction the girls were staring, and saw Rory in the doorway.

"That's where you went this morning? To the prison?" Rory asked, her voice rising.

The girls got up from the table and exited, leaving Marc to explain.

"So you and the girls went to breakfast leaving me to fend for myself, with no food in the house, and you told *them* what you were doing!"

Marc couldn't deny it; she had him dead to rights. "Yeah, I'm sorry..."

"You're sorry? Did someone ask you to evaluate this guy?"

"No, but I thought if Blake vouched for him, he was ok. I wanted to see for myself. Sam and Sarah are taking the case, and they need all the help they can get. I asked them first if they wanted me to do it and they were grateful," Marc said, skirting the truth.

"So I guess now you're the hero and I'm the villain? That's swell!"

Rory suddenly ran out of steam, and sat down in the nook, putting her head in her hands and sobbing.

Marc got up to sit next to her. He put his arms around her. "I am sorry, really. I wasn't thinking about you, and I understand why you're angry."

Alex and Kate, listening outside the kitchen, felt it was safe to come in. "We're sorry, Mom, we just weren't thinking either, and the time got away from us," Kate said.

Rory looked at them, her face fixed in a scowl, and said, "Perhaps that's because you were too busy having parties while we were gone!"

Kate and Alex looked at each other, identical 0's forming on their mouths. Neither spoke.

Marc looked both surprised and relieved.

"Are you ready to 'fess up, or do you need the incontrovertible evidence?" Rory delivered the speech as if she were in court.

"Well, I got rid of the evidence," Rory continued, "I put the towel with throw-up on it, the one that was shoved to the back of the linen closet, in the wash. It stank up the whole closet! That was the worst evidence, and there were other things out of place, and the covers rumpled in the guest room. You know, I do notice things…"

"You said we could have people over…" Kate ventured, despite a warning look from her sister.

"Yes, we did, and I believe we explicitly said, 'no parties'. We didn't realize 'having people over' really meant having a party," Marc said, happy to have the focus off him for the moment.

"Look, here's what happened," Alex began. "We asked a few friends to come over after our game. We didn't know they'd told a few other people. And before we knew it, there were way too many people here, and some of them brought beer and stuff. And it wasn't fun!"

"We had to get some friends, some big guys, to start throwing people out. There were people here we didn't know, and we knew if we didn't get rid of them, the neighbors would call the police. We even thought of calling Roland, but the kids left," Kate confessed.

The twins looked at their parents.

Finally Rory said, "Well, I guess you found out the hard way, and that's more effective than us lecturing you on it. So I think there are a few things you'll do differently if we decide to leave you alone again?"

"Oh yes, yes, we learned a lot…" Kate said.

"Actually, I'm glad it came out," Alex said, "because I got tired of feeling guilty. And that's where a lot of the food went, too. The kids who came were so disrespectful, it made me sick!"

"Lesson learned?" Marc asked.

Both girls shook their heads vigorously.

"Ok, just a week of grounding," Rory said.

They left quickly. Marc turned to Rory, "Wow! You had a lot to contend with on your first day home, and I compounded it. I am sorry."

"I did feel abandoned, especially since we've been inseparable for the last two weeks. And then the other stuff kept piling up. I guess I shouldn't be peeved that you went to see the guy, since I blew the case off."

"And I should've had the guts to tell you I was doing it. I'm as bad as the kids, sneaking around trying to keep secrets from you." Marc stopped, not wanting to go into other secrets he'd kept.

"So, you were impressed with the guy, what's his name?"

"His name is Mason Rowe, and I was very impressed. He's suffering, not only from the beating he received at the hands of other prisoners, but from the weight of the charges. He was eager to talk, for someone to listen to him. I think he felt more hopeful when I left."

"Well, that's good. You did a good thing," Rory said. "So you're sure he didn't do it? Why was he charged? They must have something."

"They have DNA evidence, but it's flawed. The report is short, and sloppy," Marc replied.

"How is it flawed?" Rory asked.

Marc had to stifle a grin as he saw her getting drawn into the case. "Well, you'll permit my lack of modesty, but I give more expert testimony on pedophiles than any other group of sex offenders. So I have seen cases where DNA was manipulated. In this case, the sperm in the sample were dead, and it was tested the day after the girl, Rachel, was molested."

"Hmm, and the report didn't address this?"

"No, it didn't. One possibility is that Rowe is sterile, but he couldn't confirm that one way or another. He offered to have his semen tested, but I discouraged him."

"Why?" Rory asked, puzzled.

"Because if he is sterile, that plays into the hands of prosecution…"

"Oh, of course, because defense would have to turn over that evidence. I hope you'll let Sam and Sarah know," Rory said, as if just realizing this was not her case.

"I'll tell them if it comes up, actually I'd like to see if they figure it out."

"It sounds like you're in for the long haul on this case," Rory replied, trying to sound indifferent.

Chapter 10

The bogeyman was waiting in his car for Carly. He wanted to be absolutely certain he wasn't spotted. An angry Gordon Howe had confronted him the night before. He'd told Gordon it was nothing and not to worry. For some reason, he didn't trust Howe, so he would be extra careful that he wasn't seen.

Carly soon came skipping down the sidewalk. He knew she was looking forward to seeing him, and he couldn't stifle his urges, beginning already. He hoped he could take it slow, but she'd had sex before, he could tell.

As she passed the car, he called softly out the window, "Carly, I'm here!"

She ran eagerly in his direction, and he reached over to open the door.

She got in, breathless, her cheeks pink.

"I told you I'd be here, Carly. I couldn't forget you, because you're such a sweet and pretty girl."

She didn't blush, she simply looked directly at him, smiling.

"I've brought you something," the bogeyman said, holding up a small box.

"You did?" she said with a gasp.

The bogeyman knew this had been a good idea; she probably didn't get much in the way of gifts. He handed her the box, and she opened it.

"Oh!" she exclaimed, as she took out a heart locket with a long faux-gold chain. "Is it really for me?"

"Of course, you silly girl! Now scoot over here, so I can put it on for you."

Carly eagerly moved over close enough for him to put the necklace on. He slowly pulled her long hair out of the way, and made much of securing the clasp, touching her as much as he could, reaching inside her shirt to touch her undeveloped breasts.

"There we are," he said, having tucked the necklace inside her shirt. "Now this is our secret. When you go home, keep it tucked under your shirt. We don't want your parents to notice it."

"They're my *foster* parents," she said looking down. "I don't think they'd notice, they don't talk to me much or anything," she said quietly.

"Ah, but you have me," he said smoothly, feeling very clever indeed for finding another needy foster child. "But keep it hidden just in case."

"Oh, I will! I don't want them to take it from me."

"Would they do that?" he asked, feigning disbelief.

"They might," she answered. "They took money from my foster brother, and he refused to tell them where he got it."

"Oh?" he asked, suddenly alert. "Do you get along with him, your foster brother?"

"Not so much," she said. "He's older than me, twelve, and he can be mean."

"Well, I'm here to be nice to you!" He grabbed her, hugging and kissing her. She hugged him back.

Sensing movement in his rear view mirror, he focused on the image. A man, a person who looked like Howe from the back, was walking rapidly in the opposite direction.

***

Rory had just spoken with Sarah and asked her to tell the others that she'd be back tomorrow. Sarah had seemed happy to hear from her, and they'd talked about many things, but not their case. That would be a difficult subject to maneuver around, but she'd find a way to do it, or she'd just address it head on. She'd decide later.

Right now, she had to focus on putting a meal on the table. She had no excuse for getting takeout again tonight. It was too hot to do anything elaborate, so she decided on chicken fajitas, a family favorite and easy to prepare.

Finishing up just in time, Rory heard the clatter of the girls' footsteps, as they blew in the front door.

"Hi Mom!" they chorused in unison.

"Smells so good in here!" Alex said, as Kate nodded.

Rory smiled, "We'll eat as soon as you father gets home."

"He brought us home," Kate said, as Marc appeared, coming in through the garage entrance.

Marc gave Rory a kiss, inhaling, and praising the aroma of dinner.

Rory smiled to herself. Perhaps they'd all realized they took her for granted. She wondered how long that would last.

They all prepared their own fajitas and headed for the breakfast nook. There was a pitcher of water already on the table.

"Really good, Rory," Marc commented, between bites. "I don't know about you, but I was getting a bit sick of eating out."

"It got old," Rory agreed, "but I didn't miss being the chief cook!"

Kate and Alex looked at each other, but said nothing.

"How's the case going?" Kate asked her dad, changing the subject.

"I, uh, don't really know. I dropped off the report this morning and haven't heard anything." He neglected to say he'd spoken at length with Sam and Sarah, especially in regard to how DNA could be compromised.

Rory said, "I spoke with Sarah a while ago, and she didn't mention it. I've decided to go back tomorrow, and I asked her to tell the others."

"I've been thinking about the case, and did some research." Rory continued, "Did you know that only 12% of child sexual abuse is reported, and one in four girls, as opposed to one in six boys, will endure some type of sexual assault before the age of 18. I realize how lucky we've been with our own girls. I'm not sure I could handle it."

The look that passed between Marc and Alex was not lost on Rory. She felt a rock form in the pit of her stomach. Silence reigned at the table.

***

Gordon Howe had seen enough. What had happened in Afghanistan was one thing. Everyone gave him a pass, considering the pressure they'd all been under. A lot of things were overlooked in wartime, and this guy was actually considered a hero. He'd saved some of their team from an IED explosion. But this was different; he couldn't excuse it. Nor could he go to the police. He still had a vestige of the bond they'd formed in Afghanistan. He needed to talk with Sam Logan, he'd know what to do.

He was headed home, and on the way took out his cell phone to call Logan. He fumbled in his pocket to find the card Sam had given him. He punched in the number. Drat! It went straight to voice mail. He decided to leave a message. "Mr. Logan, this is Gordon Howe. You said to call if I had any new information, and I do. Can you meet me at your office at nine tomorrow morning? I think we should meet ASAP." Intent on his phone message, Gordon failed to notice as the bogeyman drove by, his car window open.

Chapter 11

Rory and Marc were left in the nook staring at each other after the girls had excused themselves to get ready for their game. Doors slammed upstairs.

"I may be imagining things," Rory said slowly, "but it seemed that you and Alex exchanged a meaningful look when I mentioned how lucky we were…"

"No, you didn't imagine anything, Rory," Marc said quietly.

"Well, then what…*the fuck happened*?" She felt her control slipping away, as she was seized by a tidal wave of panic.

"Please hear me out. This isn't and wasn't easy for me, so just hold on." Marc spoke urgently.

Rory nodded for him to begin, not trusting her voice.

"When Alex and Kate went to camp, eight years ago," he began. "If you recall, I was summoned to bring Alex home because she 'was sick', or so I was told. When I got there, it was a different story. Alex had been fondled by a female junior counselor. We brought charges, the young woman was adjudicated on a misdemeanor and sent for therapy."

"Oh my God! You never told me! Why didn't you tell me?" Her anguished voice became thin and quiet. Her face had lost its color.

Marc took a breath. "You had just suffered a miscarriage in your third trimester. That's actually the reason we sent the girls to camp, to give you space to recover. You went into a deep depression, and were out of work for over a month. I couldn't see burdening you with this on top of everything else. I didn't want to lose you."

Rory was sobbing quietly, feeling a deep sense of guilt that she hadn't been there for Alex, that her own problems had overwhelmed her. She'd forgotten, or purposely tucked away much of what had happened at that time. As she thought about it she remembered feeling a sense of hopelessness.

Marc continued, "I got Alex into therapy immediately with a

child psychologist whom I admired. She did very well. The psychologist was an expert in post traumatic stress disorder, and she employed a relatively new, but very successful treatment."

"Why didn't you tell me?" Rory persisted. "I've dealt with tough situations all my life. Why didn't you let me decide? I wasn't there for my daughter! What must she think? One more secret you've kept from me all these years…"

Hearing footsteps approach the kitchen, Rory stopped.

Alex entered cautiously. "I'm going to the game now," she said.

"Is Kate going?" Marc asked.

"No, she has a headache," Alex answered, as she hurried out the door, responding to the honking horn.

Rory looked at Marc, "Does Kate know?"

"She doesn't, Alex didn't want her to; she was more embarrassed than anything. She didn't want you to know, for that matter, because she knew how upset you were already."

"So you let Alex decide who to tell?" Rory asked, incredulous.

"I let her decide about telling her sister. As far as you were concerned, I agreed it was best. Maybe I was wrong! Maybe I should've told you, but I couldn't bear how it would hurt you. I wanted to tell you! I wanted to confide in someone, but in the end, I accepted it as my burden."

"And all these years, you never once thought to tell me?"

"When? When would be a good time to bring it up? I watched Alex closely, and she continued in therapy for a year. She showed no signs of neurotic or obsessive behavior. She's seemed fine," Marc concluded.

"So the 'flute lessons' you took her to, without any evidence of improving her musical talent, they were therapy sessions." Rory said, realizing the cruel hoax that had been pulled off at her expense.

Marc nodded. Rory said, "I can't take all this in right now, but we will have a family meeting and it will all come out. I'm glad to be going back to work tomorrow so I have something else to think about."

She left Marc sitting alone in the breakfast nook, and went up the back steps to her bedroom. She barely made it to the bathroom before she retched and brought up all of her supper. Oh God, she thought, don't let this be what I think it is! But she knew. She would see her friend Sally Flynn, also her gynecologist, first thing tomorrow, before work. She'd call her now to set it up. Sally always made time for her.

As she prepared to get ready for bed, she decided to talk with Kate. She went to her door and asked, "May I come in?"

Kate gave an emphatic "No!" So Rory went to bed even sadder than she'd been. She cried herself to sleep, which thankfully came soon.

***

When Alex returned from the game, the house was quiet. Her dad, it seemed, was closeted in his study, and her mom, she deduced, was either asleep or reading in bed. She didn't want to see either of them. She needed to talk with Kate.

Tapping on Kate's door, she heard a quiet, "Come in," so she entered. As expected, Kate's eyes were red and swollen. Alex sat on the side of the bed and asked, "Can we talk now?"

"You talk, I'll listen," Kate said without emotion.

"Okay," Alex said, taking a deep breath, "When we were at camp that summer, when we were ten, I went home 'sick', supposedly. But I wasn't sick. That young counselor, Joanie, you remember her? Well, we became friends, at least I thought we were friends, and I thought it was cool to hang out with an older girl."

"Yeah, I remember how you spent time with her, and I was jealous, actually. You didn't seem to want to share her."

"It was she who was possessive, and it was starting to get on my nerves. When I tried to pull away, and spend time with other girls, she cornered me, telling me she was in love with me, kissing and fondling me. It scared the shit out of me, and I went to the camp director. That's what happened, and I was too ashamed to talk about it except to Dad and my therapist. I thought I must've led her on in some way."

"Why didn't you talk to me? We've always shared everything, or so I thought."

"I just wanted to forget it happened. I felt so vulnerable, and I didn't want to talk about it. Only in the therapist's office did I feel safe enough. I did want to tell you, but after the therapy sessions, I was so exhausted! I wanted to stay busy all the time so I didn't keep thinking about it."

"I would've been there for you. I wish you'd given me the chance..."

"I'm sorry, I'm really sorry, Katie. I love you. I would never do anything to hurt you, but I guess I did," Alex's eyes were downcast, and tears began to flow down her cheeks.

"And I'm really sorry for what you went through. But it might take me a while to understand why you didn't confide in me. I guess I just assumed that our secrets went both ways."

Chapter 12

Rory was up and out of the house before the rest of the household awoke. She'd grabbed a banana on her way out. That was the only food she'd been able to eat in the morning, and much to her chagrin, she'd recently discovered she couldn't stomach coffee.

Backing the Prius silently out of the garage, she headed to the doctor's office. Sally Flynn had been her OB/GYN since before her girls were born, and they'd become friends.

As she entered the office, she noticed that the receptionist wasn't there. She knew Sally had come in before her normal office hours, and Dr. Flynn soon appeared. "Rory, come right through." She led her to a dressing room, and said, "You know the drill, put on this lovely gown, open in the front and come to the examining room as soon as you're ready."

Rory complied quickly, wanting to get this over with as soon as possible. She entered the examination room and got up onto the table, putting her feet in the stirrups and leaning back. She wondered who'd invented this medieval torture, and concluded it must've been a man.

"Okay, Rory, you suspect you might be pregnant. When was your last period?"

"To be truthful, Sally, my periods have been very irregular, since my last checkup. I'm pretty sure I'm going into menopause."

"Have you been using birth control regularly?"

"For the most part, but I can't swear that I always did. As you know, I use a diaphragm, and it's a pain to use. I guess I figured since menopause was coming on, I didn't have to worry. Maybe I was wrong!"

"Well, let's have a look," Dr. Flynn said. "Try to relax through this." The doctor performed an internal exam. She then said, "Okay, you can go change back into your clothes and then come to my office."

Happy to be out of the awful gown, Rory dressed quickly and headed for the doctor's office.

"Have a seat, Rory," Dr. Flynn said. "Your suspicion was correct. It appears you're in the early stages of pregnancy. I didn't check, but I assume your breasts are swollen and sensitive?"

"Yes, I think so, I do remember them looking larger and at times, they hurt. I guess I was thinking menopause."

"The truth is, Rory, many premenopausal women figure they're no longer fertile, and that's just not the case. So I guess you and Marc have some thinking to do. You can let me know if you need anything." Noticing Rory's glum expression, she added, "There are options, you know."

"Yes, I know," Rory said. "Not that you'd see him, but please don't tell Marc. I need to do some thinking first. Now, I've got to get to work. Bye,"

Rory felt overwhelmed, her thoughts were scattered, her emotions in turmoil. She was trying to cope with another of Marc's secrets, and wondering if she even wanted to have another child with him, or have another child *period.* And how could she approach Alex, after all these years? She was on the verge of tears, and just at that moment, the skies opened up and poured down on her.

She ran to her car, where she'd left her umbrella, much good as it would do her there! She just noticed that the skies had grown dark as night. They were in for a big one, she knew. The clouds and the rain fit her mood perfectly, she thought.

Driving to the office in her slightly damp clothes was uncomfortable, but she didn't want to take the time to go home and change. Luckily she found a parking spot close to the office and now she had her umbrella, so she wouldn't get any wetter.

Rory was surprised to see the office in darkness. As she fumbled to get the key in the lock, her cell trilled. She saw it was Sam and picked up as she entered the office.

"Rory, it's Sam, are you in the office?"

"Just came in the door Sam, looks like I'm the first one here. What can I do for you?"

"I got a message last night from Gordon Howe. He's one of the guys who was at the poker game with Rowe. Anyway, I interviewed him the other day and asked him to get back to me if he thought of anything that might help us. So, he sounded a little uneasy when he left the message and he wanted me to meet him at the office *now*. Can you check next door and see if he's there? Just tell him I'll be late."

Although she was a bit confused, Rory gathered this was the pedophile case. "There are no lights on next door, but if I see him I'll deliver the message."

"Thanks, Rory, and by the way, welcome back!"

As she disconnected, she thought she heard whistling, and then the sound of a door in the construction area closing. Rory walked through the plastic sheeting to the next room. She couldn't see anything, so she groped along the wall to find the lights.

Before she knew it, she stumbled over something and hit the concrete hard. Rory saw stars and then, blackness.

Chapter 13

Ten minutes later, Sam entered the office. He checked for Rory but didn't see her in the main office. Curious, he went through the plastic sheeting and hit the light switch.

What he saw made him gag. Rory was lying on the floor on top of a man's body. There was blood everywhere. Both looked dead. He dialed 911, and went over to Rory. Picking up her wrist with trembling hands, he felt a pulse and breathed a sigh of relief.

He looked Rory over more carefully and tried to rouse her. She looked very pale and was breathing shallowly, but she *was* breathing. A knot was forming on her head where she'd smashed into the floor. Hearing sirens, Sam went to the office door and watched as the ambulance and police arrived almost simultaneously.

Sam directed the EMT's into the area under renovation. He pointed out Rory, and the medics immediately went to her and lifted her carefully onto a board, stabilizing her neck. Sam gave them her information and his card and they took her to the ambulance.

Two other EMT's directed their attention toward the man Rory had apparently tripped over. Sam now recognized him as Gordon Howe, the man who had asked to meet him at the office. It appeared that his throat had been slashed and blood was everywhere. There was no doubt he was dead.

The police came in and began to cordon off the area with yellow tape. The EMT's left the scene as the police took over. Sam saw Officer Jamison and went to talk with him.

"Hi Sam," Officer Jamison said. "It's pretty grisly in there." He shook his head. "What can you tell me?"

"Not much," Sam said. "The dead man is Gordon Howe, and he works for Citadel, the company doing our renovations." Sam went to make coffee. He was feeling shaky. Then he continued, "I met with Gordon a few days ago regarding a case I'm working on. A man has been accused of molesting his fiancée's daughter…"

"Oh yes, I heard about that," the officer said.

"Anyway, Sarah and I interviewed two of the men who'd been with Rowe, the defendant, the night of the incident. The men, all Citadel employees, were playing poker together. They all agreed that Rowe appeared to have had too much to drink, so he stayed overnight at the host's house."

"Was Howe the host?" Jamison asked.

"No, another guy Sarah interviewed was. I think Kraft was his name. Anyway, the two men we've interviewed so far gave essentially the same story of the evening. We left our business cards with the men we interviewed and asked them to call us if they thought of anything else," Sam said. He went to get a cup of coffee and offered one to Jamison.

Sipping his coffee, Sam resumed. "Howe left me a voice mail last night and said something about having new information. He wanted to meet with me this morning at nine. He sounded, I guess I would say, a bit scared. He got off the phone quickly."

"I was running late this morning, so I called Rory, who'd just arrived at the office, and asked her to tell Howe I would be there shortly. This was a bit past nine. She said she didn't see him, but would look next door. That's what I know for sure. The rest is conjecture," Sam said.

"So you think Rory went next door and walked in on a murder in progress?" Jamison asked.

"I don't think so. When I got here, the construction area was in darkness. I didn't see Rory here, so I went next door. I found the light switch right away and that's when I dialed 911. I wasn't sure Rory was alive and went to her first. There was blood everywhere, so I couldn't tell whose it was." Sam stopped to take a breath and drink more coffee. He was beginning to feel more himself. "It looked to me like Rory was finding her way in the dark, tripped over Howe and slammed to the floor. But I guess you'll know more when Rory wakes up." Sam said.

"I checked Rory's pulse and found a slight one, then tried to revive her. But she was out. The EMTs arrived quickly and took her to the ambulance. Two other medics took one look at Howe, and figured it was a police matter. It was then I noticed who it was and that his throat was slit." Sam shuddered.

"OK, thanks Sam. Maybe you want to get ahold of Rory's family and we'll get on with the investigation here. We'll be here for a while, I think," Jamison added.

"Thanks," Sam said. "I, uh, guess I should call Marc first…" He wandered to the front door with the phone to his ear, waving goodbye to Jamison.

On his way out, Sam almost ran into Forsythe, coming in the door, a look of alarm on his face. "What's going on?" he asked Sam.

"Uh…one of your men, Gordon Howe, was killed. His body's in there," Sam said.

"But, he's not even working on this site," Forsythe answered, looking confused.

"He was here to meet me," Sam explained, wondering why Forsythe was here since no one else was. "I interviewed him about Rowe." Sam stopped before he gave away too much.

"That's disturbing…" Forsythe said, seeming at a loss for words.

Sam considered mentioning Rory, but thought better of it. He needed to reach Marc as soon as possible. He excused himself and left.

***

When Rory opened her eyes a few hours later, Marc's face was hovering above her. She tried to lift her head up, but the pain twisted her face into a grimace. She fell back onto her pillow, closing her eyes.

Marc had tears in his eyes as he leaned over to brush a kiss on Rory's cheek. "I'm here, Rory, I'm right here," he said. He rubbed her arm, being careful not to touch the needle taped in place.

A nurse came in and Marc told him that Rory had opened her eyes, tried to lift her head and seemed to experience pain, then she fell back to sleep.

"That's good, Mr. Chandler, that's a good sign," he said. "Her vitals look good, and we're hopeful. By the way, I'm Paul Goodwin, the head nurse, so I'll be looking in on your wife. Dr. Tyler is handling her case."

"As he left the room, Goodwin said, "Oh, and call me if you need anything."

Marc focused his attention on Rory again, rubbing her arms and talking to her.

He looked up as his daughters entered the room quietly. They had similar expressions of sadness on their faces, and their slow movement was atypical.

Marc welcomed them, saying, "Your mother opened her eyes a few minutes ago and tried to lift her head, but she fell right back to sleep. The nurse, Paul Goodwin, said it was a good sign and that her vitals were good."

Kate spoke first, "Yes, he talked with us, too and said we could come in now."

"I'm hopeful that your mom will come out of it soon," Marc said, in an attempt to be optimistic.

"Well," Alex spoke up, "he also said she's on heavy doses of pain meds. She hit her head pretty hard on that concrete floor."

"So, it's probably better for her to sleep through the pain," Kate added.

"True," Marc said. "It looked like she was in pain when she tried to lift her head, so it is probably for the best," he sighed. "Why don't we let her rest now," Marc suggested. He leaned over again to kiss her pale cheek.

The girls went to her bedside to kiss her as well.

When Kate turned from her mother, tears were streaming down her face. Marc gave her a hug. "It's ok, Katie," he said using a name he'd called her as a child.

"But Dad," she stammered, "When she wanted to talk to me last night, I was mean to her!" Kate sobbed against his chest.

"Kate," Marc said, looking at her. "I know you feel bad, but this wasn't your fault," he said softly. He wished he could assuage his own sense of guilt.

Looking at both girls, he noticed that Alex, too, was crying. "Listen, your mother knows you love her. That's all that matters."

The three left the room with their arms around one another.

***

The bogeyman was pacing around his home, filled with fear. He'd never killed anyone and it rattled him. He hadn't been careful and he might get caught. He couldn't afford that; it would ruin everything.

But it had been necessary to kill Howe; he had no choice. Howe had walked past his car last night and had seen him fondling the girl.

Howe had seen him the night before and warned him. The bogeyman had followed Howe slowly in his car and had heard the call he made to that lawyer guy. That would've been the end if he told the attorney, and Howe planned to meet him, so he'd had to stop that. He'd been right to take him out before Howe blew the whistle on the whole thing.

Turning on the TV, he saw the news was flashing pictures of the murder scene, identifying the victim and giving a number to call in anonymous tips. Then there was a picture of Rory Chandler, the head lawyer in the office where he'd killed Howe. She had apparently fallen over Howe's body and was in the hospital in guarded condition. Fuck that nosey bitch, he thought bitterly. She might know something. What if she'd seen him? He hoped she'd die. If not…

***

Sam and Sarah had left the hospital and dropped the twins off at their house. Marc was the only one who stayed at the hospital and would try to sleep in the bed next Rory.

Neither was inclined to talk so they rode home in mournful silence. It was still pouring outside, which didn't improve their mood.

"Oh, God!" Sarah said, breaking the silence, "it was horrible seeing Rory like that, all pale and hooked up to those machines…"

"I know," Sam sighed. "I still can't get rid of the image of her lying on the floor over a dead man with blood everywhere."

"I'm sorry, Sam," Sarah said, her voice softening. "It must've been dreadful. You had to deal with it all. And you got help right away. I'm sure that made a big difference."

"I just sort of went into survival mode, so I don't really remember much of what I did. But I do remember my first view when I turned on the lights," Sam shuddered.

Sarah patted his leg. "We'll get through this."

"God, yes! Somehow we both got through your kidnapping last fall. It's coming up on a year and I think we're doing ok. How about you?"

"I will probably never really be *over* it, but it's receding, and your support has speeded up the process."

They drove in silence again. And then Sam spoke. "But I have to tell you I feel guilty about Rory. She went into the construction site because I was late...if I'd been on time this might not have happened."

"If you'd been on time Sam, this might be a double murder. You certainly didn't cause what happened to Rory," Sarah said. "So please ditch the guilt, it never helps."

***

Marc had just drifted off when he was awakened by Rory moaning. He jumped up and turned on the light. Rory's eyes were closed but she was thrashing and crying out. Before he could buzz for the nurse, one came through the door.

She had a concerned look on her face and went straight to Rory's bedside, saying, "Time for her meds. She's still in pain, obviously." She changed the bag of intravenous meds. Then she took Rory's temperature.

Addressing Marc, she said, "I'm the night nurse. Your wife's temp is elevated a bit, so we'll have to watch it. She seems comfortable now. Call me if you need anything, Mr. Chandler."

"I was about to call you just now, but you beat me to the punch. Thanks," Marc said.

When the lights went out, he prepared again to sleep. It was difficult with all of the images and thoughts flashing through his mind. Suddenly it occurred to him that the murder had taken this case to a whole new level. What was going on?

Sleep seemed to be elusive tonight. Marc was about to call the nurse and ask for a sleeping pill, when the door opened slowly. Huh, he thought, she's read my mind again. But it wasn't the nurse. He saw the silhouette of a man in a cap and he wasn't dressed in hospital garb. He was moving slowly in Rory's direction, and the light from outside the window glinted on something shiny in his hand.

Marc sat up, searched for the call button and hit it. When he turned back, the intruder was fleeing out the door. Marc was on his feet and nearly collided with the nurse as he reached the door.

"Get security!" he called over his shoulder as he ran after the man, who was rounding a corner several yards in front of him. When he reached the corner, there was no one in sight. He faced several doors into which the man might've gone. He opened one, an empty bathroom. Then he opened the door to a utility closet, seeing only cleaning supplies. As he prepared to look into a third, he heard a soft click from far down the hallway. It was an exit.

Marc barreled down the hallway in pursuit. Out of breath, he opened the exit door and listened. He heard nothing.

Chapter 14

The sound of hurried footsteps echoed off the walls. Marc wheeled around and faced a security guard.

"Mr. Chandler?" the guard inquired.

"Yes, I asked the nurse to call security because a man crept into my wife's room as I was trying to sleep. I chased him this far. I think he went down the stairs here, but couldn't hear anything. Can you do a lock-down or something?" Marc asked.

"I'll radio my contacts on other floors and of course, the lobby. Can you give me a description of the man?"

Marc rubbed his chin, thinking. "He was a little over six feet, had on dark clothes, jeans maybe and a dark shirt, and he wore a cap. He had something shiny in his hand. I guess that doesn't help much, but aside from seeing him enter the room in the dark, I saw him only from the back."

The guard was repeating the description over his two-way radio, broadcasting to the guards all over the hospital.

***

The intruder emerged from a supply closet on the first floor. He was wearing green scrubs, a head covering and a surgical mask over his face. He walked slowly down the hall towards an exit. A guard came around the corner, listening to his radio. The man nodded to the guard as he headed out the door.

"Hey, wait a minute!" the guard called as he realized this might be the man they were looking for. He called for back up and ran out the door. Looking around, he saw nothing at first. Then, he saw a slight movement between cars and ran towards it. He stopped dead as a mangy dog came in his direction, a menacing growl coming from its throat. He backed off slowly, putting his hand on his gun, just in case. But the dog ran off and the guard breathed a sigh of relief.

Two back-up guards jogged over. "What's up, Mike?" asked one.

"I think we lost him. I saw movement and followed it. Turned out to be a stray dog, but it ran off. Scared me shitless! Meantime, the dude probably got away. We should search the parking lot anyway. And watch out for the dog, it looked mean!"

They split up and went in different directions. After several minutes of searching, they found neither the intruder nor the dog.

Going inside, the guards reported to the head of security. They were all instructed to keep a special lookout for any unusual activity. And a guard was to be posted at Mrs. Chandler's door. She had been moved to another room.

***

Rory had continued to sleep through the move to her new room on a different floor.

Marc was trying to settle in, but doubted he'd get any sleep now. As if he didn't have enough worries!

The night nurse on this floor came in to speak with Marc.

"Mr. Chandler, I understand you had quite a scare. I just want to reassure you that there is now a guard posted outside of the door and all of the security staff is vigilant."

"Thank you. It's been quite a day, and so far the night isn't shaping up much better. I was just imagining that I'll probably be up the rest of the night," Marc said ruefully.

"I'll be happy to provide you with a sedative if you want one. I think you can feel safe in the knowledge that security has been beefed up and your wife is in a new room. What do you say?"

"I say, thanks, please knock me out." The nurse went to get the meds and Marc checked to make sure there was a guard outside the door. He introduced himself to the man and thanked him.

***

The next morning Rory awoke with a pounding head, dry mouth and no memory of what had happened and why she was in a hospital. It hurt to turn her head, but as she looked around the room she was immediately comforted by the sleeping form of her husband. Whatever happened must've been bad for him to spend the night.

A nurse came through the door. "Mrs. Chandler, I'm Gracie V, and I'll be your day nurse. How are you feeling?"

"Uh, my head hurts, and I feel pretty foggy, and thirsty. I don't remember anything that happened to put me here. But I'm happy to see my husband zonked out over there."

The nurse poured a glass of water and held it close to Rory's mouth so she could use the straw. Then she said, "Your husband was given a sedative about 1 a.m., and I think that did the trick. Now I need to take your temp. You were running a slight fever last night. She put the thermometer in Rory's ear, and then said, "It's still a little elevated but it hasn't risen, so that's a good sign. How are you doing with pain?"

"My head is throbbing, barely tolerable," Rory said.

"On a scale of one to ten?" the nurse asked.

"Probably a nine," Rory estimated.

"OK, that qualifies you for continued meds. I am happy to see you awake. You suffered a concussion, so it's important to keep you awake as much as possible, although you also need rest. But it's a very good sign that you awoke on your own." Gracie added.

"I guess you can't tell me what happened," Rory said.

"I do know what happened to you," Gracie said. "The short answer is that you tripped and fell hitting your head on concrete. Of course there's more to the story but I don't think I'm the one to discuss that with you."

"Thanks for your honesty," Rory said. "It doesn't ring any bells for me. I just have no memory of what happened."

"And that's not unusual for a patient suffering a concussion. It may take a while for it all to come back, and then again, once you know what happened you may be able to connect the dots. Ok, I'm done here for now. Do you feel up to having breakfast?" the nurse asked.

"No, I want to rest. Just talking is making me tired," Rory answered. Looking again at Marc, she said, "I'm glad my husband is here." And then she dozed off.

***

Sam, Sarah and the twins were speaking with the head nurse on what had been Rory's floor.

Sarah was asking head-nurse, Paul Goodwin, "Can you tell us where Rory's new room is?"

Goodwin shook his head, "I'm really sorry, but for security reasons, I am not authorized to give anyone that information. Mrs. Chandler and her husband are still asleep. When either of them wakes up, they can give us a list of who can visit. I've already put in a call to the nurse on her floor and she will get back to me as soon as possible. Meanwhile, I suggest you go get coffee in the cafeteria, or just wait here for the news."

Kate spoke up, "But you talked to us yesterday, you know we're her daughters!"

"Of course I know that," he smiled. "And if I could make any exceptions, it would be for you. But unfortunately, I can't. In any case, both of your parents are sleeping and that's probably best for them."

"OK," Kate said. "We might as well go get something at the caf. I'll leave my cell number so you can call me."

"I already have it," Goodwin said, "You gave it to me yesterday. And for sure, I'll call you if anything changes."

***

The intruder from the night before was hunkered down in his car, where he'd spent the night. The stupid security guys hadn't looked into the cars, at least not his. He saw no security combing the area now, but a large cluster of reporters was standing outside of the hospital doors. They were obviously waiting for an update on that Chandler bitch. Thanks to him, she was now big news. He would have to listen to the news later to find out about her condition. If only that dude, probably her husband, hadn't been in the room he'd be home free now.

Chapter 15

The bright morning light coming into the hospital room finally awakened Marc. He sat up, glancing around, momentarily disoriented. Then the events of the night before came to him in a flash like a punch to his gut.

He looked over at Rory, who appeared to be sleeping peacefully. Marc pulled himself together, going into the bathroom to splash water on his face. He would have to go home sometime today and change clothes.

He said "Good Morning," to the guard and told him he appreciated that he was there.

Marc went to the main desk. A nurse, with a nametag that read, "Gracie V., R.N., Head nurse" raised her head from the paperwork in front of her and smiled. "Mr. Chandler?" she asked.

"Yes, I guess you're the person I need to speak with."

"Right, I looked in on your wife earlier. She was awake, by the way, but you were still knocked out. I'm glad you got some sleep."

"Me too!" Marc said. "For a while there, it looked like I'd be up all night. So, how is Rory doing?"

"Very well, I would say. She sat up and spoke with me for a little while. She doesn't remember anything, and I told her only that she had tripped and fallen on a concrete floor. She asked for more pain meds, and I gave her a lower dose, because she seems in slightly less pain, and because we want her awake as much as possible. Before she fell back to sleep she said she was glad you were here."

Marc smiled. "That's good news. Does she still have a fever?"

"Her temp is slightly elevated, but it's the same as last night, so at least it hasn't gone up. Dr. Tyler will be in to see her soon, and he should be able to answer any other questions you have."

"OK, thanks, Nurse…"

"Just call me Gracie. My last name, Vivacaro, is tough to pronounce, so I just go by Gracie or Nurse V., your choice. Oh, before I forget, there are four people waiting to see your wife. Before we give out the number of her new room, we need you to authorize a list."

"That's easy. My daughters, Kate and Alex, Sam Logan and Sarah Justice. If anyone else shows up, you can just run the name by me, but I think we want to keep the numbers small at this point," Marc answered.

"I'll call down and okay the four. They should be up soon, since they arrived earlier. I'll let you know when they get here and you can meet with them out here in the waiting room until your wife wakes up."

"At some point I need to go to the cafeteria for some breakfast."

"Tell me what you want, and I'll order it from the kitchen," Gracie offered.

"That's very kind of you, thanks. I'll just have scrambled eggs and toast, and of course, coffee."

***

Marc had just received his breakfast, when his daughters, followed by Sam and Sarah came off the elevator and into the waiting room.

Kate came forward first, saying, "Don't get up, Dad, eat your breakfast. We've had ours."

Marc replied, "Hi guys. Boy am I glad to see you! Good news on Rory. She was awake and spoke with the nurse while I was still sleeping. Last night they gave me some kind of knock-out med and I was out like a light." Marc paused. "Anyway, it's good that she woke up. By the way, she doesn't remember anything so we'll have to play it by ear when we start to feed her the news. She went back to sleep. The nurse put her on a lower dose of pain meds, so she should have more awake time. We'll see." Marc finished talking and looked at his food.

"That's good news, Dad," Alex said, giving him a kiss on his forehead. "Go ahead and eat!"

"Sarah and I will be going to the office to work on the case, since there are definitely new developments. The murder certainly changes things, we'll just have to figure out how," Sam said. "I gave a statement to the police earlier, including that the murder is connected to the bogeyman. Detective Herrera is working on the bogeyman case, and that will include Howe's murder now."

Marc had finished his breakfast, when Kate asked, "Dad, can you tell us why Mom was moved to a different room? Everyone has been so hush-hush about it!"

"Oh," Marc said, his face darkening. "Have a seat everyone," Marc said as he launched into a description of the previous night's events.

"So that must be Mom's room, with the guard in front of it," Alex said.

"Right," Marc said looking up at the astonished faces around him.

"We certainly need to keep mum about Rory's condition," Sarah said. "So, the suspect must've seen Rory's face on TV last night and thought she might know something about the murder."

"Oh this definitely changes things!" Sam said. "The same person who killed Howe, came here to take care of Rory, it seems. Good you were here last night, Marc."

"Yeah, when I think that I almost didn't stay, I realize how lucky we are. But, I didn't know she was on TV," Marc said. "You're right, Sarah, no news leaks about her condition."

Alex and Kate looked shell-shocked. Marc went over to reassure them.

Sam said to Marc, "We'll be on our way. It looks like we have even more work to do on the case. Call us if you think Rory is up to a visit, and give her our best."

Sarah stopped to give Marc and the girls a hug before she and Sam left. She was frowning.

***

Sam and Sarah had just arrived at the office. They noticed that construction had ceased next door, and the crime-scene tape was still in place. Nevertheless, Forsythe came through the plastic sheeting into their office space.

"Any news about Rory?" he asked immediately.

"No, sorry, we weren't able to see Rory. Her condition is still guarded. We're sorry about your man, Howe," Sam added.

"Yeah, it's been quite a blow to all of us." He stood awkwardly, and then said, "Well, you let me know how Rory's doing, ok?"

"Will do," Sam said tersely. When Forsythe had left the room, Sam said to Sarah, "He hasn't even met Rory, why do you suppose he's asking about her?"

"I don't know, I think he's just nosey! But he seems to keep asking questions we've already answered."

"He probably doesn't like how this might affect his company. Now two of his employees are in the news, and neither is bringing good publicity," Sam answered.

Chapter 16

When he had made the other calls, Sam contacted Blake. "Hey, no reason to come in today, Sarah and I will be out meeting with the DA, police, and Rowe."

"That was quite a shock to see one of Rowe's friends murdered and Rory on the news! I tried to call you, but couldn't get through," Blake answered.

"We were at the hospital all day and into the night, and there are still more developments, but I don't want to talk about it on the phone. If we have time, maybe we'll stop by and fill you in. How's Katrina holding up?"

"She's ok, she actually thinks this murder might take the heat off Mason, since it must be related to the case," Blake said.

"It may well be," Sam answered. "There's a lot we need to piece together before we've solved the puzzle. I'll call you later Blake, bye." Sam ended the call.

When he'd finished making calls, he said to Sarah, "Now let's get out of here. We have a very full schedule."

Sam locked the office and he and Sarah headed across the street to the DA's office. Sam had been lucky to catch McClain before he got involved in other cases.

Entering the super-cooled courthouse, they took the elevator to the third floor.

McClain's administrative assistant greeted them and motioned for them to go through to McClain's office.

"Thanks, Leigh," Sarah said as they went back to the office.

McClain was at his desk, and an ADA they didn't know was seated to his right. McClain stood to shake hands and introduce everyone. "Dylan Jefferson, meet Sam Logan and Sarah Justice. Dylan will be the ADA on this case," McClain said. "We were just discussing the new developments and wondering how they may impact the case."

Sam and Sarah seated themselves. Then Sam spoke, "Well, in our view it changes things a great deal. The murdered man, Gordon Howe, was one of the alibi witnesses we interviewed. I met with him and left my card, instructing him to call me if he had anything else to add. There was a message from him left on my voicemail the night before the murder asking to meet with me at the office the day he was murdered. I was late for the meeting and phoned Rory, asking her to give him the message. Yeah, I would say they're connected."

"So, was she there when the murder took place?" McClain asked.

"We won't know that until Rory is able to tell us. She's awakened a few times, but remembers nothing of the incident. She suffered a concussion and apparently it's not uncommon for memory loss to accompany that kind of injury," Sam said.

"You must have some speculation as to what happened," McClain prodded.

"I got to the office about ten minutes after my phone call to Rory," Sam said. Then he went on to explain what he saw next. Sam stopped, having trouble continuing as the images swam before his eyes.

McClain waited a bit, and then said, "So, do *you* think she saw the murder?"

"I don't think so. If she'd seen the murder, I don't think she'd be alive," Sam informed them.

Sarah spoke up, "There was a rather serious incident at the hospital last night." She told McClain what had happened and then said, "It seems as though the murderer is afraid Rory saw something, after her picture was on TV last night. By the way, we want none of this to get out. As far as the public knows, Rory will remain in 'guarded' condition. She's been moved to a new room and has a hospital security guard posted."

"That certainly changes the case considerably." McClain looked shocked.

"We will ask for a review of bail hearing under the circumstances. It seems obvious Rowe had nothing to do with the murder of his good friend, and Howe may have been ready to blow the whistle," Sam finished.

"So it would seem," McClain said slowly. "I've just read the Court sex-offender evaluation, and while it doesn't exonerate him, it casts some doubt about his guilt. Go ahead and schedule it. Make your case and we'll see how it goes. Oh, and have Leigh make a copy of the report for you."

"Marc Chandler also did an eval, pro bono, and he believes Rowe to be innocent. Of course he can't say that in his report, but it's favorable and we'll submit it in court. We'll get a copy to you."

"Do you think we could get a different judge this time?" Sam asked.

"I'll see what I can do," McClain replied. "Thanks for the update." He shook his head. "Whew! It's a lot to take in." He stood up and they shook hands all around before Sam and Sarah left the office.

"That went well, I think," Sarah said. "Do you know Dylan at all?"

"I know of him," Sam replied. "I think he'll be ok."

***

Marc had just returned to the hospital after going home for a shower and a change of clothes. He got on the elevator and a woman entered just as the door began to close. He recognized Dr. Flynn.

"Hi, are you here to see Rory?" Marc asked.

"I thought I'd stop in and see her while I'm here doing my rounds."

They got off at the fifth floor, and when she saw the guard at Rory's door, she asked Marc, "What's up with that?"

He went on to explain the night's events.

"Oh my God, how awful!" the doctor exclaimed.

The head nurse looked up. "So you're back, Mr. Chandler," she smiled. "Your wife woke up a short time ago and your daughters are with her." She nodded to Dr. Flynn, "Are you going in to see her, Sally?" she asked.

"Yes," she answered. "Mr. Chandler and I will go in and ask the girls to leave."

Marc and the doctor went into Rory's room. Marc was happy to see Rory looking much better, and conversing with the girls.

Rory saw Marc enter and smiled at him. "I hear you went home to clean up. You look wonderful!" Rory said, motioning him over. Then she saw Dr. Flynn, and said, "Sally thanks for coming!"

Marc went to Rory's bedside and bent down to give her a kiss. "You look much better!"

Then Marc turned to his daughters, "Thanks for keeping watch while I was gone. Do you mind waiting outside? Your mom's supposed to have only two visitors at a time," he said.

"Sure," Kate said, leaning down to give her mother a kiss. Alex did the same, and the girls left the room.

As Marc spoke with the girls, Rory gave the doctor a warning look, and the doctor gave a quick nod of acknowledgement.

"So," Marc said, pulling up a chair, "how are you feeling?"

"Much better," Rory said. "My head still hurts but it's not pounding any more. I still don't remember anything, so can you tell me what happened?"

"I think it might be hard for you to take in if I tell you everything at once. What is the last thing you remember?" Marc asked.

Rory seemed to concentrate for a while before she talked. "I remember driving to the office and I think I was running late…"

Before she could finish, the doctor said, "I'll be going now, but I'll stop by to see you after my rounds."

"Bye, Sally, thanks," she said. "Go ahead, Marc…"

"Do you remember going into the office?" Marc continued.

"No," Rory shook her head, yawning.

"Look, Rory, I think you've heard enough for now. Why don't you get some sleep?"

Rory nodded off almost instantly.

Chapter 17

Sam and Sarah had managed to schedule the review of bail hearing for two days later. They'd spoken with Detective Herrera, who was assigned to the bogeyman case. He was over whelmed since the chief had added Howe's murder and Rory's probable attempted murder, to the case.

"I would welcome any ideas you have. I'm glad to discuss this case, which has become more complex by the day," Herrera said.

Sarah and Sam spent the better part of an hour discussing their views on what had happened, including their perspective on Rowe and why they were requesting another hearing to review bail.

"I guess there's no chance of withdrawing the charges…" Sam said.

"Not at this point," the detective said. "We're assuming the perp is the same actor in all three offenses. We can't afford to take anything off the table at this point. Although I think it's reasonable for Rowe to be released on bail."

"Assuming the judge is reasonable," Sarah said. And to Sam she said, "Why don't we visit Mason and let him know about the bail review."

"I guess that's about all we can do at this point," Sam replied. "You ready to go?"

Thanking the detective for his time, they took their leave.

As they were driving to the prison, Sarah spoke, "I was just thinking maybe we should interview the other two guys who were at the poker game. They must be a little scared, knowing that one of their own has been murdered."

"I think we need to tread carefully when we talk with them. I don't want them to know that Howe had called me the night before. If they know that, they'll be afraid to say anything."

"That's a good point, Sam," Sarah said, frowning. "So how do we approach it?" she asked.

"I think we have to ask the same questions we asked of the others, to get a fair assessment," Sam answered.

"But, don't you think it has to be one of the remaining three?"

"Logically, but they were supposed to be friends, they work together, play poker…"

"Maybe Mason can shed more light on this. We need to bring it up," Sarah said.

They continued their discussion until the prison rose up before them, ending the conversation.

***

Marc was still there when Rory woke up over an hour later.

"Oh, you're still here. You were starting to tell me what happened…"

"If you want to know first hand, you'll have to talk with Sam, but I can tell you what he told me."

"Please, tell me what you know, it's been bugging me to have no memory…"

"Ok, I'll tell you what I know. "You remember entering the office, right?" Rory nodded. "Do you remember talking to Sam as you entered the office?"

"No," Rory shook her head. "That I don't remember at all."

Marc went on to try and fill in the blanks for Rory.

"That's starting to ring a bell," Rory said. "I remember being confused about who this guy was, because I didn't know anything about the case."

He continued with the account Sam had given him, ending when Rory went to look for Howe in the construction area.

"I don't remember that, but go on…"

"When Sam arrived at the office about ten minutes later, he found no one in your office and no lights on in the construction area. So he went next door and switched on the lights. He found you sprawled on the floor on top of a man's body, and blood all over the floor."

"Oh, my God! Who was the man?"

"It turned out to be Gordon Howe, whose throat was slashed. At first Sam thought you were dead, too, because of all the blood. He called 911 and went to check your vitals and found you had a slight pulse."

Rory was shaking and Marc put his arms around her.

"I'm sorry, maybe you weren't ready to hear that."

"I needed to hear it. So why do they think Howe was killed?"

"Sam believes that Howe had reason to suspect someone, and he thinks it was one of the other men at the poker game. And that other person, he thinks is 'the bogeyman', that's what the little girl, Rachel, said he called himself."***

Sam and Sarah were led to the infirmary at the prison, where Rowe was still being housed.

As they arrived, the doctor was leaving his room. "I'm Dr. Cooper," she said. "Do you represent Mr. Rowe?"

"Yes, we do," Sarah replied, introducing Sam and herself.

"I think you should know that Mr. Rowe has had several episodes of waking up screaming during the night. I started to question him about it, and he said it happens occasionally, but he hasn't sought treatment. You may wish to explore that, and let me know what you think."

"Thank you, Dr. Cooper, we'll do that," Sam assured her.

The guard asked how Rory was doing.

Sarah looked surprised, so he said, "I'm Gus, me and Rory go way back, she's a good lady."

"Well," Sam answered, "we haven't been able to see her because she's never been awake when we were there. She's in guarded condition."

Gus shook his head, "She'll be in my prayers," he said gravely. Then he ushered them into Rowe's room.

Rowe had a depressed air about him, but seemed pleased to see them. "Thanks so much for coming!" he said. "We don't get much news in here, but I heard my friend Gordon was killed and Rory's in the hospital. I hope you can tell me what's going on…"

Between them, Sam and Sarah tried to piece together the events for Mason. He listened intently. Then he said, "I don't get why someone would kill Gordon. There were three other guys there besides me. What could it mean?"

"As I mentioned, Gordon had called me the night before. He sounded stressed and wanted to talk with me in the office first thing the next day. He didn't give me a hint of what information he had, but I have to assume he had a guess at who might've been responsible for molesting Rachel and pinning it on you," Sam replied. "The molester must've had a hunch that Howe was about to out him."

"Jeez," Rowe said, "It's hard for me to imagine any of those guys doing that. I mean, we go way back, we were in the war together, Afghanistan that is." He shook his head.

"How long have you known them, then?" Sarah asked.

"Hmm, about eight years, that's how we all ended up at Citadel," he answered. "I can't believe any of those guys would do that, frame me and then kill Howe. It just doesn't add up."

"Do you have any other ideas about who would be capable of this?" Sam asked.

"No, I just can't imagine, but it's probably not random…"

Changing the subject, Sarah asked, "The doctor just told us that you wake up screaming at night sometimes. Do you have any idea what that's about?"

"It started when I got back from Afghanistan. I'm on the waiting list at the VA, have been for two years, but I haven't gotten any help."

Sarah couldn't stop the frown that creased her brow. "Do you have any dreams that you remember?"

"I don't remember any of the dreams, I just wake up in a cold sweat, crying. In fact, there's much about the war that I can't remember, and I'm not sure I want to. We were in a munitions unit, so it was pretty dicey. We all got very close. That's why I can't imagine any of them doing this. We all had each other's back, that's how we survived."

"I'm not a shrink, but what you describe sounds like PTSD, I'm sure you've heard of it, since so many vets are returning from battle similarly impacted," Sarah said.

"Oh, yeah, I'm pretty sure that's what I have. I just can't get treatment."

"I don't think we'll wait for the VA, I think we can get you into treatment right away."

"But my only coverage is with the VA," Rowe said.

"No, I mean we will get you treatment, as part of your defense. There's a relatively new and very effective treatment, called EMDR. I'm not quite sure what all the letters stand for but the procedure takes you back to your traumatic memories and reprograms your brain, by a series of eye movements. It's been likened to rebooting a computer."

"I haven't heard of that," Rowe said, "but then I haven't seen anyone either. I'm not sure I want to recover those memories," he added.

"Oh, I hear you," Sarah said. "I understand that, but keep an open mind. As difficult as it might be, I think you have to confront those memories before you can get past them. You've already established your bravery by going into battle, so I'm sure you have the courage."

"I don't know how brave I am, I was scared every day over there…"

"And despite that, you did your job every day. I call that courage," Sam said.

"Well," Sarah said, "we do have some good news for you. We spoke with the DA this morning and have scheduled a review of bail hearing for Wednesday, day after tomorrow. We're hoping for a better outcome this time."

"Oh God! That is good news. I'll have to try very hard not to get my hopes up. You warned me about that. How is Rory, by the way?" Rowe asked.

Sam answered, "We haven't spoken with her. She wasn't awake when we were there."

"I'm so sorry!" Rowe said. "What's the prognosis?"

"She's in 'guarded' condition," Sarah answered. "Sam and I will be handling your case," she added, anticipating Mason's next question.

"Right," Sam confirmed, "I've been working on your case from the beginning and have a good grasp of things. I'm not as good as Rory, but she's been a great teacher."

"Thanks, man," Rowe said. "I have confidence in you and I'll be praying for Rory. I hope to meet her, since I've heard so many good things about her. And I'm sure you've learned a lot from her.

Sam stood, as they prepared to leave. "See you Wednesday and keep the faith!"

Chapter 18

It was dark when Rory awoke, having had a long nap .She assumed Marc had gone home for dinner .The light in her room was dim, but now she noticed a man, not Marc, standing at the bottom of her bed. She blinked several times, trying to get a better look as her panic rose.

The man walked to the head of the bed and took her hand. "Rory, you're awake! How are you?"

Rory sighed with relief. "Sean, I'm fine…why are you here?"

"You have to ask? I'm here because every single time I've needed you, you've been there for me," said her brother. "I had to see you for myself. Marc told me you'd probably be fine, but I came anyway."

"Oh God, do Mom and Dad know?" Rory asked.

"Of course, they saw you on TV. They called me before I'd even seen the news. So I promised I'd call them the moment I had anything to tell them. Are you up to talking to them on the phone?"

"Yeah, sure, I guess I'd best do it soon."

Sean punched in the number on his phone and handed it to Rory. Trying her best to sound upbeat, Rory spoke when her mother came on the line. "Hi, Mom, I'm fine, really…I'm just a little tired." She listened and then answered, "I know the news says I'm in guarded condition, and they will continue to say that for a while. That's because we want the murderer to think I'm out of commission…" Rory continued to reassure her mother and then spoke with her father. That out of the way, she handed the phone back to Sean and fell back on the pillow, exhausted.

"Thanks, Rory," he said. "I know you made them feel better!"

"Did Ginny come?" Rory asked.

"No, I came alone," he said, a smile playing around his mouth.

"Why the smile? What's up?"

"Sorry, I can't keep a secret any longer. Ginny's pregnant!" His smile was huge.

Rory held herself in check. She needed to give the right response. "That's wonderful news! I didn't know you guys were even trying…"

"We weren't, it just sort of happened, but we're ecstatic!"

"Well, I guess! Give me a hug," Rory said.

They hugged and she gave him a kiss. "That's for Ginny and the baby."

"I'll deliver it, although I wasn't supposed to tell you."

"Why not?"

"Ginny didn't want to take the focus off your recovery."

"Well, you can tell Ginny that's just the news I needed to take my mind off my situation."

"I'll tell her, but she'll still accuse me of not being able to keep a secret."

"Well, that part's true," Rory teased. "How old was I when you told me there was no Santa Claus?"

"You were at least five and I was tired of keeping up a front."

"Do Mom and Dad know?"

"No, Ginny wanted you guys to know first."

"Well, now you can tell them!"

Just then there was a tap on the door. Dr. Tyler came in with Marc right behind.

Rory sat up. "Dr. Tyler I'm glad you're here. I want you to know I feel fine and I just need my walking papers."

"I'm happy to see your spunk return. I think you've rounded the corner and will soon be ready to leave. But first your temp needs to stabilize and we need another MRI to make sure there are no visible lasting effects."

"In case you haven't heard, someone tried to kill me, and I've got a murdering pedophile to catch!"

***

In the hospital parking lot the man sat in his car and watched as Marc left the hospital. So she was still there. Her husband wasn't looking especially happy, so maybe she was unconscious and he was still safe. He supposed that after his failure to take her out, she was probably under guard. Going back into the hospital was too risky, and he needed to cut his losses.

***

Rory had sent everyone home, and had just finished her dinner. It was not gourmet fare, but her appetite had returned, so she'd eaten every morsel. Now she felt sleepy. There'd been a lot of excitement today and she'd overestimated her stamina. She wouldn't tell the doctor that, but she probably did need to be in the hospital for at least another day.

As she started to doze, her cell rang. Reaching for it she saw it was Sarah, and smiled. "Hi Sarah, how are you?"

"I'm fine, the question is, how are *you*?

"Oh, you know, just lazing around letting people wait on me!"

"Still have your sense of humor, I see. Good! It's great to hear your voice. You managed to be asleep whenever we were there, but I'll try not to take it personally."

"I was drugged up pretty good, for sure. My pain meds have been lowered considerably, and I have much less pain. I should be out in a day or two."

"That's great news! But we'll keep up the fiction we've been putting out. Officially you're still 'in guarded condition'. Now, about that other rumor I heard..."

"I don't know what you're talking about," Rory said innocently.

"I'm waiting…"

"Well, I may have mentioned that I might like to catch whoever tried to kill me, and I assume that person and the 'bogeyman' are one and the same. By the way, how did he get that creepy name?"

"He's a creepy guy, and actually he told Rachel, his first victim, that was his name. It fits!" Then Sarah gave the thumbs up to Sam, and Rory heard wild cheering on the other end.

Chapter 19

The next day, Sam and Sarah came into Rory's room just as she was finishing her breakfast. She was drinking her tepid tea, which she found unappetizing, but she couldn't stomach coffee.

Sarah ran over to her bedside and bent down to give Rory a hug. "I hope I didn't hurt you! It's just that I'm so happy to see you. You look great!"

"Thanks, Sarah, no you didn't hurt me, and it's good to see you, too." She turned to Sam.

"Hey, Sam, how's it going?" He came over to give her a kiss.

"It's going much better now that you've joined the defense, not that we weren't prepared…"

"And it will get Forsythe off our backs, I hope," Sarah said.

"Forsythe?" Rory asked, looking confused.

"Oh, we need to get you in the loop," Sarah said. "Forsythe owns Citadel, and he's been bugging us about the case. He claims Rowe is his best foreman, and he's paying for his defense. He really wants you on the case."

"Funny, I've never met him, even when we signed the contract with Citadel."

"Once you meet him, you'll wish you never had!" Sarah said, grimacing.

"He's that bad, huh?" Rory asked.

"Only if it bothers you to have someone up your ass with every move you make!"

"Is Sarah exaggerating, Sam?" Rory asked.

"Nope," Sam replied at once. "But if he's paying, I guess that's part of the deal."

"Well, I'll put off meeting him as long as possible. Once I get out, I'll probably work from home for a bit. But you can go ahead and tell him I'll probably take the case when I'm better."

"Ok, but we won't tell him how to reach you," Sarah said.

"So," Rory said, "What's the strategy? What have you guys been up to so far?"

Sam and Sarah took turns filling Rory in on what they'd done and what they were planning to do.

"We'll give you copies of the discovery, and the court eval done on Rowe. By the way, Marc's was much more thorough, so you might want to look at that. Marc was impressed with the guy, and so were we when we met him."

"His review of bail hearing is tomorrow, and McClain said he'd try to get a different judge," Sam said.

"Let me guess," Rory said, "You got Dickenson, and that DA…"

"Bingo!" Sam said, "We got the 'gargoyles' again, and they performed as expected. But to be truthful, we didn't think he had much of a chance. With them, though, he had zero chance of getting out."

"We should do better this time, what with the murder, which implicates the bogeyman, and the court eval, while not as extensive as Marc's, is not unfavorable. I think we'll put Marc's eval in for balance. Rowe might just get out tomorrow," Sarah predicted.

"You guys will do fine with the hearing. It should be pretty cut and dried, and certainly easier than the last one."

"Thanks, Rory," Sam replied, "I'm not sweating it, but I don't want to be overly optimistic."

"Oh, really?" Rory laughed. "Who'd you hear that from?"

"We heard it from the top!" Sarah said. "And it's proven to be true quite often."

"By the way," Rory said, "here's another piece of advice, if he does make bail, have a side-bar with the judge, and request this…"

***

The bogeyman was sitting in his car near the playground. Carly had not come for the last two nights and he was panicked. He'd given her the necklace, and that might have been the reason for her disappearance. He'd arrived earlier than usual, but most kids had left the playground. He was sure she wanted to see him, and just as sure that something else was going on.

The last of the stragglers had passed and he still hadn't seen Carly. He knew where she lived, so he decided to drive by and see what he might learn. He pulled up and parked across the street from her house where he had a good view. Almost immediately, he became aware of the problem. There was a county vehicle, with CYS, (Children and Youth Services) on the side. Of course! She was a foster child and had been placed by CYS. This meant that some nosey bitch caseworker would be checking on her. He was fucked. And he was furious.

He knew too much about the foster care system, having been a victim of it himself.

Just as he prepared to leave, the door to the house opened and out walked Carly, with a suitcase. She was being escorted by a young woman who looked like she was just out of college. She had her arm protectively around Carly and a concerned look on her face. It looked like Carly was crying.

When the CYS car drove off, the bogeyman was not far behind.

***

Rory had dozed off after dinner. She'd had a busy day. Besides spending a good hour with Sam and Sarah, she'd had a visit from her brother and her daughters. It had been wonderful to see everyone, but it did tire her out.

Marc came in and found her sleeping. He sat and watched her, wondering if he should just let her sleep, or wait to see if she woke up.

A nurse came in to check on Rory, so the decision was made for Marc. Rory woke up while the nurse checked her vitals. She saw Marc and smiled. "How long have you been here?" she asked.

"Not long, I was just wondering if I should leave…"

"I'm glad you didn't," she answered. And to the nurse she said, "What's the prognosis?"

"Well, your temp has come down, but is still a tad elevated, perhaps because of all the visitors?" she asked with a smile. "You're improving in all areas, but tomorrow you'll have the MRI and that will help Dr. Tyler decide if you're ready to go home. I'll stop in again before bedtime," she said as she left.

Marc came over to sit next to Rory. "You did have a lot of company today. How was it?"

"It felt good to be part of the defense team. I'm glad I made that decision, with some *subtle* help from you."

"From me?" Marc said innocently.

"Uh, yeah! You know me well, and you played your ace with that eval."

"Is that what did the trick?"

"That was part of it, but when that bastard damn near killed me, that pushed the envelope. But if you hadn't vouched for Rowe I wouldn't have touched it. I don't think I could defend a verifiable pedophile. And, since you got me into this, could you give me some info about pedophiles? The short version, since I do know some things."

"All right, I'll do my best to fill in the blanks. First of all pedophiles are attracted to prepubescent children, of either sex, although girls are more often their targets. All pedophiles do not become child molesters; in fact it's a small minority of offenders who do. The child molesters, in addition to having a predisposition (probably because of an abnormality in the hypothalamus) toward pedophilia, have other mental health issues and/or have been abused themselves. The most serious and chronic child molesters show signs of antisocial behavior early on. Am I boring you yet?" Marc asked, smiling.

"Not at all," Rory said. "Please continue."

"It is believed by some psychologists that serial killers have similar profiles to serial child molesters. Of course, they would be referring to the most serious of those offenders. By the way, our bogeyman may be in that category, especially since he's now murdered someone. I believe he will be labeled as a 'predator', if he's found guilty, and that would buy him a lifetime in prison. There really is no cure for pedophilia, and those deemed predators are the most dangerous."

"Wow!" Rory said. "I guess I knew he was dangerous, but that gives me chills."

"On another subject, can you tell me how DNA can be compromised?"

"I've done this long enough to have seen several cases where DNA was either manipulated or mismanaged in the lab. In this case, I have some ideas. The dead sperm are a red flag. Unless he's sterile, and we don't know that, his sperm could've been collected and used to incriminate him. Sam and Sarah need to question him about his method of birth control."

***

Marc was tired when he left the hospital. Rory was looking and, it seemed, feeling better. He knew that soon they'd have to discuss difficult matters. Rory's accident had put them on hold, but the issues were unavoidable.

Alex's molestation was paramount. The twins were still a bit chilly towards each other, but had banded together to support their mom. Getting Rory to be okay with it was another matter entirely. So much to think about. He would have to learn to put things in perspective. And he missed Rory. They'd had such a good vacation, and as soon as it ended, it seemed they'd had hell to pay.

Marc wasn't paying attention, and had walked past his car. He hit his fob a few times until he saw the flashing lights. Then he went towards the car and got in quickly.

Before he could start the engine, a cold steel object was pressed to his neck.

"Don't turn around, *Marcus,*" came a raspy whisper. "You better make sure your wife doesn't say a word, or I'll be back!"

"She's in a coma for God's sake!" Marc wailed, and soon the back door slammed.

Chapter 20

Marc was upset, but managed to keep his cool. From his rear view, he saw the intruder run off. Immediately, he called the head nurse on Rory's floor and asked that she alert security.

Then he called Sam to ask who he should call at the police department to report the incident.

"I think it's better if you go in person. It's Detective Herrera on the case, but why don't I meet you at the station?" Sam offered.

"Thanks, Sam, I'll be there in about ten."

As he drove, Marc realized he was shaking. He pulled to the side of the road until he felt more like himself. Was that the bogeyman he'd just encountered? It felt like a knife had been pressed to his neck, and wasn't Gordon Howe killed with a knife? Who else could it have been?

Then he thought about protecting Rory when she came home. He checked himself for over- thinking the situation. He would have to deal with this most recent encounter first. He drove back onto the highway.

Arriving at the police station, he parked the car and decided to wait for Sam. In the meantime, he called the head nurse again to inquire about any further developments. She reported that nothing suspicious had occurred and Rory's guard was doubled. Marc breathed a sigh of relief. He could handle himself, but if anything happened to Rory, he was pretty sure he'd fall apart.

Sam pulled up next to Marc, and the two went in to speak the detective.

***

Sam was up early the next day. It had been late when they'd left the police station. Herrera had been very helpful and was taking the threat to Marc seriously. He'd also promised to contact the Nether Providence police, because Marc and Rory lived in their jurisdiction, to ask for their cooperation in routinely patrolling Rory's neighborhood.

Sleep had been a long time coming for Sam, and now he had to present a cogent defense for releasing Rowe on bail. He had told Forsythe that Rory would take the case when she was better, but for now he and Sarah were on it. Forsythe was coming to the hearing, and would post bail, if allowed.

Sarah walked sleepily into the kitchen and found Sam scribbling notes. "You're pretty prepared for this, so why are you still writing notes?"

"You can't be too prepared, Sarah. I just want to cover all the bases."

"I thought we'd done that." She answered, stifling a yawn. "Did this keep you up all night? I noticed you tossing and turning."

"My mind was just racing after meeting with Herrera. Marc was pretty upset about his close encounter with probably the bogeyman. Now we're worried about Rory's safety when she gets out of the hospital, which could be today."

"Oh, you're right, Rowe and Rory could both get out the same day…"

"And the case gets ratcheted up another notch or two."

"Ok, Sam, here's some of your advice coming back at you, 'take one thing at a time.' "

"I know, it's just sometimes hard to do what I know is best. But thanks for reminding me!"

"Can I fix you some breakfast? That will probably make you feel better."

"Yes, I think you're right, thanks for offering."

Sarah went into the kitchen to make a nice, big breakfast for Sam. She was feeling guilty because she had something to tell him, and wasn't sure when the right time would be. Her father had called her a few weeks before, and invited her to come visit him. Initially, she'd told him no, but left the door open for consideration. Now, with Rory getting out of the hospital she felt she could take the time.

No matter when she went, it would be tough on Sam because he was so overly protective of her. She needed to get out from under that for a bit, and she thought it would be best for both of them. Plus, she would love to spend time with her father, especially since their relationship had improved incredibly following her kidnapping.

***

When Sarah and Sam left the office to walk to the courthouse for the hearing, they were overwhelmed by the press milling around outside. "Well, at least they won't be outside the hospital if Rory leaves today," Sarah noted.

There were three major news vans parked in front and more reporters than they could count. Sam made the decision to go in a side door, which they could access with a key card. They hoped no one would notice as they walked away from the main entrance to the courthouse.

At least one person noticed. It was the bogeyman.

***

Entering from the side door proved to be a good strategy, since reporters weren't allowed access to the courtroom. Sam led Sarah to the third floor and they made their way to the courtroom.

Sam took a deep breath and said to Sarah, "I've got to see who's sitting today." He walked into the courtroom and asked the bailiff.

"I think it's Judge Jenkins," he told Sam.

"Great, thanks," Sam said, feeling a load lift.

He was smiling when he came out.

"Oh, good!" Sarah said when she saw his smile. "Who is it then?"

"Judge Jenkins," he said, with a grin. "At least that's what the bailiff thinks."

"That is good news," Sarah said. "She's fair, and that's the best we can hope for."

"She also likes to get started early, so we might as well go in and wait in the back."

They had taken their seats when they heard someone come in and turned to see that it was Forsythe. They had no choice but to acknowledge him.

Forsythe came over and looked ready to sit with them.

"Sorry," Sarah said, "but this side of the courtroom is reserved for court personnel." It was a total fabrication, but Sarah just blurted it without thinking.

Sam recovered without laughing out loud, and said to Forsythe, "Is there anything we need to discuss before the hearing?"

"Just the bail stuff," he answered.

"Let's not jinx ourselves. If he gets bail, we'll talk then.

"Ok," Forsythe said as he reluctantly took his seat across the aisle.

Sam tried to frown at Sarah, but found he couldn't do it.

More people entered the courtroom, and Sam turned to see the same guys from Citadel. He thought that was a good sign, and must make Rowe feel better. Although, noticing the scowl on his face, Forsythe didn't seem to approve.

When the bailiff said, "All rise..." it wasn't Judge Jenkins who entered. It was the dreaded Judge Dickenson, who'd presided at the last hearing.

"We're sunk!" Sam hissed in Sarah's ear. "Now what?"

"Can we ask for a continuance?" Sarah suggested.

The judge asked the bailiff, "If the prisoners have arrived, please bring in," she stopped to consult the files before her, "Rowe, for the review of bail."

The bailiff answered, "They have arrived and I will have Rowe brought in."

Sam took his seat at the defense table, and Sarah sat behind him on the first bench, since there was only one other chair at the table.

Sam greeted the DA, Dylan Jefferson, whom they'd met at McClain's office. "Any idea why we got *her*?" Sam whispered.

Dylan shook his head, "McClain tried and we thought it was Jenkins, but this happened last minute. McClain can't control who the judge is, but he did appoint me to handle it from this side. She wanted to bring her 'toady', I'm sure, but don't worry about me, I'll go along with you."

"Great, there's a recommendation I would like you to make at sidebar." He went on to tell him.

Rowe came in escorted by the sheriffs and took his seat next to Sam.

He looked much better, Sarah thought. His color was better and some of the bruises were fading. She prayed he'd be released today, but had doubts because of the judge.

Jefferson introduced the case, and nodded to Sam to address the court.

"Good morning, Judge Dickenson," he began. "As the state has indicated, this is a review of bail hearing. I would direct Your Honor to the memo and evaluations which accompany this case."

"I have read them, Mr. Logan. You may proceed."

"Your Honor, we have scheduled this hearing because circumstances have changed since the arraignment. First, both sex-offender evaluations present Mr. Rowe as nonviolent. Neither labels him a 'predator'. The second, and in our opinion, the most compelling reason is that one of the men who'd been at the poker game the night of the molestation, and thus an alibi witness, has been murdered. I interviewed Gordon Howe, the murder victim, a few days before his murder. The night before his murder, he left a voice message asking me to meet with him at our office because he had news to tell me. His tone was grave, and he seemed upset. My assumption is that this man was killed because he was willing to out the so-called 'bogeyman'. From the beginning, it was our opinion that one of the other men at the poker game was the bogeyman. For these reasons, we are requesting that Mason Rowe be released on bail."

"Thank you, Mr. Logan," the judge said. "Does that complete your remarks?"

"Yes, Your Honor," Sam said, as he took his seat.

"And your rebuttal, Mr. Jefferson?" the judge asked, almost smirking.

"Your Honor, the state does not oppose the release of Mr. Rowe on bail, and for the purposes of this hearing we believe he has met the criteria for said release."

The judge was not smiling now. It would be unprecedented for her to override the DA's argument, or lack thereof, and would appear unprofessional.

"Your Honor, may we approach the bench?" Jefferson asked.

"You may," she said, appearing confused.

Jefferson made the suggestion that Sam had asked him to make, and it was accepted.

"The ruling in this case is that the defendant, Mason Rowe, be released on one-hundred thousand dollars bail, ten percent real." She banged the gavel a tad harder than necessary, and left the bench quickly.

Sam clapped Dylan on the back and thanked him.

Chapter 21

A young woman was ushered into Detective Herrera's office. She had told the duty officer that she had some information that might be related to the 'bogeyman' case.

The detective offered her a seat and without any preliminary chitchat, asked her to give the information she had.

"Well," Ms. Hunter said, "I work for CYS, and my area of specialty is to place appropriate children into foster homes. Some of these homes are temporary, others may be permanent. I also check in periodically with the children." She stopped to take a breath.

Detective Herrera nodded, and said, "Continue."

"I'm working with a girl of nine who has been in several foster homes. She was removed from one home for alleged sexual abuse by the foster father. So I try to be especially careful where I place her. At a routine visit the other day, I noticed she was wearing a necklace I hadn't seen before and I asked her about it. She smiled and said, 'Charlie gave it to me.' There is no 'Charlie' in this foster home, so I asked who he was. She told me she met him at the playground, and then once sat in his car with him. She told me he was 'very nice' to her. Of course alarm bells were ringing, so I checked with the foster parents, and asked if they were aware of this 'Charlie', and if she'd ever gone to the playground alone. They were unaware of Charlie, but did admit that she had gone to the playground unescorted on a few occasions."

"And, your conclusions?" the detective asked.

"I think she may have been dealing with the 'bogeyman'. I immediately removed her from that home, and have her in a group home until I can find a permanent home for her. I asked her a few questions about Charlie and she became defensive, so I'm not sure what information she'll be willing to give, but I can bring her in for questioning if you think it's appropriate.

"By all means, bring her in. See the duty officer to arrange an appointment. And thanks."

***

Mason Rowe, in his street clothes, was escorted by two police officers, along with Sarah and Sam, out the back entrance of the courthouse. His release would be big news so they had to avoid the press.

The five quickly got into a squad car, and took off. But their exit strategy had been anticipated and a small crowd of the press and some hecklers blocked their way.

Calls of "pervert" and "baby-fucker" rang out from by-standers, as the press took pictures and held their microphones aloft.

The officer reacted quickly and authoritatively. Lights flashing and siren blaring, the driver sped up, forcing the crowd to disperse.

Rowe sat in the back between Sam and Sarah, head in hands, covering his face. He looked up as they left the chaos behind.

"I was so relieved to get out, I didn't even think how people might react," he sighed. "I guess I should go right to my apartment, even though it may seem to be a prison. I don't mean to sound like an ingrate. I appreciate so much what you've done for me. Thank you both," Rowe said, looking from Sam to Sarah.

Sam spoke first, "I got the impression Forsythe wants you back on the job, right?"

"Yes, he did say that. But he said I should come back when I'm ready. I'll have to see how much courage I can muster."

"Is there any place you could stay besides your apartment?" Sarah asked. "It might be easier if your whereabouts were unknown."

"My brother Greg has a bachelor pad in the city, it would be kind of a long commute, but...well, that's all I can think of."

"For now, why don't we go back to your apartment? You can get what you need, call your brother and come up with a plan," Sam suggested.

"Is there a back way out of your apartment?" Sarah asked. "If there is, I can get dropped off at home and come back with the car when you're ready."

"Yes, there is, that sounds good," Rowe answered.

Sarah spoke to the officer, "Can you drop me off at 44 South 5th street?"

"Certainly," he agreed. "We're almost there."

"Sam, you'll call me when you're ready?" Sarah asked as the car drew up in front of their apartment.

"Sure, I'll be in touch. Go on, get in there quick and lock the doors!" Sam instructed, as he looked around for any reporters.

Chapter 22

Rory was sitting anxiously in her hospital bed. She'd had her MRI after breakfast, and was waiting for Dr. Tyler to give her the all clear to leave. She was being optimistic, she realized, but she really did feel better and she was getting antsy to get home. She hadn't heard from Sam or Sarah, so didn't know whether or not Rowe had been released.

Her phone rang and she grabbed it, expecting either Sarah or Marc. It was neither; it was her friend, Don, who was an adult probation officer, and at times, her unofficial private investigator.

"Hey, Rory, I've been worried about you, but wanted to give you a few days before I violated your privacy. Are you up to talking?"

"You bet I am!" Rory said. "Actually, I'm waiting for the doc to let me go. I'm feeling much better and want to get into the 'bogeyman' case."

"Wow! I'm glad you're so much better. The reports haven't been all that positive," Don said.

"I know, I know, that was intentional, so the murderer, who isn't sure whether or not I saw the murder, doesn't try to off me. He tried once, the first night I was here!"

"Jeez, that's serious! Aren't you afraid to go home?"

"I can't wait to go home. I think we'll keep up the fiction that I'm in the hospital."

"It's sounding more interesting by the moment! Hey, it's my kind of case; can you use my undercover talents?"

"I'm sure I can, Don, but I have to get into the case first, once I get home. I'll call you as soon as I have anything."

"Promise?"

"Promise, just wish me luck getting home. I can't take it much longer!"

"Hey, feel better and keep in touch!"

“Will do, and thanks for calling! I’m sure I would’ve enlisted your aid anyway. Bye.”

Rory started to get out of bed, when her friend Roland sauntered in. Roland was a State Trooper who’d developed a friendship with Rory over the years. What cinched it was that she defended a gay friend of his in a school board hearing. Rory had saved his friend’s job, and their friendship had blossomed. Not many people knew Roland was gay, and as a trooper, he needed to keep it that way.

Roland came straight to her bedside and leaned down to give her a kiss. “You look good! Marc has kept me informed of your progress, and he seems to think you’re getting out today.”

“Did the doc tell him that?” Rory asked.

“No, it’s not official yet, but he wanted me to be here, in case the press was outside, as it’s been. Although today, I think they’ve reassembled at the courthouse. Have you heard how that case went?”

“No, I haven’t but I have high hopes that Rowe and I both get out today!

***

Mason Rowe was in a state of shock. What he’d prayed for since his incarceration had finally come to pass. And now he had a whole different set of circumstances to deal with. He hadn’t considered that he’d be so reviled. He looked slowly around his apartment, realizing that most of his things were at Dara’s, but he couldn’t go there. Perhaps she could bring some things to him later.

He walked as if in a trance from room to room, unable to focus on anything. Sam noticed his predicament and tried to help. “Ok, Mason, what do you think you will need to take with you? Do you have work clothes, toiletries?”

“I can wear anything to work, unless I’m meeting with clients, so I’m sure I can find some stuff for now. I’ll have to ask Dara to drop some things off…”

“She can bring them to the office, and we’ll deal with them from there. You may actually be working at the office. It would be convenient for all of us, and I’m sure Forsythe would be on board.”

“Yeah, he’s really stepped up. I don’t understand, but I appreciate it.”

Sam’s phone buzzed and he saw it was Sarah. “Hi Sarah, no we’re not quite ready…sure, lunch sounds great! Hang on.” Sam asked Mason, "What would you like for lunch? Sarah's going to stop by on her way over."

"Oh, I get to choose! I've been dreaming of a cheese steak, with onions and ketchup. That would be heaven!"

Sam got back on his cell, "Make that two cheese steaks with onions and ketchup, oh and get it at Vinnies. Outside of Philly, they're the best. Thanks, see you soon, come in the back way."

"Jeez, I just realized how hungry I am," Mason said, seeming to come alive. "Let me gather up some stuff while we're waiting."

By the time Sarah arrived, some ten minutes later, Sam and Mason were sitting in anticipation like lions at feeding time. They got up immediately as she entered.

"Hungry, eh?" She laughed, as they virtually ripped the bag from her hands.

"I haven't eaten a decent meal since I went to jail. There were only a few things I could eat." Mason shook his head in disgust.

"Then you'll be happy." Sarah said, "that I got you two! One for now and one for later. I wouldn't try to eat too much on an empty stomach, though," she cautioned.

"What about me?" Sam whined dramatically. "Why do I get just one?"

"Did you bother to look in the bag?" she asked.

He looked and found an extra one. "Oh, I thought that was yours…"

"No, mine would be the lowly salad on the bottom. I got two for you so I don't have to make dinner tonight."

"Works for me!" Sam said, tucking into his sandwich.

"Mmm," Mason said, his mouth full.

***

Marc had asked Roland to bring Rory home in his cruiser, to avoid the press and any other unforeseen events. . When Rory got the final OK to leave the hospital, it was lunchtime. Roland phoned Marc and alerted him to their imminent arrival. He suggested Marc have some lunch waiting for them.

With all the paperwork finished, and prescriptions filled, they left the hospital. "We're going out the back way to avoid any members of the press who may be hanging around. "

Rory followed Roland as they took the elevator to the basement. As the elevator door opened, Rory was stopped in her tracks by the horrendous smell. "Oh Jeez," she said "What is that *smell*?"

"Uh, that would be formaldehyde, the morgue is down here. I get down here a fair amount on the job, so I hardly notice it," Roland answered.

Rory had her hand over her nose as she quickly followed Roland out of the building. Even though the air was humid, it smelled good to Rory. When Rory was settled in the car, Roland took off. They were in the middle of a conversation, when Rory abruptly stopped talking. Roland smiled as he saw that her head had dropped to one side and she was fast asleep.

***

Dara Keene hadn't been able to attend Mason's bail hearing, but she was pleased to know he'd been released. He wouldn't be staying at his apartment, however, because he was afraid of repercussions such as he'd encountered when leaving the courthouse. He was staying with his brother in Philadelphia for the time being. They'd keep in touch by phone. Until this whole trial was over and done with she thought it best not to see him.

She'd just gotten off work and was on her way to pick up Rachel. Thoughts of Rachel made her happy. Her little girl had made such strides in therapy. She may not have entirely forgotten her encounters with the 'bogeyman,' but she seemed to be more herself.

Getting out of her car at the daycare, Dara noticed that the kids were outside playing. She scanned the yard for Rachel, who was wearing a bright yellow top and blue shorts. She should be easy to spot, Dara thought, but she didn't see her.

She walked up to one of the aides. "Are some of the children inside? I don't see Rachel."

The aide looked surprised and said, "Mrs. Keene, your husband picked up Rachel over an hour ago. I checked and he is on the list as one of the approved caretakers. Was there a miscommunication?"

Dara could hardly speak, she felt as if she'd been sucker-punched. "He's my ex, I guess he's still on the list, but he's been living out of town. And he certainly didn't notify me of his intention to pick her up. I'll have to call him, thank you."

Dara stumbled to her car, trembling. Paul wouldn't do this, would he? Why would he pick her up without consulting me first, she wondered. When her hands had stopped shaking, Dara punched up his cell number. It went right to voicemail, not a good sign. Perhaps he'd wanted to surprise her and was waiting at home with Rachel.

Driving home as fast as was safe, she arrived at her place in a few minutes. Paul's car was not there. She parked the car and raced to her house, fumbling to get the key in the lock. As soon as she entered, she began calling, "Rachel, Paul, are you here?" The silence was deafening.

She checked the entire house and found no sign of either of them. She did find some open drawers in Rachel's room, which she did not take as a good sign. As she came back through the kitchen, she noticed the answering machine light blinking. She raced for it and listened to the message.

"Dara, it's Paul, and I have Rachel. Just don't go ballistic, she's fine. I got an anonymous message on my phone from someone who told me Mason's been released from jail. He suggested that Rachel wouldn't be safe with Mason on the streets. Sorry, Dara, but I just had to do what's best for Rachel. I hope you understand."

Chapter 23

Blake and Katrina were just sitting down to dinner when Katrina's cell buzzed. She looked at her phone and saw it was Dara, so she took the call.

"Katrina, I need your help! Paul took Rachel from daycare today and he won't tell me where they are. He said he had to keep Rachel safe because Mason was released from jail. I don't know what to do!" Dara wailed.

"Sit tight, Dara, we'll be right there!"

Getting off the phone, she spoke urgently to Blake, "We've got to go to Dara's, she's freaking out! Paul took Rachel from daycare and won't reveal where they are."

Blake took a last bite of dinner and looked at it longingly.

"We'll eat later," Trina barked, "let's get a move on!"

Blake sighed as he got his keys and followed Katrina out the door.

As he drove, Katrina filled him in a bit more. "Paul said he got an anonymous call from a guy who told him Mason got out, and warned him that Rachel wouldn't be safe. So apparently he reacted impulsively, as usual, and took off with Rachel."

"How come the daycare released her to him?"

"Dara didn't say, but he does have visiting privileges and was probably still on the daycare list of approved care-takers. And I know Rachel was happy when he stopped at the house to see her about a week ago, so she wouldn't have reacted negatively to seeing him."

"Jeez," Blake muttered, "how can we possibly help? Any ideas?"

"The only way we can help right now is to listen to her and maybe prompt her to think of any place Paul might've taken Rachel."

As soon as they drew up to Dara's house, Katrina jumped out of the car as Blake parked.

Dara was waiting at the front door and nearly collapsed into Katrina's arms. Katrina guided her to a seat in the living room. They just sat with their arms around one another. Dara shook convulsively as she sobbed.

Blake entered and closed the door behind him. He felt useless and stood with his hands in his pockets. Trina was much better with this emotional stuff than he was. Blake thought about creeping out of the house and taking off. That was what he wanted to do, but knew he couldn't. Katrina would kill him, and really, Dara had been through so much.

As the sobbing ebbed and slowly ended, Dara looked up and saw Blake. She went to him, her arms outstretched. As he hugged her, she said, "Thank you Blake, I know this is a sacrifice for you, being interrupted at your dinner hour." She almost smiled.

"Oh hell, Dara, you come first! I'm really sorry about Rachel. Did Paul leave you any clues as to his whereabouts?"

"He just left a message on my house phone, the coward! He knew I wouldn't be home when he called. And he also knew I'd be panicked. But it's hard to believe that he acted on an anonymous call."

"That is tough to understand," Katrina said. "Has he ever done this before?"

"Well, yeah," Dara said. "When he came here last week, he'd gotten an anonymous call about Rachel being molested. I should maybe call to talk with someone at the daycare."

"That makes sense," Blake agreed.

Before Dara could make the call, her house phone rang. She ran to pick it up.

***

Hayley Singleton, a rookie reporter for The Daily Times, sat at her desk, bored. She'd been assigned to report on the Mason Rowe trial, but he'd disappeared shortly after his release, so she didn't have much of a story. She wanted very much to be a star reporter, but so far she hadn't caught any breaks. That's all it took, she thought, just one.

Her phone rang and she answered immediately. "Listen carefully," the unidentified caller said, "I'm only gonna' say this once." Hayley grabbed for her pen and notebook.

"Go ahead," she said.

"Rowe was just released from jail, and now his fiancée's daughter is missing. Is that a coincidence?" The line went dead.

"But, but…" Hayley said, to no avail. She quickly dialed *69, but the number came back as blocked. "Shit!"

Taking a few moments to calm down, she tried to think it through. She looked through the file she'd put together on Mason Rowe and found the address of Dara Keene, Rachel's mother. She decided that was a good place to start. Grabbing her briefcase, she ran out the door.

***

Dara picked up the phone. It was the day-care director, Mrs. Roberts. "Mrs. Keene," she said. "I understand there was a mix-up today about Rachel. I do hope it was straightened out."

"It was," Dara said reluctantly. "Paul and I just need to communicate better," she lied.

"I'm relieved," the director said. "I saw her leave with her father and she seemed very happy, so I was sure all was well."

"Yes, it was. By the way, I'm off tomorrow, so Rachel won't be coming to daycare. Bye now."

Dara looked at Katrina and Blake. "I don't want to go off half-cocked and make this a bigger deal than it is…"

"Do you have any idea where he may have taken Rachel?" Katrina asked.

"I've thought and thought, and the only place I can think of at all is a house his parents left to him outside of Lewes, Delaware. We used to go there, but with all of the problems Paul's had with staying sober, and then the divorce, we haven't been there in years, and the house must've fallen into disrepair…"

"Well, Lewes isn't far, is it worth the trip?" Blake asked.

"Yes, I guess it is, but how do we get him to give her up?"

"I can call Trooper Johnson, see if he can help," Blake offered. Dara nodded, and Blake called Roland on his cell. It was his private cell and he answered quickly.

"Blake, what can I do for you?"

Repeating the scenario, Blake asked for Roland's help.

"You understand," Roland said, "that I can't act in an official capacity once I reach the Delaware border. But, I do carry a weapon and can be persuasive. Why hasn't Dara involved the authorities?"

Blake didn't know the answer to that question, so he asked Dara to explain to the trooper.

"Trooper Johnson?" Dara began, "I don't believe my husband means to harm Rachel. He did leave me a message that he has her because he's afraid of what might happen to her with Mason out of jail. He's impulsive and often irrational, but I don't believe he would ever hurt Rachel. I just want her back, but he won't answer my phone calls, so I think I have to do this in person."

"Okay, I understand," Roland said. "Give me your address and I'll be there shortly."

"Thank God!" Dara said, as she hung up. "At least we're doing something."

***

Across the street from Dara's house, Hayley Singleton sat in her beat-up Kia watching. All the lights were on in the house and she could see movement of shadows behind the curtains. But she hadn't seen anything that was noteworthy. She didn't have anything else to do so she decided to follow her hunch and wait.

She was rewarded for her patience, when, in about ten minutes, a late-model Dodge Charger slowed down, came to a stop and parked near the house. The driver got out, and walked to the front door.

Didn't cops drive Dodge Chargers, she thought, as she watched the tall, well-built black man enter the house. He looked like a cop, Hayley thought. There was definitely something going on. Her caller was right!

A few minutes later, several people emerged from the house, a man and two women, along with the cop. She identified one of the women as Dara Keene. The other woman, a redhead, got in the 'cop car' with Dara and the two men. The car took off.

Hayley hesitated, then pulled out and followed the Charger from a distance.

***

Rory's house was quieter than usual at this time of night. The twins had made dinner and were staying in for the night. This was a huge sacrifice on their part, Rory thought, but she knew their solitude wouldn't last. Still, it was nice of them and they were being so helpful. She wondered momentarily if there was something she didn't know about her diagnosis, but automatically banished the thought from her mind. She didn't have time for negative thinking. She had too much to do.

Dozing off on the couch as Marc, a news -junky, watched CNN, Rory was jolted awake as she overheard her daughters arguing, and then doors slamming. Everything was back to normal. She wondered though, if they were still arguing over Alex's undisclosed molestation. They would have to have a family meeting. Rory sighed.

Marc reached over for her hand. "You ok? Glad to be home?"

"Oh, beyond glad! The last few days were torture," she said. "I am feeling quite tired, though, just like the doc said. Yes, I'll take it easy," she added as she saw that Marc was about to speak.

Marc shook his head. "Your idea of 'taking it easy' and mine are worlds apart!"

"True, but I will try and I can't go anywhere for the duration, so all my work will be done at home."

"Oh, I know you'll try, Honey, but can you succeed? Look, I don't want you back in the hospital. That's the bottom line, so I hope you'll listen if I tell you to pull back. I really missed you." He leaned over to give her a kiss.

"I know you missed me," she said softly. "But I'm not quite ready for sex," she said ruefully. "Sorry."

"Oh, well in that case, you might as well go back!" he said in mock horror. "Actually, your doctor told me we should lay off for a while, but I brought you home anyway!"

***

The conversation in the car had tapered off. Roland had been watching his rear-view mirrors for the past several minutes. They were on I 95 south. The red Kia had been following him since he'd left Dara's house. The car was now several lanes to the left of him, but not far behind.

"Hang on, kids!" Roland said, as he made a quick exit onto 495, which detoured around the city of Wilmington, rejoining 95 several miles south.

"Sorry about that!" Roland said, "but I don't like that red Kia that's been on our tail for a while." Checking his rear-view, he said, "Don't see her now."

"You know it's a *she*?" Katrina asked.

"Yep," Roland answered, "unless it's a man with a wig or really long hair." He laughed. "I know a back way to Rt. 1, so we won't be going back onto 95." He exited at the next interchange.

***

"Shit! Shit! Shit!" Haley yelled her frustration. Now she was sure it was a cop she'd been following. What were her options? She thought about staying the course until 95 joined up again. But what was the point, she wondered. She thought she'd best cut her losses and head back to the office.

As she drove, she thought about what she would say. Yes, she would write an article. After all, she had information no one else had. She would piece together a probable scenario and go for front page. That would get the readers' attention. She could envision the accolades as her career took off.

Chapter 24

Dara glanced at her watch. It was just before nine pm; they were making good time. She hoped she would recognize the house. Roland had punched the address into his GPS, so that should help. But still she worried that something would go wrong. *Suppose she was totally wrong?* Too late for worries, they should arrive in a few minutes. She looked out the window, willing the house to appear.

"Shouldn't be too long now," Roland observed. "You might want to look out for the house, Dara."

"I'm looking," Dara answered, "and trying to remember how far it was from the road. It's been a few years since I've been here." She continued staring out the window. "It's so dark it's hard to see anything!" She heard the panic in her voice and tried to quell her fear.

The GPS pinged, "You have reached your destination." Roland pulled the car to the side of the road. "Well, it's got to be somewhere around. Shall we get out and walk around?"

Dara followed Roland's lead and got out of the car, while Blake and Katrina stayed with the vehicle. It was unexpectedly chilly and Dara shivered. She peered through the darkness, thinking this area looked somehow familiar. "I think it's set back from the road a bit, but we should be close."

"Should we look for a driveway?" Roland asked.

"There was never much of a driveway," Dara replied, "and by now it would probably be over-grown." Dara stopped, looking around. Then she pointed. "I think it's right back there!" She picked up the pace and in a few moments they were close to an almost completely overgrown house, nearly invisible from the road because it blended in so well with the field and trees.

Roland motioned for silence, and indicated that Dara should stay where she was. He walked around the side of the house and soon disappeared from view.

"Oh God," Dara moaned, "what if they're not here?"

***

Dara sat bolt upright in her own bed, awakened by a surge of anxiety. Her heart beat double-time, until she saw the small form of her daughter, asleep next to her. It took a few moments for Dara to calm down as she reviewed in her head the events of the night before.

Her instinct had been right. Paul and Rachel were in the house in Delaware. Trooper Johnson didn't have to pull out his gun. Paul had had time to reflect on what he'd done, and was remorseful. He was grateful to Dara for not involving the authorities. And the trooper had made Paul well aware of what the consequences could have been.

Hearing noise in the kitchen, Dara got carefully out of bed so as not to awaken Rachel. She put her bathrobe on and went to the kitchen.

Blake was looking around, presumably for coffee. "Morning Blake, how'd you sleep?" Dara asked.

"I slept great! How about you?"

"I fell into a deep sleep, but my mind must've been working over-time. I woke up having a panic attack, thinking that Rachel was still missing. Thank God it turned out like it did. And thank you for staying. I was a bit leery about Paul staying over-night, but it didn't make sense for him to head back to the half-way house so late."

"Can he go back? I mean, will they let him?" Blake asked.

"He had the good sense to call them last night and they will accept him back." Dara set about making coffee as she and Blake conversed.

As they talked, they heard a small thud on the front door.

"That would be the paper," Dara said. "Do you mind bringing it in? I'd like to see how the bail hearing played out in the paper."

Blake went for the paper, but didn't return immediately. Dara heard him in the hallway. "Damn!" he said.

Dara's stomach knotted for the second time. "What is it?" she asked, not really wanting to know.

Blake turned the paper so that she could read the headlines.

ROWE RELEASED FROM JAIL: RACHEL KEENE GOES MISSING!!

***

Rory slept until ten a.m., a radical departure for her. When she woke up, she was momentarily disoriented, and then relief washed over her. She was in her own bed! No wonder she'd slept so well. She snuggled back under the covers, enjoying the sensation of comfort, emotional and physical, her bed gave her.

A few moments later, Marc appeared in the doorway. "I thought I might've heard you waking up. You seemed to sleep deeply all night, at least when I woke up. Are you ready for breakfast?"

"I did sleep well, and yeah, I'm ready for breakfast. I'm starved! But don't give me too much. I don't think my stomach can take too much food yet. Just a couple of eggs and toast sounds good," Rory answered.

"And coffee?" Marc asked.

"Hmm, maybe tea," she said, hoping Marc wouldn't question it.

"OK, one more question, do you want breakfast in bed?"

"No! I've had breakfast in bed for the last three days! I'm getting a shower and then I'll be down," Rory answered.

"Ok, see you downstairs in a few," Marc said as he left the room.

Rory luxuriated in the warm spray as she cleansed the last traces of "hospital smell" from her body. They'd been wonderful to her at the hospital, she had to admit. But she truly believed in the old adage, "There's no place like home." Although she felt like staying in the shower, she was hungry. Rory dressed quickly and went down the back stairs to the kitchen.

"Good timing," Marc said as he put the plate of food in front of her.

Rory slid into the breakfast nook, another place she'd sorely missed. She felt something on the seat, and pulled out the morning paper. Interested, she looked at the front page.

Rory gasped, "What the fuck is this?"

***

Sam and Sarah were at the office, and had read The Daily Times earlier. They'd put in a call to Blake, and he'd told them the whole story. He said he'd be in the office later to discuss the ramifications of this news.

Sarah said, "Jeez, I'm surprised we haven't heard from Rory."

"Oh, for sure we'll hear from her the moment she sees the paper, unless of course, Marc got to it first. Man, that reporter's in a world of trouble! She got some of it right, but thank God Rachel's home safe. Who do you think put her up to this?" Sam asked

"I think if we knew who it was we'd have the perp. Who else would've pulled a stunt like this, and who benefits from Rowe being blamed?" Sarah replied. "I wonder if Hayley would divulge her source? She may have to if the police question her."

"In fact," Sam reflected, "it might be a real good idea if we paid a visit to McClain. He'll already know, of course, that it wasn't Rowe because he's got the leg bracelet on, and he can't make a move without them knowing."

"Which is to his benefit in terms of his own safety and proof of his innocence. Rory's suggestion that he go on the electronic home monitor was a good one. And keeping it quiet was a good idea, too, so the person responsible for all of this mayhem doesn't know about the monitor," Sarah said.

"Let's give McClain a call," Sam said as he walked towards the phone.

Before he could pick up the phone, it rang. He looked at the number of the in-coming call, and scrunched his face, mouthing, "Guess who?"

Picking up the phone, he held it out from his ear.

A familiar voice demanded, "OK, tell me what you know!"

***

Dara Keene marched into the main office of The Daily Times, trailed by Blake and Rachel. She strode to the front desk and introduced herself, quietly demanding to see the editor.

Moments later, she was escorted to the editor's office.

Dara sat on the edge of the chair she'd been offered across from the editor's desk. Ms. O'Brien had a look of contrition on her face as she offered coffee or water.

Water sounded good to Dara, so she accepted it. Her mouth was beginning to feel dry now that she was face-to-face with the editor. She had gone over what she wanted to say in her mind, and she would strive to do that without anger.

Taking a sip of water, she began. "I, that is my family and I, were egregiously misrepresented in your paper. We felt violated and exposed and it was all for a big headline. We need you to issue a retraction as soon as possible." She went on to explain that Rachel had been with her ex-husband, Rachel's father.

Ms. O'Brien listened, nodding gravely. When Dara had finished, she replied, "Ms. Keene, I agree that you do need an apology. I'm not sure how this got by the evening editor, and I'm not trying to pass the blame, because ultimately, it's my responsibility. And I will get to the bottom of it. I can call a press conference right now if you like. I'm as eager as you to get this over and done. And again, you have my deepest apologies."

Dara was at a loss for words because she had expected push back. But it was exactly what she needed. She said, "Thank you, Ms. O'Brien, and I agree a press conference would be the best way to go. My daughter is in the waiting room with a friend. You can come out and meet her if you like, but we won't be part of any press conference. We would like to go back to our regular lives, as much as possible."

"I can assure you that none of my reporters will be following you. Ms. Singleton will be on official probation, taken off your case, and she will have to fight to keep her job." She stood, and said, "I'd like to meet your daughter, and I assume she's unaware of any of this."

"Right, she just took a short vacation with her father and came home last night."

Ms. O'Brien led the way to the waiting area. Blake stood and shook hands with her when Dara introduced them. "And, this is my daughter, Rachel."

Rachel stood up and shook Ms. O'Brien's hand, saying "HI!"

"Thank you for coming in, Rachel," Ms. O'Brien smiled at the little girl.

Dara said to Blake, "We came to an understanding and a quite reasonable one, I think."

She smiled at Ms. O'Brien, who smiled back.

To Rachel, she said, "So, let's go get some breakfast!"

"Yea!" said Rachel, for whom it was a big treat to go out for breakfast.

Chapter 25

Things were not going so well for Hayley Singleton, who sat mutely in her office, tears staining her face. She'd been moved to a cramped office, far away from the action. Instead of getting kudos for a story well reported, she'd gotten a dressing-down from the editor, who'd put her on probation! She was seething with anger, but hadn't sorted out yet with whom she was angry. What she didn't want to face, but knew, was that she'd acted impulsively with hopes of rising quickly to the top. Why did someone feed her inaccurate information? What did they hope to gain? And who was it? Of course she'd been asked by the police who the "anonymous source" was, and had to admit that she didn't know. But when she'd gone to the Keene house she'd seen what appeared to be covert actions and a sense of urgency.

So now she was "officially" off the case. But she would find out who had given misinformation and she *would* clear her name.

***

There was one person who was ecstatic with the headlines. He read them over and over. He'd certainly picked a winner, and he would feed her more 'information.' She was just the kind of fame-seeking idiot who would do his bidding. Before he was done, Rowe would be maligned by the press, and never have a chance at a fair trial.

Unfortunately for him, he left for work before hearing the press conference.

***

Rory and Marc sat in the breakfast nook, as they waited for Sarah and Sam to come over. Marc had managed to calm his wife down, to a degree. But he was secretly pleased to see her spunk returning. Her eyes were sparkling and she was ready to get right into this case.

He went to the door to let the expected visitors in, and ushered them into the kitchen.

Sarah went straight to Rory and gave her a hug. "So glad you're home! And you're obviously ready for work." She smiled and sat down next to Rory.

Sam and Marc slid in across the table from the women.

Sarah spoke first, "Look we saw the headlines this morning and called Blake straightaway. He knew what was going on because he was involved in it." Sarah went on to explain the intricate details, as she understood them. "Blake will be here later, but he's still with Dara. He took her to the Daily Times office, so he should be able to fill in any of the details I didn't get."

"Wow!" Rory said, "what a hot mess!"

"Oh yeah," Sam said. He looked at his watch and said, "Maybe you want to turn on the TV, any channel. There's a press conference and the editor of the DT is going to apologize and give a retraction."

"That's huge!" Marc commented, as he got up to turn on the TV.

Sam was right; it was on all the channels. He chose ABC and sat down to watch. It hadn't started, and the anchorwoman was discussing what might happen. They had surmised that a retraction would be forthcoming.

Soon, a very poised Evelyn O'Brien appeared at the podium. "Ladies and gentlemen of the press and viewers, I am here to issue both an apology and a retraction of the headline in this morning's paper. I have no excuse to offer, nor will I point any fingers. It is ultimately my responsibility what goes out in print. And I apologize to the family most affected by this misinformation. I spoke with Dara Keene this morning, met her daughter Rachel, who is fine, and gave her my most sincere apologies. Also, Mason Rowe, who is innocent until proven guilty, and now out on bail, deserves our apology. The press has no right to vilify a man alleged to be guilty of a crime, nor attempt to skew the jury. I can promise you, that to the best of my ability, this kind of journalism will not prevail in my newspaper while I am the editor. Thank you."

As she left the podium, she was assailed with questions, but made it clear that her statement had spoken for her.

It was quiet in the Chandler kitchen. Marc turned off the TV and sat down.

"That was quite a statement," Sarah said. "No equivocation there!"

"You're right," Rory agreed. "She did a great job. I can only imagine the pandemonium that must be taking place at the newspaper."

"So," Sam said, "Sarah and I were speculating about who would've misled this young, vulnerable journalist. Tell them your theory, Sarah."

"Ok, well, it seems obvious who would benefit from bringing negative attention to Rowe, now that he's out on bail. The most sensible answer is *the perp*. Keep in mind, that he isn't aware, thanks to Rory's advice," she nodded to Rory, "that Rowe is on the electronic home monitor. Rowe's every movement is known by the authorities."

"Makes perfect sense," Marc agreed. "Bet he's pissed off at such a quick reaction by the editor."

"Yeah, he may be feeling the noose tightening, so he could be getting more dangerous. Any ideas?" Rory asked.

Sarah answered, "Well, Sam and I will continue to interview other Citadel employees, but we'll first focus on the other guys who were at the poker game. Some of them might be afraid to say much because, you know…"

"Has anyone interviewed Forsythe? He seems awfully interested in Rowe, and he did post bail for him," Rory pointed out.

"Uh, we try to avoid him," Sarah said. "He's always popping up with more questions. Doesn't he have a business to run?"

"By the way, does he know I'm out?"

"No!" Sarah shook her head vehemently. "He asks about you every day, too. We give him nuthin'! But we did tell him that you would probably take the case in the event of your recovery."

"I'm glad about that. And the headlines today sort of took the heat off me, so at least the press isn't at the hospital I guess. But," Rory said, "it might be really helpful if one of you could try to put aside your antipathy towards him and engage him in an interview."

Sarah made a face, and Sam said, "I guess that will be me."

Chapter 26

Hayley Singleton was still brooding at her desk when her phone rang. She hesitated to pick it up, expecting more blowback from her story. She noticed the caller was "unknown" and picked up immediately. If this was her anonymous source, she needed to give him a piece of her mind.

"Ms. Singleton," she answered without emotion, though her heart was racing.

"Well, well, we put you on the front page," the man said. It sounded like the same person as before. "You're welcome!" he said sarcastically when Hayley didn't reply.

Wait a minute, she thought; he probably didn't see the press conference. So she decided to play along. "Oh, I'm forgetting my manners! Thank you so much! Do you have any more news?" she added.

"Well, I just might…"

"Go ahead then," Hayley urged him. "It's got to be something even bigger!"

He laughed, a nasty mirthless laugh. Hayley cringed.

"How about this? Rowe hasn't been picked up by the police and I know where he works!"

"Ok, that's good. Look I need to meet you someplace where we can talk in private, you okay with that?" she asked, immediately wondering why she'd suggested it.

Silence on the phone. Then he said, "OK, meet me at the Aston ice rink, like in a half hour; it's not too busy before noon."

"How will I know you?" Hayley asked, feeling suddenly vulnerable.

"Oh, don't worry Honey, I know you!" He laughed again before he hung up.

Hayley felt a tremor of fear, *or was it excitement*, run up her spine. She would go, what choice did she have? She had to confront the person who'd tried to tank her career. All the better that he didn't know about the press conference.

***

Sarah sat with Sam in Rory's office with the door closed. "Okay, Sam, let's talk about what to say to Forsythe."

"We don't need to have that discussion, unless there's something specific you want to ask. I mean, *you* could do the interview," he teased.

"Oh no!" Sarah put her hands up in front of her. "I'm not interested in that. Sorry I brought it up."

"Fine," Sam said, smiling. "I'll do it, but I'm going unscripted. I'm not sure what I'll say, but the words aren't really as important as the vibes I pick up."

"What, so you're a psychic now?" Sarah laughed. "Or are you just bullshitting?"

"Better watch your step, Missy, or this will end up in your lap!" Sam was only half-kidding. "I mean, for someone who doesn't want to do this interview, you sure have lots to say about it."

Sarah got up without a word and left the office, closing the door behind her.

Sam wondered, is she angry or just deciding to butt out? He sighed, thinking that women, judging from Sarah's behavior, were mercurial. He got up to steel himself for the interview, deciding that putting it off wasn't productive.

Walking through the reception area, he blew a kiss to Sarah, and went into the construction zone.

Sam was surprised to see how much the crew had accomplished. The three offices had been framed up and the drywall was starting to go on. He strolled around and began looking into the offices.

He startled when he heard a voice behind him. Turning around, his jaw dropped as he faced Mason Rowe. "Hey! Didn't know you were back to work, good to see you!" Sam said.

"It's good to be here, I've had enough down time. I really needed to get back."

There was an uncomfortable silence for a moment, as Sam wondered whether or not to mention the headlines.

Rowe read the silence and said, "Yeah, it was tough showing my face after reading this morning's paper. But Dara called and told me to watch the news. God bless her!" He sighed, "I definitely wouldn't be functioning if it weren't for her. I can't even begin to know how she must feel, but she's a brave woman and still loves me." He shook his head, as if in disbelief.

"She is quite a woman," Sam said.

"By the way, how is Rory doing?" Rowe asked.

Sam looked down, hesitating. He hated lying, even a white lie.

"That's ok, man, I understand if you don't want to talk about it. I'm sorry."

"Thanks for understanding," Sam said, relieved to be off the hook. "By the way, I came over here to see Forsythe, do you know if he's here?"

"He's not," Mason replied, "but I think I heard one of the guys say he'd be back this afternoon. Should I tell him you want to see him?"

"That would be helpful, thanks. Good to see you," Sam told Rowe as he left the area.

***

Rory was sitting alone in her kitchen nook with her thoughts whirling in every direction. She'd convinced Marc to go back to work and the girls had gone to their softball camp. She hoped that with peace and quiet she'd be able to think her way through this perplexing case. Rory was not sure where to start. She was getting caught up in the case, and forgetting what Rowe had been charged with. But she was too far in to back out now. And she surprised herself that she didn't feel uncomfortable.

She sighed with relief when her cell buzzed, hoping to have something else to focus on. Seeing it was Don, she took the call. "Hey, Don, I'm home!" she blurted.

"Great!" he said, "I guess the latest headlines took the heat off you. So what's up with that? At least I know I didn't plant that headline," he joked, referencing salacious headlines he and Rory had been responsible for in a previous case.

Rory laughed, "No, it sure wasn't us, and I wouldn't want to be in Ms. Singleton's shoes!"

"But I'm betting you know something about today's headlines. Am I right?" Don asked.

"Why don't you come over and I'll spill the beans. You might try to bribe me with some lunch!"

"You're pretty brazen for a woman who was at death's door a few short days ago!" Don said, only then realizing how insensitive that sounded. "Hey, I'm glad for that, just messing with you!"

"You needn't worry about me developing a thin skin since my accident. I'm still the same. So, are you coming over?"

"Wouldn't miss it! Do you have any special lunch requests?" Don asked.

"Egg salad on rye sounds good to me. Nothing else, I still can't eat much," Rory replied. "See you soon, bye."

***

The man had left work early, feigning illness. He had some time to kill, so to speak, before he met that dimwit reporter at the rink. He thought he'd just drive by Rowe's lawyer's house. He'd looked her up on the net. She lived in a nice area more or less on the way to the mall. He hadn't heard any more news about her, so turned his radio to the all-news station as he cruised through Rory's neighborhood.

He slowed down so he could see the house numbers, many of which were obscured by an abundance of large trees. The houses were all big, he noticed, not the 'McMansion' types. These were large, older houses. He slowed almost to a stop in front of her house. It was set back from the road, and there didn't seem to be any activity, at least none he could see.

Suddenly something on the news caught his attention. What was that? He listened closely as they aired the press conference taped earlier in the day. The man's jaw dropped as he took in the full account. Then it dawned on him: *that bitch is playin' me!*

He floored it, did a quick U-turn and sped off, nearly colliding with a blue Subaru. He slammed on his brakes, avoiding the car, whose driver had also stopped. The two eyed each other suspiciously. When the Subaru driver appeared ready to exit his vehicle, the man sped off.

***

Arriving at Rory's, Don got out of his blue Subaru, juggling the lunches he held. He was shaken. Who was that fuckin' idiot who'd almost crashed into him head-on? Rory might know. He'd ask her.

Get a grip! Don said to himself as he noticed his shaky legs and racing heart. But, man, that was one scary dude. He took a few breaths to calm down before he walked up to Rory's door.

She opened the door on the second knock and welcomed Don. "Hey, stranger!" Then she did a double take and said, "Are you sick or something? You look like you've seen a ghost!"

"Yeah," he said slowly, "I almost saw my own!" He handed her the lunches and sat on a stool.

"What happened?" Rory asked, looking concerned.

"You have a neighbor drives a big white pick-up?"

"Not that I know of," Rory answered. "Why?"

"Just as I drove into your street, this white truck comes screaming past your driveway and almost crashed into me head-on. Guy stopped, then, as I started to get out, he took off, fast. Scared the shit out of me!"

"I can see that. Did you get a look at the guy?" Rory asked

"We looked at each other, but he wore sunglasses, so I didn't see much of his face." Don answered. "I was in shock, disbelief. It's a damn good thing we both stopped or it could've been a nasty accident."

Rory was deep in thought. Where had she seen a white pick-up? Why did that resonate with her? And had the driver been on the way to her house?

Chapter 27

Getting out of her red Kia, Hayley arrived at the rink ten minutes before they'd agreed to meet. She wanted to have the edge, wanted to be there when her informant arrived. She was counting on being able to turn the tables on him, get him to give her real information, or she would go to the police. That would show him. But maybe he did know things that were being covered up. What if he was right and the others were lying?

She'd just play it by ear. She didn't see anyone at the counter, and there were no skaters on the ice. The place seemed deserted.

When their meeting time came and went, she was getting nervous and needed to pee. Hayley headed down the long hall to the bathrooms. Her footsteps echoed eerily as the sound bounced off the walls. She quickened her steps as her fear increased and the urgency to use the bathroom intensified.

In a show of faux-bravery, she flung open the door and switched on the lights, heading straight to a stall and slamming the door closed behind her. She locked it with a loud *thun*k. Thank God, she'd made it in time. She sat there, chiding herself for being afraid. That was until she heard the distinct cadence of footsteps echoing off the walls in the hallway, coming closer…

***

Rory and Don were discussing the morning's headlines. Rory gave him the complete story, as she'd heard it from Sam and Sarah.

"So, basically the reporter is in deep shit," Don said in his typical lingo. "But it doesn't make sense that she'd stick her neck out if she had no evidence, do you think?"

"It didn't work in her favor," Rory agreed. "It seems that if she'd offered up evidence to her editor, she wouldn't have been hung out to dry."

"So she gets an anonymous call, from whom? Who would benefit from giving her that kind of info?"

"Well, Sam and Sarah seem to think it's got to be the perp, and I have to say I agree with that theory. And Rowe's covered, by the way, because he's on the monitor. I'm not bragging, but it was my idea to keep that secret."

"That was a nice touch," Don said. "But as for the reporter, I'm thinking that guy will probably try to get to her, maybe even take her out. She could be in real danger," Don said, "especially if the police have questioned her."

"So, what can we do?" Rory asked. "I'm out of my league here. This seems more like your kind of behind-the-scenes drama."

"Call it what you like," Don said. "But I am going to see if there's something I can do. And, keeping an eye on her might lead us to the 'bogeyman.' "

"Well, be careful! He's proven to be dangerous, and not only to little girls," Rory cautioned.

***

Hayley yanked her pants up as she eased quietly out of the bathroom stall. She tiptoed across the floor, switched off the lights, and stood behind the door. She held her heavy tote bag aloft, waiting for the door to be opened.

The door opened slowly and the lights were switched on. Hayley was ready to swing her bag with all of her might.

The uniformed security officer jumped back, holding up his hands. "Whoa! I'm just checkin' everything out, no problem," he said, backing away. "I saw the lights go off and nobody came out, so I had to see was there a problem."

Hayley dropped the bag and whooshed a sigh of relief. "I'm sorry officer; it's just unusual for the rink to be so empty. I got scared when I heard steps coming down the hall."

"Ok, I gotcha'. Sorry if I spooked you. Can I escort you out?"

"Yes, I'd appreciate that, thank you," Hayley replied.

The guard took her to the entrance she'd come in and bade her goodbye.

"Thanks so much!" Hayley said, heading towards her car. Once inside, she sat for a moment, shaken. And she started to think about what might've happened if a different person had appeared. She wondered if he'd even shown up. Did he see her escorted out by a security guard? She wondered. What a fool she'd been to think about meeting a stranger at the rink, however public it might be.

She jumped when there was a tap on her window, and was relieved to see the security guard. Rolling the window down, she asked, "Is there something else?"

"I was just watchin' to see that you got off ok. Is everything all right?" he asked.

She decided to trust him. "Well, I was supposed to meet someone here, a man. I didn't see him anywhere. Did you see anyone hanging around?"

"There was a guy, over by the counter. He had his back to me when I was going to check the bathrooms. But he was gone when we came out and I haven't seen him since. Think that was your guy?" the guard asked.

"Don't know, never met him before. I know, it was a really dumb idea," she said, noticing his expression. "It's not what you think, but it was a dumb idea anyway," Hayley concluded.

"Look," he said, "you seem like a nice girl, you're pretty, you got a lot going for you. Just be careful, ok?"

She thanked him, and then rolled her window up, waving as she drove away. She could still see him in her rear-view mirror when she reached the street.

***

The man had indeed seen Hayley being escorted out of the rink, and had quickly exited. It didn't look good for him, he had to admit. He should've moved more quickly, should've gotten to her when he first saw her. But the fuckin' security guy ruined his plans. Now he had even less reason to trust her, since he'd heard about the press conference. He'd have to proceed carefully.

Hunkered down in his truck on the other side of the parking lot, he saw Hayley get into her car, but she didn't leave immediately. Then he saw the guard come out and speak with her. What was it they were talking about? Had he called the police? It was time for him to cut his losses and vanish, for the time being…

***

Hayley had learned a valuable lesson, she thought as she drove back to the office, and would live to tell about it. Thank God for the security guard!

Parking her car in the lot, she went in the back way to her office. She looked all around her, making sure no one was following her. She hadn't noticed a tail as she drove, but knew she would have to be extra cautious,

She went straight back to her stuffy little office, which was a constant reminder of her reduced status with the paper. It would take her a while, but she would find a way to build herself up gradually and achieve her goals. There would be no instant notoriety, or rather, *positive acclaim*. She was notorious now, for sure.

Hayley opened the door to her office, which she'd left unlocked and gasped as she saw a strange man seated in front of her desk.

Chapter 28

Sam finished interviewing Forsythe, and went back to the office to talk with Sarah.

"Hey, Sweetie," Sam said, happy that they had worked through their earlier disagreement during lunch. "What's going on?"

"Not much here, I've just been reviewing all the notes I've compiled, and so far nothing has jumped out at me. How'd the interview go with 'Chief Citadel'?" Sarah asked.

Sam laughed, "Actually that's an apt nickname. I have to admit he seemed to be pulling rank on me, oh so subtly. He was in charge of the interview, I suppose because that's what he's accustomed to doing. Frankly, I didn't learn much, but I did pick up an undercurrent. I think he's hiding something. That makes him 'a person of interest,' in police jargon. It wouldn't hurt for us to keep tabs on him. Come to think of it, seems he's keeping tabs on Rowe by having him work here."

"Yeah, I thought of that, too," Sarah said, "but in a different context. I thought he might be trying to keep him safe."

"Ever the optimist," Sam replied. "Not that it's a bad thing," he hastened to add, "and you may be right. I want to keep an open mind, but it can't hurt to keep an eye on Forsythe. You said nothing jumped out at you from your notes. Do you have any idea of possible suspects? Maybe we should go down our list and see what we have?"

"Good idea, but why don't we head over to Rory's and brainstorm with her?"

***

Leaving her door open and starting to back out, Hayley was ready to scream. The man in the chair made no move to stop her. Instead he calmly pulled out what looked like a badge.

She hesitated, and then said, "Bring that over here, please."

He got up and she noticed he was tall and burly. She was glad she'd left the door open.

As he got about a foot away he stopped, handing her the badge. He smiled and she noticed for the first time, that although he was a big guy, he looked more like a teddy bear.

Hayley looked closely at the badge, noting the name, Don Mandel, and learning that he was a parole officer in Adult Court. She cocked her head and said, "Don Mandel, what interest can you possibly have in talking to me?"

"Nice to meet you, Hayley," Don said companionably. "This is not an official visit, and it has nothing to do with my day job. But I'm friends with Rory Chandler, who's representing Mason Rowe, and we got to talking about why you were given misinformation and who would benefit from it. We concluded it had to be the perp."

"Wait a minute, isn't Ms. Chandler still in the hospital in guarded condition?"

Don thought, *oops! what have I done now*? Then he said, "Look, I'm here because I think you might need protection and you might lead us to the actual bogeyman, who seems to have also murdered a witness."

"OK, I get that and thank you. Is this just a sideline for you? And by the way you didn't answer my question about Ms. Chandler." She looked him in the eyes.

*Reporter*s, Don thought belatedly. "Yes, doing investigative work for Rory is a part-time gig for me. And yes, I did speak with her today. You must promise that this does not get into the paper…"

"Are you kidding? Do you think I'll go down that road again?" She snorted a laugh.

"Ok, I'll trust you. Rory is recovering. We have reason to believe the perp is after her, too. He's not sure if she saw the murder. So for Rory's protection you can understand why it's kept quiet. And frankly, your headline basically took the focus off Rory, even though it didn't work out for you,"

"I'm glad someone benefitted from that," Hayley said without bitterness.

"And if we can solve the case, you'll be in on it and have first crack at reporting it. So maybe we can help each other. But the real reason I came to see you is because we think you could be in danger and I'm willing to keep an eye on you."

"How can you do that with your full-time job?" Hayley asked.

"I'm very flexible. And I can stay in touch with you by cell. All you have to do is call. I assume you'll be at work much of the time, and when you're not, let me know where to meet you. I have a secure cell number which I'll give you, and you might want to get a disposable phone, too."

"I'm still not sure what your motivation is…"

"You'll start to get it as you spend time with me. I really like the behind-the-scenes stuff that gets things moving. I've helped Rory before and we've pulled off some wild things. You just have to be willing to think and act outside the box."

"OK," Hayley replied. "I don't really have anyone in my corner now, and I'm unwilling to ask the police for help, because that's death for a reporter. I did have a brush with the person who must be 'the perp', just this morning. I'd arranged a meeting with him at the ice rink, and, well, to get to the point, thank God the place has security guards, because I might've ended up like his last victim. I realized, almost too late, that meeting him was a bad idea."

"Did you see him?"

"No, but the security guard probably saw the back of him," Hayley said.

"What if he tries to get in touch with you again?" Don asked.

"You think?" she asked. "That's a good point. What do you think I should do?"

"I think he will contact you and try to meet with you, and I think you should call me immediately," Don answered without equivocation. "I am licensed to carry," Don added.

***

Rory opened the door wide for Sam and Sarah. "I'm so glad you came! I was getting a little squirrely, what with all the information…"

"We just thought it was a good time for us to lay out all the evidence and discuss it," Sam said.

"And maybe make a list of possible suspects," Sarah added. "By the way, Rowe is back to work."

"That's good news," Rory said as they all gravitated to the nook and took seats.

"Coffee, anyone?" Rory asked. Marc had made it but she hadn't had any.

"No thanks," Sam said and Sarah agreed.

Rory took her seat and said, "Before we get started, I have to tell you about a strange incident when Don came over this morning." She went on to tell how he narrowly missed the truck speeding out of her driveway. Having finished, she said, "So what do we have?"

"Wonder if it was a Citadel truck," Sam muttered, almost to himself.

"That's what I was trying to remember, why the white truck sounded familiar. Hmm, something to consider, go ahead, Sam."

"Well, to get you up to speed, I interviewed Forsythe today. I didn't learn anything, but I got the feeling he was hiding something," Sam said.

Sarah asked, "Getting on, who else is suspect?"

Rory said, "I think you guys are correct in looking at the guys at the poker game first. Who have you interviewed? You may have told me, but please reiterate."

"OK," Sarah said as she turned to a new page in her notebook. "So, we have Forsythe, Gordon Howe, who unfortunately died, and Jordan Kraft. We should see the other two guys before someone gets to them."

Rory and Sam both nodded. Sam said, "Is there anyone else who's been remotely suspicious?"

Rory answered, "I think until we prove otherwise, we have to interview the remaining two, who are?"

"James Quinn and Alistair Caldwell," Sarah replied, looking at her notes.

"I agree," Rory said, "I think the answer might lie with the other men in the room that night."

"That's what we have to go on for now. Let's just hope the killer doesn't start knocking off the others. I'd rather not find out by the process of elimination," Sam said

Rory's cell buzzed. She saw it was Don and answered at once. She listened, frowning, and then smiled. "Wow! Wait 'til I tell the others, Sam and Sarah are here now."

***

It was late and Hayley was having a tough time getting to sleep. She was quite shaken by her apparent brush with the killer. She'd taken meds for sleep but was too worried for them to work. She'd mulled over her discussion with Don Mandel and had concluded that he was who he seemed. He could be funny and quirky, but she believed he was genuine, and in fact, one of a kind. She'd also 'googled' him and found that he had a presence on the net.

Don was quite appealing, with his ready smile and kind eyes. She trusted him. And in her position, there weren't many she could describe as trustworthy. If her story had been legit, she would've had friends galore, she thought with bitterness.

Hayley had just decided to get up and make some warm milk, when her cell buzzed. Her heart was in her throat as she saw 'caller unknown' come up on the screen. She was compelled to answer.

"Hello," the now- familiar voice came on the line, sending a shiver down her spine. "Sorry we *missed* each other today," he said, his words dripping with sarcasm. "But I have information you should know. There's been another abduction attempt on a young girl. I'll be happy to give you the details, if you meet me..."

"Out of the question," Hayley replied, trying to keep her voice strong. "We're done."

"Oh, I hardly think so, I'll come to your place," he said as the phone went dead.

Chapter 29

Don was out of bed and dressed in a flash. He glanced at the bedside clock and was not surprised to see it was one a.m. His heart was racing as he mentally pictured how to get to Hayley's apartment. He hadn't been there, but he'd gone on Google maps to find it. She lived on the other side of Media from him.

He got into his Subaru, and took off. Trying to concentrate without coffee was daunting, but he was afraid to take the time to stop, and he had no idea how far the killer was from Hayley's apartment. Fortunately, he didn't have far to drive.

As he neared her place, Don called Hayley's cell. She answered immediately and he breathed a sigh of relief. "Any word from him? Any strange noises?" Don asked.

"Nothing!" she answered, her voice trembling.

"I'm in your parking lot now. Should I come up or wait here and see if I can spot him?"

"Please come up!" she said without hesitation.

"Ok, I'll come right up. I'll text you when I'm ready to be buzzed in," Don said.

Getting out of his car, Don looked around furtively. He didn't see any white pickups or any movement, so he proceeded to her door. She buzzed it open when he gave her the signal, and he went in, closing the door quickly and looking behind him.

Walking up to the second floor, he knocked on apartment 202. "It's me," he said quietly.

Hayley opened the door and quickly ushered him in, turning the deadbolt. "Thank God!" she said, falling into his open arms. She sobbed into his chest and he patted her back, until she calmed down. She pushed away, embarrassed, when she realized what she'd done. But Don didn't seem to be uncomfortable.

She offered him a seat on the couch and sat down across from him as she described the call and the abrupt hang-up. She'd been completely undone.

Don suggested, "Can I make you some tea or something? You might try to get some sleep."

Her response was to laugh, almost hysterically. "I doubt I'll be able to sleep," she answered finally.

"Well, I'm going to stay and keep watch, so you may as well try to sleep. Have any herbal tea?"

"Yeah, I do, that's not a bad idea. I'll show you where it is." He followed her to the kitchen.

She sat on a stool at the island while Don put the kettle on. "So, do we have a plan for if he shows up?" Hayley asked.

"I'll have a nasty reception for him if he does," Don said calmly. "For some reason, I think he won't show up because I'm here. I'm guessing he's very careful, and has gone to great lengths to avoid detection."

"What makes you say that?" she asked.

"I'm not sure, it's just a feeling I have. I've learned to trust my instincts, they're usually right. I think he might be watching your apartment, and he may have seen me come in. He won't risk coming after you unless he's sure you're alone."

"Well," Hayley said, "I'm not always with someone. I mean how is that even possible?"

"I'll escort you to work tomorrow. If you need to go out, call me or grab a friend you can trust."

"What about your family?" Hayley asked.

"My wife and I are separated."

"I'm sorry."

"It's not going to be one of those horrid divorces. We're still friends and will share custody of our sons."

"Wow, how adult that sounds," Hayley commented.

Don laughed, "I'm not usually praised for my maturity, but thanks. We just realized that our marriage wasn't working and we agreed to get out."

"How are your sons with that?" she asked.

"They're ok, I think. We've talked about it a lot and they're both pre-teens, beginning to spend more time with friends."

"That's really important you're not angry. My parents divorced when I was four, and it was awful! I became a toy to be tossed back and forth at their whims. And they made no secret of their animosity towards each other."

"Yeah, that's sad." Don was dunking the tea bag and asked, "What do you want in your tea?"

"Just some honey, it's right there on the counter."

Hayley was reaching for the teacup when the apartment went dark.

"Oh shit!" Hayley blurted. "Now what?"

Don answered calmly, "Go to your room and lock yourself in. Do you have a flashlight?"

"In the drawer right there," she pointed as she raced for her room, knocking over a chair on the way.

Don took a moment to let his eyes adjust to the darkness. He noticed the street lights were on, so some light came in and that meant it wasn't a local power outage. He walked over to the front door and looked out through the peephole. He couldn't see much because the hall was dark. He took his gun from his belt and held it at the ready.

The lights in the apartment flashed on and off a few times. When they came back on, the fire alarm sounded, with an ear- splitting, insistent screech.

Hayley came out of her room with her bathrobe on and covering her ears. "I guess we have to go out…"

"Yes, we do, but let's not be the first in line. I think this is part of the drama our suspect has in store for us." He looked out through the hole and saw people in various states of undress congregating in the hall, grumbling. They soon began to walk down the stairs.

Don and Hayley waited until it seemed everyone from their floor had left the hall. "Make sure to lock the apartment," Don said. She did as Don suggested, and then they went out slowly, looking around. As they approached the first floor, they saw the line of people backed up on the stairs. The alarm bell stopped abruptly, and the silence stunned them.

Someone who appeared to be in charge yelled, "Go back to your apartments, go back! This was a false alarm; the emergency box was smashed. We'll be investigating. Sorry for the inconvenience."

"That's the super," Hayley said. "He's pretty much on top of things, and I think he'll get to the bottom of this."

"Maybe," Don said, "but I don't think he'll catch the guy, he's too smart. That was a message to us, the bogeyman was messing with us!"

***

The man sat in his car, a nondescript old Chevy. The truck had already been seen, so he couldn't use that. He was pleased that he'd caused a disruption, but not happy that Hayley hadn't emerged from the building. If that fuckin', nosey building super hadn't come on the scene so quickly, he might've gotten a glimpse of Hayley.

He'd seen the blue Subaru enter the parking lot, and the timing was right, if Hayley had called someone to rescue her. His laugh sounded like a snarl. So, maybe she had a boyfriend, a boyfriend who was also friends with that Chandler bitch. He was convinced that the Subaru guy had been headed to Chandler's house when they almost crashed. That would make it harder, but not impossible. Everyone lets his guard down sometime. *Except for me*, he thought. It was true, he trusted no one.

When she saw tomorrow's headlines he thought she might regret not seeing him.

***

Detective Herrera got a late night phone call. It was from Marilyn Hunter, the CYS worker with the little girl in foster care.

"Ms. Hunter," he began, "I assume you have some pressing news to call this late."

"I do," she said, her voice constricted. "Carly, the little girl I told you about?"

"Yes, I remember, go on," he encouraged.

"Well, someone tried to get into her room by slitting the screen. When one of the staff made a routine check on the rooms, Carly was standing by the window talking to someone. Whoever it was fled, and Carly has refused to say anything about what happened."

"Well, sounds like our bogeyman has been busy. I'll get someone over there to dust for prints and other evidence. I think this has to go into the papers. I want this guy to know we're onto him."

"That's fine with me," Ms. Hunter said. "I'm taking her home with me tonight, since it's too late to find a suitable place for her."

"Is your home secure? I wouldn't rule out the possibility of him following you. He found Carly once…"

"I think it's pretty secure. It's an apartment complex that has a gate around it with card access, and you have to get buzzed in the front door. I live with my boyfriend, too, so it's not just me."

"Ok, it sounds pretty good. You have my number if you need it. Oh, and Ms. Hunter, please bring Carly in first thing tomorrow."

"Yes," she said, "I'll do that. Good bye and thanks."

Chapter 30

Rory was reading The Daily Times, as Marc came into the kitchen. She was interested in the written retraction from yesterday's news conference. She automatically handed Marc the other paper, The News of Delaware County.

He perused it as he went for coffee. "Oh my God!" he said, reading the front page.

"What?" Rory demanded, looking up.

He walked over with the paper, "Look here," he pointed.

"Jeez, another possible victim of the bogeyman! I guess the Times stayed away from that one, after yesterday's fiasco. But I wonder how The News got the story. It might be interesting to find out."

"It says," Marc read further, "Detective Herrera gave the information, so it should be legit. He's in charge of the bogeyman case. I spoke to him the other night…" He stopped, realizing he hadn't told Rory.

As expected, Rory jumped on it. "And you saw Herrera why?"

"I was threatened, probably by the bogeyman, when I left the hospital the last night you were there," Marc said, waiting for the barrage of questions to come.

"Did you see him? Did he do anything? Tell me what happened!"

"The bastard was waiting in the car for me. He pressed what felt like a knife to my neck, and said I should tell you he'd be back if you said anything. Then he left and I saw only his back in the rearview. I called the nurse on your floor immediately…"

"That would explain the second guard the next day," Rory mused. "And you were planning to tell me, when?" Her voice was rising and her face was red. "Is this another one of your secrets meant to protect me?"

"Look, there was so much going on, it just slipped my mind…"

"That's pretty lame!" Rory was shouting now. "You didn't think to tell me to be extra careful?"

"The Nether Providence Police are surveilling our neighborhood."

"Well, they weren't here yesterday when a white truck nearly smashed into Don's car when he was just up the street. And the truck drove off like a bat out of hell," Rory said harshly.

"And that's something you chose not to tell me? You know, the road goes two ways, Rory."

***

The night had passed uneventfully for Marilyn Hunter, though her sleep was ruined. She got up a bit later than usual and woke Carly. Her boyfriend, a personal trainer and a big guy, was waiting to leave for work until he could escort Marilyn and Carly to the car.

"Looks like you didn't get much sleep either, Ryan, I'm sorry."

"It's ok," he said, blowing it off. "I'm glad I was here, and I hope you can find a safe place for Carly, poor kid," he said. "I'd like to get my hands on that bastard! I just can't stand to hear when kids are abused!"

"Yeah me too," Marilyn said. "That's why I do the work I do, but it's depressing that even when I'm doing my best, bad things happen."

"Look, that's true, there's a lot we can't control, but your heart's in the right place."

They ended their conversation as Carly walked into the kitchen.

"What would you like for breakfast, Carly?" Marilyn asked brightly.

"I'm not really hungry," she said with downcast eyes.

"You need something in your stomach. Would you eat some toast? With peanut butter?" She thought that might entice the girl.

"Ok, just one piece," Carly answered.

***

Rory called Don as soon as Marc left for work. Their argument had ended in a tentative truce. Rory wasn't happy about Marc withholding information from her, especially important info. That really rankled, but she realized she did it too. After all, she still hadn't told Marc about her pregnancy. Why hadn't she? The answer was, she realized, she still didn't trust him. She wished they could rewind and go back to Ireland. Things had seemed much easier there.

She thought about the day they had driven through the rain for several hours, and when they'd arrived at the Cliffs of Moher, the sun suddenly appeared. There were many magical moments like that…

Don answered on the fourth ring, breaking into Rory's memories. "Hey, Rory, what's up?"

"Hi, Don, I was just wondering if you saw today's News of Delco?"

"No, that's a rival paper, so Hayley doesn't get it. I'm at her place. She got a call from the bogeyman late last night and called me, so I stayed. Anyhow, what's in the paper?"

"An attempted abduction of a little girl in a group foster home. The intruder, assumed to be the bogeyman, slit the screen to her room and was interrupted in time by a vigilant staff."

"Shit! When the guy called her last night, he said he had information about another attempted abduction, but she hung up on him. He said he was coming to her place, so I came over. Wait 'til I tell her! I'll catch up with you later, Bye."

***

Marilyn and Carly arrived at the police station by 9:30. Herrera was waiting for them at the front desk. Marilyn introduced Carly to the detective. The little girl nodded and shook his hand stiffly.

"Ms. Hunter, could you escort Carly with me? Just follow me down the hall."

They stopped at the end of the hall. The detective spoke to Carly, leaning down to be at eye level with her. "I'm taking you in to meet Mrs. Scott. I think you'll like her." He led Carly into the room where a matronly woman welcomed her with a smile.

"We can go back to my office and talk," Herrera said to Ms. Hunter.

"Ok, good," she replied. "Mrs. Scott looked very welcoming. I hope she can get Carly to talk."

"If she can't, then we're in deep trouble," he said. "In addition to being a cop, she has a degree in Psychology. She's been successful with our most reticent victims."

Chapter 31

As Don neared Rory's house he slowed and looked around carefully to make sure the white pickup wasn't in the vicinity. He realized, however, the perp undoubtedly had another vehicle, one he probably drove last night. Don was sure the molester had orchestrated the scene last night. And he was probably waiting to see who Hayley came out with. Well, they'd deprived him of that, but he was sure to come up with something equally unnerving.

He pulled into Rory's drive and parked at the top of the incline, pulling the car in under a tall stand of oaks.

Rory was waiting at the door and opened it before he knocked.

"Hey, thanks for coming. I thought I'd heard you drive up, but then I didn't see your car. You really tucked it away, huh?"

"Well, there was that white pickup yesterday…"

"Oh, right, we've decided it was a Citadel truck, they use white pickups with a red logo of a fortress-looking thing on the door and 'Citadel' underneath. Do you remember seeing that?"

Don thought and tried to picture the scene. "Everything was a flash in my mind, so I really didn't see anything besides my imminent death. I was in survival mode."

"I can understand that," Rory said. "But it would make sense that it was a company truck, since it was during the day and we're assuming our suspect works at Citadel and was at that poker game."

"I'm pretty sure the guy has another vehicle, too. When I went over to Hayley's, when she called me at one in the morning, I looked around before I went in and didn't see a white pickup."

They went to the nook as they talked. Now Rory said, "What was that all about?"

Don went on to explain what had happened the previous evening.

"So the bogeyman must've tried to abduct that little girl before or after he was at Hayley's. She was a lucky little girl; an alert staff prevented it." She tapped her pen on the tablet she was holding. "We have to catch him before this happens again!"

"And before he threatens anyone who's in the way," Don added. "Hayley is definitely a target, and you, too, except you've gone off the radar for now."

"But he was here yesterday, Don, when he damn near killed you, and I'll bet he took note of your car."

"Not much I can do about that since I don't have another vehicle. I'll be careful, though, and I am packing," Don added.

"Guess that's not a bad idea," Rory said, chewing her bottom lip. "Just be *extra* careful, I hate getting my friends involved and seeing them get hurt."

"Don't worry," Don replied, "I'm always on the alert because, as you know, I thrive on this shit!" He got up to leave, saying, "Now I really do have to get to my day job. Lock the door after me."

***

Hayley was tucked away in her stuffy little office, and trying to focus on the low-level assignment she'd been given. Reporting on the events taking place in Rose-Tree- Media school district was hardly her idea of news reporting. But she knew she had to pay her dues or be out of a job, so she'd suck it up.

Then she thought, why should I take the fall? She determined to go to her editor and make a case for putting her back on Rowe's case. What had happened the previous night should be made public. It seemed Detective Herrera was working the case for the police. She would work with him, and try to put pressure on the bogeyman, if her editor agreed…

***

Dara had become unglued when she'd read the newspaper at work. She didn't get this paper at home so she hadn't known. She talked with Katrina about it. Right now they were having a coffee break in the nurses' lounge.

"Oh God, Trina, is this ever going to go away? I know the bad guy is still out there and I wonder if I can keep Rachel safe. I'm thinking of going to my sister's in the city and maybe taking a leave of absence from work…"

Katrina didn't answer, because she knew this was something Dara had to work out for herself.

"You think it's a bad idea, don't you?" Dara asked.

"I think," Katrina spoke slowly, gathering her thoughts, "that only you can decide what's best for you in this difficult situation. I can't tell you what to do."

"Well, you sure haven't held back before!" She put her head down on the table and began to sob. When she lifted her head she said, "I'm sorry, you're the best friend I have, you didn't deserve that!"

"Look, I know you're under incredible stress. And your situation is very tricky. Honestly, I'm not sure what I'd do."

"Can you just think about what you *might* do, I'm looking for something," Dara said.

"Ok," Katrina relented, "I'll give you my opinion. In the first place, I think you want things to stay as normal as possible, whatever that means. I think it's important for you to keep working, even if you cut your hours. And I think it's important for Rachel to stay in school."

"Thank you, Trina! I just needed to hear what you think. I value your judgment. And mine sucks right now." Dara almost laughed. "What about staying with my sister?"

"Has she offered her home to you?" Katrina asked.

"Yes, yes she has. In fact, she's been very supportive, surprisingly so."

"In that case, why not go there, at least part of the time." Katrina put her hand on Dara's. "I know things are awful now, but in time…"

"I know it will sort itself out in time. I agree with everything you've said, it's really helped to pull my thoughts together. And I think Rachel would find it an adventure for us to stay with her Aunt Claire for a few days a week."

***

Rory was watching the Media Police Chief, Arnold Helms, give a televised interview regarding the recent attempted abduction. Herrera stood next to him. Many of the questions pertained to whether the police were looking at Mason Rowe as the perpetrator.

Helms did not look particularly at ease with public speaking. He held the podium tightly and gave single word answers. Rory understood that the press felt frustrated. Why had he consented to an interview if he had nothing to say, she wondered.

Finally the chief seemed goaded into giving some information. He said, "At the present time, Mr. Rowe is not a 'person of interest.' We can account for his whereabouts since he's been out of prison. We are gathering evidence, questioning possible witnesses, and pursuing this suspect with due diligence. That is all I have to report for the time being. Should there be additional news, I will be happy to share it. Thank you," he said as he released his grip on the podium and strode into the station house without a backward glance.

Rory switched off the TV. At least no one had asked about her, thank God! She was happy to think that perhaps they'd forgotten her. That was fine, she was just sorry that it had taken a new attempt on a child to divert the attention of the press.

***

The killer had just watched the press conference. He was livid. What did they mean they could account for Rowe's whereabouts? They hadn't been to work to check on him, because that would've gotten around. How were the police so certain he hadn't tried to do it again? What did they know? This was very upsetting. He'd counted on Rowe taking the fall for anything that happened after he got out. Of course, he'd had to kill Gordon Howe *before* Rowe got out. Was it possible that they'd connected his death with Rachel's molestation? He didn't think they were smart enough to do that. He would lie low for a while. And last night's attempt was frustrating. He'd come so close to getting Carly, and she was willing. He just hoped she wouldn't talk to the police. And that bitch of a caseworker, he'd have to get to her. But there had been too much publicity. He'd have to be careful.

***

Don picked Hayley up from work. She skipped out the back door to meet him and got quickly into the car. She smiled, "Well, I've decided to ask my editor to put me back on Rowe's case. The bogeyman threatened me, and I want to write about it, put pressure on him."

"I'd want to check with Herrera first," Don cautioned.

"Oh, I plan to, before I talk with Ms. O'Brien."

"Have you decided where you're staying tonight?"

"No, we should probably talk with Herrera first, but I need to stop by my apartment to get some things I left in my car."

Don drove to her apartment and pulled up next to her car. Watching her get out, he noticed Hayley was staring at her windshield, and then her hand went to her mouth.

He jumped out of his car and went to stand beside her. There was a note under the windshield wiper, in big block letters, which said: SORRY YOU DIDN'T WANT THE STORY. MAYBE I'LL GIVE YOU THE NEXT ONE.

Chapter 32

Sarah had stopped at Rory's house while Sam went on to the office to talk with Rowe.

Rory and Sarah were sitting in the nook having breakfast and discussing the latest events.

Sarah had come specifically to tell Rory about her upcoming trip to her father's, but she was reluctant to do it. Deciding not to beat around the bush, she blurted, "Rory, I'm going to visit my dad soon. He wants us to spend some time together before I start work full-time, and he wants it to be just the two of us. It's sweet, but I hate to leave you guys…"

"You have to go," Rory said. "That will give me reason to get off my lazy ass and get back to work!"

"You're anything but lazy!" Sarah scoffed. "I haven't been putting in many hours either, what with studying for the bar…"

Reading her mind, Rory said, "And none of that Catholic guilt! Just focus on having a nice visit with your dad. And you'll probably have time to study there, too."

"Speaking of guilt, I still haven't told Sam, and I know he won't be happy. To tell you the truth, I think I need to get away from Sam for a while."

Observing Rory's astonished expression, she said quickly, "It's not that I don't love him! It's just that he's over-protective. I need to get some of my independence back, and this is a good start. He's just… everywhere, constantly trying to make sure I'm not in the least bit of danger. I get that, it was very scary, but this just can't be my 'new normal', I need to get on with my life."

***

Sam was in the office speaking with Rowe. He felt a bit nervous about the subject he was broaching, but it needed to be discussed. Marc had suggested he pursue this line of questioning. He began,

"So looking ahead to your defense, I think we need to focus on the DNA with the dead sperm in it."

"Okay, do you have any ideas?"

"Well yes, Marc has been talking to me about the many ways in which DNA evidence can be compromised. He suggested that I ask if you use birth control, and what method, if any." Sam felt like a coward putting it on Marc, but it had been his suggestion.

"I use condoms, always have," Rowe said, looking confused.

"Do you mind my asking how you dispose of the used condoms?"

Rowe smiled. "Well, Dara has forbidden me to dispose of them in her house, ever since Rachel found one floating in the toilet, and asked Dara why there was a balloon in the toilet. So, I am very careful about not leaving them in the house. Once, when I forgot to leave it in the outdoor garbage can, I took it to work in a lunch bag and tossed it in a dumpster. A friend of mine saw me and asked why I was tossing my lunch out. It's become sort of a joke at work…" He stopped mid-sentence. "Oh, I see where you're going with this. Yeah, I have no idea how many guys know about this. Once it got around, lots of guys comment on my sex life."

"You've just given me a powerful answer as to how your DNA was found on Rachel. Unfortunately it doesn't narrow the field, but it's a start."

***

Don and Hayley were in DA McClain's office with the note that had been left on Hayley's windshield. He was surprised at how quickly McClain had made time for them and his interest in the evidence. McClain had made a copy, and told them to be sure to give it to Detective Herrera, who was investigating the case. McClain shared his own view that the latest crimes diverted attention away from Rowe. But there didn't seem to be much evidence with which to find the perpetrator.

Don informed McClain that he thought Hayley needed to be kept safe.

"Do you think the police should get involved?" McClain asked.

"I'm going to see if Herrera can help with that."

"OK, well, good luck with Herrera; he's a sharp detective from what I've seen. And he'll welcome the evidence. Thanks for coming in," McClain said, ushering them to the door.

"Ok," Don said, "off we go to see the detective, but first I need to stop by my office and check messages."

They walked to Don's office in and adjacent building. Hayley followed Don into his office and took a seat as he played back his several messages. He jotted notes as he listened. All at once he stiffened, then played back the last message and put it on speaker so Hayley could hear it.

"Well, well," a voice said, dripping with menace, "You know you can't follow little Miss Hayley everywhere. You'll have to drop the cape and mask sometime. I'll be waiting!" His laugh echoed eerily through the office.

Hayley shuddered, "Oh, God! He's everywhere!"

***

The suspect had been aware of Don's and Hayley's movements, if not exactly with whom they'd made contact. His growing alarm had prompted him to call Hayley's 'escort' and put some fear in him. It didn't escape his notice that Mandel could be his parole officer if things didn't go his way, and he knew it was dangerous to take down someone in his position.

From his car, he watched them leave the Courthouse, and leaned over as if to pick up something from the floor, as the two passed by the car's partially open window. They were talking as they walked, and he heard only snippets of conversation.

Mandel dominated the conversation, no surprise there, he thought. What he heard made him twitch in discomfort.

"...have to see what the detective has to say...wonder what McClain made of the..."

So they were cooperating with authorities and had probably turned in the note he'd left on Hayley's car. That had been a bad move, he thought, chastising himself. He thought he'd been careful, but what if he'd left a print? He'd acted in anger, knowing they were getting too close.

Their footsteps faded away as did their voices, though he'd heard only Mandel. They'd seen the DA and were going to see a detective. That was not good, not at all. He could feel rage rising in his body, demanding release. But what could he do to stop them? He could at best try to scare them off. But so far his tactics hadn't worked.

***

It was late in the day but Detective Herrera made time to see Don and Hayley.

Don took the lead and handed the note found on Hayley's windshield. He followed that up with a tape from his office messaging system. "I thought you should hear this," Don said, handing over the tape." This was on my office voicemail. I'll let you draw your own conclusions."

The detective inserted the tape and listened to the message. His eyebrows went up. "So, now we have his handwriting, and possibly a print, and his voice. I think it's gotta' be the bogeyman, don't you?"

"Yes, we do," Hayley answered for both of them. "It was the same voice who called me. And he has it in for me because he thinks I tricked him. And since I plan to write articles about my contact with him, if the editor approves, I'm afraid he'll respond in some way. What do you think, Detective?"

"I think it could work, but you will have to be extra cautious," Herrera answered.

"I'm worried for Hayley's safety, too, and I wonder if your department can help with that?" Don asked.

"We have a number of people working the case already. I suppose, we can provide surveillance, but I don't know we can guarantee absolute safety. We don't have safe houses like the FBI does, but can you stay somewhere besides your own apartment, since he knows where that is?"

Don said, "She can stay at my place if you think it would protect her. I have very good security at my town house, and I'm licensed to carry. I can escort her to work and back."

"What do you think, Hayley?" the detective asked.

"I would definitely feel safer, since the bogeyman has already been to my apartment and I live alone."

"Ok, Mr. Mandel, if you think it can work, we'll do surveillance at your place, just leave your address, and tell us when you'll be there."

"Thanks, Detective," Don said, scribbling the information on a piece of paper.

Herrera stood up, and said, "Please don't hesitate to call." He handed a card each to Hayley and Don, saying, "This number will bypass 911 and come straight to me, any time."

They shook hands with Herrera and thanked him, taking their leave.

***

The bogeyman was parked on the street not far from the police station. His worst fears had come to pass. They were now talking to the police, and they were in there for a while. He was not happy, he was very angry. I'll find a way to get around all of their barriers, he thought smugly. They can't be 100% safe all the time, and I'll be ready.

Chapter 33

Sarah had hardly touched the breakfast Sam had made for her. She was pushing eggs around on her plate, pretending to eat.

Sam brought down her bags and placed them next to the front door. "Is this everything?" He asked brightly, probably too brightly, he thought. Sarah could read him, and he was hardly pleased that she was leaving. He noticed, too, that she'd hardly eaten. This would be tough on both of them.

"Thanks Sam," Sarah answered quietly. "Yep, that's it; packing light for a change." Her laugh sounded false.

"Sweetie, I'll miss you, you know that," Sam said, "I want you to enjoy the time with your father, and just relax. We'll keep in touch by phone." Sam was sounding more positive than he felt.

Sarah came silently into his outstretched arms and hugged him fiercely, taking in his scent. He'd become such an important part of her life. He was right, though, she should enjoy the time with her dad.

"There is…"

Before she could finish her sentence, there was a knock on the door. Looking out the front window, Sarah saw the limo her father had sent parked out front. With one final kiss and embrace, Sarah squared her shoulders, and headed for the door. Sam followed with her bags.

With quick efficiency, the driver took Sarah's bags and stowed them in the trunk as she got into the car. Sam couldn't see her through the darkened windows, and he wasn't sure she could see him, but he blew her a kiss anyway, as was his habit. He walked back into the apartment, missing her already. This would be the first time they'd been apart since Sarah's kidnapping, nearly a year before.

"Damn!" he said, punching a wall and hurting himself. "I should've made her stay*!*" But he knew in his heart that this was something she had to do.

***

Rory was waiting for Sam and Don to arrive, so they could do some brainstorming. She knew Don had been trying to out the perp with Hayley as bait. Of course he wouldn't see it that way, but that's how she saw it. Rory knew Don could be reckless, but she also knew he wouldn't compromise Hayley's safety. And, frankly, there was little else to go on.

She started at the knock on her door and got up to look out. She'd been careful about answering the door since the hospital intrusion. It was Sam and he looked dejected. She opened the door immediately, and held out her arms to him. He gave her a quick hug and tried for a smile, which never came.

"I gather Sarah just left," Rory said.

"She did," he sighed. He sat down in the nook and put his head in his hands. "I don't know what I'll do without her," he mumbled, almost to himself.

"It must be tough," Rory said, sitting across from him. "Is there anything I can do?"

"Well, you could've told her we needed her on the case! You might have refused to give her time off!" Sam replied bitterly.

Oops, Rory thought. She knew Sam would be a wreck, but she also knew Sarah needed to get away. She remained quiet, hoping it would sort itself out.

The silence had stretched out, when there was a knock on the door.

Sam roused himself and got up to answer it. Seeing Don outside, he opened the door and shook hands with him. "Come in, we've been waiting for you."

Rory called from the nook, "Hey, Don. Get yourself some coffee and join us over here."

Don refilled the large mug he carried with him everywhere, and offered coffee to Sam.

"No thanks, man," he said. He went to the fridge for water and asked if anyone wanted any.

"I'll have some," Rory said. "The doc says I should hydrate."

When they were all seated, Rory spoke. "Don, I've told Sam about your investigation and involvement with Hayley…"

"Define 'involvement'," Don said with a laugh.

"Why don't *you*?" Rory taunted, smiling.

"I wish!" he said. "Seriously, it's all business and it's serious, I think. Not only has Hayley been threatened by this asshole, I have, too! Now he's really in for it." Don wasn't smiling now. He went on to tell them about Hayley's brush with the perp at the ice rink, the failed entry into her apartment, the note on Hayley's windshield, the message on Don's phone at work, and their discussions with the DA and Detective Herrera.

"That does sound serious," Sam replied, showing interest in the case.

"Oh yeah," Don said. "And I sense a good amount of desperation in his threats. I don't know if that's good or bad, it's hard to say what he'll do. So far he hasn't stopped going after kids, and we know he's capable of murder. I think he's a psychopath, we should ask Marc what he thinks."

"He has mentioned that word in relation to the perp," Rory said. "Although that was just an off the cuff remark," she added.

"How's Hayley holding up?" Sam asked.

"She's ok and she keeps me in the loop about where she is and what she's doing. She's mostly at work, and after work she comes to my house. He hasn't tried to enter my fortress; I'm pretty well armed with locked gates and security cameras…"

Rory smiled, "No surprise there," she commented. "But I guess you need it, what with all the covert activities you take on."

"Absolutely! As you know, Rory, that's what I live for! Not that I'm happy about the current state of affairs, but it certainly does call for my attention."

"By the way," Rory asked, "what did the detective say about you guarding Hayley? Did they offer to take that on?"

"He said they could provide surveillance, and asked Hayley if she felt safe in her apartment. She said she didn't and he asked where she might stay. I told him she could stay at my place, and he was ok with that, and will surveil my place. And he wants me to stay in touch. They're running prints on the note, and should have the results in a few days. At least that's something."

"The guy's smart, I'll give him that," Sam said.

"Oh I think we know that," Rory said. "But collectively, I think we can take him on."

***

Initiating a conversation with her editor, who'd been kind enough to listen, Hayley had apologized profusely for her lapse of judgment and expressed appreciation for being kept on the job.

The groveling over with, she told Ms. O'Brien how she'd been threatened by the bogeyman, and requested to go back on Rowe's case. She mentioned that she'd spoken with Detective Herrera and was willing to cooperate with him. He had agreed that the press ramping up its coverage of the bogeyman would put pressure on him. And maybe he would get careless.

Ms. O'Brien listened with apparent interest. Then she said, "It seems you've learned the hard way about checking sources. At this point, my concern is for your safety if you go after him in the news."

"He's already stalking me. I do have a friend who is letting me stay at his place. He's an adult parole officer, and keeps a secure home. Herrera has offered to help with security."

"Ok, Hayley, I'm willing to give you another chance. If you do this, it's important to continue working with the detective. For your security here, we'll move your things back to your old office."

Hayley left the office, pleased her editor had given her the go ahead. She was prepared to attack Rowe's case and had saved the notes she'd previously made.

Back in her cramped office for the time being, she was completely engrossed in her writing, when she heard muted footsteps come stealthily down the hall towards her office. Hayley froze.

Chapter 34

Hayley's mind flashed to the incident in the mall when she heard the footsteps. She had misread that situation, but this was something else. Her skin crawled as she searched frantically around her small office. Her only hope was hiding next to an oversized file cabinet, which had a small space on the far side of it, next to the wall. Grabbing her purse and papers, she scuttled over to it as quickly and quietly as she could. She nearly ceased breathing as she heard the door open quietly. Then, someone was pulling open her desk drawers, rifling through them as she sat hunched in the tiny space on the other side of the filing cabinet.

She heard him move to the filing cabinet and begin opening and closing drawers. He was so close to her she could hear his rapid breathing, but she dared not look up. There wasn't much in the filing cabinet or the desk because this was the office she'd only recently used when she was placed on probation. What could he be looking for, she wondered.

He was muttering angrily as he ransacked her office. As she'd suspected, it sounded like the same man who'd been stalking her. "Nothing here, nothing important!"

She heard him move back to the desk and it sounded like he was scribbling something. Abruptly he left the office, letting the door close behind him.

Hayley didn't move, still immobilized with fear that he'd come back. Thank God she'd brought her purse with her. She quietly removed her cell phone and hit Don's number. She texted: "Please come to my office NOW! He's been here."

A few minutes passed and he hadn't returned, so she called the front desk and asked the receptionist to come to her office. He seemed surprised but agreed.

A moment later, a knock came at her door and a voice called, "Hayley, you in there?"

She recognized the receptionist's voice and squeezed out of her hiding place to open the door.

"Thanks for coming down Ray. I just wondered if anyone asked for directions to my office recently."

"No," he said, frowning, "did someone come in to bother you?"

"Someone came in unexpectedly and I was wondering how he found my office..."

"Do you want me to call security, see if they saw anything on surveillance?" Ray asked.

"That's a good idea, thank you, Ray." Hayley said.

"Ok, I'll go do that, let me know if you need me for anything. I'm sure no one got by me, he must've come in the back way," Ray said.

"I'm sure that's what happened, thanks Ray."

As Ray was leaving the room, Don came in. Hayley introduced the two, and Ray acknowledged, "I've seen you here with Hayley before."

Then Ray said, "I'll go notify security now," and he left the office.

Don had a look of alarm on his face. Hayley said, "Sit down, I'll tell you what happened."

Hayley went on to describe the event. When she told him where she'd hidden, he got up to take a look.

"It's a good thing it wasn't me trying to hide there! I never knew there was space between the file cabinet and the wall, it's a pretty small space."

"Oh I know that, but I really didn't have another choice, and I honestly can't believe he didn't find me." Remembering that she'd heard him scribbling, Hayley looked down at her desk for the first time. There, tucked into the blotter, she saw a note on an index card. It had the same large block letters as the last note: I AM GETTING CLOSER.

***

Sarah found it relaxing to have a luxurious, comfortable back seat and tinted windows. Before long she was fast asleep. The trip to Branford, Connecticut, near New Haven was just about four hours.

It seemed like minutes rather than hours when the limo drew up in front of her father's house and came to a stop.

Sarah awoke quickly and was somewhat disoriented. It took her a few moments to realize where she was.

The driver turned around and smiled. “Looks like you had a good sleep, we’re at the judge’s house.”

Sarah smiled back. “This car is such a smooth ride! I think I got back the sleep I lost last night.”

Her dad was hurrying out the front door towards the car. He opened the door and helped her out, giving her a big hug as she stood up.

“It’s so good to see you Sarah! I’ve cleared my schedule, so you can stay as long as you like.”

“That’s great, Dad, I’m so happy to be here!” She found she couldn’t hold back the tears, the happy tears, that flooded.

As she looked up at her father, she noticed a sheen of unshed tears in his eyes. He had certainly changed, in a good way.

“Let’s get your things in,” he said.

The driver was holding her luggage, and the judge directed him to take it into the house, tipping him generously before he left.

The two walked into the house.

“Something smells good in here!” Sarah said, realizing she felt hungry.

“Oh yes, Maria fixed us something good for lunch, I’m sure. Are you ready to eat?”

Sarah nodded and the two went into the kitchen.

Taking her favorite seat, which looked out over the sound, Sarah said, “It’s so good to be here. It really feels like home.”

“Of course it is your home and I’m glad you’re happy here.” He smiled and then added, “I’m so proud of you! I wouldn’t have pushed you into law, but I must say I’m glad you followed in the ‘family business’, as it were.”

They ate slowly and carried on minimal conversation.

As Maria cleared their lunch plates away and left the room, Carson spoke, “I have some news for you that I wanted to deliver in person. Of course, that’s not my only reason for inviting you here.”

Sarah was surprised, and felt a lump form in her stomach, as she waited for bad news.

“Sarah, honey, you look sad,” her father said. “Nothing is wrong; it’s just that I’m not good at discussing things.”

"Go ahead, Dad," Sarah urged, trying to prepare herself.

"Well, I should've told you this before, but I'm just getting used to our relationship. Ok, here goes, I've been seeing Geneva, the woman who worked forensics during your abduction." He was flushed.

"I remember meeting her, Dad, she's gorgeous! I think that's awesome."

"Well, we're getting serious, and I wasn't sure how you'd feel about that…she's black, you know."

"No shit, Dad! Sorry for the language, but you and Mom raised me right, so how could you imagine that would be an issue for me?" She laughed, "After all, I was the one involved with a Mexican drug-lord!"

"I'm happy, very happy. You certainly deserve having someone to love, besides me, of course," Sarah joked.

"But I think you've given me the courage to become more involved with life, and love. I don't think I could've made that change without you. You're so expressive, and loving, like your mother…"

"I hope you do get married. Surely you don't think I'd disapprove of that. I know you loved Mom, and she would want you to be happy. You've been alone for too long."

"Thanks, Sarah, now I'm wondering why I thought you might be upset."

"Look, Dad, I'll always remember my mother, and you will, too. I don't think Geneva would have a problem with that."

"I'm sure not. She wanted me to tell you months ago, when we started considering getting engaged."

"Well, are you engaged?"

"Geneva wasn't comfortable with it until I spoke with you."

"That's very sensitive of her, and you can tell her you both have my blessing."

"Well, is there anything else?" Sarah asked.

"Yes, since you mention it. Another reason for this trip now, is that my marshals have been in contact with the FBI. Your 'savior,' Jesus, is coming through town on his way to another safe house. He's been in California, and they felt it best to move him farther away from Mexico, as the cartel seems to be back in business."

Sarah's breath caught. "I'd love to see him, and there's so much I'd like to know! That's wonderful!"

***

Don whipped a plastic baggie out of his pocket and slid the note and the pen from Hayley's desk into it, without touching it. He looked at Hayley and said, "This goes to the police. But before we leave here, we're going to have a heart to heart with your editor. We will also speak with security, and maybe look at surveillance. And we *will* have you placed in another office, not this one way down in the bowels of this building where you're a sitting duck!"

"OK, Boss! I like it when you get angry!" She smiled for the first time today.

Don chuckled, "You think I'm over the top? Honey, you ain't seen nothin' yet!"

"Thanks, but I already spoke with the editor, who was quite reasonable, and she agreed I could go back on Rowe's case, and for my safety, I'll be moved back to my old office.

"But sooner rather than later!" Don said.

Just then there was a knock and a voice called "Security."

Don opened the door and a security officer came in. Hayley knew him and said, "Jim, this is my friend, Don." The men shook hands.

"I requested security because a man came into my office about a half-hour ago and didn't check in at the front desk. He must've come in the back way. I wonder if we can look at security tapes for about that time frame from the back entrance."

"We can do that, but can you give me an idea of who we're looking for? You know, like height, weight, etc.?"

"Well…" Hayley started to explain.

Don interrupted, "The guy's been stalking her, he's left threatening notes, but we've never seen him."

"Have you gone to the police?" the guard asked.

"We have," Hayley answered, "And we'll go back today, but first I want to see that tape."

They followed the officer down to the surveillance office. The guard found the screen for the back entrance. There was static on the screen. He sat down to fiddle with the monitor, but couldn't remove the static. "I'm going around back to have a look at the camera, come if you like." With Hayley and Don trailing behind him, Jim said, “Sometimes the cameras get thrown off by wind or falling objects.”

They arrived at the camera by the back entrance, and looked up together to see that the camera had been smashed to bits.

***

Don and Hayley had spoken with Evelyn O’Brien to bring her up to speed on the security breach, and to request that the move take place immediately.

Hayley ended the interview by standing up. She said, “Thank you so much for helping, Ms. O’Brien. I think we should pay a visit to the detective with our new evidence. I’ll be back later.”

“In the interim, we’ll have your things moved to your old office, close to security,” Ms. O’Brien said. To Don she said, “Very nice meeting you, Mr. Mandel, and I appreciate all you’re doing on Hayley’s behalf.” Then she surprised him by saying, “The sooner we get this pervert the better!”

Don laughed, “Couldn’t say it better myself, except maybe I already have! Bye now and thanks!”

***

Detective Herrera did not keep Don and Hayley waiting, and for the second time, Don handed the detective the newest evidence.

“Maybe we’ll get lucky with prints, again,” said the detective.

“You got prints on the first note?” Hayley asked, surprised.

“Yes, well a partial, it was enough to lead us to a felon in the data base. We got his DNA, too.”

“Anyone we know?” Don asked, on the edge of his seat.

“No, the name was ‘Christopher Bell’, probably an alias,” he said shuffling his papers. “Bell jumped bail over ten years ago in St. Louis. Charge was attempted molestation of a child. Looks like it could be our guy. It’s a cold case there, but I’ve requested the files. They dropped the ball on that one.”

“By the way,” the detective asked, “how is Rory? I know she’s out of the hospital, but that is still not common knowledge.”

“She’s back on the case from home, and doing well. You know there was a guy in a Citadel truck checking out her house, right?” Don asked.

“Yeah, she’s under surveillance, mostly undercover cops in

unmarked cars. He hasn't been back, so far as we know. It looks like the perp has trained his focus on you and Hayley, and he may be running scared by now. He should be, and I hope we're closing in. We've got the evidence we need; we just need to find him."

"Let's get on it then," Don said, standing. "Thanks, Detective!"

***

When they'd left, Herrera called Rory and gave her the information on the partial print and DNA.

"Wow, that's great news!" Rory said. "How can we help with that?"

"Well, you can ask your staff to be vigilant, if anyone tosses out a used coffee cup, or water bottle. For that matter, a dirty mug in the sink; grab it and we'll check it out."

"Ok, I'll put the word out, and while I have you, there's a question about evidence that hasn't been cleared up. The DNA report mentioned that there was an 'unknown substance' in Rachel's vagina, in addition to the dead sperm. Could you have that tested and see what it is?"

"Sure, I'll do that. Report's a little sloppy, don't you think?"

"Yes, I do!" Rory agreed wholeheartedly.

Chapter 35

Rory, Blake, and Sam were strategizing at Rory's house.

Rory told them what she'd learned from Herrera, including that they had a viable print from one of the threatening notes to Hayley. "He's interviewing all of the guys at the poker game again, since they were questioned before the murder. I asked him if we could help and he suggested we be vigilant and try to notice them disposing of coffee cups or water bottles, and also when someone puts a used cup in the sink."

Sam said, "If we manage to get prints, we could solve this thing!"

"For sure!" Blake weighed in. "We have the DNA and prints, if this is the 'Chris Bell' who jumped bail ten years ago."

"It's the best lead we have so far," Rory said.

"So why can't the police just print everyone when they come in for the interview?"

"Good question, Blake. The men would have to give their permission to have prints taken, and that would tip off the perp to leave town. Plus, if we want the charges to stick, and not give defense a loophole, we have to do everything strictly by the letter of the law."

"Yeah, should've known that," Blake said. "I guess I have more studying to do before I take the bar."

"But, if they happen to leave prints, that's a different matter. So now we need to get down to interviewing these guys," Rory said.

Blake said, "I could help with the interviewing, Sam."

"You can help Sam with the office interviews, and trying to collect prints, but I'll do the follow-up interviews. When Sarah left I told her I would take up the slack. And I'm better and ready to do that."

"What about your cover, you know, you being in the hospital…?" Blake asked.

"We're beyond that," Rory said. "I'm not sitting home any more. It was bound to get out anyway. Look, Hayley has been stalked by this asshole, too. It's just a question of being smart, and careful," she added.

"Fine," Blake said, "I'll split the office interviews with Sam."

Sam looked at Rory saying, "I understand you have a need to be more involved. I also know you tend to push yourself. That's all I'm going to say about that, but please pace yourself, and let me know if it gets to be too much. The case is starting to gather momentum."

"I know! Jeez, you sound just like my husband!" Rory said, scolding Sam. "It's just what I need to get back to my game. And I promise you I will try to pace myself."

"Ok, Rory, I'll take you at your word," he said, "Now let's go over the questions Sarah and I came up with. And feel free to add or change anything."

"Speaking of Sarah," Rory asked, "have you heard from her?"

"Not yet."

Rory sighed, "I'm sorry, Sam. Would you like to have dinner with us tonight? I've been a bit neglectful not to invite you sooner."

Sam laughed, "She just left yesterday," he reminded her. "But who can turn down a free meal?"

***

The perp was growing restive. He'd been unable to find Hayley at work or at her apartment. He was sure she was staying with her boyfriend, the parole officer. He knew where Mandel lived, but the guy kept a low profile and he couldn't get the number of his unit. Not to mention that it was gated and locked.

Marilyn Hunter, Carly's caseworker, might be an easier target and he might even threaten her into giving up Carly.

***

Marilyn had gone back to her office while Carly spoke with Mrs. Scott. The detective said it could be a rather long session, especially if the officer could get Carly to talk. Marilyn looked at her watch, and noticed it was close to eleven. That was probably good news.

As if on cue, her cell buzzed and it was the detective. "Hello, Detective," Marilyn said. "I'm hoping for good news."

"You bet!" he answered. "We don't disappoint. Officer Scott is really remarkable, and she's established a good beginning relationship with Carly. Can you come over to the office so we can discuss things?"

"I'll be right over!" she said as she ended the call and collected her things. Running out to her car, she jumped in and took off for the station. She never noticed the white truck following her.

***

Sam finished interviewing James Quinn, who declined coffee, but took hot tea. Sam tried to keep him long enough to finish the tea. The interview itself provided nothing new, but at least he had put Quinn somewhat at his ease, having a pleasant conversation. And now he had his DNA and possibly his prints. He'd retrieved the cup from the trash and marked Quinn's name on the bottom. It was in a bag in his drawer, hopefully awaiting the others.

He'd asked Blake to interview Forsythe, and felt guilty about it. At the same time, he rationalized that he'd had enough dealings with the man.

Now Sam called Blake into Rory's office, which he'd taken until her return. "So, two down, how'd the interview with Forsythe go?"

Blake made a sour face. "Well, apart from treating me like a peon, he had his own agenda and sort of turned the tables on me. He wanted to know about Rory and how the case was going, but really gave me no new information. Plus, he came in with his own coffee mug, so, I might as well admit, it was a bust."

"Damn! He's a tough one, and thanks for taking him on. Maybe you could check later and see if he's left his unwashed mug in the sink. That might work. I doubt any of us, except maybe Rory could get any more out of him."

"Ok," Blake answered, "I'll check on the mug later."

Sam looked at his watch, "It's eleven, so would you mind getting Caldwell from next door and I'll see him?"

"Sure," Blake said.

Chapter 36

Sarah and her father were finishing a leisurely breakfast, chatting and looking out over the sound. It was a clear day and promised to be a comfortable 80 degrees, with low humidity. June was more pleasant here, Sarah remembered, at least when she was a child. Summers seemed to be getting worse every year. But she would just enjoy today.

"My kind of weather!" Sarah said. "It's too damn hot and humid in Philly, we live too far from the ocean. That's one of the things I love about Branford."

Remembering something, Sarah said, "Dad, where did I plug in my cell phone? It was dead when I got here, and I never called Sam!" She was feeling guilty, but at the same time, she realized this was part of creating some distance between Sam and herself.

"I believe you left yours over there," he said pointing to a hutch in the corner of the kitchen.

Sarah went to check and found that it had charged. She punched in the numbers, and listened as it rang four times and then went to voicemail. Disappointed, she left a message.

"Sam, sorry I didn't call as soon as I got in, but my phone was dead and I went to bed early. So, I'm here and fine. There are a couple of things I meant to discuss with you before I left, and they're too involved to leave in a message. So, please call back. I love you!"

***

Sam finished his interview with Alistair Caldwell. This guy seemed genuinely concerned about Rowe, and Sam had seen him talking to Mason as they worked together. He also provided more information than the others.

Caldwell said he met Rowe and all the guys at the poker game when they had served in Afghanistan about eight years ago. They'd formed a close bond during that time, but he and Mason were bunk mates, so were probably closer to each other than some of the others.

Caldwell had finished his coffee and threw the empty cup into the trash. The interview ended shortly after.

Blake came into the office when he saw Caldwell leave. Sam held up the cup like a trophy, then labeled it and put it in the bag with the other one.

"This is the best interview I've had, and he gave me lots of information. He was the first one to admit the guys all met in Afghanistan eight years ago, like Mason told us. He seems pretty genuine, but then, Quinn was better than he was last time I spoke with him, too," Sam said.

Checking his watch, Blake said, "You want to go out for lunch?"

"Not really, I want to write this up, but would you mind getting takeout?"

"No problem, just tell me what you want," Blake said.

As soon as Blake left with his order, Sam looked at his phone. He thought he'd felt a vibration during the interview. As he'd hoped, it was from Sarah. He was relieved as he listened to the message.

***

Detective Herrera was waiting for Marilyn Hunter when she entered the police station.

"Come right back," he invited, and she followed him to his office.

Sitting on the edge of her chair, she listened.

"Well, I told you Mrs. Scott was good, but she seems to have really connected with this child. Carly, it seems, is extra needy and Mrs. Scott was able to address some of her needs. Mind you, she hasn't broached the subject of the bogeyman yet, but she will, gradually."

"That's great news!" Marilyn said. "Now, if only I can find a safe place for Carly to live…"

"Well, I have a proposal for you. Officer Scott, Erin is her first name, has offered to be a temporary foster mother for Carly. Her children are grown and she's a widow. Apparently she's thought about being a foster parent, and this seems to be a good opportunity. I don't know how that works with CYS, so you'll have to enlighten me."

"I do home studies, and they take a bit of time, but mostly because of the security checks we have to do. But she must have up to date checks to be working here…"

“Not only up to date,” the detective said, “but considerably more in depth, I suspect.”

“So, that’s great,” Marilyn said. “I can easily expedite it so that Carly can go home with her today, if you think Mrs. Scott is ready.”

“I get the feeling she is, but why don’t you talk with her and I’ll chat with Carly.”

They walked down the hall to Mrs. Scott’s office, and Herrera introduced the women and asked Carly to come to his office. Carly reluctantly left the office with a backward glance at Mrs. Scott.

“I’ll see you in a few minutes, Carly,” the woman assured the child, with a warm smile.

***

Sarah was walking in the back yard, enjoying the balmy weather. When her cell buzzed, she saw it was Sam and immediately picked up. "Sam!” she said breathlessly, “thanks for calling back. I’m so sorry I didn’t call you as soon as I got in…”

“That’s ok,” Sam answered. “I’ve been really busy and I think we may be onto something. But, first, tell me what you need me to do.”

“I never got Rowe hooked up with a therapist, as I promised. So, if you can find my therapist’s card…”

“I have one,” Sam interrupted, “because we saw her together at times.”

“You’re right!” she said. “Ok, just call Dr. Grant and ask her for the name and number of the woman who does EMDR therapy. See if she can expedite getting an appointment for Rowe.”

“All right, done. Now if your next question is *how is the case going*, I have some news.

Sam went on to explain the print Herrera tracked down and how this impacted the investigation.

“Wow, I’d say you got a lot done. Of course we can’t just test all the suspects’ DNA, without their permission…”

“True, but Herrera suggested that if we can get ahold of a discarded cup or water bottle, and mark whose it was, those prints would be legally obtained. So, we’re offering coffee or water to the guys as we interview them.”

“Brilliant!” Sarah said. “Have you collected any yet?”

"I have two cups, of course we won't know if they yield prints until they're tested."

"It sounds like you at least have something to move on, that's good."

"Yeah, so we're busy and that keeps me from missing you so much. But I do miss you, Sarah."

"I know Sam, and I miss you, too, but I also think it's good for us to have some time apart…"

"Well, I hope it's good for us, and I'm glad this case is keeping me busy. And Rory's feeding me."

"You know damn well how to cook, Sam! You should be inviting them over, considering how many meals we've mooched from them."

"Maybe I will," he said, knowing it wouldn't happen. "Gotta' go now, Blake came back with lunch. Love you."

"Love you, too," Sarah said, but the connection was broken.

I guess he's taken exception to my suggestion, Sarah thought. Too bad.

Chapter 37

Rory was having a well-deserved shower after a hot sweaty day of hard work. It felt good to be on the case, but she had to admit that it tired her. And her hormones were still raging, not to mention the nausea. Moreover, she wasn't any closer to reaching a decision about the baby. Still smarting over Marc's omission around the discussion of Alex's molestation with her, ratcheting up her trust issues over his affair, Rory found herself emotionally depleted. She couldn't make any decision in this state.

She came out of the bathroom with only a towel around her and was surprised to find Marc in bed, reading.

"Well, well," Rory said, "what brings you to bed so early?"

He gave a wicked grin, closed his book, and said, "Why don't you come over and find out?" He whipped off the covers, to reveal his nude body, with the beginning of an erection.

"Marc, I'm really tired, I had a busy day…" she began.

Moving to the side of the bed he tugged at her towel, and pulled her down next to him. He began to caress her breasts, which were very tender.

"Marc, that kind of hurts," Rory said, hoping to stop him.

"Sorry," he said, not sounding sorry.

"Look, I really meant it when I said I was tired. I'm not up for this now!" Rory could feel the anger building.

Marc said nothing. He calmly got up, put his clothes on and closed the door a tad loudly as he left.

"God damn him!" Rory muttered. She flung his book against the door and then broke down sobbing.

***

Having placed Carly with Mrs. Scott the previous night, Marilyn Hunter was feeling pleased with the situation. Additionally, she'd secured an appointment with the therapist of her choice. She and

Carly were sitting in the waiting room. Across from her was a woman who looked vaguely familiar. Where had she seen her?

As Carly was called into the office, Marilyn recalled she'd seen a picture of the woman in the newspaper. Her daughter was the first reported victim of the bogeyman. She had so many questions for her, but didn't want to impose. Finally, her curiosity got the best of her.

"Excuse me," she said, sitting next to Dara Keene, "I don't mean to pry, but I'm just wondering if you think the psychologist is as good as advertised."

"I'm very pleased," Dara said. "Is that your daughter who just went in?"

"No, I'm a caseworker for CYS, and that poor child has been through so much abuse…"

"Well if anyone can help her, I think Dr. Singh can. My daughter showed signs of improvement in a few weeks. Of course, it will be a long process…"

"Thanks, I hope things go as well for Carly." Marilyn lowered her voice, "I'm afraid the bogeyman has begun a relationship with her, and we're doing our best to stay ahead of him. It's scary."

Dara drew in her breath. "The bogeyman is after her?" she asked.

"We can't know for sure, but we know he's still on the loose, and pedophiles are obsessed, they don't heed the warnings that regular people do," Marilyn said, with a shiver.

Dara spoke softly, "I know how you feel."

***

Rory came into the office on her first day back to work feeling grumpy about the unfinished business with Marc, who had slept in the guest room and left for work before she got up. And she was slightly apprehensive about being back to the office. The last time she'd been here, well, she didn't want to think about that. And it still bugged her she didn't remember what happened before she blacked out.

Rory appreciated that Blake and Sam had brought pastries to welcome her, but she knew she couldn't stomach them, or the coffee for that matter.

"Hey, thanks guys," she said, without her normal enthusiasm. "It's good to be back," she lied. "I'd best get on with it. Maybe we should discuss where we are with the case," she said, leading the way to her office.

She found her office newly cleaned and in order. "Cleaner than I left it," Rory said.

Sam asked, "Mind If I get some things from your drawer?" With her assent, he reached into the bottom drawer and pulled out the bag with three styrofoam cups in it, waving it aloft. "We got everyone but Forsythe," Sam grimaced. "He came to the interview with his own mug and left with it."

"I looked in the sink later to see if he'd left it there, but no such luck," Blake said. "He's a creepy guy."

"I can't wait to meet him," Rory said without enthusiasm.

"Careful what you wish for," Blake cautioned.

As if scripted, they heard the rustle of plastic, and saw Forsythe emerge from the construction area. He walked directly towards Rory's office, as Sam jammed the cups back into the drawer.

Entering the office, he said, "Rory Chandler, I presume," offering his hand. "I'm Chad Forsythe, don't get up," he strode towards her. "I'm so pleased you're better, and more than happy you're taking Mason's case."

"Thank you, Mr. Forsythe," Rory said, with as much grace as possible. "It's good to be back."

"Yes, the press reported you were in a very bad way," Forsythe said.

"Well, I was, for a while. It took me longer than expected to wake up from the concussion. To this day, I have no recollection of what happened." She added the last remark for good measure.

"I wish the offices had been finished when you came back, but we had several days of work stoppage while the police collected evidence. Bad business!" he said, as if regretting he'd gone there. "Well, I'll let you get back to work. Talk to you later," Forsythe said as he left.

When the plastic curtain had whooshed shut, Blake quietly closed the office door. "You don't think he heard us, do you?" he asked.

"I don't really give a rat's ass," Rory said. Sam and Blake smiled as if to say, *She's Back*!

***

Carly came out of Dr. Singh's office with a smile on her face. Marilyn breathed a sigh of relief, but knew enough to refrain from asking her questions. "Hi Carly, are you ready to go back to Mrs. Scott's?"

"Yes!" she said with more enthusiasm than Marilyn had seen earlier in the day. "I really like her, Miss Hunter, she's the nicest lady. She's the best foster mother I've ever had!"

"I'm happy for you, Carly. I like her too." She thought glumly about the procession of foster parents who hadn't worked out for Carly, and acknowledged that it was very hard to find good people.

Marilyn and Carly walked out of the office. As they approached the car, Marilyn looked more closely. It appeared there was something on her windshield.

She buckled Carly into her seat and then went to take the paper from under the wiper. It was an index card with block letters, which read: YOU TOOK CARLY FROM ME AND YOU WILL PAY!

Chapter 38

A half-hour later, Marilyn was sitting with Detective Herrera, having dropped Carly at Mrs. Scott's. She was taking family leave so she could settle Carly in.

The detective was examining the note, which he held by one corner. "It's the same guy," he said as he looked at the other notes on his desk. "This guy is really brazen! He doesn't have the sense to back off," Herrera said.

"He's bound to make a mistake with his reckless behavior," Marilyn said. "Of course, that is typical of pedophiles, isn't it? He'd been grooming Carly, and she was a willing participant, I'm sure. Anyone who shows her kindness is like a magnet to Carly. Poor kid hasn't had a chance! But she does like Mrs. Scott," she said, turning optimistic.

***

Rory had learned all she needed from her discussion with Blake and Sam. Despite her reluctance to work on this case, it was time for her to get down to business, namely get on with interviewing the men, including Forsythe. In fact, she would start with Forsythe, since he seemed the most challenging.

As she pushed her way through the plastic, Rory had a strange sensation, a visceral reaction that left her off balance. She blacked out for a second and would've fallen to the floor, had not Forsythe been there to catch her.

When she came to and saw Forsythe's hands on her, she yelled, "Get off me!"

Sam, followed closely by Blake, came into the room and pulled Forsythe off Rory.

Coming to her senses, she said, "Sorry, sorry, Mr. Forsythe."

"Let him go," she said to Sam and Blake. "I don't know what came over me, I just…don't know."

With a look in Forsythe's direction, Sam said, "I think you came back to work too soon, Rory. You should see the doc."

"I'm fine, really!" she said frostily. "I need to do some paper work." She walked somewhat unsteadily to her office.

"What happened?" Sam asked Forsythe with an accusatory tone.

"I have no idea; one minute she was walking through the curtains, and the next, she was falling."

"Did she say anything?" Blake asked.

"Not until she told me to get off her. Her eyes were sort of unfocused. I didn't do anything, except catch her!" Forsythe was angry.

"Ok, well, thanks, I guess," Sam said. "And sorry." Sam's lack of authenticity was apparent.

Blake and Sam headed back to the other side, leaving Forsythe with a frown on his face.

When they were out of range of Forsythe's hearing, Blake said, "What do you make of that? Should we insist Rory see the doctor?"

"You're kidding, right? Insist that Rory do anything against her will?" Sam snorted. "When she's ready, she'll come and find us."

***

Fifteen minutes later, Rory opened her office door, motioning for Blake and Sam to join her.

They wasted no time following her direction, and were soon seated across from her desk.

"I think my memory of that awful day is coming back. As soon as I went through the curtains, I got an odd feeling, and had a flash, a quick one, which left me blacked out. I think my memory might be starting to come back, and I hope, all of it."

"You sure you don't need to see a doctor?" Sam asked.

"No, I don't. But I do need to see Forsythe, and get on with the interview." Rory stood up.

Sam and Blake followed her to the curtains, to make sure she made it this time.

She entered without incident and walked to Forsythe's door.

He looked surprised when he answered the door. "Are you ok?"

"Much better, thank you. I owe you an apology, and my thanks for catching me. Sorry we got off on a bad footing."

"I'm glad I was there to help. I'd hate to see you back in the hospital on your first day back to work."

"Where I could've easily landed, but for you."

"But now, to business. As you know, I'm late coming to this case, so I need to get my own perspective. My associates have interviewed all of the men at the poker game with Mason Rowe, and I understand they interviewed you, as the employer of the men. So I'm going to go over the same ground."

"Ok," Forsythe said, looking a bit reluctant.

"Do you know how long these men have known each other?" Rory asked.

This seemed to throw him, and he hesitated. "Well, they didn't all start work here at the same time. I could look up their dates of employment…"

"I just wondered if you knew of a prior relationship they may have had?"

"No, not that I know of," Forsythe replied, squirming in his seat.

"So, to your knowledge, they've known each other only through their current employment, correct?"

"Yes," he answered, without giving further information.

"Are they a tight group? That is, were they a tight group, including Gordon Howe?"

"They played poker together, I don't know of anything else outside of work."

"Were any of them particularly close?"

"I really couldn't say," Forsythe said.

"One last question," Rory said, realizing she wasn't getting much. "Can you imagine any of these men framing Rowe to hide his own involvement?"

"Certainly not!" Forsythe said, far too quickly, Rory thought.

"Ok, that's all for now. I should see Mason Rowe, is he here?"

"Yes, he is. Would you like me to bring him in here?"

"No thanks," Rory said. "I'll take him to my office. I don't want to impose on you any longer."

***

Marilyn Hunter stopped by to see Carly at Officer Scott's house, a snug brick home on a tidy block with sidewalks. There was a long, tree-lined driveway that gave the house a sense of privacy. It was within walking distance of the Borough of Media and Marilyn knew Carly wouldn't have to change schools. That was one fewer obstacle.

It was also far enough from her previous foster home, and the notorious playground. But she knew that Erin Scott would not be allowing Carly to go out alone for any reason.

Erin answered the door, and gave Marilyn a smile. "Come, have a seat. Carly's playing in her room, and I'll let her know you're here. I think we need to talk first, though."

Marilyn heard her speaking to Carly with an affectionate tone. "Ms. Hunter and I are going to talk for a bit, and then I'll bring her in to see your room, ok?"

"Sure, that's ok, Mama," Carly said.

Coming back into the room, Erin said, "I asked Carly what she wanted to call me, and she said 'Mama.' What could I say?"

"She desperately needs a Mama," Marilyn said.

Then she discussed pertinent details with Erin, including speaking with the principal and counselor at Media Elementary before the next school year began. Marilyn also told her about the note she'd found on her windshield, and cautioned her to be exceedingly careful about the bogeyman's ability to find Carly.

"Well, my dog, Pepper, should be quite helpful." She whistled and a large Rottweiler galloped into the room, arriving at Erin's feet, as if awaiting instructions. She patted his head and said, "Go see our guest."

He obediently trotted over and sat at Marilyn's feet. "Well, Hello, Pepper," she said scratching him behind his ears. He wagged his tail and licked her hand.

"What a sweetie!" Marilyn exclaimed.

"That's true, but had I issued another command, it would've been a different story! He will attack on command."

"That's perfect!" Marilyn said. "How do he and Carly get along?" she asked.

"I told him to protect Carly. And he does not take that lightly. Plus, she loves him, so he just naturally follows her around. He sleeps in her room now, and it's next to mine. So," she concluded, "between Sargent Pepper and my Glock, I think we're prepared. But not complacent!" she added.

"Hopefully you can teach her not to trust indiscriminately!" Marilyn noted.

"Well, that's true, I'll do my best. I'm quite taken with the girl."

"I can see that!" Marilyn said. "Now can I see her room?"

"Follow me," Erin said.

Marilyn's exclamations about the room were totally genuine. "Oh, my goodness, what a lovely room." It was large and filled with light. There was a motif of teddy bears trimming the top of the walls, and the bears themselves, scattered around the room. Carly was playing contentedly with two dolls.

Marilyn smiled at Carly and Erin, as she said "Goodbye." Then she said, "Can I come play 'Barbies' with you sometime?"

Carly's face lit up as she said, "Sure."

As she left the house, she took a good look around. She didn't want to have this freak following her.

Chapter 39

Rory ushered Mason Rowe into her office. He was tall and lanky, with dark brown hair and expressive green eyes. He was quite attractive, Rory thought. The bruises on his face and arms had begun to heal, and his hair was growing back, but she imagined that the emotion of the event was still with him.

He took the proffered seat, and looked straight at Rory. Before she could begin, he said, "I just want to thank you, and your associates, and your husband. Everyone has been very considerate, and I can't imagine going through this ordeal without all of you. Thank you."

Momentarily speechless, Rory weighed his words and found she was impressed by his sincerity. Accustomed to lots of BS, she found it refreshing to hear genuine appreciation, without embellishment. And she began to feel better about taking his case. She just realized she hadn't thought she'd like him.

"I'm happy we can be of service to you Mr. Rowe," she said. "I'm sure you've tired of all the questions, but I'm new to the case, so I need to start fresh."

"Makes sense to me," Rowe said.

"Thank you for understanding," Rory said. "I'm afraid we have to start with the night of the poker game. Can you tell me in your own words what happened that night?"

Rowe went into a fairly lengthy description of the evening. He expressed confusion about his allegedly being drunk that night. Although he felt dizzy, he knew he'd had only one beer.

Rory interrupted, "I've heard that the other men said you were impaired, but that you were not a big drinker. So I have to wonder if someone put something in that one beer to mimic a drunken state."

"I've wondered that myself, but I can't really see any of them doing that to me. We were very tight in Afghanistan, and we relied on each other. Christ, one of the guys saved me from an IED!" He lapsed into silence.

"It must've been bad over there," Rory said quietly.

"It was beyond bad, beyond anything I've ever experienced. And we went through it as a team."

"And you're still having nightmares, I'm told," Rory said.

"Yes, I still relive it sometimes at night. I wake up screaming, but have no recollection of what I saw."

"I'm not a shrink," Rory said, "but my husband is, so maybe I've picked up some stuff. It seems to me that until you purge some of this from your memory bank, it will come back to haunt you."

"Yeah, I believe that's true. And Ms. Justice suggested I go for EMDR, whatever that is, to treat it. Sam set up an appointment for tomorrow. I'm scared to go, but I will," he added. "I'll do anything to get rid of those dreams."

"Would you like someone to go with you?" she asked.

"No, it's something I have to do on my own, but thank you," Rowe said.

"I can tell you a little about EMDR, an acronym which stands for 'eye movement desensitization and reprocessing'. I know it's a mouthful, but it's often described as rebooting a computer. I think you're walked through the traumatic events by the therapist, and then your eye movements are directed by the therapist. It's not an instant cure, it may take several visits, but it's a proven method. You'll still have the memories, but they lose their ability to immobilize you.

"It sounds good, but I'm still scared. I'll let you know after my first appointment what I think."

***

Hayley Singleton was on pins and needles. She'd been given the go ahead to write the article about the bogeyman. It would be an editorial, because her thoughts and feelings would be included. She'd already scrapped two versions. She got up to pace around the office. That helped sometimes to start her thought process. She was definitely blocked, but she had to find out why.

As she walked to her office, she came to terms with her feelings. She was scared witless of this guy, and afraid this editorial would further provoke him. That was the intent, but she didn't like that she was bait. But, she reminded herself, she had Don and Herrera on her side. She felt the load lighten a bit, so went back to her desk.

This time, she wrote with a vengeance, and the words just flowed, as she felt lighter with each paragraph.

***

When Rowe came out of Rory's office, after about an hour, Sam went in to retrieve the cups so he could deliver them to Herrera.

"How'd the interview go?" Sam asked.

"It went well, he's easy to interview, and he seems very open, somehow."

"Yeah, I found that, too," Sam said. "I really like the guy."

"By the way, he's afraid of the appointment tomorrow. I spent some time telling him what little I know of the process, including what EMDR stands for," Rory said.

"What does it stand for?" Sam asked.

"Ask him, I think he wrote it down," Rory joked.

"I could go with him if he wants," Sam said.

"He doesn't want, I already asked. He feels he has to go it alone."

"Well, that makes sense, I guess," Sam replied. "Oh, before I forget, the reason I came in was to get those cups in your bottom drawer."

Rory opened the drawer. There was nothing there besides her files. "Are you sure you didn't move them?"

***

It was still light out, but Carly had had a very busy day and looked sleepy. Although she'd seemed happy coming home after her first therapy session, it had definitely tired her, Erin Scott noticed.

"Carly, how about I read to you?" she asked. "You get to pick the books."

"Thank you, Mama, that would be fun." She began to peruse the shelves of her bookcase, which was jammed with books. "Who read these books before?" Carly asked.

"My own children" she said. "We did lots of reading together."

"You have children?" Carly asked.

"Yes, but they're not children anymore, they grew up on me and moved out."

"I'll never move out, Mama. I will always be here so we can read together."

She smiled at Carly, saying, "You'll get to meet them Carly, they live close by and they stop in often."

"Oh, good!" Carly said, still searching the shelves. She finally picked a few and took them to Mrs. Scott.

They sat on the floor and Carly's 'Mama' read to her. Before long, Carly's head drooped and fell against Erin's shoulder.

Erin looked lovingly at the sleeping child, but kept reading until she was sure Carly was fast asleep. Then she carefully lifted her onto the bed, covering her with a light blanket. She kissed Carly's forehead, and the girl said, "Thank you, Mama," without waking up.

As she left the room, she patted Pepper's head, and told him, "You stay." He put his head on his paws, and did as he was commanded.

Glancing at her watch, Erin noted with satisfaction that it was time for one of her CSI shows. She sat in her favorite chair, put her feet up and directed the remote to the TV.

The show had barely begun when she started dozing.

She didn't know how long she'd been asleep when Pepper's furious barking woke her with a start. With surprising agility, she got out of the chair and ran to Carly's room. She saw Pepper, with his paws on the windowsill, barking. The window was closed and locked.

Officer Scott had an idea who might be out there, so she silenced the dog, went to get her Glock, and closed Carly's door. Miraculously the child had slept through it.

She leashed Pepper, and the two went out the back door, locking it behind her. They walked quietly in the direction of Carly's window. Erin saw a figure nearby, and released Pepper, with the command, "Sargent, attack!"

The dog raced in the direction of the intruder, who was running now, almost out of Erin's sight. She could hear Pepper snarling, and then she heard a yelp.

She ran towards the noise, and found Pepper on the ground, bleeding in the area of his shoulder. Looking closer, it appeared to be a puncture wound. She could no longer see the intruder, but fired a shot into the air to let him know she wasn't playing. Damn, she thought, that man was the one who deserved to be stabbed.

Chapter 40

Marilyn had been working late, finishing up the paper work for her placement of Carly in Mrs. Scott's home. There had been no doubt that it would be approved, but the necessary documentation was overwhelming. As she finished up, she noticed the sun had set and it was getting dark. She appeared to be the last one here.

She gathered up her things quickly, having no desire to remain in the empty office. The security guard who was usually at the front door was not there, and his replacement had not shown up. Marilyn tried to quell her fear as she headed out of the building. Unfortunately, her car was parked a distance from the office. She put her hand into her sweater pocket and strode to her car, trying to appear unafraid, though her knees were knocking.

As she got closer to her car, she swept her gaze over the surrounding lot. Seeing nothing, she quickened her step, hit the fob to unlock her door and made her way swiftly to the safety of the car. As she was getting in, she was pulled from behind by her hair so hard it brought tears to her eyes.

Her tormenter whispered harshly in her ear, "You will get Carly for me or you will not survive."

Marilyn tried to turn around to look at him but he pulled her hair harder until she gave in, or appeared to. She was able to reach into her pocket, and take out a can of pepper spray, doing her best to aim it at her attacker's face. Apparently, she'd made contact because he released her hair immediately, screaming, "You fucking bitch!" and swiping fiercely at his eyes as he ran off.

She kept spraying at his retreating back. Thank God her boyfriend had insisted she carry pepper spray.

Sinking to the ground, Marilyn dialed Herrera's cell. He answered immediately and when she described the situation promised he'd be over. "Go back inside and wait for me," he said.

As she was walking on trembling legs back to the office, she continued to look around, holding her pepper spray. She was nearing the front door when she heard rustling in the bushes, and then heard a moan, "Help me!"

***

Erin Scott was cradling Carly, who had finally awakened with all the commotion going on in the house. Her dog lay at her feet, fighting sleep. Erin had a friend who was a vet, and she'd offered to come over and treat the dog. The wound had been dressed and the dog had been given antibiotics and pain medication.

Now Carly asked, "Mama, why is everyone here? What happened?"

Not one to sugarcoat the truth, she told Carly what happened.

"Carly, someone tried to get in your window, but Pepper scared him away."

"Is that how Pepper got hurt?"

"Yes, the person stabbed Pepper."

Carly started to cry, and hugged the sleepy dog. "Who was it?"

"I don't know, he ran off before we could catch him. But the police are looking for evidence."

Carly had a concerned expression on her face.

"What's wrong, Honey, why do you look sad?" Erin asked gently.

"Well, my friend Charlie tried to come get me from my window before but the staff scared him away. He's my friend and he gave me a necklace."

"My dear Carly, whoever tried to get in your window tonight is not your friend. And anyone who would stab a wonderful dog like Pepper is not your friend, or someone you can trust."

"Maybe it wasn't him, then," Carly said.

"Maybe not, but I hope the police find whoever it was. I will keep you safe. Our brave dog will keep us safe."

***

Herrera had left the crime scene at Erin's to drive the short distance to the CYS office. He found Marilyn inside with the wounded security guard, who'd been found lying in the bushes. The EMT's had been called but hadn't yet arrived.

The guard told Herrera everything he could remember. "I was running late for my shift, so I parked my car and was walking to the front door. I had called the guy I was relieving, and told him to leave. As I almost reached the door, I didn't see or hear anything, but something struck me hard from behind, and I went down. Don't remember anything, until Ms. Hunter revived me and helped me in here. Sorry I can't be more helpful."

"Any information is helpful," Herrera said. Hearing approaching sirens, he said to the guard, "Looks like your ride is here."

After the guard left, Herrera went to Marilyn. "This guy really has it in for you!"

"Yeah, he wants Carly, and he promised to harm me if he didn't get her."

"Evidently he's had a busy evening. I took your call from Erin's house, where he'd tried to break in through Carly's window"

Marilyn's hand flew to her mouth, "Please tell me he didn't succeed! What happened?"

"No, he didn't get her. If he had, he probably wouldn't have paid you a visit."

"Of course, I didn't think of that. Thank God Carly's safe!"

"Erin will go to any lengths possible to protect Carly. She set the dog on the guy, but he stabbed the dog. Then Erin ran in his direction, but he got away. She did fire a warning shot, to let him know what to expect if he comes back."

"Is Sgt. Pepper ok?" Marilyn asked.

"Who?" Herrera asked.

"The dog, is he ok?"

"He'll be ok, he's been seen by a vet. I thought his name was 'Pepper.' "

***

Sam was talking to Sarah on the phone after work. He was upset and Sarah always soothed him. He was telling her about the cups, which may have had fingerprints on them. "I swear to God I never moved them, but they were gone! I searched everywhere, but couldn't find them. Now I look like an ass, since I told Herrera I'd bring them to him."

"Calm down, Sam," Sarah said quietly. "This gives us more evidence that the bogeyman is in the group we've been interviewing.

It's got to be someone at Citadel. Who's had access to Rory's office?"

"Too many people. I mean the place is wide open with the construction going on…"

"I'm sorry that happened, Sam, but it's not your fault."

"Whose, then? I put them in the drawer, and forgot about them when Rory came back. But I showed them to her, I think. And I had every intention of taking them back today. I blew it!"

"Stop beating yourself up!" Sarah said forcefully. "All you can do now is to try harder to find the bogeyman. Apparently, he's right under your nose."

"So near, and yet…" Sam stopped, saying to Sarah, "How's your day going?"

"I spent some time studying for the bar while Dad did paperwork. And later today, an FBI guy is bringing Jesus over, so we can talk before he's placed at a new safe house. I have lots of questions for him," she added.

"That should be interesting, if you think you're ready to hear it…"

"I'm ready, and it should help me put this behind me."

"How many days until you come home?" Sam asked, changing the subject.

***

Rory's day had been fruitful, excluding Sam's meltdown when several searches of the office yielded nothing. That had kept her from finishing her interviews, but she'd do them tomorrow. She needed to talk with Alex and now was the time. Marc was working late in the city, and Kate had gone out with her new boyfriend.

Light came from under Alex's door, so Rory knocked softly. "May I come in, Alex?"

"Sure, Mom, come in." She sat up in bed and closed the book she'd been reading. She patted the bed next to her and said, "Come sit here."

Rory sat down and as soon as she opened her mouth to speak, she started sobbing. Alex waited until her mother had found control. Then Rory began to speak.

"Alex, I'm so sorry about what happened to you, and I'm sorry I was too self -involved to notice your pain. I don't know how to make it up to you…"

"Mom," Alex said, putting her arms around her mother, "It wasn't your fault. I didn't want to talk about it, except in therapy. In fact, I still don't want to talk about it. I'm sorry it came up, honestly."

"I have to give you your space. If you ever want to talk about it, I'm here. And I love you."

"Love you, too, Mom."

Rory left the room, still worried about Alex, but with the realization she had to leave it alone. Damn Marc for keeping her in the dark for so long!

Chapter 41

The Daily Times was delivered to Don's early, as usual. He was up and waiting for it, his coffee already in hand. He went out, looked around carefully, and picked up the paper.

Sitting at the kitchen counter he opened the paper and scanned it for the editorial. As promised, it was not plastered on the first page. He found it on the third page, and began to read it while Hayley slept. It was good, and very few, if any changes had been made. He was proud of Hayley for writing it, knowing it would enrage the bogeyman. Don was ready for that, and perhaps the bogeyman would get sloppy. The angrier he got, the more likely he was to be caught. And Don hoped that would be soon.

Don was just putting the paper down, when a sleepy Hayley came into the kitchen. "You're up early…" Then she noticed the paper and seemed to wake all at once. "Oh, did you read it?"

"I did, and it's on page three; I think you should be very pleased. Come here and give me a hug. She walked into his arms and they hugged. Don leaned down, and gave her a kiss, a real kiss. She came up for air. "Congratulations," he said, and handed her the paper. "Here, read it."

She sat at the counter and delved into the editorial.

"Coffee or tea today?" Don asked.

"Oh, why not coffee," she said. Then she went back to her reading.

Don poured a cup for Hayley, added milk and set it in front of her.

"Thank you," she said distractedly. Without looking at it she picked up the cup and took a sip. "Whew, hot!" she said and stuck her nose back into the paper.

When she'd read the entire editorial, she looked up, pleased. "I don't think anything was changed. That's remarkable!"

"Well, it's a remarkable piece of writing. Well done, Hayley!"

Hayley began to cry. Between sobs, she said, "I don't know why I'm crying. I'm happy and relieved, but also scared, very scared."

Don put his arms around her, and spoke in her ear. "What you did was very brave, and we can expect blow back, but we'll be ready for it. And I'm going to keep you very close."

***

Mason Rowe was sitting in the waiting room. He had the first appointment of the day and he'd arrived early. He wanted to get this over with. He'd spoken on the phone with Dara the previous night, and she'd been extremely supportive. She'd wanted him to go for treatment for some time, and she'd offered to pay out of pocket. When Mason told Dara that the law office was paying for it, she was surprised and pleased.

He'd looked Dr. Reynolds up on the internet, and read about her and the treatment. This procedure had been around and been studied for several years, but was coming into its own as so many people like him returned from war psychologically scarred.

A nurse appeared at the door and called him in. She chatted with him, took his weight and blood pressure, which was a bit elevated. "Is this your normal pressure?" she asked.

"No, it's a little high today. I'm a bit nervous," he admitted.

"That's not uncommon," she told him. "This procedure had been practiced for several years, but people don't understand it too well, so it worries them."

"Why do you take weight and blood pressure, since Dr. Reynolds is not an MD?"

"Dr. Reynolds is a nurse practitioner, as well as a psychotherapist. She likes to see what shape her clients are in, and it helps if she needs to prescribe meds for her patients."

"That sounds like a good idea."

"I think Dr. Reynolds will put you at ease. She'll be in shortly." Before she left the room, she said, "I just want to thank you for putting yourself out there and going into battle. Now that takes courage."

Mason was surprised, in a nice way, and he was feeling better already.

A few moments later, Dr. Reynolds came in. She introduced herself and shook his hand.

Mason was surprised that she looked no older than he was. She was tall, with chin length auburn hair, and was quite attractive. She reminded him of Rory.

***

Rory was working at her desk when Jordan Kraft appeared in her doorway. She looked up, and said, “Come in Mr. Kraft,” Rory stood up and shook his hand, “I’m Rory Chandler, thanks for coming in. Have a seat.” Jordan Kraft was incredibly handsome, breathtaking, in fact. He was very tall and lean, with dark curly hair and bright blue eyes, and a smile that lit up his face. She thought, *he’s probably gay*, like all the gorgeous guys, and immediately chastened herself for the thought.

“I’m sorry to take your time for more questions, but I’m new to the case,” Rory told him.

“I have no problem answering questions. I want to get to the bottom of this as much as you do. Rowe’s a good guy, and he needs to be cleared. For that matter, Gordon was a good friend, too.”

“Thanks, I appreciate that,” Rory said. “You were in a unique position the night of the poker game, since you hosted it.”

“Well, yes and no. As the host, I was in and out of the room a lot, so I could’ve missed something. Rowe did stay overnight on the couch because the guys seemed to think he’d had too much to drink. That was odd, because he’s not a drinker, and I’ve never seen him drunk.”

“Do you remember who first called attention to that, his having too much to drink?”

Jordan thought for a moment, and then shook his head. “When I came into the room, it was already an accepted fact, and he did look woozy, but like I said, that was unusual for him.”

“Did you wonder about it at the time?”

“No, not really, it was like the decision had been made, so I felt compelled to let him stay.”

“Do you have any way of knowing if he left during the night?”

“Like I told Ms. Justice, I’m a heavy sleeper and it’s tough to wake me up. I even have a dog sleeping in my room, and I’ve gotten accustomed to him barking during the night, so I’ve been told by my neighbor, and that doesn’t wake me up.”

"So, you wouldn't remember if he barked that night?"

"No, sorry, I wish I could be more helpful."

"Did it ever occur to you that someone put something in Rowe's drink that night?"

"Yeah, I wondered about it afterward, especially because it was very difficult to rouse Mason the next day. But we're a tight group, with a bond formed years ago, in Afghanistan, so it's hard for me to get my head around that. But I do have questions, especially since Gordon was killed. It can't look good for us as a group, but I just don't know..."

***

When Jordan left Rory's office, he went out the front door, headed for his truck. Before he reached his truck, he saw one of his co-workers sitting in a Citadel truck. He tapped on the window, and the man at the wheel unlocked the door.

"What's up Kraft?" the man asked tersely. "You just meet with that nosey bitch, Chandler?"

Kraft was a bit taken aback, "How do you get off calling her that? She's just trying to get to the bottom of this, and clear Rowe."

"Suppose he did it?" the man shot back. "He makes us all look bad."

"I don't get it," Kraft shook his head. "I thought we were all in it together."

"Maybe not," the man said, "maybe we all need to save our own asses!"

"Well, I'm not worried about my ass!" Kraft said, getting out of the truck and slamming the door.

He gave a backward glance to the driver of the truck, and watched as the man accelerated and sped off. He'd never had a chance to ask the man what he thought about the situation, but he guessed he'd gotten his answer anyway.

What's going on? Kraft wondered, as he thought back to Afghanistan. They had bonded there, but maybe for some it was stronger than others. He had some thinking to do.

***

Sitting at her desk after a hurried lunch, Rory heard someone come in, and soon Sam appeared at her door. "I was hoping to talk with you, got a minute?" Rory asked.

"Sure," Sam came in and sat down.

"I was pleased with my interviews this morning. Kraft and Caldwell seemed genuine and cooperative. What was your experience?"

"Sarah interviewed Kraft, and seemed to like him. When I saw him, I wondered if she wasn't taken in by his looks," Sam admitted.

"I didn't notice," Rory lied.

"Yeah, right, like any woman between the ages of seventeen and seventy wouldn't notice!"

"Well, I guess…" Rory relented.

"So, what about Caldwell?"

"I liked him, he seemed comfortable, nice guy."

"Ok, thanks, I just wanted to check with you."

***

Hayley had been busy and lost track of time. Work was just what she needed to take her mind off her worries. She looked up at the clock and realized she was late; Don had said he'd meet her at 4pm, and it was almost five past. She quickly gathered up her papers, stuffed them in her briefcase and hustled out the front door.

The hot, humid air hit Hayley in the face as she went outside. The familiar blue Subaru was not out front where she had been meeting him lately. This made her nervous. Maybe since she was late, he'd gone around back. Hayley called him as she walked to the back lot. He didn't answer, so she left him a message. "Sorry I was late coming out. Since you weren't out front, I'm checking around back."

Before she could look up from her phone, she was pulled from behind by her hair, and dragged across the parking lot towards the woods that abutted it. She tried to look around and see her assailant, but he just pulled harder on her hair.

He muttered harshly as he continued to drag her. "Writing lies in the paper! You think you're so clever, well, that's the last one you write!"

He pulled her up as they reached the end of the lot. She still couldn't see his face, as he had a hat pulled down and dark glasses on. He started smacking her, and then dropped her as a car approached.

Don's Subaru was headed straight for the bogeyman.

Chapter 42

It took a great deal of control for Don to hit the brakes. Every fiber of his being yearned to run over the bogeyman and be done with it. But he knew he couldn't risk hitting Hayley.

Leaping out of the car, he followed his instinct and gave chase, his hand on his revolver. He didn't have time to check Hayley, but she was sitting up, so he hit 911 on his cell as he ran. The area adjacent to the parking lot was essentially a swamp, filled with muddy water and a tangle of briars. It had recently rained, so he was slogging through water up to his ankles. It was slow going and the suspect was far ahead of him.

The 911 operator came on and asked, "What is your emergency?"

Don gave the location and described what had happened. "Send an ambulance at once!" he said as he hung up.

He'd lost precious time talking to the operator, but Hayley was his priority. Looking around and seeing no movement, he punched in Herrera's number and headed back to Hayley.

Herrera answered promptly, and Don told him what had happened and asked if he could send officers to the area behind the lot. The attacker should be easy enough to pick out, with mud all over him.

Finding Hayley still sitting up, and seemingly in a trance, he ran to her side.

"Are you ok, Hon?" he asked, taking her hand.

"That was the bogeyman, but I couldn't see him. Damn!" Hayley exploded.

"Get a grip Hayley, you're lucky! I'm sorry I was late, and by chance I was almost out front when I got your message."

"Thank God you're ok! You *are* ok, aren't you?" Don asked.

"I'm probably in shock and my head hurts like a bitch because he dragged me by my hair. The bastard!"

Soon the sirens pierced the air, announcing the approach of the cops, or the EMT's. As it turned out, they arrived in tandem.

***

Rory was the last one to leave the office. She took time to breathe in the cooler air, a smile on her face. Damn, she thought, it felt great to put in a good day's work.

Unlocking her car, she leaned in to drop her briefcase. Noticing a slip of paper on the seat, she picked it up, expecting it to be her grocery list. It wasn't.

The note, in an unfamiliar script, read, "You're on the right track, keep up with the interviews."

It wasn't signed, but Rory believed it was from one of the men she'd interviewed. So, it might have been from Kraft, Caldwell, or Forsythe. She wondered if she could devise a way to get handwriting samples. That would probably go as well as the fingerprint fiasco had, she thought, discarding the idea.

Noticing the front windows were open a crack, she surmised that was how the note landed on her seat. Well, at least it wasn't a threatening note, like Hayley had received.

Maybe they were on the right track, or maybe it was misinformation. She'd talk it over with Marc tonight.

***

The bogeyman had hunkered down behind a large rock, surrounded by grasses. He'd just emerged from the swamp area, and had heard the sirens. He knew there was a good chance that the cops would be searching the area soon, and he didn't want to take any chances.

He thought bitterly about the attacks against him. That cop had sent her dog to get him, and the damn dog had nipped his leg, drawn blood. He had to stab the dog to get him off. Then he had to run on an injured leg while she shot off her gun, like a warning. He knew she was a cop, so of course she had a gun.

And to top it off, that so-called 'caseworker', Marilyn had tried to knock him out with pepper spray. And all of this because he wanted to befriend a little girl who really liked him.

And now, Hayley's boyfriend tried to run him over. He needed to lay low for a while and heal himself.

He realized he should give up on Carly. That big bully who was 'protecting' Carly wouldn't let him near her.

He heard the barking of dogs growing close and knew it was time to make a break for it. For some reason, he didn't hit it off with dogs.

***

Hayley had been taken to the hospital, while Don stayed behind to talk with Herrera.

Herrera shook his head, "Three attacks in two days, and we still have squat!"

"Maybe we're wearing him down," Don suggested. "I think he barely got away today."

"He should be running scared," Herrera said, "but I don't know if that's good or bad."

"I guess you want to go to the hospital, see how Hayley's doing," Herrera said.

"Yes, I do. She looked good to me, but he was beating on her when I got here. I wanted so bad to get ahold of him! See you soon, Detective."

***

Marilyn was sitting at Erin Scott's kitchen table. Carly had gone to bed and they were having a glass of wine and talking.

"I'm really pleased with Carly's response to living here, and I think she's ready to give me some information about her friend, Charlie, especially regarding his appearance. I have to tread carefully there; she still feels some loyalty to him. I think soon our relationship will trump hers with Charlie. I know she loves being here and having her own room. And she loves Pepper."

"So, how are you doing after your encounter with bogeyman?" Erin asked Marilyn.

"Truthfully, it felt so good to spray him, it was almost worth it. I'm so glad my boyfriend made me carry the pepper spray. And now, he's escorting me everywhere, won't let me out of his sight!"

Chapter 43

Don spent the night at the hospital. Hayley had sustained a concussion. She'd been in and out of consciousness all night, as he'd sat by her bedside. He'd been instructed to keep her awake as much as possible. This had proved difficult, because Don kept dozing off.

She was sleeping now, so Don went in search of coffee, real coffee, not the machine kind. He spoke to the nurse at the desk, inquiring about same.

"You look like you could eat some breakfast. Why don't I order you some from the kitchen? They'll be bringing the trays up soon anyway."

"You are an angel!"

She smiled and said, "Hungry men say the damnedest things!"

"Don't we!" Don agreed. "Do you have any idea when Hayley can come home?"

"She'll need to stay awake for a prolonged period, and she'll need an MRI. We'll know more when she wakes up. Did you have any conversations with her during the night?"

"None that made much sense," Don answered. "She kept asking where she was and how she got here, but when I tried to explain, she drifted off."

"That's not unusual. We'll just have to see how she does today."

The call button for Hayley's room lit up. Don followed the nurse quickly into her room.

Hayley was sitting up in bed, and said, "I'm hungry! Can I get something to eat?"

***

Rory was driving to the office, and thinking about the note she'd found in her car, and her subsequent discussion with Marc. He agreed it could be taken two ways, as an attempt at misdirection or as authentic concern. Her reasoning was the interviews had gone well, except for Forsythe, who remained a bit elusive. And Forsythe probably wouldn't be urging her to do more interviews. But the other two men appeared genuine. It was something she'd have to figure out.

She was early to work, so she parked reasonably close to the office. She unlocked the office and turned on the lights. Rory blinked as she had a déjà vu experience. She remembered Sam's call on the day of the murder. She remembered him telling her to look out for Howe and tell him Sam would be late. She'd noticed the lights in the construction area were off, but she'd heard *something* and then a door closed next door, so she went through the plastic curtain. Her foot had hit something before she could turn on the lights, and she had tripped, mentally falling into a deep black hole.

Rory sat down, shaking. She'd just remembered what had happened before her fall. She hadn't seen the murder or the murderer. She had probably arrived just after the murder, and heard the murderer make some noise and then close the door. She was glad she was remembering, but it wasn't enough to solve the murder. What was that noise?

She made a pot of coffee. Even though she didn't feel like drinking it, she needed it. The nausea had lessened somewhat, and she was glad to be able to tolerate one mug of coffee.

***

A new contingent of Herrera's officers was combing the swamp behind the newspaper parking lot. It was a nasty job, no doubt about it. And it was mostly rookies who'd been chosen. A more senior officer would oversee the operation, without getting wet feet.

One of the rookies had decided to take the job seriously instead of complaining. She was determined to find something useful in this mess. After all, the alleged bogeyman had been pursued through this swamp, so she might get lucky and find something. She was looking for something, anything. She'd been concentrating her attention downward, but decided now to look around her. The area was loaded with brambles. Anything could catch on that, she thought, as she looked closer.

Her patience wasn't rewarded immediately, but within five minutes, she spied something in the brambles. Upon closer examination, she saw it was a piece of fabric that had snagged. As she went to pull it off the bramble, she noticed something else. A pair of sunglasses was caught in the bush as well.

"Hey! Over here!" she called.

***

Marilyn Hunter had just brought Carly to Erin's house after her second therapy session. Carly was looking better all the time. She seemed to be thriving under Erin's care.

The two women sat at the kitchen table having a cup of tea, while Carly played with Pepper in the next room.

"I think Carly is close to helping me draw a picture of Charlie. We've talked about it, and the next time we draw together, I plan to offer to draw Charlie if she provides the details. I'm torn about it though, because I'm manipulating her, and not being truthful."

"It sounds like a good idea," Marilyn began. "But I think it would be better to talk it through with her therapist. We don't want to do anything to upset that process."

"Good point," Erin said. "I have to remind myself that I'm not her therapist."

"You know, she might want to see you anyway. Let me give you her office number and you can call and talk to her. Maybe you should take Carly to her next appointment," she added.

"Well, I'll call her and see where we stand, and then I'll let you know," Erin said. "Oh, by the way Herrera told me the blood they found near where Pepper was stabbed, is human blood. That will give us DNA. So, whenever we find a suspect, we can check his blood against the sample we have. Or if he happens to leave any prints around."

"That's good news, Erin!" Marilyn said. "It looks like the case is moving forward. Any more bogeyman sightings?"

"Not that I know of. I think we've outgunned him recently, or at least put some fear in him. One thing I know for sure is that he hasn't come near Carly."

***

Herrera was going through his files, trying to find the DNA report from the man who'd skipped town in St. Louis. What was his name? Here it was, Christopher Bell, probably an alias. He found the DNA report, and… Bingo! It was a match! Now they didn't have to assume the connection, they knew this was their man. Now if only they could nab him. They'd come so far!

***

"How'd the interview go with Quinn?" Sam asked Rory.

"It was okay, except for his reticence... I have a feeling he's an introvert, but he seemed cooperative. I just didn't learn anything new. He didn't mention the men had met in Afghanistan. But, according to the anonymous note in my car, we should keep interviewing."

"I just don't know what we can gain by continued interviewing," Sam wondered.

Chapter 44

Mason Rowe had just finished his second appointment with Dr. Reynolds. He knew he was getting close to remembering something he wasn't sure he really wanted to know. He did want the raging nightmares to stop though, so he would try to stop fighting the process. Dr. Reynolds was calm and patient, and he was grateful that he'd found someone both competent and compassionate to help him.

As more of his feelings became uncovered he realized how much he missed Dara and Rachel. He'd spoken with them on the phone, but that almost made things worse, because he ended up in tears after saying 'Goodbye.' He hadn't cried in years, since…since before Afghanistan, he thought. The war had stripped him of so much! He hoped this therapy would bring back some of what he'd lost. He would go forward with treatment. It was his only hope.

***

Rory was driving from her doctor's appointment to her meeting with the detective. Her friend, Dr. Sally Flynn, had pressed her to make a decision about the baby. If she intended to keep it, she and Marc needed to have a discussion, and she needed to slow her pace at work.

As much as she trusted her friend, she didn't welcome her advice. She was already scolding herself about not telling Marc, and about putting off calling Ginny to congratulate her brother's wife on her pregnancy. And, as for working too hard, that was her salvation! She could never give up her work, or slow down. Hell, she'd just gotten back to work after an aggravating injury.

She arrived at the police station on time, and went in to find Herrera waiting for her in the reception area. "Rory, good to see you!" He strode forward to shake her hand. "I haven't seen you since you got home, but you look wonderful!"

"Thank you, Detective, it's so good to be back to work!"

He led her back to his office. "So, you have some news for me?"

"Well, it's not earth shattering, but I'm happy to have begun getting my memory back." She went on to describe her déjà vu experience.

"It's good you remembered," he said. "Maybe in time, you can remember more."

"I think there's more, I definitely heard something, but I'll have to be patient. Have you had any breakthroughs with the case?" Rory asked.

"Well, yes I have. The biggest one is that we now have DNA from blood left outside Officer Scott's house. It was human blood and it matches the DNA of one Christopher Bell, a man charged with child molestation, who'd skipped town in St. Louis ten years ago, then he went off the radar. So, if we have any suspects, and can get DNA, we could solve this case. As you know we already have the prints."

"Damn!" Rory exploded. "You know we had gathered cups from three of the men we interviewed, and when Sam went to get them, they were gone. We might have already solved the case!"

"I know, Sam called to tell me. But it seems to prove your theory that it's someone in the Citadel organization."

"I wanted to tell you the day I interviewed three of the men, there was an anonymous note on the front seat of my car, urging me to continue interviewing. What do you think?" She gave him the note.

Looking at the note, he said, "I think it's a good idea, and there is at least one person at Citadel who is wondering about his co-workers."

"And we're beginning to interview the men again, since Howe's death."

"Too bad we can't just DNA test them all," Rory said. "Of course as an attorney, I shouldn't even say that."

"Yeah, that was a red herring the DA was chasing. There are too many ways to contaminate DNA, but that doesn't seem to be common knowledge."

"That's what my husband said," Rory answered.

"Well, he should know," Herrera commented.

"Is there anything else?" Rory asked.

"Well, I'm not sure if you've heard through the grapevine..." And he went on to fill her in about the bogeyman attacking Ms.

Hunter, trying to lure Carly from her room at Officer Scott's, and the stabbing of her dog. And the most recent attack on Hayley.

"Oh, so that's where the blood came from, I was confused. My God, he's just showing up everywhere!" Rory exclaimed.

Herrera's phone rang and he answered, "You found something in the swamp? " He listened, then said, "Good work! Bring the stuff back with you ASAP."

He smiled at Rory and said, "They found sunglasses and some fabric in the swamp where the bogeyman was chased yesterday."

"He's getting careless," Rory said. "And maybe more dangerous."

Chapter 45

Sarah and her father had been having a relaxing vacation. Today, however, was the day they would see Jesus, the former drug runner who'd helped Sarah escape from the others. In return for his testimony regarding the Corizon Cartel, he'd been given sanctuary, and placed in the Witness Protection Program. Sarah hadn't seen him since the day of her rescue, almost a year ago. She had much to say to him.

After lunch, a car pulled up in front of the house. It was a black SUV with dark tinted windows. This must be the FBI escort, Sarah thought. Soon the front passenger door opened, and out stepped an agent they knew. He opened the back door and quickly herded Jesus into the judge's house.

Carson Justice addressed the agents. "Thanks for setting this up, we really appreciate it.

The agent, Truax, said, "He's getting moved to another safe house soon, so this might be your last opportunity to see him. He's doing very well and is grateful to be protected from the cartel. The cartel is rebuilding, according to our sources, so we wanted to get Jesus as far away from them as possible."

"Well, the cartel killed his brother and then took over his identity. He told me the only reason he joined was to find a way to avenge his brother's death," Sarah said.

"Well, he's done a good job of that," Truax said.

***

As promised, Herrera phoned Forsythe, reminding him he and the other witnesses had interviews with police the next day. "Nine o'clock sharp," he said. "I hope you've given them notice."

"I guess I can get everyone to come, even though it will slow down the renovations on Rory's office," Forsythe agreed grudgingly.

Herrera smiled when he said, "Oh I think Rory will understand that a murder investigation trumps a few hours of work."

***

Alex and Kate surprised Rory by making dinner. As she opened the front door, she inhaled the distinct aroma of pesto.

Heaping praise on her daughters, Rory said, "It's so nice to come home to such wonderful smells, and, I assume, dinner in the making. I've had a long day, and I could use a shower before dinner."

"Go ahead," Alex offered. "Dad won't be home for another half hour, at least, depending how the trains are running."

"Oh, I might take a long bath, even better! You girls are angels, remind me I said that next time you annoy me," Rory said laughing.

Once the bath was ready, Rory slid into the bubbly water and began to relax. Or at least she would've relaxed if she could silence the thoughts in her head. Paramount was the decision to tell Marc she was pregnant. Looking down at her stomach, she was surprised to see the distinct baby bump. She would tell him tonight, she vowed.

She thought about her conversation with Herrera, and that he would be interviewing the Citadel guys who were possible suspects. That could move the case forward considerably. If the men hadn't taken Rory and her staff seriously, another police interrogation should certainly get their attention.

Her déjà vu experience came back to her. How could she use that to move the case along, she wondered? In a flash, she decided she would talk openly about how her memory was coming back to her. She figured she was already a sitting duck, and probably on someone's radar. Why not give them more reason, she rationalized.

She was deciding to get out of the cooling water, when she heard the summons from the kitchen.

***

Hayley was just finishing her dinner when Don came in. He came to her bedside and gave her a kiss. "How's it going?" he asked, sitting in the chair next to the bed.

"Not so good, I'm still here!" she pouted. "I still have the mother of all headaches, so I guess I need to be here, but it's beyond boring!"

"I'm sorry, Hayley, it can't be fun. I'm just grateful you're alive, and not badly injured. I do miss you at home; it's quiet. What does the doc say about you coming home?"

"She says it's easier to manage the headaches in the hospital, and she wants to get an MRI before I leave."

"Anyway, I've decided to write while I'm in here. I called Ms. O'Brien and asked if I could write about the attack from the bogeyman. She said I should go ahead and do that. But I don't have a computer here…"

"That's no problem," Don said. "I can go home and get my laptop. Do you want me to go now?"

"No, you just got here," she protested, grabbing his hand. "I won't start until tomorrow anyway, so maybe you can drop it off on your way to work."

"Ok, I'd rather stay anyway. By the way, Herrera called to see how you were, and he also said one of his officers had found sunglasses and a bit of fabric in the brambles behind the parking lot."

"That's good news," Hayley said. "Anything else new?"

"Well, you weren't the first one attacked by the bogeyman lately. There were three assaults in two days, yours being the last."

"Wow, that's scary! Who else did he get?"

Don went on to tell Hayley about the attempt to take Carly, the stabbing of the dog, and Marilyn's quick brush with the bogeyman. "But Marilyn had pepper spray with her and apparently he dropped her pretty quick once he got sprayed. And she kept spraying until he ran off."

"Good for her!" Hayley said. "Can you maybe get me some pepper spray?"

"Not only can I get you pepper spray, I can get a discount, with my badge!"

***

The bogeyman was in a panic. Just before he'd left work, he'd heard through the grapevine he and the other guys at the poker game had to see Detective Herrera first thing in the morning. He was pissed that everyone tried to interfere with him seeing Carly. But he'd find a way, that bitch cop couldn't watch her every second of the day!

To be truthful, he'd expected the police interrogation sooner, but now it was upon him. He'd have to be careful. If he were caught, it wouldn't be pretty. He'd do whatever it took to stay out of jail.

***

Erin Scott had accompanied Carly to the appointment with Dr. Singh. The doctor had spoken with Erin before seeing Carly. Erin gave as much information as she had about Carly and answered all of Dr. Singh's questions. Then she asked what the doctor thought about her trying to get a description of 'Charlie' by trying to draw a picture.

"Ms. Hunter said I should run that by you before we do it, so we don't work at cross purposes," Erin explained.

"If you can do that without getting Carly upset or defensive, do it. I'd like to see it if you can manage it," the doctor said. "And now, I think I'll see Carly, unless there's anything else you want to discuss."

"No, I'm good," she said. "I'm pleased to see Carly's improvement. It's about time some luck came her way," Erin said, as she left the room.

***

Marc and Rory did the dishes, since the girls had made the meal. "I could get used to this," Rory said, handing a rinsed plate to Marc.

"I like doing dishes with you," Marc said, smiling as he slid the plate into the dishwasher.

"Well you've certainly kept that a secret!" Rory laughed.

"What do you mean? C'mon, I help out a lot!" he said, mentally calculating but coming up short.

"Sure, if you count Thanksgiving and Christmas, oh, and Mothers day…"

Marc was saved from answering when Alex came into the kitchen. "Do you have some time to talk to me?" she asked.

Rory and Marc looked at each other, surprised, but Rory said, "Sure!"

"I'll just get the last of the dishes in," Marc said.

"Shall we sit in the nook?" Rory asked.

"That's fine," Alex said, as she walked over to it.

When they were all seated, Rory asked, "Did you want Kate to join us?"

"No, she's ready to go out anyway."

"Ok," Marc said, "Go ahead, Alex…"

Alex took a deep breath, and launched into her issue. "You know,

Kate has a boyfriend, and I'm happy for her. But at the same time, the idea of having one myself makes me nauseous. I don't really know what's going on with me! I know, Mom, I told you I was fine and had put that whole mess behind me, but I'm afraid it's coming back."

"We could arrange for you to see the therapist again," Marc suggested.

She sighed, "I think I should. See, I'm not sure I'm even attracted to guys. I sort of think that counselor came on to me because she had me pegged as a lesbo!"

"And is that thought repugnant to you?" Rory asked quietly. "Because, it's not like you to use those labels."

"I know, I'm just all fucked up, and I'm trying to figure out who I am!"

"It's tough being a kid today," Marc commented. "And you have a history that makes it tougher. We'll support you, whatever happens."

"We hope you know that," Rory said.

"I know that, of course, and I appreciate you listening. I know it's my job to figure it out, but it's good to know you're here. By the way, Mom, I think I might want to talk to Alicia..."

"I can give you her number, but I haven't talked with her lately," Rory said, remembering that Alicia's partner was a woman who lived with her. Alicia's mother, Rory's friend, had been murdered over a year ago because she knew too much about a case Rory was investigating.

"Ok, thanks," Alex said as she left the kitchen.

Marc had a confused expression, and looked to Rory for an explanation.

"Alicia and her partner, Vanessa, had been a couple before her mother was killed. They had told Helen and she was supportive. They're living together in Helen's house now. Remember?" Rory asked.

Still looking confused, he said, "I guess, but does that mean Alex thinks she's...a lesbian?"

"That's what she's trying to figure out, I think," Rory said. She realized her news about the baby would have to wait.

Chapter 46

Herrera and several of his best lieutenants were ready when the men arrived from Citadel. Caldwell and Kraft arrived together. Forsythe and Quinn arrived a few minutes later, separately.

Each was escorted by a different officer to be interviewed in a private office. Herrera would confer with his interviewers and perhaps see some of the suspects himself.

He wondered again why these men had not been interviewed more intensively when Rowe was first charged. That was before he took over the case. He was sure the reason was that the DNA 'made the case'. He didn't believe that.

He found himself unable to concentrate on anything while the interviews went on, so decided to call Officer Scott and ask how things were going with Carly. Erin was one of the few people who still had a landline, so he called that number. She answered on the second ring.

"Hey, Jorge, what's up?"

"Well, I'm sitting here on pins and needles, waiting for my staff to interview all of the Citadel suspects. So, how are you and Carly doing?"

"We're fine," she said. "How come you're interviewing them again?'

"Circumstances have changed since Howe was murdered. Besides, they should've been interviewed more intensively when the case first broke. Sloppily done, I think."

"So what do you hope to accomplish?" she asked.

"As you know, the more often suspects are interviewed, the more likely they are to show signs of stress, and we get more info. I plan to interview some, maybe all of them, after I talk with the guys who saw them. It's a shame I can't use you; you're the best!"

"So why can't I do it?" Erin asked.

"Well, it's bound to have gotten out that Carly's with you…"

"And, that would, what? Prejudice me? I don't think so. And it might put the fear of God in them, which isn't a bad thing."

"Hey, if you're willing, why don't you come in? Where will you leave Carly?"

"Hmm, I think I'll take her to my sister's. See you in about a half hour?"

***

Mason Rowe was at his third appointment with Dr. Reynolds. He'd arrived early and was pondering the reactions of the Citadel guys who were being interviewed. He'd tried to gauge their feelings. Forsythe seemed extremely fidgety, more than he normally was. The other guys brushed it off as a formality. But was it one of them, as the investigators seemed to believe? Rowe was not convinced.

His reverie was interrupted, when the nurse called him.

Dr. Reynolds put Rowe at ease, carrying on a mundane conversation before they began their work.

"So, getting back to where we were at your last appointment, I'd like you to try and remember what you were feeling that night in Afghanistan, the one you keep going back to in your dreams. By the way, are you still having those dreams?" she asked.

"I am, and I seem to be getting closer to what's at the center. I wake up after the dreams, but I'm not screaming and sweating."

"That's a good sign. It seems you're beginning to trust yourself with the truth."

"Well, whatever it takes to get better."

***

Erin Scott took a circuitous route to her sister's house. She'd been vigilant for any cars that might be following her. Ever since the bogeyman had almost taken Carly, she had been hyper-cautious.

"How're you doing, Carly?" she asked looking in the rearview mirror.

"I'm fine, Mama," she said. "I like to go to Aunt Lucy's house. I get to play with her cat and her dog. And sometimes we read together," Carly said.

"That's good, Honey, I want you to be comfortable when I drop you off."

"Where do you have to go today, Mama?"

"I'm going into my office," she answered.

"That's at the police station, isn't it?" Carly asked.

She'd never told her she was a police officer, but somehow Carly had figured it out. Maybe because she could read the sign on the front of the building, Erin thought, feeling stupid. She knew Carly was always alert, probably because of the uncertainties in her past.

"Yes, it is," she answered simply.

"Is he a nice guy, your boss?" Carly asked.

"Yes, he is. What do you think of him, Carly?"

"He was nice to me," Carly answered.

Well, that's a step, Erin thought. Having arrived at her sister's without noticing a tail, she said, "Well, we're here. I'll take you in."

***

Herrera was pleased Erin was coming in; she really was the best at questioning suspects. He'd already decided he'd put her in the interrogation room that had a two-way mirror and sound access. He wanted to see her do what she did best, and he hoped to notice some things she might miss. He doubted she'd miss much, but still ...

Forsythe was the first to finish round one of questioning. He was asked to sit in the waiting room.

"I thought I was done," Forsythe said. "I do have a business to run." He sounded irritated.

Herrera stepped in, saying, "We will not keep you a moment longer than we have to. We know your business is important," he said, trying to soothe the man. Forsythe didn't answer.

Herrera didn't really have any more to say to him, so he was glad when Erin arrived. "Officer Scott, thanks for coming in!"

"Sure thing, boss, shall we go to my office?"

"Let's go," he said, with a backward glance at the officer who'd interviewed Forsythe. "Curt, you'll stay out here?"

The officer nodded.

***

Rory was in her office with the door closed. She was thinking about her decision to offer herself up as bait, by putting out the word her memory was returning. She was a bit frightened by her decision, but she might feel better if she got pepper spray, or better yet, if she borrowed Marc's revolver. She'd always been against guns, but Marc had insisted she know how to use his if she needed it.

She thought of her friend, Roland, a trooper who'd watched her back in the past. He was the only one she'd tell, she decided. She'd have to endure a lecture from him about not letting Marc know, but she felt sure he'd do as she asked. They were very good friends. She got on the phone.

"Rory! Hey, stranger, how're you doing? Are you back to work?"

"Oh yeah, you know me, Roland, I have to work. I have a little favor to ask of you, so how about we meet for lunch?"

Roland groaned. "I'd love to meet you for lunch, but I don't like the sound of this!"

"All will be revealed," Rory replied enigmatically. "Meet you at 12:30 at 320 Deli." She ended the call before he could ask more questions.

***

Herrera had missed lunch and was hungry. He saw little to be gained from further questioning. Officer Scott and his other officers had done a good job of interviewing the men. They all gave the same story of that evening, except for Forsythe, who hadn't been there. He'd been the least cooperative, perhaps for that reason. He hadn't been there that night, and didn't understand why he was included in the questioning. For a bright man – he assumed he was intelligent, owning a prosperous business – he sure could seem dense sometimes. Perhaps that was intentional.

Erin stopped by Herrera's office. "Ok, if I go now? Sorry I didn't get any confessions," she joked.

"You did a great job. It's just these guys have had over a month to get their stories together."

"You think they're all in it together?" she asked, sounding surprised.

"Look, this is a very serious charge. Understandably, none of them wants it pinned on him, so…"

"I get it, but if they're all innocent, why don't they talk?"

"They work together, moreover, they served in Afghanistan together. One of them, I'm not sure who, saved Mason's life. So, there's a lot going on."

"What about Mason Rowe? Would he have any idea who might have done the crimes?"

"According to Rory, he trusts these guys implicitly. He is, however, in therapy to treat his PTSD. He may remember something he's blocked."

"Let's hope he does, and soon! Let me know if you need anything. I've got to pick up Carly. I'm hoping today's the day she'll consent to letting me draw a picture of her friend, 'Charlie.'"

"Good luck on that, I need to get back to rereading these interviews, see if I've missed anything. Bye."

He walked back to his desk and sat down heavily, sighing. He realized he was staring at a piece of paper he hadn't noticed before. He picked it up and read, 'Why don't you do a line-up?' He riffled through some papers until he found the note Rory had left with him. Comparing the two, it was obvious the writer was the same. The handwriting was identical. *Why didn't I think of that?*

He picked up his phone to call Forsythe, who'd just left the building.

Chapter 47

Erin had picked up Carly, who seemed happy to see her. She was full of news about her stay with Aunt Lucy and chattered on from the back seat as Erin drove. It was good to see Carly so happy. She hoped that was a sign Carly might be willing to let her draw Charlie.

As soon as they got home, Pepper was released from the house. Carly ran around behind Pepper while the dog sniffed everything in smelling distance. He was picky about where he relieved himself.

The house phone rang, and Erin felt she should answer it. Then again, she did have an answering machine if it was important. She stayed outside and listened to the message from the doorway. It was Herrera, and the message was simple, "Call me back ASAP!"

It sounded urgent, so she decided to call him right back. She pulled out her cell, but it wasn't charged.

"Carly!" she called, "I need to make a phone call from the house. If you want to stay out, stick with Pepper."

"Ok, Mama," she replied.

Erin went into the house as Carly continued following Pepper, when suddenly he bolted off towards the back of the yard. She heard him yelp and ran towards the sound.

She found Pepper lying on the ground and started to cry.

" Carly!"

She recognized the voice. Charlie was waiting behind some bushes and he opened his arms wide.

"Carly, I missed you so much! Come here, let me see you!"

Carly was unsure what to do. "My dog, what happened to him?"

"Oh, he's just sleeping, he'll be awake soon. Come over, I need you to do something very important. And I promise, if you do this one little thing, we can be together, forever!"

She walked forward into his open arms. He hugged her fiercely, whispering in her ear. When the back door slammed, Charlie quickly left. "Don't forget!" he said over his shoulder.

***

As Forsythe and some of his men returned from the police station, they began to drift into the construction area, grumbling. Rory went through the vinyl curtains, and sought out Forsythe. Walking straight to his office, she knocked. “It’s Rory, can I come in?” she asked.

“Come in,” he said with less enthusiasm than usual.

She entered and asked, “How did it go? Seemed like you were there a long time.”

“Yeah, it was a long time, and I’m not sure what was accomplished. I don’t know what we can do to help their investigation. And now Herrera is scheduling a lineup with all of us. He called on my cell just as we were leaving. I can tell you, the other guys aren’t happy.”

“Oh, that sounds serious.”

Forsythe shrugged, with a look of distaste on his face. “I don’t understand why he’s targeting us.”

“Hmm,” Rory said. “Why don’t you ask him?”

She left his office quickly and returned to her own.

Closing the door behind her, she flopped into her chair. She’d hoped to start the news that she was remembering. But perhaps there was a chance the lineup could flush out the perp.

She’d had lunch with Roland, and, as expected, he was skeptical about her idea to use herself as bait. He encouraged her to discuss it with Marc, which he assumed fell on deaf ears. In the end they reached a compromise. Roland would put a tracking device on Rory’s car and she promised to call him the moment she suspected anyone or anything suspicious.

***

Erin came running outside as soon as she finished her call. She didn’t see Carly anywhere. She called, “Carly! Where are you?” She was unable to hide the fear in her voice.

“I’m way back here!” Carly answered.

Erin ran to the back of the yard, embracing Carly as soon as she found her. “I was afraid you’d wandered off!”

“I was just following Pepper,” she said.

“I thought I heard him yelp earlier, did he?”

“I didn’t hear it. Look, he’s right over there. He was taking a nap.”

Pepper was rousing himself, and when Erin called him, he came walking unsteadily towards her.

"Come here, Baby," she urged, hugging him as he got nearer. "Are you sure nothing happened to him?" Erin asked.

"Nothing happened to him. He just lied down to have a nap," Carly said, looking at the ground.

"Well, let's get inside, then, maybe he's hungry," Erin said, feeling a lump starting to gather in her stomach. In those few moments, she'd lost Carly.

***

The bogeyman was raging with anger, fear, and lust. He was being thwarted at every turn. The snotty detectives asked endless questions, which had pushed him almost to the brink. But he had stayed cool.

And now! Now, they were ordered to report for a lineup first thing tomorrow! He was filled with doubt. Should he leave, make a break for it? He should've taken Carly when he had the chance. She was somehow different with him. Had those fuckin do-gooders turned her against him? Could he trust her to do what he'd asked? He just didn't know what to do, but he certainly couldn't risk going back to her house.

***

After putting Carly to bed, Erin called Herrera. "Hey, Jorge, I haven't told Carly what she needs to do tomorrow; I'm not even sure how I'll do it. I think something happened when I was on the phone with you. I lost sight of her. When I found her she was way in the back of the yard and Pepper was lying down. When he got up he was really shaky, and when we got inside, he drained his water bowl, and then went to his bed for a long nap, without touching his food."

"My vet friend, Vicky, came over to see him and found a small puncture in his thigh. She took a blood sample and will let me know if it reveals anything."

"What do you think happened in the few moments we talked?"

"Well, you know the call was brief, but in my darkest thoughts I believe the bogeyman made contact with her, but for some reason didn't take her. Thank God! But Carly was a different girl when we came back inside. She hardly talked, didn't look at me, and didn't finish her supper. Something went down and I can tell you it wasn't good!"

Chapter 48

At nine a.m. sharp, Herrera was ready to start the lineup. He'd invited Rory to be present, and she eagerly awaited the outcome. Hopefully, they were near the end of this nightmare.

Officer Scott had come in earlier with Carly and had taken the silent child into her office. Herrera knew Erin's job of explaining what they were asking of Carly would be difficult. He'd been shocked when he saw the little girl, who'd been steadily improving, and looking happier with passing time. He agreed with Erin, that something had definitely happened to return her to the silent, frightened child he'd met weeks ago.

The men straggled in, as though this were an unimportant event, which they need not make a priority. Herrera figured this attitude came from the top. Forsythe made no pretense of cooperation.

When the four men came in, they were assembled in the interrogation room. They were lined up in no apparent order, and a few of the officers, in street clothes, were added. At the last minute, Rowe joined the others, wanting to make a statement. When they were ready, Herrera went to get Erin and Carly.

Rory joined them on the other side of the two-way mirror. Herrera spoke softly to Carly, who appeared to be frozen. He told her that no one could see her, and that Mrs. Scott would always keep her safe. He asked her to look at each man carefully and tell him which one, if any of them, had tried to take her from Mrs. Scott's house. He'd purposely made no mention of Charlie.

"Whenever you're ready, Carly, you can tell me which man you think it might be. If you need one of them to step closer, just tell me which one, and I'll do it. Do you understand what I need you to do?"

The little girl nodded solemnly, still not looking up, her eyes fixed on her shoes.

The men in the lineup were growing restive, moving and grumbling.

Herrera spoke into the microphone, “We will get started shortly. I need your cooperation to stand quietly until our witness is ready. Do you understand?”

They nodded and straightened up.

Carly looked up at the detective, and whispered, “Do I have to do this?”

“Of course you don’t have to,” he said calmly. “It’s just that there’s a man out there, maybe one of these men, who is hurting little girls like you. We want to find him so he doesn’t hurt any more girls. I would ask you to just look over these men; remember, they can’t see you, and if any of them looks familiar to you, let me know. Then you can leave with Mrs. Scott before we let the men go.”

“What will happen to the man I pick?” she asked.

“We will talk to him and see if this might be the man. We will have to investigate more.”

“Okay,” she said, looking up, “It’s that man in the plaid shirt, the one with a 3 on his chest.”

Herrera spoke into the mike again, “Would number 3 please step forward?”

Jordan Kraft looked stunned, but complied and stepped forward.

“Please say for me, ‘Hello, how are you?’” Herrera said into the mike.

Kraft complied, looking like a deer in headlights.

Herrera asked Carly, “Does he look and sound like the man who came to Mrs. Scott’s house?”

“Yes,” she said, looking once more at her feet. She did not elaborate.

Herrera said to Erin, “You’d best leave now and let me know on the secure line where you end up. Thank you, Carly, I know this wasn’t easy.”

After they’d left, Herrera had a few more men step front and speak. He bought another ten minutes to give Officer Scott time to make her getaway.

Then Herrera went into the room and excused all of the men except Kraft, who was asked to remain behind.

***

Erin Scott, who’d packed a few suitcases, and plenty of food for Pepper, was on her way to her family’s hideaway in the Pocono

Mountains. It would probably be a journey of three hours. She hadn't been to the cabin in a long time, not since her husband died, she thought with a sudden pang of grief. But she figured it was far enough away to keep Carly safe until the bogeyman was caught. Carly sat in the back seat, with Pepper's head in her lap.

Erin didn't believe Carly had chosen the right man. And she thought she knew why. That was the reason for their hasty departure. She would call Herrera as soon as they were settled. He would be the only person to know their whereabouts.

She spoke to the silent child, "You did well Carly, and I know you didn't want to do it. I'm proud of you."

"What will happen to that man I picked?" she asked.

"Well, Detective Herrera and the other officers will talk to him and try to figure out if he's the one who hurt you and other girls."

"He didn't hurt me," Carly said.

Erin was thrown by this response and wasn't sure what to say. She settled for, "Tell me more."

Before Carly could answer, Erin's cell phone rang. "Hello?" she said tentatively.

"Hi," came the answer, "it's Vicky. I just wanted you to know that there was a trace amount of Ketamine in Pepper's system. I believe the intention was to knock him out quickly, but not for long…"

"Well," Erin said. "Thanks so much, Vicky. This confirms what I suspected. Will Pepper be okay?"

"Yes, he'll be fine, I'm sure, but check the site of the dart entry for any infection."

"Thank you so much, I'll talk to you later. Bye."

Erin heaved a sigh as she disconnected.

Of course Carly had been listening from the back seat. "Is Pepper ok?" she asked, sounding worried.

Before she answered, Erin considered that Pepper was cherished by Carly. This might be a chance to move her back from the dark side. "The vet just told me that Pepper was shot by a dart that had medicine in it to put him to sleep. Pepper wasn't just having a nap yesterday. He'd been drugged. I don't know who would do such a thing, but I'm very upset. Suppose he'd missed Pepper and hit you?

That is very scary. Did you see anyone near Pepper?" Erin asked, hoping not to shut the child down.

"But will Pepper be ok?" Carly asked with a trembling voice. She didn't answer Erin's question.

"I hope so, Honey," Erin said, her voice softening. "The vet said we should keep close watch on where the dart hit. It could get infected."

Carly sobbed quietly in the backseat, patting Pepper. And Erin knew she'd have to wait for another time to question Carly.

Chapter 49

The detective had Kraft in his office. He had been fingerprinted, DNA swabbed, and a mug shot had been taken. Forsythe had stayed behind and offered to post bond. He was told to leave, that charges had not yet been brought, and if they were, he would be notified. He'd left in a huff.

Kraft looked angry, very angry. He sat with his arms folded over his chest, not speaking. Herrera wondered how long he would keep up his façade.

As the men sat in silence, a fingerprint expert was comparing Kraft's prints with the ones they had of Christopher Bell. The detective would bet his next paycheck, not that it was a king's ransom, that the prints were not a match. The way Carly picked him out, without any equivocation, was unusual. He'd presided over countless lineups, and it ordinarily took the witness/victim a rather long time to make the final call. Carly was reluctant to do it at all, and that was, he thought, because she was torn. She'd had a 'relationship' with the bogeyman, who had no doubt been in the process of grooming her.

Herrera was brought to the present by Kraft's shifting in his seat. Kraft sighed loudly, but said nothing. The detective could wait. He hadn't asked anything of Kraft, he just wanted to see how long it would take for him to talk. He'd instructed the fingerprint expert to take his time, an explicit stalling tactic.

Herrera spoke now, "Mr. Kraft, can I get you coffee or water?"

It first appeared that Kraft would stonewall, but then he seemed to have a change of heart and said, "Coffee would be great!"

Herrera smiled and said, "Well, I can't promise great coffee around here, but I will get a fresh pot made for us. What do you take in it?"

Kraft smiled back, and said, "Just milk."

He called the front desk and asked the duty officer to make a fresh pot of coffee and bring two mugs. "One with milk, and you know how I take mine."

"How do you take yours?" Kraft asked.

"I don't like that to get out, but it's a bit heavy on the sugar. My excuse is that it helps sweeten the job."

Kraft smiled, but said nothing further.

The silence stretched out until the coffee arrived. Then each focused on his coffee for a bit.

Herrera was surprised when Kraft started to speak. "I guess I should ask if I'm going to be charged…"

"I don't know yet," Herrera said truthfully. "I'm waiting to have some evidence corroborated. If you wish to speak, I should give you your Miranda rights and offer you an attorney."

"I'll waive all that until and unless I'm charged," Kraft said.

"But you know that anything you say…"

"Yes, I know, but there's nothing I could say that would incriminate me. The only reason I'm here at all is because I was at the poker game, and in fact hosted it."

"That's true. If you feel comfortable speaking, go ahead," Herrera urged.

"Ok, I think you guys are on the right track, not by singling me out, but by looking at our group. I've had my own suspicions, but haven't come up with a definite person. The note that was left on your desk yesterday was from me. Ironic, isn't it that I was the one to be chosen. I also left a note for Rory to keep hammering away with the interviewing. Would you like a handwriting sample?"

"Sure," Herrera said, pushing over a tablet and pencil. As he waited, he located the notes he'd previously received.

Kraft scribbled something and pushed it back to Herrera. He'd written 'Why don't you do a lineup?' and the handwriting was identical to the other notes.

"Yeah, they match. Why did you write them?"

"I don't have the necessary evidence, only suspicions, so it's not that I can do anything. But I hoped that you and Rory could."

"Well, now we have the word of a young and very scared little girl, that you're the one who tried to break into Officer Scott's home."

Kraft looked surprised, “I didn’t know the little girl was staying with one of your officers.”

“Ah, well, the grapevine isn’t always accurate,” Herrera said. “Do you know the little girl’s name?”

“No, I don’t,” Kraft said. “Look, not everyone knows this, I’m gay, but I’m not a pedophile!”

“Well, I certainly know that being gay has nothing whatever to do with being a pedophile.”

“Let me ask you this,” Herrera said, “Do you think it’s possible that one of the men at the poker game could be the bogeyman and that he framed Mason Rowe?”

“I’m coming to that conclusion,” Kraft said, “but it pains me to say that, to even think it! We were a ‘band of brothers’ on the battlefield, and I believed that bond would be unbreakable.”

“On another subject, what do you make of Forsythe’s interest in this case, his willingness to bail you out?” Herrera asked, not expecting an answer.

Kraft’s reply threw him for a loop.

***

Rory returned to the office ahead of the Citadel employees. She hunkered down in her office with Blake and Sam, discussing the surprising outcome of the lineup.

“Do you think he’s the bogeyman?” asked Sam.

“Not for a minute!” Rory said emphatically. “It’s a gut feeling, really. First of all, I think he was very open during our interviews. Secondly, I was watching Carly as she made the choice. Unlike most witnesses, she at first wouldn’t even look at the men. And when she did, she made her choice quickly, looking down at her feet as soon as she’d said it. I think she has a relationship with the bogeyman, and I think he was grooming her.”

“She’d been sexually abused before, hadn’t she?” Sam asked.

“Yes, she had, and it’s uncertain how often and for what duration, because she would never name her abusers,” Rory answered. “I have a hunch that somehow he got to her before the lineup.”

“So, what do you think will happen to Kraft?” Sam asked.

“Well, Herrera has prints and DNA on Christopher Bell, which we assume is an alias. The DNA at Officer Scott’s house matches

'Christopher Bell,' and prints that match. So if either matches Kraft, then he's our man, and if not, it's back to square one!"

***

Mason Rowe was in Dr. Reynolds's office. He was replaying the dream he'd had the night before. He told the doctor, "Gordie, he's the guy who was murdered, and I were in the desert and we went to another guy's tent. We didn't announce ourselves, we just walked in. The guy, I couldn't see his face in my dream, had a naked little girl on his lap and was fondling her. I woke up from the dream and almost threw up."

"So you think that may be what you've been suppressing all these years?"

"I think that was a biggie. And after that whatever happened is a blur in my mind. You see, I always thought my stepfather was abusing my younger sister, but I never said anything. I lived with the shame of that for years, but this is the first time I've thought of it since I got back from Afghanistan. And I never talked with my sister Gwen about it." He hung his head.

"That's quite a lot to take in," the doctor said calmly. "Are you ready to go deeper?"

Rowe shook his head. "I don't know, I just don't know!"

Dr. Reynolds waited quietly, knowing that he would have to make the decision.

***

Erin and Carly had arrived at the cabin. It was much cooler up in the mountains, and she and Carly walked around outside for a while, enjoying the cool air and letting Pepper sniff.

Carly spoke for the first time in nearly an hour. "It's so beautiful up here! How did you ever find the place?"

"My parents built this cottage many years ago, when I was about your age actually. It was our family retreat," she answered.

"What means 'retreat?'" Carly asked.

"It means a place where you can get away and just relax, without all the hustle and bustle."

"Oh," Carly said, smiling. "I thought it meant something good to eat."

"Yeah, sure I understand that, you were thinking it's a *treat*. Well, it actually is a treat to be here, but not something you can eat!"

"Mama, thank you for bringing me here. I'm sorry if I upset you this morning.

Chapter 50

Sarah and her father were having breakfast outside, overlooking the sound. They'd met with Jesus the previous day and Sarah had learned many things about 'Henrique' and her abduction. It helped her to have some closure and open a new chapter of her life. It had actually been liberating. Today, though, she missed Sam. She missed him on a deep level and she literally felt empty space in her body.

Her dad knew she was grappling with something, so he asked, "What's wrong, Honey?"

"Oh Dad," she said, "I'm grateful you invited me to come home, and it was wonderful seeing Jesus. I feel quite free, in a sense. But I also miss Sam almost more than I can bear."

He could see she was on the verge of tears, and he wanted to help. "Sarah, you can leave whenever you want. Or you can ask Sam to come here."

Her face brightened immediately, as if the sun had just emerged from behind a cloud. "I don't want to disappoint you. I never got to see Geneva. I would like Sam to come up, but I think the case is in a crucial stage right now."

"You and Sam should plan to come as soon as the case is wrapped up."

"Perfect!" she said. "I'm not going to tell Sam, I'll just wake him up tomorrow."

***

Herrera said to Kraft, "Can you repeat that, I'm not sure I heard you right."

"Oh, I think you heard me, I said, Forsythe was our Lieutenant in Afghanistan. He got out before we did and had a business to return to; his wife had run it in his absence. He hired the five of us when we got out. So he's got an interest in what happens in this investigation. He may suspect one of us is the bogeyman, so he tries to stay on top of everything."

Herrera was silent for a moment. "Do you think his 'interest' would include shielding the guilty party from prosecution?"

"I wonder about that myself. I've noticed him micromanaging everything, wanting to know what's going on. But I have to admit he's not as sharp as he once was. Maybe Afghanistan left its mark on him, too. He was older when he joined up, and he did it because his younger brother had been killed in Iraq by an IED. So he got into the munitions unit and basically what we did was defuse them, if we found them in time."

"Very interesting," Herrera said. "So if he suspected someone, he may or may not give us the info?"

"I really don't know. Forsythe's job was to protect us in Afghanistan, and when a few men were blown up by an IED, he mourned for months. He took it as a personal failure. I really don't know how far he'd go to protect a guilty person. He does have a conscience."

Herrera's cell buzzed, the secure line, and he asked Kraft to wait in the hall while he took it.

***

Rowe and Dr. Reynolds were deeply involved in his therapy session. Mason had let himself drift back to where the dream had left off. He went over and over the same scene, but he was stuck.

Dr. Reynolds said, "I want you to open your eyes now, and maybe I can get you unstuck."

An involuntary shudder went through Rowe's body, but he complied.

"Now follow with your eyes as I move my finger, do not break eye contact."

Rowe tried to follow, but was unable to keep from losing eye contact.

Always patient, Dr. Reynolds said, "Try again, and breathe your way through it."

The breathing relaxed Mason, and soon he found he was able to follow her movements with his eyes. He was back in that tent in Afghanistan and this time he felt as if a boulder had been moved off his chest. He finally saw the face of the man holding the little girl. "Oh, my God! It's him, he's the bogeyman!"

Without a word to his therapist, he bolted out the door.

***

The bogeyman was pleased with this morning's main event. He could trust Carly, and would find a way to have her. He'd been fantasizing all morning, hardly paying attention to his work. He'd been biding his time until he could leave for lunch.

When lunch time came, he bolted for his truck, driving to Officer Scott's house to wait for his opportunity. He parked on the street, far from the house, and walked the distance. There was no car in the driveway. He stealthily peered into the garage, which was empty.

He walked closer to the house, and then to Carly's window. The blinds were down. He circled the house, looking for a way in, for a clue as to where Carly was, and he was also waiting for that damned dog to start barking. On that subject, he thought, I should've killed him when I had the chance.

But he saw no sign of the dog. Even the bowl of water left outside for him was gone. So where would they have gone and taken the dog? It perplexed him, but he would wait here for his entire lunch hour in the hopes of taking Carly, by force if necessary.

***

Herrera answered his secure cell phone. As expected, it was Erin. "Hi, I assume you've arrived safely?"

"We have, and the closer I got, the calmer I felt. It seems Carly feels the same. She thanked me and apologized for disappointing me this morning. What's important now, I think is to just give her peace and quiet and distance from the bogeyman. I'm not going to pressure her in the least. If by chance she gives me anything useful, I'll call. In the meantime, the only calls I'm taking will be from you. I did take a call from my vet on the way up and she told me there was a trace of Ketamine in Pepper's system. By the way, I'm in the Poconos, at our family retreat. I won't tell you where it is in case you're tortured!" She laughed. "Oh, one more thing, please contact Marilyn Hunter. She has a right to know where we are, but don't tell her. I'm sure she'll trust my reason for getting Carly out of town for now."

***

Mason Rowe finished his work day without, thankfully, seeing the man he was now sure was the bogeyman. It had taken every ounce of his restraint to get through the day. His thoughts were centered on taking down his adversary, the man who had abused Rachel and framed him. He would find a way to catch him, and then…

Chapter 51

Rory woke early, her mind reeling with all the details of the case. She felt they were on the verge of a breakthrough, but had no idea how that would manifest itself. As she got up to take a shower, she remembered Sam had spent the night in the guest room. He'd looked so sad after dinner, and frankly had drunk too much wine, so the decision was made for him to stay. Sarah's absence had taken a toll on him, and Rory hoped they'd be reunited soon.

As she showered, she thought about the discussion between Sam, Marc, and her. They were in agreement that the bogeyman was operating under their noses, hiding in plain sight. The bugger of it all was they didn't have a clear path to finding him. Rory had her own secret plan, and had put out the bait, but hadn't gotten a nibble. She would continue to broadcast that her memory was slowly returning.

Rory recalled Marc's further discussion of child molesters. He'd said, "Child molesters have a strong, and sometimes irresistible desire to have sex with children. Their judgment is overcome by the repetitive, to the point of compulsive, sexual behavior with children. This seems to be the case with the bogeyman; he puts himself in increasingly risky predicaments from which he barely escapes. That is, at least, so far. His self defeating behavior will get him ensnared, and let's hope soon!"

***

Mason Rowe hadn't slept well, but it wasn't the dreams that kept him awake. He was planning a way to catch the bogeyman in the act. He knew where the man lived, and would begin to shadow him. His first problem had been the ankle bracelet. He certainly couldn't have free rein with that on his leg. This was where his experience as a munitions expert came in handy. He'd figured if he could defuse an IED, he could take on the much simpler mechanism of the monitor. He'd gingerly tinkered with it the night before, and had been able to remove the device without too much difficulty. And there'd been no repercussions, so he assumed he'd done it successfully.

Now he phoned Forsythe to report that he was taking a sick day. The phone went to voicemail and Mason left his message, happy he didn't actually have to talk to Forsythe.

He had to keep his brother in the loop so he knew what was going on, in case it all went south. They talked over breakfast. "Greg, I just want you to know what's going on. I took today off from work. I'm going out, however..."

"What about the monitor?" Greg asked.

"I was getting to that. I was able to detach it last night. If it had triggered the system, we'd have known by now," Mason explained.

"Why'd you do that?" Greg demanded, his face flushed with anger.

"Calm down, man, this is my problem, not yours. I've got to find the guy who molested Rachel, and now I'm sure I know who that is."

"You're involving me by virtue of leaving without the monitor, and why can't you just go to the police? Why do you think you're the only one who can do it?" Greg's voice had risen by several octaves.

"I can't explain it to you, but I gotta' do it my way. The police haven't done shit! They had a lineup yesterday and arrested the least likely person. I mean the guy is gay; he doesn't go for females of any age! They're fucking it up, so I doubt they would listen to me saying, 'it came to me in a dream,' but that's the way it happened."

"Okay," Greg relented. "Look, take care of yourself, and don't get in over your head. Call me if anything goes down. I got your back." He clapped Mason on the back and watched him go out the door.

***

Jordan Kraft had spent the night in a cell. Herrera hadn't decided what to do about Jordan. Of course the prints were not a match, as he'd suspected. It would take longer to get the DNA, but the prints were enough to go on for now. He had no reason to keep him, but he didn't want that information to get out. Kraft had agreed to cooperate with the plan, at least in the short term. They both hoped it would end soon. Herrera had told Forsythe Kraft would remain in custody until they could complete their investigation. He knew Forsythe wasn't happy, but he'd expected that.

First thing in thing in the morning, Herrera opened Kraft's cell, and gave him the breakfast he'd brought. While Kraft ate his meal, Herrera drank his coffee. Then he asked, "Have you come up with a plan yet?"

"I've been thinking about going up to my ski cabin on Blue Mountain. It's only an hour or so from here, and at least I'll be out of your hair."

"That's not a bad idea, but I'm afraid Forsythe will demand to see you if you're gone too long. Should we let him in on it?"

"No!' Jordan replied. "I don't know why I feel so strongly about that, but it's a gut feeling. If he starts meddling, tell him to send a lawyer. Actually, tell him to send Ms. Chandler, she's already working for him. I think she'd go along with it."

"She probably would, that's a good idea. Think you can get out of town without being seen?"

"I can sure as Hell try!" Jordan said. "The sooner the better! I'll be in touch."

"Let me give you the number of my secure phone," Herrera said, scribbling the number on a piece of paper. "Good luck."

***

Sarah arrived at the apartment by seven. The limo driver got her bags and delivered them to her apartment on the second floor. She gave him a big tip and thanked him.

Unlocking the door slowly and quietly, she managed to get her bags in without making too much noise. Her cat Jewel ran to Sarah, and meowed loudly at her feet.

"Shhh, Sarah said, wondering why Sam hadn't woken up. She strode quickly to the bedroom, unable to restrain herself. She flung open the bedroom door about to announce her presence, but then she found the bed hadn't been slept in. She wandered around the apartment, just in case he'd heard her and was hiding. He wasn't anywhere to be found.

Where could he be? Sarah was overcome with disappointment, just when she realized how much she'd missed him.

She would call Rory. If anyone knew where he was it would be her.

Rory answered on the second ring, “Sarah! Where are you calling from?” Sam was sitting in the nook with Rory, so she put the phone on speaker.

“I’m home! I came home early because I missed Sam so much and he’s not here! Do you know where he is?”

Sam was beaming, and gave Rory the ‘zip it’ signal, deciding to surprise Sarah.

“Gosh, I don’t know, Sarah. He doesn’t usually go to the office this early. Tell you what, why don’t you just come over and we’ll find him together. I can’t wait to see you!”

She disconnected before Sarah could disagree. “Sam, you’re a wicked boy!” Rory chided, although she was in on it.

Chapter 52

Rory was at the door to welcome Sarah, and gave her a hug as soon as she entered.

"How was your trip? Come on in and tell me about it!" Rory led her to the nook. Want some breakfast?" she asked.

Sarah's face fell, "I'm not hungry, Rory. I just have to find Sam!"

"Come sit down, and we'll try to think of where he could be."

Sarah did as directed and took a seat in the nook. As she tried to move to the end of the bench, she found that something prevented her. Then her foot was grabbed and she screamed, pulling away.

Rory watched in amusement as Sam unfolded himself from under the table and scooched up to sit next to Sarah.

Sam folded Sarah in his arms as she sobbed on his shoulder.

When she realized the two had pranked her, she said, "What the hell! You were both in on this, and you knew I was upset!" She punched Sam in the shoulder.

"I'm sorry, Baby, it was my idea. I was so happy you were home, I wanted to have a little fun with it."

"Sarah, he stayed over last night because he'd tried to drown his sorrow, you know, so we wouldn't let him drive home."

Partially mollified, Sarah said, "Well, you at least deserve a hangover." But she smiled.

"Trust me," Sam said, "the punishment is brutal. Now, how about you tell us about your visit with your dad?"

***

Rowe was at the suspect's house, and the truck and car were still in the driveway. He waited for at least a half hour, thinking the man was already late for work. His patience paid off when he saw the man exit his house and get into his car, an older blue Chevy. It was nondescript, and not the car Rowe remembered him driving. Perhaps he had more than one that he used during his crime sprees.

It was after rush hour, so following the Chevy wasn't too difficult. Rowe was alert for any indication he'd been spotted. The car Rowe was driving was borrowed; he'd traded with his brother. He had no idea where his prey was headed, but it seemed to be the heart of Media. Odd, he thought, as the man pulled up next to the Children and Youth Services office.

Initially confused, Rowe had an 'aha' moment, when he realized that the little girl was a foster child, and would have a caseworker. Rowe thought he would try to get info from the caseworker about the little girl. Knowing the boogeyman's tactics, he was leery of what would happen next. What could he do? He couldn't call the police, since he was actually AWOL. But he would call the police and leave an anonymous tip if he saw criminal activity. He anxiously awaited the bogeyman's next move.

***

Carly was up early playing with Pepper. The change in her was gratifying for Erin to see. She had returned rather suddenly to the child she'd recently become, active, curious and, best of all, happy. Erin felt her own heart expand with love as she watched the child and dog interact. She'd decided that she would do nothing to try and prod information from Carly. She would just let her be.

"Carly, are you ready for breakfast?"

"I'm starved, Mama!"

"I hope I can help you out; what's your very favorite breakfast in the world?"

Carly closed her eyes tight and thought. It didn't take long for her to say, "French toast!"

"It shall be yours," Erin said, smiling. "And in the meantime, can you please feed Pepper? I'm sure he's hungry, too!"

"Okay, Mama, didn't I hear you say that *Sargent* Pepper was his real name?"

"Yes, it is, and he answers to both. He's named after a famous album put out by the Beatles, have you ever heard of them?"

"No," she replied frowning, "and what is an 'album?'"

"Oh boy," Erin said, "I have a lot to teach you about the 'good old days,' and maybe we'll talk over breakfast. But for now, here's Pepper's food."

***

Sarah had eaten a large breakfast once her appetite returned at the sight of Sam. They sat, still in the nook, holding hands.

Watching them, Rory felt a pang for that lost feeling of young love. There was nothing like it. Not that she and Marc weren't still in love, it was just, well, complicated,

Now she said, "Ok, Sarah, you've been fed, now will you tell us about your visit home?"

"Ok," Sarah said, thinking. "Well, it was wonderful to spend time with my dad, he's turned out to be such a nice person; well, I guess he always was. It took him a while to get over my mother's death. But, anyway, he's found someone, a forensic expert who helped during my abduction. Her name is Geneva."

"Oh, I remember meeting her at your welcome home party," Sam said. "She's a knockout! And she also seems very nice," he added in response to a sharp look from Sarah.

"She is both," Sarah continued, "and they're getting engaged! I'm really happy. Dad invited us to come visit once this case is over."

"Anyway, that was part of the reason for the trip, and also it was to celebrate my graduation. But the reason I went when I did was because Jesus Alvarez is about to be moved to a new safe house and he asked to talk with me before he left."

"Wow!" Rory interjected, "That must've been very interesting."

"It was that, and more, much more. His English is much improved so he was able to fill in a lot of blanks for me. For instance, he told me that the Corizon cartel had sent Henrique/Pedro to the U.S. and paid for law school. When he flunked out, he was afraid to face them without giving them something, some information. So, he used me, devised a plan that would help the cartel and advance his own agenda. The plot took a while to develop, but Pedro was behind it all. Jesus got himself involved because he had a huge grudge against Pedro, for killing his brother, the real Henrique Alvarez."

"So you finally got the full story," Rory said. "How does it sit with you?"

"It took quite a weight off, and I'm feeling like I can start anew. And I realized how much I missed Sam after only a few days apart." She smiled at Sam.

Rory bit her tongue before she could say, 'Get a room!'"

***

Marilyn Hunter was sitting at her desk with mounds of paperwork. She'd just spoken with the detective, who'd told her that Officer Scott had taken Carly away after the lineup. She was relieved that Carly was out of the area, and she was covered legally because the detective believed her safety was in jeopardy.

Her phone rang twice before it registered with Marilyn. It was the receptionist.

"Marilyn, while you were on the phone I got an emergency message from Ryan's gym. It seems he's had an accident with a heavy weight falling on him. He was taken to Riddle Hospital. I'm sorry, Marilyn."

"Thanks for the message, I'm leaving..." With that, Marilyn tore out of the building.

Rowe watched as a young woman, blonde hair flying behind, bolted from the building and headed for the parking lot. Something was up; he knew the bogeyman would make his move, and he did.

Marilyn rushed towards a parking lot behind the building, which was surrounded by trees. Rowe watched as the bogeyman jumped out of his car and ran in pursuit of the woman. Rowe had to get out of the car in order to see around to the back of the building.

He saw the suspect get Marilyn in a chokehold and drag her to the back of her car. He put something over her face, after which she flopped in his arms. Opening the trunk with the keys he'd taken from Marilyn, he threw her in and slammed the lid shut. Then he tossed aside something he'd taken from her. It all happened in about a half minute.

Without thinking Rowe jumped into his car, ready to follow. His overriding thought was to save the girl.

Chapter 53

Forsythe was tired of getting the runaround from Herrera. He'd called several times, offering bail, and insisting that Kraft be freed. He called Herrera again, and said, "I'm coming down to see Kraft, and you need to answer some questions!"

Herrera was annoyed but had been ready for the call. "Don't waste your time. You won't be allowed to see him. Since you already have Ms. Chandler on retainer, why don't you send her? She's sure to preserve his Constitutional rights. Have her call me," Herrera said as he rang off.

His blood pressure had gone up only a few ticks, not bad.

Rory's call came in quickly. "Good morning, Detective, I guess you know Forsythe is putting pressure on for Kraft's release. I'm still at home, but I could be there, in say, a half hour, ok?"

"That sounds good, thanks."

***

The bogeyman was on an adrenaline high, things were falling into place. He'd got the girl, and would not let her go until she told him where Carly was. She must know where Carly was, and he would find out.

He was looking behind him; earlier, he thought he'd spotted a tail, and he was afraid it could be Rowe. He'd been watching him intently at work. So, he called the sheriffs' office and said, "I think I saw Mason Rowe and he wasn't at work." He hung up quickly. If it's Rowe, that should fix him. He chuckled.

The ether he'd put over Marilyn's face should keep her out for at least an hour. He'd obtained quite a few drugs that were proving helpful. Quite by chance, he'd found an abandoned veterinary supply warehouse that had a busted window. He'd grabbed a bunch of drugs, and though they were old, they seemed effective.

He was driving to an abandoned warehouse he'd found near the vet supply place. All of the buildings in that area were in disrepair and abandoned.

***

Rowe was still following the bogeyman, and wondering where the hell he was going. They'd left the Blue route, and turned on to I-95. This road was heavily traveled at any time of day. But he welcomed it. He could hide behind cars and keep an eye on the Chevy.

He checked his gas, which was one quarter full, hoping it would hold out until the bogeyman arrived at his destination. They were headed into Philadelphia, far out of Herrera's jurisdiction. Rowe wasn't sure how that worked, but they could figure it out. His main objective was keeping the woman safe. He hoped she could hold up. The bogeyman had been intent on bashing women. It was only little girls he could intimidate.

They passed the airport, threading through heavy traffic. The bogeyman was still five or six cars ahead, but within sight. Unexpectedly, Rowe's prey exited at the sign for the Walt Whitman Bridge. Jesus! Did he plan to take her to New Jersey? That would take this to another level if he crossed state lines. And Rowe's tank would undoubtedly be empty.

***

Ryan Benson had been trying to reach Marilyn on her cell phone, but she never picked up, nor had she returned a call or text. He'd been concerned that she hadn't gotten back to him. And he cursed himself for not driving her to work just because he'd had an early appointment at the gym. Now he called the front desk of CYS.

The phone rang for quite a while, but he was determined to get through. Finally the receptionist answered, saying, "Children and Youth Services, please hold," before he had a chance to speak. Shit! Nothing was going his way today. The early appointment didn't even show, and now this. After five minutes of waiting, he hung up. The only alternative he could see was to go in person, but it would have to wait until he finished with his last client of the morning. Frantically, he left an urgent text message for Marilyn.

***

Rory was dressing after a hasty shower. She'd enjoyed hearing about Sarah's visit and the new info about Jesus, but now it was time to get to work. She'd sent Sam and Sarah home to 'take a nap', like that would happen! She did enjoy watching their relationship bloom, and wondered how long it would be before the wedding date was announced.

She dressed casually for work, since she had no court appearances. She was curious about Herrera's call. He said Forsythe was worried about Kraft's civil rights, since he hadn't yet been released from custody. Herrera was an interesting man and a very competent detective.

Grabbing a bottle of water from the fridge, she checked the wall clock at the same time. Well, it looked like she would be a tad late for her appointment with the detective. She hated being late, but she knew she'd been inattentive lately, more inattentive than usual.

There were many things on her mind, she thought as she drove. She still hadn't found a good time to tell Marc she was pregnant. She wondered how Alex's chat with Alicia had gone, and she worried about the rift that appeared to be pushing her daughters apart. And then there was this daunting case, which was spinning wheels.

Arriving at the police station, Rory checked her watch and saw that she'd made up some time by speeding. She was only five minutes late.

As she'd come to expect, Herrera was in the lobby waiting for her.

Waiving aside her apologies, he said, "Hey, I'm lucky to get you at all, as busy as you are, come on back."

Rory followed him to his office and took a seat. He told her about Kraft's case, and how Forsythe was being a royal pain.

Then the detective said, "I hope I'm not on shaky ground legally. I mean Kraft is cooperating, and he very much wants to see the case resolved." He went on to say that Kraft had been released on his own recognizance, and was staying out of town for a while, to throw the bogeyman off.

"I've been convinced of Kraft's innocence almost from the beginning, so I'm glad that the evidence pointed elsewhere. We all believe the bogeyman is affiliated with Citadel, but the answer is just not coming. It's frustrating," Rory concluded. "Oh, and Forsythe is incredibly annoying."

Looking at her watch, Rory said, "I need to get into the office. I'll make up some BS for Forsythe about Kraft's rights. Thanks for putting me in the loop. Bye now."

***

Rowe was relieved that the bogeyman didn't take the bridge to New Jersey. Instead, they were slowly winding their way through the labyrinth of streets and alleys in South Philadelphia. He'd spent a lot of time in the city, and his brother's place was not far, but none of these streets was familiar. He'd almost lost the man on a few occasions, because he had to stay far behind. He certainly didn't want to get trapped in one of the narrow one- way streets.

Finally, the suspect pulled into a large area of abandoned buildings, warehouses apparently, that were surrounded by a chain link fence, which hung open on rusted hinges. Rowe did a quick u-turn and pulled up to a position where he could see what the man was doing. Of course, he couldn't go into the fenced in area, at least not yet.

He watched as the Chevy pulled up to an enormous building that appeared deserted. In fact all of the buildings, some falling down, were in a state of abject disrepair.

Bogeyman was opening the car's trunk, having parked very close to the building. He hauled the woman, who appeared to be unconscious, out of the trunk. Flipping her over his shoulder like a rolled up rug, he looked around furtively before entering the building.

***

Hayley was still in the hospital. Don had brought his laptop in so she could write her articles. She was indebted to Don for so many things, she thought as she typed. She started to wonder what she'd done before she met him. She thought her life had been full, with plenty of friends and enough casual dating. But he'd taken the idea of relationship to a whole new level. From the very beginning, he'd been protective of her and she trusted him. No, it was more than that, she loved him.

She felt her face get hot, and was sure it was not a pretty sight. Well, that and the fact that she hadn't washed her hair or applied makeup since she'd arrived. When she realized she'd been typing without thinking, she stopped to look at the screen. "I love Don" was written several times.

Oh shit! I need to get rid of that, she thought, just as Don walked through the door.

She slammed the lid down a tad harder than intended, and Don noticed.

"Hey, Baby, what's up, getting frustrated with your writing?" He walked to her bedside and gave her a quick kiss. Then he opened the computer, saying, "It can't be that bad…"

Chapter 54

Ryan Benson hurried his workout with his last client before lunch. He went into the locker room and hastily changed his clothes. The longer he went without a call or text from Marilyn, the more he panicked. He'd tried to call CYS, but they were closed for lunch, fuck that! He'd just drive over to the office and find out from someone where Marilyn was.

His anxiety grew as he drove, trying not to go too far over the speed limit. He still blamed himself for not driving her to work. He'd promised he'd never leave her vulnerable again after she was attacked by the God damned bogeyman. She'd been insistent he go to the gym and keep his early appointment. And then the bastard didn't show up!

Ryan tried to call the man back, but a recorded message said that the number was out of service. Wait a minute, he thought, what if this whole thing was planned so he didn't take Marilyn to work? What if this was no coincidence? The more he thought about it, the more convinced he was. He ignored the panic rising in his chest.

When he finally reached CYS, he parked out front and bolted in the front door.

He saw the receptionist he knew as Janine look up at him in surprise. "So, you're ok then! We got a call that you'd been taken to the emergency room. Marilyn was so worried when she raced out of here..."

***

Rowe had been waiting no more than five minutes and was about to go into the building, when he saw the bogeyman come stealthily and quickly out of the building. He got into his car, driving away, as Rowe stayed hidden behind a huge bush. He waited for a few minutes to make sure this wasn't a trap, and the bastard wasn't coming back.

When he felt that enough time had elapsed, he reached into his car and took out a few bottles of water. If the woman was coming to, she'd be thirsty. Or she may need cleaning up. In any case, he was going in. He squared his shoulders, and took a deep breath before surveying the area around him. Then he walked quickly and resolutely toward the warehouse.

Entering the door the bogeyman had gone in, he took a moment to let his eyes to adjust to the dimness of the interior. He noticed it had a musty, dank smell about it, and had apparently been closed for many years. He looked around for closed doors, and saw many partially opened doors, finally noticing one was closed. He went straight to it, listening for any sound. The handle turned, but the door didn't open. He pulled on the knob a few times, but it wouldn't budge.

Looking and feeling around the edges of the door, he discovered that the door had been held closed by a simple mechanism, a rubber door wedge, commonly used in homes. He kicked it away and opened the rusty door that creaked noisily on its hinges.

Taking a deep breath, he entered the room. It was even darker in here, where there were no windows. He took in the room quickly and headed for what looked like a bundle of rags in the corner of the room.

Kneeling down, he found a young woman with blonde hair, who appeared to be unconscious. He started a conversation, "Hey, I saw what happened to you, and I'm here to help you." He felt her pulse, which was faint, but steady. "Are you okay? I want to get an ambulance for you." He looked closely at her face and her arms and saw bruising. He couldn't tell if this was from rough handling of her or if she'd been hit. At least she wasn't bloody, from what he could see.

He punched in 911 and gave the address as he could best figure it. "Stay on the line, we're sending an ambulance," he was told. He put the phone in his back pocket.

Looking back at the woman, he saw her eyes fly open. "Who… who are you? You're him! You're Rowe! Please don't hurt me… I…"

"It was the bogeyman who took you, I think," Rowe said trying to calm her down. "I'm here to help you. An ambulance will be here shortly."

She calmed and then said, "I've never seen him, but this is the second time he's attacked me. The first time I pepper sprayed him, but never saw his face. This time, I didn't open my eyes when he dropped me here, although I was awake. He just kicked me a few times and left. When you came in, I thought he was back." She spoke quietly and with some effort.

Hearing the sirens close by, Rowe said, "Look, I'm going to leave now. Please don't describe me or say my name. I'm tracking the bogeyman and I need to do it my way. I'll also put in an anonymous tip to the police. Here," he said, as he handed her a bottle of water, "this should help stave off a bad headache. Drink as much water as you can."

"Thank you, I'm Marilyn," she said. "And God bless you. I won't describe you, except as a good Samaritan."

Rowe went through to the back of the building and found a way to exit, as he heard the ambulance pull up out front.

Finding a gap in the dilapidated fence, he made his way through the underbrush and back to his car, remaining behind it until he saw the EMT's carry Marilyn out to the waiting ambulance.

Once they were gone, Rowe got back into his car and took off. He was looking for some little dive with a pay phone. God knew there weren't many pay phones left! But he couldn't place an anonymous call from his cell phone.

He saw a run- down corner store that advertised a pay phone. Entering the store, Rowe asked about the phone and was directed to the back of the store. He found it and dialed the number of the Media police. When the duty officer answered, he said, "I have a message for Detective Herrera. A woman named Marilyn was kidnapped and taken to a warehouse in south Philly. She's now on the way to the nearest hospital." He hung up and went quickly out to his car.

As he got in, his cell phone rang. The caller was his brother, so he picked up. "Hey, Greg, what's up?"

"Man, you gotta' get home, like now! I just got a call from the sheriff, and they're coming by for a check on you, 'cause you didn't go to work. So haul your ass on home!"

"I'm not far from home. Do me a favor and make sure the window to my bedroom is unlocked so I can come in that way."

"Ok, man, just hurry the fuck up!"

"No worries, Bro, I'll be there," he said with a confidence he didn't feel.

He floored it and took all of the back streets he could to avoid traffic and allow speed.

Rowe made it in ten minutes, a new record, he was sure. Parking in the alleyway behind his brother's house, he went directly to his bedroom window on the first floor. Slipping in easily and closing it behind him, he found the ankle bracelet and reconnected it, hearing it click into place. Then he stripped down to his underwear and got under the covers.

As it turned out, he had seconds to spare. He'd no sooner gotten into bed when there was a loud knock on the door.

"Mr. Rowe, we're coming in!"

Chapter 55

Ryan was in a state when no one at CYS could give him any idea where Marilyn was. "I gave her the message that you'd been taken to Riddle Hospital. She took off right away…"

"I guess the person didn't give a name?"

"No, and because it was an emergency, I reacted quickly and told Marilyn. But that was about two hours ago, so she should've been back by now when she discovered you weren't there."

"Does anyone have an idea where she parked her car this morning?" Ryan asked, grasping at straws.

"Yes, I know that because we came in at the same time this morning. I'll show you if you like," Janine said.

"Yes, please," Ryan replied.

Janine came out from behind the desk and Ryan followed her outside to the parking lot.

The lot was in the rear of the building, surrounded by trees. There were no windows facing it, Ryan noticed. Perfect place for an abduction, he thought, frowning.

Janine pointed to an empty spot at the corner of the building. Ryan went immediately to the area, searching for anything that might leave a clue. The parking spot contained nothing, but Ryan bent down, looking under the adjacent car. He saw something, but couldn't reach it. Looking around, and finding a long stick, he tried again. This time, a small canister rolled towards him. It was a can of pepper spray.

***

Marilyn had been taken to Jefferson Hospital, and was in the emergency room having her wounds treated. She'd been kicked in the ribs, but nothing was broken. Except for that, all of her injuries had been superficial.

A Philadelphia detective was waiting outside her cubicle to meet with her as soon as her treatment was completed.

She had no purse or cell phone with her, and thus no health care card, but was treated anyway. Marilyn was also dehydrated, so there was an IV in her arm. They'd taken blood to determine what drug had been used to knock her out. The attending nurse suspected the virtually forgotten drug ether, because he'd smelled a slight whiff of it, and it had a distinctive smell. But a proper blood analysis would be needed for police evidence.

When the nurse had finished with Marilyn, he went to the detective. "Hello, I'm Ty Carter, and I just finished treating Ms. Hunter. She'll have to remain here until we're sure she's stabilized, but you can see her now.

"Thank you, I'm Detective Soloman," he answered. "Can you tell me about her injuries?'

"Yes, I can. She has abrasions to her face, her wrists and arms, and major bruising on her lower rib cage, but no broken bones. She's still in an acute state of shock, and she's dehydrated, probably due to the drug that rendered her unconscious. A blood analysis has been ordered."

"Thank you, Dr. Carter," the detective said.

Ty didn't bother to correct him, and say that he was a nurse practitioner. He grinned to himself. Because he was a man, even though he was black, he was often mistaken for a doctor.

The detective went into the curtained off room where Ms. Hunter was sitting up. He identified himself and showed her his badge. "Are you up to answering some questions Ms. Hunter?"

"I am, Detective."

As she answered his questions, the story of her abduction unfolded. Their discussion was interrupted when the detective's cell phone buzzed. "Detective Soloman," he answered. "Yes, yes, I'm with her now. It looks as though there are two jurisdictions working here…sure, you can come in and see her. I'll be here for a while."

"That was Detective Herrera, and I gather you've been working with him."

"Yes, I didn't get to that part yet. I guess he's coming here?"

"He's on his way," the detective said. "We'll be working together. I got information from the ambulance driver as to the location where you were found, so I sent two officers there. They'll be dusting for prints, keeping an eye out. Do you think he'll be back?"

"I'm certain he will be. I feigned unconsciousness, so he couldn't get any information from me. I know what he wants."

***

Rowe responded to the banging on his door, with a feeble sounding, "Come in." Sitting up in bed he managed to look disoriented and disheveled.

The two sheriffs entered, and one of them gave the direction, "We need to see your bracelet."

Rowe pulled his left leg from under the covers so they could see it. "Is something wrong?' he asked groggily.

"You didn't report to work today," the larger of the two sheriffs said.

Rowe looked intentionally confused, "But I called out sick from work."

"You're supposed to call our office, so we came here when we didn't find you at work."

"I'm sorry I've made extra work for you," Rowe apologized. "I honestly wasn't aware of the need to notify your office, but you can count on me doing it in the future. The way I'm feeling, I may not be in tomorrow, but I'll be sure to call if that's the case."

The sheriff grunted, "Ok, we'll take you at your word," as he handed Rowe a business card, and, along with the other sheriff, left the room.

Rowe flopped down on his pillow, actually feeling sick with fear. The sheriffs seemed to be genuinely disappointed that he was home with the bracelet still on. Thank God he'd been able to get back in time. Moreover, he'd saved the woman. Now he had to address the root cause of all the problems.

***

Herrera had spoken with the Philly detective, and was headed into the city. This could be a real break in the case, especially if Marilyn could describe her abductor. In any case, there would be more evidence to process. He understood that Detective Soloman had sent some forensic guys over to the warehouse to comb the place.

His cell buzzed and he answered without looking at the number. "Detective Herrera," he answered.

"Detective, this is Ryan Benson, I'm Marilyn Hunter's boyfriend. I called your office and was told that you'd left, but they wouldn't give me any other information. I believe Marilyn was kidnapped by the bogeyman and taken, in her own car, but I have no idea where. When I went to the spot where she'd parked this morning, I found a canister of pepper spray that had rolled under the next car. It's her pepper spray, but she didn't get to use it this time. Can you help me find her?" Ryan waited tensely for an answer.

"You know where Jefferson Hospital is? Meet me there, in the emergency room."

"Yes, of course I'll meet you there, is she ok?"

"She's conscious and alive, that's about all I know."

***

The bogeyman was on his way back to the warehouse. He'd ditched Marilyn's car, after wiping off his prints. He drove the blue Chevy now, in an abundance of caution. But he wasn't worried, really, because he'd been careful, very careful. And no one would find her in this deserted area. And she *would* give him the information he sought, sooner or later.

His confidence began to wane as he drove closer to the site. He squinted to make sure he wasn't mistaken. There were cars, two of them, parked right outside of the warehouse! How could this happen? He'd taken care of Rowe, and he hadn't seen any tail the entire time during the drive here.

He drove past the area, making a U-turn and pulling off the road to get a better idea of what was going on. As he watched, he saw a uniformed officer exit the warehouse, from the door he'd left less than an hour before. It looked as if the officer was leaving. He backed the car up as far as he could to avoid detection.

The officer drove off, and the bogeyman sighed with relief. Then he got angry. "Fuck!" he yelled, pounding on the steering wheel. How could they possibly have found her this quickly? He knew Rowe was somehow behind this, but he couldn't figure out how.

He sped off in a panic.

Chapter 56

Rowe's brother burst into his room. "Man, I almost shit myself! I tried to stall them; I took my time getting to the door, told them you were pretty sick, and all but blocked their passage. I can tell you, they're not a happy couple!"

"Yeah, I noticed that, too. I think they were disappointed to find me here. And, thanks to your diversionary tactics, I got in with seconds to spare. Thanks, Bro, I owe you one, well, more than one..."

"Just promise me you won't do this again!"

"I can't say I won't, but I won't do it from here. It's very easy to dismantle the bracelet, so really I can do it anywhere."

"But I worry about you, Mason! I don't want you to get hauled off to jail."

"Neither do I, trust me. I'm happy I was able to accomplish something important today. I actually thwarted the bogeyman!" And he went on to describe what had happened.

"Shit! You're a fuckin' hero, man, I mean it!"

***

Ryan had run a few red lights in his haste to get to Jefferson Hospital. There was always traffic to contend with in Philly, but it seemed worse today, probably because he was intent on reaching Marilyn, and at the same time, afraid of what he might find. The detective hadn't given him much to go on.

Screeching to a halt as he approached a red light, he realized he'd just dodged a bullet. A Philly cop was now crossing the intersection, and gave him a hard look as he passed. *Ok, note to me, slow down.* He tried taking deep breaths, like Marilyn always suggested, and soon he arrived at Jefferson.

At the ER reception desk, Ryan asked to be directed to Marilyn Hunter's location.

"She's with the police now," the nurse told him.

"Could you call back there and tell them Ryan's here. Detective Herrera told me to meet him here."

"I'll check, why don't you have a seat?"

Ryan wasn't pleased with her dismissive attitude, but certainly didn't want to make a scene.

When she hung up the phone, she nodded to Ryan, "Sir, you can go back now; she's in cubicle 3. You should've told me you're an officer," she added.

Ryan had to suppress a grin as he thanked her, and gave a mental nod to Herrera.

When he reached the right room, he walked in, shocked to see Marilyn's pallor, which was accentuated by bright red spots and bruising on her face. He went straight to her, seeing no one else in the room. As he got close he touched her face, gently. Then he nuzzled her ear. "Thank God you're safe!"

Slowly, he became aware of the officers, when Marilyn tried to introduce them.

Ryan pulled away from Marilyn and said, "Sorry, I wanted to make sure she was ok. Thank you both for being here."

Both detectives acknowledged him, and asked him to have a seat.

Detective Herrera spoke first. "She's been very helpful, except she really hasn't seen this man, even though he's attacked her twice. He's being very careful, but I doubt he expected us to find her today."

"How *did* you find her?" he asked.

Marilyn answered, "A good Samaritan must've seen him carry me into the warehouse. He gave me water and called 911. It was so dark in that cell where he left me, I couldn't really see the man, and he left quickly. I owe him my life. If this gets on TV, I want to thank him." Tears began to trickle down her cheeks.

Ryan left his chair to sit on the bed next to her. "You're very brave," he murmured. "And I'd like to shake the stranger's hand." He went on, "You know, there aren't enough people willing to get involved."

Detective Soloman spoke. "You might be surprised at the number of tips we get from people without giving their names. But you're right, most people don't want to actually go into a dangerous situation, like this man did."

***

Word had traveled around in the construction area of Rory's office, after the sheriffs had come in like gangbusters, demanding to know where Rowe was. Forsythe, predictably, had argued with the sheriffs, saying that Rowe had called in sick, and was entitled to his sick time undisturbed.

Rory was in the office alone, having sent Sam and Sarah home. Blake had taken off to study for his law boards. She wanted to share this new development, but didn't want to disturb the others.

She had heard one of the sheriffs roar, "Well, our office never got a God damn call from him and that's the rules! So now we have to hike our asses up to Philly and check on him."

"Why?" Forsythe had asked. "Did he go off your radar? I doubt he'd do anything to jeopardize his bail. Besides, there's a flu going around and some other guys are out today."

The sheriffs had left without answering Forsythe, who reacted by storming into his office and slamming his door behind him.

Rory wondered if it was true that there were other guys out, and if so, was there a connection between them. She didn't get far with that line of thought, so dropped it for the time and went back to slogging over the evidence.

She'd put in a call to Herrera a while ago and was told he'd left the station hurriedly, and said he was going to Jefferson Hospital in the city. Rory had left a message for him to call her back. Was this connected to the case, or was this a family matter? Once more she found that she had more questions than answers.

Trying to get back to work, she heard the front door open, and saw her friend, Roland. "Come on back!" Rory greeted him.

The trooper closed the door behind him and took a seat across from Rory. "Hey, Girlfriend!" He greeted her, as was his custom. He lowered his voice to a whisper, and asked, "How's the plan going? Any nibbles yet?"

"No, but there's been some drama going on in here…" Rory said mysteriously. She went on to explain about the sheriffs coming in and demanding Rowe.

"Are you aware that the sheriff's office needs to be notified?" Rory asked.

"I didn't think so," Roland answered, "but the county sort of makes its own rules." He shrugged. "Anyway, how can I help?"

"To answer your question, there have been no nibbles, but I'm dropping hints about my memory returning. I don't really think I've remembered everything…"

"You mean," Roland said with a stern glance, "you're still intent on putting yourself out for bait."

"Well, yes, more or less..."

"Well, you know I've got your back. And you know I put a tracking device on your car, that's the best I can do."

"Yes, and you know I appreciate that."

"Look, I know you well enough to assume you will do this with or without me. And I suspect you haven't told Marc…"

Rory didn't answer.

"I take that as confirmation. And I know it's none of my business, but you need to get your shit together with Marc. He's too good a guy to lose."

"I know that, and I intend to. And I do appreciate your help."

Roland sighed. "But you must promise to let me know the moment you think you might be in danger."

***

Dara Keene and Rachel had just come from an appointment with Rachel's therapist. Rachel was doing well, Dr. Singh told Dara. She warned Dara, however, to watch for nightmares, or temper fits as Rachel remembered more of the incidents.

"I cannot tell you with any certainty how often Rachel was visited by the bogeyman, or over what period of time, but it's clear that it happened more than once. He could've been grooming her for some time," Dr. Singh had said.

"But," Dara said, feeling like an inattentive mother, "she's never been out of my sight except when she's in daycare, or with her father."

"I'm not criticizing your parenting skills," the doctor had said, "It's just that pedophiles are real pros at getting kids' attention in a moment when no one is watching. Perhaps when the kids are playing in the yard at daycare, or possibly someone you know who has visited your home…"

"Gosh, I never thought in my wildest dreams, or rather,

nightmares, that this could happen to my child. And I'm pretty vigilant," Dara said.

"And it's good that you are, but be careful not to be over-protective. I know that's a tall order and there's a fine line, but you're a good parent, and you need to trust your instincts. By the way, has Rachel seen her father lately? She seems to talk about Mason and how much she misses him, but not much about Dad."

"Her dad is still in a half-way house upstate. He has seen her a few times since this happened. But frankly, she's closer to Mason. We haven't seen him, and we won't until the bogeyman is caught, but we've both talked with him on the phone."

"You might get her dad to bring Rachel in to one of her appointments when he next visits. I like to get a picture of the family constellation. At some point, if you and your fiancée stay together, I'd like to see him, too."

"Sure," Dara said. "See you next time."

Dr. Singh's words had troubled Dara. It seems that the doctor would be scrutinizing the two men in relation to Rachel's molestation. She'd never considered that either man was the perpetrator, but …

Chapter 57

As it turned out, Marilyn had remained at Jefferson Hospital overnight. Ryan had been allowed to stay with her. The attending physician thought it best for Marilyn to have him with her because she was still suffering the effects of shock. Ryan felt as if he were in shock as well. It had been an extremely stressful day.

Marilyn was on a tranquilizer, and Ryan wished he could have one, too. It was evening and she'd dozed off after her dinner, some of which he ate because she wasn't hungry. He wandered out to the nurses' station and was surprised to see a security guard outside of the door. He asked the nurse about it.

She said, "That detective, not the Philly one, asked for a guard because of a previous incident when the suspect actually came into the patient's room. But her husband was there to protect her."

"Well, I'm happy to have security," he said. "By the way, do you think I could have a sleep aid?"

She smiled, "I can give you an OTC sleep aid, not one that requires a prescription. I hope that helps you get to sleep in the chair." She handed him two tablets and said, "There should be a pitcher of water in the room."

"Actually, I think Marilyn finished it," he said. "She's been real thirsty."

"That's good, and will help her recover more quickly. I'll bring you a fresh pitcher," she offered.

"Thank you," Ryan said as he walked back to her room, nodding to the officer at the door.

***

The bogeyman had tried to calm down, but he was in a high state of agitation. He couldn't stay away from the warehouse, driving past it a few more times before it turned dark. He'd noticed police cars coming and going, but at least one remained, and there was crime scene tape everywhere.

This was Philly's jurisdiction and they were bound to do a more thorough search than that detective from Media. What had they found, he wondered. He hadn't paid much attention to detail because he couldn't believe she'd be found. He'd thought he was home free and would soon have Carly back. Now, he saw no clear path to Carly. Well, she was off limits to him for now, maybe later…

***

It was late when Rory got around to calling Rowe to find out why the sheriffs had come to the office. She called from home after she'd had dinner.

Mason answered on the second ring, "Hi Rory," he said, "How are you doing?"

"The real question," Rory answered, "is how are *you*? I knew you'd called out sick today, but then these sheriffs came to the office and raised hell! Were you aware of that?"

"No, but I woke up quick when they pounded on my bedroom door this afternoon! And oddly enough, they seemed disappointed that I was here, in bed with the bracelet intact."

"That doesn't surprise me, but I'm not sure why they came to your house if the bracelet didn't trigger it," Rory said, wondering aloud.

"They told me that I had to call their office with any change, but honestly, I don't remember reading that in the paperwork," Mason said. "But I sure as hell won't make that mistake again!"

"Maybe I should call them. As your attorney, I have a right to know what's going on. And to me, it seems highly irregular. I'll get back to you if I find out anything. Do you think you'll be in tomorrow?" she asked.

"I'm really not sure. That whole invasion thing didn't help my health, or my brother's for that matter. I'll let you know…"

"Okay, I'll let you get some sleep. I'm sorry if I woke you. Bye."

She was still sitting in the nook, phone in hand, when Marc wandered into the kitchen.

He did a double take as he walked past her. "Rory, you okay?"

"Yeah, I just spoke with Mason and he told me the sheriffs came to his brother's house today because he wasn't at work and hadn't called to tell them. I've never heard of that happening unless they got a signal that the monitor had been tampered with. I can't believe the rules have changed."

***

It was early morning when Don went out to pick up his paper. He was anxious to read Hayley's story, which would be in today's paper. Once inside, Don got his coffee, and sat down to read the paper.

Hayley's article was on the front page, along with her picture. This was a good article. Don got Hayley on the phone, "That's a damn good article, and it's on the front page! On the down side, this will piss off the bogeyman even more, and I don't want him going after you when you get out. I have some ideas, and I'll talk to you when I come to get you. When's check out?"

"Once I get my papers, I can leave. It's usually about eleven, but it's really up to the doc. I'll call you the minute I get my walking papers. Thanks for calling, Bye now."

As he thought of other options for Hayley, his mind went to his sister, Jean, who lived alone in Cape May, NJ. That would be a perfect place for her to recuperate. And his sister was a nurse. He picked up his cell.

***

Erin Scott was more than pleased with Carly's progress. Each day she seemed to grow more comfortable and happy. Erin never mentioned the lineup, nor did she mention 'Charlie.' This damaged child would need to develop an enormous ability to trust before she could give up 'Charlie.'

The officer had daily conversations with Herrera, when she was sure Carly couldn't hear. Erin had been shocked when Marilyn was abducted, and so grateful she'd been rescued before the bogeyman could inflict more harm. There was no way she could tell Carly what had happened to her caseworker.

More than ready for the case to be resolved, Erin knew it couldn't be at the expense of Carly. Certainly the child had the most information about the bogeyman, but was not yet ready to impart it.

She was willing to wait as long as it took.

Chapter 58

The next day Rory was at work early and her first order of business was to call the sheriff. She dialed the number and got the receptionist. "Hi Gayle, this is Rory Chandler, could you connect me to Sheriff Clark, please?"

"Just a moment, Rory, I'll try to track him down."

"Sheriff Clark here." He didn't address Rory directly, but that was his way. He was a bit officious, and perhaps he wouldn't answer her question.

"Good Morning, Sheriff, this is Rory Chandler. I have a question you may be able to answer. My client, Mason Rowe, is on an electronic home monitor and called in sick to work yesterday. Later in the day, two sheriffs showed up at his brother's house in Philadelphia, where he's staying, to check on him. Is this standard procedure?"

"Well, you do know, Ms. Chandler that it is our prerogative to check on anyone who's on the monitor. This may have been just a routine check."

Same old pompous ass, Rory thought, before she spoke. "Of course I know that," she stressed, as if speaking to a child. "It's just that Mr. Rowe was told, when they found him sick in bed with the monitor still on, that he had failed to call their office, in addition to calling his employer. I thought standard procedure was to call the place where he was supposed to be."

"Not necessarily. It is possible they called his home and he didn't answer."

"So you don't have specific information about what happened yesterday?" she asked.

"It would not be necessary to contact me on such a trivial matter," he said. "And if you have nothing further, I have plenty to occupy my time. Goodbye."

"Goodbye to you, too, *dick!"* Rory muttered when she heard the click. She knew that if the sheriff hadn't been notified, the two deputies would have hell to pay. He tried to stay on top of everything.

Her takeaway was that this was not standard procedure, but he'd never admit that. So she wondered, did someone who would benefit from putting the spotlight on Rowe, put in an anonymous tip? And if so, why? As usual, there were more questions than answers.

***

Don called Detective Herrera, and was put right through. "Good Morning, Detective," Don said. "Have you seen Hayley's article today?"

"Yes, I have, and it's quite good," he said. "Is she out of the hospital yet?"

"No, but she'll probably be released today. That's what I'm calling you about. The bogeyman will not be happy with her unflattering portrayal of him in the paper and I'm thinking of getting her out of town. What do you think?"

"Might be a good idea," he said. "You may not know this, but he attacked and kidnapped Marilyn Hunter yesterday, and she's in the hospital."

"Never heard that, it must've been kept quiet!"

"Well, he took her to a deserted warehouse in Philly, and she's now at Jefferson Hospital. So if it was reported, and I'm sure it was, it would be in the Inquirer. Anyway, to answer your question, the bogeyman must be running scared, and becoming unhinged. Anything could happen. So, yeah, it may be good to get her out of town."

"Man, she was lucky to get out of that alive! How'd you find her?"

"We didn't find her. A 'Good Samaritan,' as she described him, found her, called an ambulance and then tipped our office. We have no idea who it was, but it was a good outcome!"

"For sure!" Don said. "Well, I appreciate your information. Now I need to get an Inquirer and call Rory!" He rang off.

***

Marilyn woke up and asked Ryan to help her to the bathroom.

"I'm friggin' tired of peeing in the bedpan!" she said. "Plus, I never hit the mark and the bed gets wet."

Ryan helped her out of bed, as she winced. "Jeez, I hurt all over! That bastard!"

"It's okay," Ryan soothed her. "He's bound to be caught soon!"

"That's what I thought last time. I should've sprayed him 'til he dropped!"

Entering the bathroom, Marilyn happened to glance in the mirror. "Oh my God! How can you stand to look at me?" Tears were forming in her eyes and dripping down her cheeks.

"It upsets me," Ryan said, "to see how badly you were hurt, but I'm happy you're alive! And you're still beautiful."

"That's a lie, but it's sweet, Ryan," she said, as she sat on the toilet.

"Well, I have to say, what I want to do to the bogeyman is anything but sweet! How dare he mess with you, twice!"

"All the more reason to feel thankful. I've got to make sure there isn't a third time."

"We'll have to talk about that, keeping you safe," he said as he helped her back to bed.

***

Mason Rowe decided to go to work, figuring the bogeyman would be lying low for a while. Of course, there was the possibility of running into him at work, but he'd deal with that if it came up. As he drove to work, he mentally reviewed yesterday's events.

He'd talked with Dara for a long time the previous night, and longed to see her, hold her. He missed Rachel almost as much. It helped staying in touch by phone. He'd told her about the episode with the sheriffs, and she seemed angry about it. He was sorry he couldn't tell her the truth. He worried about Rachel's safety, now the bogeyman had been thwarted and couldn't get to the little girl who was a foster child.

He also told Dara about Marilyn's brush with the bogeyman and urged her to keep Rachel safe. He'd read an article in the Inquirer about the kidnapping, and it had been on the morning news. Marilyn had publicly thanked the 'good Samaritan' who'd saved her, without giving any description as he'd requested.

Before he knew it, he'd arrived at work. He braced himself for whatever might come his way. He didn't enter the construction area. Instead, he went straight to Rory's office.

"Good Morning, Rory," Mason said, as he entered. He noticed she was the only one in the office.

"HI Mason, come right back," Rory said. "I'm so glad you're better today."

He thought he might have detected a hint of sarcasm, and that didn't surprise him. He knew she was pretty sharp. "I'm happy to be back to work. I got tired of lying in bed all day, but I guess it helped. Did you see the news about that caseworker being kidnapped by the bogeyman?"

"I sure did! Wow, was she lucky! That's twice she's gotten away from him. I hope her luck holds out. Imagine, a stranger saved her! What did she call him, a 'good Samaritan?'" She looked directly into Mason's eyes as she said it.

Yep, she knows, he thought. He was pretty sure he couldn't fool her, and he was glad she was on his side.

***

Dara had called her ex-husband, Paul, and asked if he could get away for a brief visit, and accompany Rachel to her therapy session. "Dr. Singh would like to talk to you, to get a clearer picture of what's going on with Rachel."

He sounded alarmed. "Why? Does she think I might be a pedophile?" he asked.

"No, Paul," Dara explained. "Up to this point I'm the only person from her family who's spoken to the therapist. You will have a different perspective, and it's important for her to see that."

"But, we're together in this," he said. "I'd never say anything against you, I hope you know!"

"Of course I know that, but it's really not about pitting us against each other. It's all about helping Rachel."

"Oh, okay, when's her next appointment? I'll be there for it," he said, sounding calmer.

"Well, it's later today, I didn't mean for you to come on such short notice, the next appointment is fine."

"That's ok, I can get away today, just tell me when and where."

Chapter 59

The food on the breakfast tray in front of her was getting cold, but Hayley was too excited to eat, hoping she could go home today. The doc hadn't appeared yet and she was getting antsy.

To break the monotony, she switched on the TV and found a local news station. After the weather report, which predicted, no surprise, another heat wave, she saw Marilyn Hunter, all bruised up, talking with a reporter from her hospital bed. "Oh my God!" she murmured. "The bogeyman got to her again!"

Just then, Hayley's doctor came through the door, followed by Don.

Hayley's face lit up and she said, "Looks like I'm getting out!"

Then she said to Don, "Did you hear what happened to Marilyn Hunter?"

***

Rachel was waiting eagerly for her daddy to pick her up at daycare. She stood by the playground fence, looking for his car to enter the parking lot. She didn't notice a man standing under a tree near the fence, until he walked towards her.

"Hi," he said in a friendly manner. "Are you looking for someone? Maybe I can help…"

Before he could say more, an observant staff member called Rachel over, and the man disappeared immediately.

"Rachel, Honey, you do know not to talk to strangers, don't you?"

"Yes, my mommy tells me about it all the time. But he was nice…"

"Sometimes people who seem nice aren't really nice. It's best to be safe and just not talk to someone you don't know. What did he say?" she asked.

"He just asked who I was looking for, and said maybe he could help me find him."

"Does he know your daddy?" the teacher asked, confused.

Before the teacher could say more, Rachel's father walked over.

"Hey, how's my little girl?" he asked, swinging her up into his arms.

"Daddy! I been looking for you and here you are!" She hugged him.

"Anything wrong?" he asked the staff person, who seemed flustered.

"Not really, I just had to remind her not to talk to strangers..."

"What do you mean?" he asked.

"There was a man by the fence just a minute ago, and she was over there waiting for you, so I just called her over to remind her."

"Did you talk to the man?" her father asked Rachel.

"No, he just said hi, and asked what I was doing, and then she called me. He was nice,"

He looked at the teacher and said, "Do you know her history? You should find out, if you don't. She shouldn't be anywhere near the fence. But thanks for being alert and calling her over."

Rachel's father continued talking to his daughter as they left together. And after he secured her in her seat, he surveyed the area, seeing no one, which was in a way more concerning. The guy had left quickly.

***

Marilyn Hunter's doctor was examining her. He told her they were able to detect ether in her system, and it was a fairly potent amount for someone her size. He asked if she had a headache.

"I do, but compared to last night, it's much better. Do you think I can go home today, Dr. Smythe?"

"I don't see why not, since you don't have a fever and your bruises will heal soon enough. How about the ribs? Any pain there?"

"Only when I laugh, and I haven't been doing much of that lately," she joked.

"I can give you something for pain," he offered.

"No thanks, I don't need it. I need rest."

"And plenty of fluids. You can take Ibuprofen for the headache. I'll prepare your discharge papers, and you'll be good to go in about an hour."

"Thank you, doctor, I appreciate it," Marilyn said.

"Keep yourself safe," the doctor added, a concerned look on his face.

He went out to speak with Ryan and reiterated what he'd told Marilyn. Then he said, "I do hope you have somewhere she can be safe."

Ryan was pondering what to do as he walked into Marilyn's room.

"Why so somber? I'm getting out!"

"I'm happy about that, but the doc mentioned your safety, and I'm not sure what to do. I thought I was doing everything possible, and he still got to you. And he still wants to know where Carly is, so what's to stop him?"

The smile had slipped from Marilyn's face. "You're right, I'll be scared to be alone, but I can't ask anyone to stay with me all the time!"

Both were lost in thought with frowns on their faces when Ryan's cell beeped.

***

Rachel's father waited while his daughter was seeing the therapist. He was looking through a magazine, but his mind really wasn't on it. He was worried that the bogeyman was still out there and still wreaking havoc. Had it been he who was talking to Rachel this morning? He didn't plan on asking Rachel too many questions, but he had managed a quick aside to the therapist before Rachel went in.

When the hour was up, Rachel came out smiling. "Hi Daddy! The doctor wants to see you now."

"Okay, Honey, I won't be long, but remember what we talked about."

"I won't forget, Daddy. The doctor said the same thing."

He kissed her cheek before he went in to see the doctor, noting the receptionist was at her desk.

Soon after Paul went in to the therapist's office, the receptionist left her desk to go to the bathroom. She said to Rachel, "I'll be right back."

The little girl was intent on looking for a book when the door opened quietly and a man came in. It was the same man she'd seen at the fence, and she knew she shouldn't talk to him.

"Hi," he said. "Didn't I just see you at the playground?"

She stood stiffly, not knowing what to do. The man approached her and she screamed.

The receptionist raced back to the waiting room, but the man had left, and the door was open. She went straight to Rachel and was holding her in her arms as Paul and the therapist came into the room.

Paul went right to his daughter and asked, "What happened, Sweetie?" as he took her in his arms.

"It was the same man who was at the fence, and you told me not to talk to him so I didn't and he was walking over to me when I screamed."

Paul glanced at the receptionist, asking, "Where were you?"

"I was just in the bathroom for a quick minute, it happened that fast. I'm so sorry!"

"Did you see the man?"

"No," she answered, "he'd gone, but the door was open. I don't know how he knew…"

"Well," Paul said, surveying the room, "we are on the first floor, and there's a window right there." He pointed to it. "Please call 911 now! Tell them we may have had a bogeyman encounter."

***

Rowe was waiting when the bogeyman came rushing out of the office. As the man passed by Rowe's car, the door was flung open, knocking him down.

Before he could get up, Rowe was all over him, smashing his head into the pavement. He pulled him up by his hair and hissed in his ear, "If I ever catch you within spitting distance of Rachel again, it will be your last breath."

He let the man's head slip from his grasp and it hit the pavement. Far from being cowed by the encounter, the man struck back, elbowing Rowe in the gut, and knocking the wind out of him. When he fell over to catch his breath, the attacker kicked him in the ribs and aimed a final blow at Rowe's head, before running off.

Knocked out momentarily, Rowe cursed himself when he recovered. "Fuck! I should've taken him when I had the chance," he muttered. Looking at his injuries, he knew he couldn't go back to the office now. He'd have to call Forsythe and tell him he didn't feel as good as he thought, and was going home. Fortunately, the bracelet he'd removed was hidden outside of the office. He hoped he could get to it without being seen. And for God's sake he had to remember to call the sheriff's office.

As he drove off, he surveyed the parking lot for any sign of the bogeyman. Seeing nothing, he left the parking lot. His cell buzzed, and, since it was Dara, he took it.

"Mason, I'm so glad I caught you! The bogeyman just tried to take Rachel while her dad was in the therapist's office, but she screamed and he didn't get her..."

"Thank God!" Mason tried to react the way he would've if he hadn't already known. "Was she left alone in the waiting room?"

"The receptionist was there, but left her desk for a minute..."

"Oh boy, not good! What can I do?" Mason asked.

"I guess there's nothing you can do. Paul will report the incident to Herrera. I just wanted you to know."

"Well, she's safe for now. What can you do to keep her safe?"

"Maybe we'll stay at my sister's tonight, and I may take off from work for a few days."

"That sounds like a good plan. Maybe you should leave work early," Rowe suggested.

"Good idea," Dara said. "Dear God, when will they catch the monster?"

"Soon, let's hope soon," he told Dara. He thought just maybe he'd have to kill him next time.

Chapter 60

Marilyn was in the bathroom dressing when Don and Hayley arrived at Jefferson Hospital.

Ryan was standing just inside the door and spotted them. He walked out the door, and said, “Hi, I’m Ryan, and you must be…”

“Don and Hayley,” she said as they took turns shaking his hand.

“Good to meet you,” Ryan said. “Marilyn is in the bathroom, but she should be out soon. But then, it could take longer if she decides to try and hide the bruises on her face,” He smiled.

“I know what she’s going through,” Hayley said. “And you can see how well my makeup works.” She grimaced.

Marilyn emerged from the bathroom. “I heard you talking, so I thought I’d join you.” She walked over to Hayley and hugged her. “I know you understand how it feels to be attacked, Hayley.”

“I do, but what happened to you, Marilyn, is really scary! I’m not sure what I’d have done.”

“Honestly, I’m glad that I was drugged, because I don’t really remember much of what happened. The bugger is, I didn’t ever see him.”

“Me, neither, that’s how he keeps getting away with his attacks.”

Don interrupted their conversation, and introduced himself to Marilyn. Then he addressed the other three. “Out of concern for the safety of both of you,” He nodded to Hayley and Marilyn, “we’re proposing to take you to stay with my sister in Cape May. She’s a nurse and welcomes the company.”

“But, I, Ryan, do you agree with this? Did you agree without consulting me?”

“I, uh, well, Don just called me a while ago, and I thought it sounded like a good idea. I failed to protect you today, despite my intentions.”

“I appreciate your offer, really,” Marilyn said. “But, can you give Ryan and me some time?” Marilyn asked Don and Hayley.

"Certainly," Hayley said. "Out in the hall, Don." The two left and closed the door.

Marilyn spoke first, "I really hate the idea of leaving you and my home! Hayley seems very nice, but there must be another solution."

"Do you have any ideas?" Ryan asked. "My priority is to keep you alive. I was terrified I'd lost you."

"I get that, it was a pretty scary day, what I remember of it. I can take a leave from work, hell, sick time for that matter, but I'd like to be somewhere familiar. I have a sorority sister who lives in Malvern, she might be willing to let me stay."

"Apart from being in a different place, how would you feel safer?"

"She lives in a gated community, and it's a pretty cohesive neighborhood. People watch out for one another. And it's far from the bogeyman!"

"Why don't you call her?" Ryan suggested.

"Ok, I will…" Marilyn got out her cell and called. "Darcy, hi, how are you?"

Ryan walked out into the hallway as she talked to her friend, and began a conversation with the guard.

A few moments later, Marilyn emerged and told Ryan, "It's all set, we can stay at her place. As it turns out, she's leaving on a cruise in a few days and welcomes our presence. We can take care of her cats."

***

Driving to the police station, Paul Keene was not happy, and wasn't looking forward to talking with the detective. He'd been on the other side of the police a few times, when he'd been charged with DUI. It made him nervous to be in a police station for any reason. But he had to do this for Rachel, he reminded himself. Dara was planning to meet him there and he hoped she got there first.

As he pulled into the parking lot, he was relieved to see her car.

When Dara spotted him driving in, she ran to the car, and reached in for Rachel the second the car stopped. She hugged her tight to her body and whispered in her ear. "Mommy's here, darling."

"I'm okay, Mommy, nothing bad happened. This man just wanted to talk to me, but I knew I shouldn't, so I screamed. And he left."

"That's good Honey, but he might not have been a nice man, so we have to tell the police."

"The police!" Rachel wailed, "What if they arrest me if they think I talked to him?"

"You're not in trouble, Honey. You didn't do anything wrong. The man did."

"Uh, maybe we should go in and meet the detective," Paul suggested. He half expected Dara to blame him for letting the bogeyman get near Rachel. And he thought she was over-reacting, probably because she felt guilty.

She put Rachel down. "You're right, we need to get on with this."

Herrera met them at the front desk. By prearrangement, Paul went to Herrera's office with the detective. He would give the details of the event, while Dara sat with her daughter. Rachel sat still and her eyes got big as she looked around the room, seeing pictures of wanted criminals. "Are those bad guys?" she asked her mother, as she pointed.

"Well, they've been in trouble with the law. But you can't really tell if someone is a bad guy just by looking at him. That's why we always tell you…"

"Not to talk to strangers," Rachel answered with a giggle.

"And never go anywhere with them. As long as you remember that, you should be fine." Dara only wished she believed that narrative.

***

The weather in the Poconos had been beautiful, especially when compared to the weather in Southeastern PA. So far it had been a very hot June in the Philly area. Erin was watching closely as Carly walked out waist deep into the lake. "Look at me, Mama!" Carly called, grinning hugely. "I'll swim to you."

Erin waded into the cool water to catch Carly.

The child swam quickly and surely, out of breath when Erin pulled her up. "You did great! What a quick learner you are!"

"Can I do it again?"

"Of course, I'll wait here for you." Erin found she had a catch in her voice as she spoke. She couldn't believe the strides Carly had taken in just a few days.

As it turned out they repeated this exercise several times, and each time Carly went into deeper water.

Looking at her watch, Erin said, "Ready to take a lunch break?"

"Just once more, ok?"

"Ok, just once," Erin said.

When Carly had finished her last swim, Erin wrapped her in a towel and hugged her tightly. "You should be so proud of yourself! I can't believe how fast you learned to swim!"

Carly beamed, looking longingly at the lake as Erin carried her into the cabin.

"Don't worry, Sweetie, the lake will be here after lunch."

After lunch, Erin told Carly they needed to rest and digest lunch before going back to the water. "And while we rest, why don't we read? What do you want to hear?"

Carly didn't answer at once, and then she said, "One of those Ramona books, and I'll read."

As Erin searched for a book she tried to hide her excitement. Carly had never wanted to read before, and she wondered if the child knew how. But she'd soon find out. "Here's one, 'Ramona the Pest,' how does that sound?"

"It sounds good," Carly answered. She was curled up on the couch. "Just come sit next to me in case I need help with some words."

"Okay, then," Erin said as she sat next to Carly, "here it is, read to me please."

"Yes, Mama, I will." And she began reading, struggling with some of the words, but not asking for help. The more she read, the better she got. Then she stopped to ask a question, "Why does Ramona's sister, Beezus, have such a funny name? I never heard of such a name!"

"Well, you're right, it is a funny name, and you'll find the answer to your question on the first page." Erin turned back a few pages and she pointed to the sentence.

Carly read, "Beezus, whose real name was Beatrice." She looked up at Erin, "Mama, so it's like another name for Beatrice?"

Erin had to smile at the way Carly drew out the name 'Beatrice.' She said, "That's right, Carly, and it's called a nickname. Have you heard of that before?"

"Yes, yes I have, Mama, but I never knew what that meant. I thought it was a kid named Nick!" She laughed, "How silly of me! But I don't like the name Beatrice any more than I like Beezus!"

"Me, either!" Erin concurred.

***

Rory had eaten lunch in the office, while the others went out. She wasn't feeling well, and didn't want to go anywhere, except maybe home for a warm bath. She felt cramping in her stomach and wondered if it was indigestion. Of course she knew what it was and didn't want to admit to anyone what was wrong. She was tired of carrying (literally!) her secret around and confiding only in her OB/GYN. As much as she liked Sally as a friend, she wasn't up for medical advice.

She stood up and walked around her office, trying to work the cramps out. It actually felt better than sitting. She walked over to her window, which looked out onto Olive Street. Not much action on the street today, she thought, blaming it on the hot, humid weather.

As she turned to leave the window, she saw movement and was drawn to it. Someone was bent over picking up something. He looked familiar, so she continued to watch, and realized it was Rowe. He stayed in a bent position for a while, and when he stood up he pulled his left pant leg down. She saw just a glimpse of his ankle bracelet before his pants covered it.

She went back to her desk, deciding to wait until he came in. But he never did.

Hearing Forsythe's cell phone buzz a few moments later, she crept closer to the work site. "Forsythe here…yes, of course you can take a half sick day, you probably came back too soon. Oh, and Rowe, don't forget to call the sheriff's office. I don't feel like having those bozos come back here like the third Reich!" He laughed.

Rory went back to her office and sat down to think. Now Rowe had just been here, so why wouldn't he come in and tell Forsythe he wasn't coming back to work. She was reasonably sure what he'd done was to remove his bracelet and then, just now, reattach it. That was what he was doing when she saw him. And he'd probably done it yesterday when he followed the bogeyman and then saved Marilyn. She'd wondered how he'd pulled that off, and then got home ahead of the sheriffs.

So, if her suppositions were correct, Rowe knew who the bogeyman was. Perhaps he'd had an epiphany in therapy and was playing vigilante. She would have to ponder this some more and see just what he was up to.

Rory's thoughts were interrupted as her staff came in from lunch. It seemed as though they were having a serious discussion. She wanted to be in on it, so she called, "Hey, guys what's up?"

Blake led the group as they straggled in and took seats. Blake wasted no time spilling his news. "Well, Rory it looks like the bogeyman struck again, or almost, like yesterday. Katrina called me at lunch to say that Dara had called her…"

"And," Rory said, circling her hand, "get it out!"

"And, Rachel was with her father at the therapist's office, when the bogeyman, we assume it was he, came into the waiting room and tried to take Rachel. She screamed and he ran off. That's all she wrote."

"Lots of questions come to mind, like, why was she alone in the waiting room, and how did he know she was alone? You know regular questions, like that," Rory said.

"I asked Katrina," Blake said, "and she said it was all 'like the perfect storm,' you know when events just happen all at once."

"I'm still not getting it," Rory said.

Sam tried to explain it. "Okay, so Dad is in with the therapist for a few minutes, and the receptionist goes to the bathroom, and voila, bogeyman enters and tries to grab, or at least walks toward, Rachel and she screams."

"OK, Sam it's getting better, but how did Dad enter the picture?"

"The therapist wanted to see him," Blake said. "Anyway, they went to see Herrera and he spoke with them and tried to get a description of the man. You know, three-year-olds are not real good at describing what they see, especially since she was scared. And Herrera thought it would be pointless to do another lineup, given that she couldn't give the most rudimentary description."

"So the bastard struck again, and we still got nuthin'!" Rory said. But she had a good idea what Rowe had been up to.

Chapter 61

Kraft was going stir crazy at the ski cabin. It wasn't ski season, and there really wasn't much to do up here without snow, besides hiking. And he'd left in a hurry without his dog, so he had no company. He'd been thinking, and probably over-thinking, the bogeyman case. He had his suspicions, but that didn't get him squat. He needed to be back in the action, or at least back to work. He was sure he knew and worked with the suspect, but had no evidence. That seemed to be what stood between law enforcement and the predator.

He needed to call Herrera, tell him he was coming in. Herrera picked up. "Hey, it's Kraft, I've gotta' come home, can't take it up here much longer!"

***

Rory was late getting to the office. She'd stopped to see her doctor/friend, Sally Flynn. She just wanted something for the cramping; it had kept her awake the night before.

Sally was kind and gentle with her, not asking whether or not she'd told Marc. Rory appreciated that. She figured Sally knew there was no point endangering their friendship by delving into Rory's marital situation.

She'd said, "Unfortunately, the only medication you can take is Ibuprofen. I don't know if that will give you relief, but that's our only option. Well, that and bed rest, which I know doesn't fit into your schedule."

"Actually, I've been napping after work every day, instead of jogging."

"That's good, and you may want to put heat on the area. Oh, and elevate your feet."

"Thanks, Sally," Rory had said, "for everything!" She hugged her before leaving.

Pulling up near the office, she began looking for parking. A car pulled out of a prime space just in time, and she congratulated herself. Rory was feeling better since her visit with Sally.

As she entered the office, she soon discovered Sam and Blake were next door in the construction area. She hadn't seen it for a while, so she went through.

Forsythe and several of his men were there, discussing last minute details.

Walking into the office and looking around, Rory said, "It looks wonderful!"

Forsythe looked pleased. "Well, we're trying to bring it in on time and under budget," he said. "It should be finished in a week."

"Hmm," Rory said, "Maybe I should give up my office and move over here!" She was only half kidding. Citadel had done a very classy job with the new offices.

When they'd finished the tour, Rory thanked Forsythe. Walking back to the other side, she said to her associates, "By the way, did I tell you my memory is coming back bit by bit?" She hoped this did not fall on deaf ears.

Blake and Sam looked at her quizzically.

'I'm wondering how quickly, since you've already told us at least twice," Sam joked.

***

The bogeyman was beyond angry: he was livid. Every way he turned he was thwarted. All of his enemies had survived and somehow had been spirited away. Rowe was responsible, he was sure of that. It was getting to the point where he'd have to leave town. Now it seemed Rory might be on to him. What could she remember? Did she see the murder? Is that what she'd remembered? No, if she had, he'd be gone. But it could happen any day now.

And that bitch reporter had written another awful, lying article about him, but she was nowhere to be found.

Forsythe was on his case about missing too much work. He'd had to remind Forsythe of the dirt he had on him, from Afghanistan, and his boss was none too happy about that threat, but it shut him up for the moment.

And what about Carly? Was she gone from him, too? She was the perfect partner, and she'd been taken away by those do-gooders! He'd made her happy and she would've satisfied him, for a while…

Perhaps he could find another willing girl before he left town, so it wasn't all in vain. He had much to do before he left.

Chapter 62

Carly was beginning to talk with Erin about 'Charlie.' The woman was pleased and surprised the child trusted her enough. She listened to Carly, keeping any judgment to herself. But each time Carly opened up, Erin listened intently, writing notes when Carly was sleeping. She had to hold back on any questioning because it was a tentative trust and could easily be destroyed.

She spoke with Herrera daily, always when the child was asleep or otherwise distracted. Carly, she knew, had an uncanny ability to hear what was going on around her. She no doubt developed this hypersensitivity out of necessity, given her background

As she thought about Carly, Erin had an epiphany; she could not give this child up. She would have to talk to Marilyn as soon as things got back to normal. She would either be Carly's foster mother indefinitely, or, better still, adopt her. She would say nothing to the child until it was certain. Carly had already met with more broken promises than any child should have to bear. Still, she had incredible resilience.

***

Sam was mulling over the accumulated case notes and reports. He was as frustrated as anyone about the abundance of evidence and dearth of results. He had to get out of the office, so he decided to re-interview the men who'd been at the poker game. That would include Rowe, he thought. Rowe might have some insight into the bogeyman's identity. But, he thought he'd start with Caldwell, so he went to Forsythe's office to find out where the man was working. While he was at it he asked about Rowe and Quinn.

"Caldwell is working at the new construction on Baltimore Pike, near the Sterling Pig, you know, that brew pub. Mason is working here today, but he's out at the moment, and Quinn took today off."

"I do know where that pub is," Sam answered. "So I guess Caldwell is the only one I can see right now. Will you let me know when either of the others is back?"

"Will do," Forsythe said, turning back to his paperwork.

After leaving the office, Sam decided to walk the several blocks to the work site. He liked walking in Media, and at least they weren't in the middle of a heat wave today.

Arriving at the work site, Sam tried to figure out who the foreman might be. He went up to the person who seemed to be in charge, and identified himself, asking to see Alistair Caldwell.

"Sorry, he's not here," the foreman said.

"Any idea where I might find him?" Sam asked.

"No idea; he wasn't scheduled to work here today."

***

Hayley was taking notes as Marilyn talked about her abduction. This would be a very good article, Hayley thought. The bogeyman would become more unhinged when he read it. She would have it to her editor by day's end and it would go into tomorrow's paper.

When the interview was finished, Hayley said, "We'd better get on the road, Don."

"I'm ready," Don said.

They said their goodbyes to Marilyn and Ryan. "Thanks for the interview, and stay safe!" Hayley added.

***

The bogeyman watched as that bitch Chandler and Kraft emerged from the police station. They stood for a while on the front steps talking. What were they saying? He wished he were close enough to hear. They were probably gloating over Chandler's brilliant move, springing her client from jail.

Why had he been released? Was he wearing a bracelet, like Rowe? Not that it made any difference, Rowe could ditch it whenever he wanted to, *whenever he decides to follow me*, he thought bitterly. Even the stupid ass sheriffs hadn't been able to catch him, despite the tip.

Kraft presented another obstacle, and was on the bogeyman's shit list. He needed to find out what he was up to, if he was suspicious.

***

Kraft offered Rory a ride back to the office, but she preferred to walk. He told her he'd be at the office later. As she walked, she thought about the ton of evidence they'd discovered. All they needed was a person to match it with.

Rory thought of all the things she'd put on the back burner as she pursued this case. Marc was a niggling worry that was always there, and the more time elapsed the more difficult it became. Before long she'd be showing, surely she should tell him before that happened.

Her pregnancy made her think of Ginny, and she realized that although she'd meant to call her sister-in-law several times to offer congratulations, she hadn't done it. She decided to walk into town now and get her something, maybe a teddy bear, and send it with a card.

Suddenly, she felt, rather than saw, someone following. When she stopped walking, another set of footsteps stopped. Well, she'd decided to do this, and at least it was daylight and she was in familiar territory. She ducked down an alley and upped her pace. Then she cut through a parking lot, and came out on another street.

She looked in one direction, and when she turned to look the other way, she came face to face with a man. "Why Mr. Caldwell, fancy meeting you here!"

Chapter 63

Jordan Kraft got into his late model red Mustang and left the police station. He was planning to go into the office, but first wanted to stop by his house to drop off his stuff, pick up his dog from his neighbor, and maybe get a shower. He was tired of the cold showers at the cabin. He lived outside of Media, not far, but far enough to feel like the country. He actually rented one of the stately old houses in Ridley Creek State Park. He'd recently become aware of a vacancy and was happy to move there. The rent was low, the house was in decent shape, but most of all he had privacy. He sat far back from the bike trail and had trees and wildlife to entertain him.

Kraft had to get out of his car to open the gate to the park's bike trail, which was never locked. Out of the corner of his eye, he saw another car pull in, hanging back a bit. Was he being followed? If so, he could take the guy on a merry run around the park; he knew it like the back of his hand. Deliberately leaving the gate open, he drove slowly down the bike trail, careful to watch for walkers, joggers and bikers. It was, after all, their trail.

As he went up a hill and rounded a bend, he hazarded a peek in his rearview. Yep, there was a blue Chevy behind him, still a ways back. Ok, game on!

He drove to the park mansion, the previous owner of which had willed all of his land, including the mansion, to the state. He meandered through the parking lot and parked close to the mansion. The place wasn't packed but there were cars scattered throughout.

Getting out of his car, he stretched, surreptitiously glancing around. He saw the blue car park a few rows back. Kraft walked deliberately into the mansion, now the park office. Once inside he took his time looking at pamphlets and maps. Then he walked around the first floor, which was open to the public, admiring the carved paneling, huge fireplace, and large leaded windows. He peered out one of the windows now, but couldn't quite see the blue car. Maybe he'd imagined it, maybe not.

Getting back into his car, Kraft decided he was ready to go home now, with or without a follower.

The blue car appeared again as Kraft neared his home. He would soon see whether or not this was a coincidence. There were two homes back here off the long drive. He drove to his house, got out of the car and walked to the neighbor's house to retrieve his dog. Riley was jubilant at Kraft's return, running circles around him and barking. Jordan took him into the house, along with his backpack and other items he'd taken to the cabin.

***

Sam was walking back from the construction site, wondering why Caldwell hadn't been there. He was talking with Sarah on the phone, asking if she wanted to take a break and meet him in Media.

"Sounds like a good idea," Sarah said. "I've about had it with torts and Supreme Court decisions; I'm afraid my head will explode!"

"Yeah, definitely time for a break. Why don't we meet at Seven Stones, and then we can decide what to do about dinner, ok?"

"Ok, as long as dinner doesn't involve me lifting a finger!"

"Deal!" Sam said, "I'm headed there now."

As he approached Seven Stones Café, his jaw dropped. There sat Rory and Alistair Caldwell at an outdoor table, apparently having a serious talk.

He hesitated, wondering if he should interrupt their discussion. Rory, facing him, looked up and seeing Sam, motioned him over.

"Hey!" he said. "Good to see you. I was just looking for you, Alistair, at the construction near the Sterling Pig."

Caldwell looked surprised. "I'm off today; who sent you there?"

"Forsythe," Sam said.

Alistair shook his head, frowning. "I don't know, but Forsythe is missing a lot these days. Maybe the pressure of the investigation…"

"Is that why he's always asking questions?" Sam asked.

Rory nodded, "I think he's losing it."

"It's sad, really," Caldwell said, "he's always been a bright guy and a good leader."

"Anyway," Sam said, "how'd you and Rory end up here?"

"I was looking for Rory, wanted to have a few words with her," Caldwell said.

***

Dara and Paul Keene, along with their daughter Rachel, had, just left Herrera's office.

The detective was amazed that the bogeyman was still around and eluding capture. His gut feeling was that the bogeyman would be caught soon. This case was odd in that they had accumulated a mountain of evidence, but they needed to find the right man.

His secure phone buzzed, and the caller was Erin as he'd expected. He spent a few moments bringing her up to speed on the latest news of the bogeyman.

"Jeez," she said, "With all the mayhem he's perpetrated, you'd think someone would be able to ID him!"

"There's the rub," he said. "The adult victims of his attacks didn't see him, because he usually attacks from behind. And Rachel is too young to give any kind of viable description. Your girl Carly is probably the only person alive who knows who the bogeyman is."

"Well, then I guess it's a good time to hear that Carly's begun to talk about 'Charlie.'"

***

Rachel was taking a nap, while Paul and Dara discussed how they would keep her safe.

"I could stay the night," Paul offered. "Then, maybe you can take off some time from work and go to your sister's. How's it been working out staying with her?"

"It's gone surprisingly smoothly, and she's been very welcoming. We're closer than we've been in years."

"I'm glad to hear it," Paul said. "Life's too short to hang on to anger and disappointment, especially in the family."

Paul was talking about them as a family, and Dara was reading between the lines. Sadly, she couldn't go back to a marital relationship with Paul, even if things didn't work out with Mason.

Dara's cell buzzed, and seeing it was Mason, she excused herself to take the call in her office.

"Hi Dara, just calling to see how you and Rachel are doing. Are you at your sister's yet?"

"We'll go tomorrow, Paul's staying tonight. Rachel is fine, she's napping now."

Chapter 64

Jordan Kraft had been looking out the top floor window with his binoculars, waiting to see if the bogeyman, he assumed it was he, was coming for him. He could just make out the car, hidden in deep woods, off the drive, as the sun glinted off the windshield. The driver was not visible, but he continued to watch for any movement. His loyal dog sat by his side looking out the window as if he knew what was going on. Perhaps he did know, Kraft thought.

Kraft saw a flash of white, as two deer ran off into deeper woods, and he immediately commanded, “Shh!” to the dog before he could bark. Now he tried to focus on what had spooked the deer. Soon he saw the stealthy movements of a person who didn’t want to be seen. He stopped often, and sometimes it was difficult to see him until he moved. Clearly his pursuer was not in a hurry, and was obviously trying to take Jordan unawares.

When the intruder came within sight of the house, Kraft made his decision. “Come, Riley,” he commanded and the dog followed him down the steps.

Opening the front door, he gave the command, “Sic him!”

***

Having finished her conversation with Caldwell, Rory had stayed at the café with Sam until Sarah arrived. She’d been glad they were able to ‘kill two birds with one stone’ so to speak. Caldwell had wanted to speak with Rory out of the office to express his concern that the bogeyman might be one of them. After chatting with them, and asking Sarah how her studies were coming, Rory took her leave.

As she walked, she weighed Caldwell’s words. Again, the dilemma was whether this was misdirection, or was Caldwell legit? She was second-guessing herself and coming up short.

She stopped at the Hallmark store to buy a card and a little bear for Ginny. Then she went to the post office to box and mail it. That was a big item to check off her list and she felt better for it.

Before she went home, however, she wanted to stop by the office and talk to Kraft. She thought he might have an idea who the bogeyman was, and she'd try to get it out of him. He'd been very forthcoming so far.

As she walked, she called Alex on her cell. "Hey, Mom, what's up?"

"Alex, I hate to ask, but…"

"You don't have to ask. I already know what you want." She didn't sound pleased.

"Yes, well, you and Kate, if you don't mind." Rory said

"Kate's out with the bf, and does it matter if I mind?" Alex asked, clearly not pleased at the prospect.

"Ok, just never mind!" Rory said angrily.

"I'll do it!" Alex said, hanging up.

"Damn!" Rory said, feeling guilty. She knew Alex was going through an identity crisis.

They hadn't really talked any more about Alex's situation, but her daughter seemed to be doing ok. And she was back in therapy.

The office was empty when Rory arrived, but she heard some noise in the construction area. She walked through the curtains and saw only Forsythe, at his desk doing paperwork. He looked up, "Yes, um, Rory?"

"I was looking for Jordan Kraft. He said he was coming back to the office after he stopped at home for a bit."

Forsythe looked shocked, "He's out?"

"Yes, I met with Herrera today and we arranged for him to be released. He was asked not to leave the area."

"Why didn't you tell me?" Forsythe asked.

"Well, I didn't want to tell you before I went because I wasn't sure it would happen," Rory improvised as she spoke. "And I expected Kraft would tell you himself when he came in. But perhaps he decided not to," Rory said.

She walked back to her office, as she heard Forsythe punching a number into his cell.

"He's not answering!" Forsythe yelled from next door.

Rory walked back to address him. "You know, maybe he's just really tired, he's had a rough couple of days. I'm sure he'll be back tomorrow."

She sounded more confident than she felt. She was sure that Kraft had been planning to come back to the office, so why hadn't he? She was a bit nervous, but felt Kraft could handle himself.

***

The bogeyman was running for his life. That fucking dog had taken a chunk out of his leg, and it was bleeding. The dog had chased him all the way to the car, and he'd finally pushed him off when he got into the car. The dog had tried to get into the car, and was barking furiously. He'd never gotten along with Riley, even when he was the 'company dog,' in Afghanistan. He'd kicked him a few times, and he was sure the dog hadn't forgotten.

He had to get out of there quick before the neighbors heard him. It took a bit of maneuvering to back out of the woods, but he was motivated to leave. In his haste, he almost ran into a jogger, who turned and shook his fist.

Oh, fuck, that's all I need, an angry jogger, he thought, as he drove off in the opposite direction, being careful to go slowly and not bring unwanted attention. He wasn't sure where he was going since he had just followed Kraft when he came in, but sure as shit he wasn't asking for directions.

He saw the sign for the park office, and figured that might be a way out.

***

The angry jogger flagged the park ranger's car as it drove by. The ranger stopped and rolled down his window. "Can I help you?" he asked.

"I'm not sure if you can, but some asshole, sorry, this jerk, who was parked in the woods back there, just about ran me over!"

"Did it just happen?" he asked.

"Yeah, less than a minute ago, back there by the driveway. Follow me, I'll show you," the jogger said.

As he followed the jogger, he phoned the main office, calling to the jogger, "What was the color and make of the car?"

"An older model blue Chevy, I think," he answered.

The ranger called in the description of the car and asked to be apprised if they found it.

He got out of the car and walked over to the jogger.

“It was right here,” the jogger said. “See, you can tell where he drove off the driveway.” He pointed to the deep grooves in the mud.

Jordan walked down to the ranger and jogger. “Yeah, there was another ‘tourist’ here. It happens a lot, and sometimes I have to send the dog after them. That usually works.”

Jordan walked back to his house, sure that it had been the bogeyman, but he hadn’t seen his face. Although he was pretty sure Riley had left an impression.

Chapter 65

Mason was upset when he ended the call with Dara. Why was Paul staying at the house? Was it possible he and Dara were reconciling? Were they sleeping together? He couldn't abide the thought.

Not that he'd blame Dara if it happened. Paul was getting his act together, and being responsible. While he had been unable to see her, hold her…he had to stop the other thoughts that came to him.

She didn't know he'd been out every free moment trying to track down the bogeyman. He couldn't tell her that no matter what, the bogeyman wouldn't have taken Rachel from the office, because he was there watching.

It was late, but he had to talk with Dara. She answered on the second ring.

"Mason, is something wrong?"

"I just had to tell you how much I love you!"

"I love you, too, and I miss you…why don't you come over? Everyone's asleep, just come in quietly."

Apparently, she hadn't thought about the monitor, and he was glad she hadn't asked.

***

Rory went into the office early the next day, even though she'd been up late. She and Marc had stayed up for a while talking after Sarah and Sam left. It was good to have Marc's opinion on the case and his insight. But with all the drama going on, Rory had still been unable to discuss with Marc her most pressing matter. She'd have hell to pay later, but for now…well, she had so much to attend to.

Rory went straight to her office to do some paper work. She had a backlog of cases, since she'd been focusing almost entirely on Rowe, not that she had much to show for it. Sam had taken over many of her cases when she was on vacation and in the hospital, so the load was lighter than it would've been.

She was in the process of scheduling cases for court when her phone rang. “Hello, Detective, how are you?”

“I’m fine, thanks, I just wanted to tell you I finally got the results back from the lab test on the ‘unknown substance’ that was found in Rachel’s vagina. Don’t know what took so long. Anyway, it turned out to be lubricant used on condoms. Figure that one out!”

***

The bogeyman was burning up with fever. He might have rabies for all he knew. He felt like shit, and certainly couldn’t go to work. Forsythe had been a real jerk when he’d called him, saying he’d heard all the excuses before and he needed to get his ass to work. Forsythe had hung up on him. How dare he! Apparently, he’d forgotten the dirty little secret he would tell Forsythe’s wife. He was sure she didn’t know her husband went both ways.

His leg really needed attention, and he couldn’t go to any major hospital. He wondered if he could go to ‘Minute Clinic,’ in one of the pharmacies, but figured they’d send him to an ER because they probably weren’t equipped to do stitches. He wondered if he could do them, but he almost threw up at the thought.

He knew some guys who operated under the radar; maybe they knew shady doctors. Before he could make the call, he fell back to sleep, exhausted.

***

Dara had taken her time getting ready to leave for her sister’s. Last night after Mason called, he came to the house, and more importantly, to her bed. She had yearned for him, so she was happy to see him and make intimate contact. She realized he took a risk coming to her, but he assured her it would be fine. Their time together had been more than just physical; they had talked for hours. The doubts she’d been having seemed to evaporate when he was with her. Since Paul was sleeping on the third floor in the back of the house, she doubted he’d heard anything. Not that she really cared. She was engaged to Mason, after all.

Everything seemed to be normal with Paul as they sat at breakfast. She’d known there was no future with Paul, and seeing Mason had confirmed it. Mason had told her he was afraid that she and Paul might be reconciling. When she told him that wasn't happening, he'd been relieved.

Paul was leaving after breakfast. He asked Dara to call him when she arrived at her sister's.

"Rachel, come say goodbye to Daddy," Dara said now.

The child ran to her father and gave him a hug and kiss. "Bye Daddy, love you."

After he'd left, Rachel asked, "When can I see Mason?"

Chapter 66

Rory called Rowe in when she saw him enter the office. "Good morning," she said. "You're looking chipper today. Getting lots of sleep?"

"Yeah, it helps. What's up?"

"I just heard back from the detective. He finally got the lab report on the 'unknown substance' found in Rachel's vagina. It's condom lubricant." She let that sink in as she watched confusion, and then recognition appear on his face.

"So that means, the guy was wearing a rubber, so why was there semen found?"

"Bingo!" Rory said. "That obviously gives credence to the idea that the semen was planted, especially given the method of your condom disposal."

"Yeah, kind of stupid of me as I think about it," Rowe said, looking at his feet.

"I'm not sure too many people think about what happens once they dispose of their condoms. What happened to you was pretty unlikely, but certainly possible, given the mind of the bogeyman."

"Anyway," Rory continued, "I want to schedule your case for court, and if you agree, we'll have it heard by a judge, no jury."

"You can do that? I've never heard of it."

"Most people haven't heard of it unless they're in the legal system."

"So, tell me about it. Why would we do it?"

"There are many advantages in your case. First, your case has gotten a lot of publicity, so a jury is bound to have some preconceived ideas. Second, I can get it scheduled quickly. Third, the judges, and there are only a few, chosen by the president judge to do these trials, are experienced. Lastly, the process moves much more quickly. What do you think?"

"It sounds like a no-brainer. There must be some drawbacks."

"The major drawback is that your fate is held in the hands of one person. But frankly, having seen some of the juries' decisions over the years, I'd opt for this."

"I have to trust you on this. How soon can we do it?"

"As soon as I can schedule it, and we can schedule it more quickly because there's no jury to be picked. We've gathered a lot of information, so it's a question of scheduling it and getting our witnesses. And of course, I'll have to run it by the DA."

"Just how risky do you think this is?" Rowe asked.

"Honestly, when you consider that most of the people on juries have no knowledge of the law, are easily swayed by the often dramatic antics of district attorneys, and come with their own prejudices, this seems far less risky."

"So, I guess you don't want to wait until the bogeyman is caught?" Mason asked.

"Frankly, I'm tired of waiting for that to happen. I think you deserve an acquittal, and I think we can make that happen. Why wait?"

Rory continued, "It's your decision. I've spoken from my own bias. And, before you ask, I have been pleased with the outcomes of the non-jury cases I've pled. I've done only a handful, but it's my preference. I think the DA will agree that your case qualifies."

"Ok, I say let's do it!"

***

The bogeyman had been out of commission for a day, but he'd found a 'doctor'-- he hadn't asked questions--to stitch him up, for an outrageous sum. The money was really 'hush money,' he understood. And he did feel much better, although a bit woozy from the narcotics he'd been given. Still, his leg hurt like a bitch from that damn dog! He really had bad luck with dogs.

He'd have to lay low for a bit, but soon he had to get out of town, whenever he could get his things together, even though it meant leaving a lot behind. He had to stay free to play another day. He'd burned his bridges here, although he might be able to find a little girl to take with him.

***

Erin and Carly were growing more attached every day. Sometimes, after she'd put Carly to bed, Erin looked at the sleeping child and wondered what she'd do without her.

Carly was playing with Sgt. Pepper, rolling around on the floor. Suddenly, she sat up and said, "Mama, I love you so much!"

Erin went to the girl and knelt down next to her. "Give me a hug," she said to hide her tears. "I love you more!" she said, trying to make a joke.

"No, Mama, you don't understand, I love you more than I ever loved anyone." She said it quietly, as if she just realized it was true. "You're the only person who never hurts me. And even when you ask me to do things I don't want to do, I do it because I trust you."

That word, 'trust,' Erin wondered that Carly had any idea what it was, but apparently she was learning.

Then Carly began to sob, a wracking, deep sobbing.

"What's the matter, Sweetheart, what happened?" Erin asked, rubbing Carly's back.

The child couldn't catch her breath long enough to speak, so Erin rocked her, making soothing noises, until Carly finally settled.

Carly looked at her Mama and said quietly, "I have something to tell you. But I'm afraid you won't love me anymore."

"Carly," Erin said, cupping her chin and looking her in the eye, "I don't think there's anything you could say that would stop me from loving you."

"But I lied," she said. "And you tell me it's best to tell the truth."

"That's true, it is. It always makes you feel better when you tell the truth."

"But it was a big lie, and it hurt someone."

"I'm sure whoever it hurt will forgive you," Erin said, wondering what was coming next.

Carly took a deep breath, and then blurted out, "You know the day Sgt. Pepper fell down and you said somebody gave him drugs? Well, Charlie did that, he was there in the yard. And he told me when I went to the lineup I should pick the tallest guy, so I did. But that was wrong and I knew it was wrong."

Not believing what she was hearing, Erin took a moment.

Taking the silence as a bad sign, Carly's chin began to tremble. "I knew you'd be mad at me."

"I'm not angry at all," Erin said, pulling her close. "I'm so pleased you're brave enough to tell the truth!"

"It was hard," Carly acknowledged, "but I didn't like myself. And I didn't like Charlie for hurting Sgt. Pepper. And I might get him in trouble, but what he did was wrong."

Erin nodded, feeling there was more to come.

"Charlie was in the lineup, he was number 1."

Erin couldn't remember who number one was, but she was sure Herrera would know immediately.

"I guess you know, Carly, I have to tell the detective, that I would be dishonest if I didn't tell him. This is a secret I can't keep."

"Yes, Mama, I know. And I trust you. I figured out Charlie wasn't really my friend because he hurt my dog and asked me to lie. But why did he pretend to be my friend?"

"He probably doesn't know how to get friends," Erin said simply, knowing there was much more.

***

Herrera had received Officer Scott's news, and could hardly believe his good fortune. Now he knew, or surmised that he knew the identity of the bogeyman. This was a tricky situation, though, especially since Carly lied at the lineup. And though he trusted Erin's professional judgment, he could tell she loved this child, and that would certainly affect the way she looked at the situation. If he took the wrong man into custody, it would tip off the real perp, who would then, in all probability, leave town. That was, if he hadn't left already. There'd been a day without a bogeyman sighting. He was glad, but it wasn't as simple as it seemed.

He would certainly put the man under surveillance 24/7. They would have to play this carefully if they wanted the charges to stick.

Herrera decided to also beef up surveillance of the remaining suspects. He called in a few of his best men, and swore them to secrecy. They would proceed with caution and not allow this news to get out.

***

Rory had scheduled Rowe's case for court. She was surprised at how quickly it had been arranged. Rowe would have his day in court in just a few days.

Sam helped Rory get the witnesses subpoenaed and together they compiled the evidence that had accrued. He'd contacted Don, who was on his way to bring Hayley back home. Rory was fairly certain she had a solid case. And whatever happened with the bogeyman, it was important that Rowe be cleared in court.

Rory wondered if the bogeyman had left town. He hadn't attacked anyone recently, at least as far as she knew.

Chapter 67

By the day of Rowe's trial, the bogeyman had still not been seen or heard from. It prompted Rory again to wonder if he had left town. She'd also heard rumors that Herrera had upped surveillance on the remaining suspects.

Whatever was going on with the bogeyman was not at the forefront of Rory's mind. She had been preparing for trial, and was elated and frightened at the same time. She knew Judge Jenkins was presiding over the trial, and was relieved to know that, although there was always the niggling worry that it might be the horrid Judge Dickenson. She put that thought out of her mind so she could review her case notes.

Rowe entered her office, looking very handsome in his suit and tie. He had a worried look on his face, and began to pace the office.

"Mason," she said quietly, getting his attention. "Of course you're worried, there's much at stake. Do you have any questions before we go over?"

"I don't really know what to ask, but the obvious one is 'will we win?' And I know you don't have the answer to that."

"No I don't, but I have faith. I think we've covered all the bases. I'm not sure yet if I want you to testify, we'll just see how it's going, ok?"

"You're the boss, I trust you to make that call. And I'm prepared to go on the stand if you think it will help."

"All right, I think it's time we head over, ready?"

"As I'll ever be," Rowe said, with a resolute look on his face.

***

The bogeyman was ready to go. True, he would have to leave many of his belongings behind, but that wouldn't matter. He had some cash, but he planned to get his last paycheck from Forsythe before he left. He'd wait until the end of the day, since Forsythe usually was the last to leave the office.

His car was in the garage; he'd ditched the blue Chevy because it had probably been seen too much. He opened the door leading to the garage from the house and put more boxes into the trunk.

Glancing out the small garage window, he saw a car, which he immediately suspected was an undercover police car. He watched as it cruised slowly up and down the street. Surveillance, for sure, he thought.

Fuck! Maybe he wasn't ready to leave. He would have to think of something.

***

Sam and Sarah met Rory and Mason Rowe outside the courtroom. Sam was second chair, and Sarah would sit behind them in the body of the courtroom. Since this trial was handled by a judge without a jury, it had a specific time to commence.

"I guess we can go in and get settled," Rory said.

They entered the courtroom and Rory, Sam and Rowe sat at the defense table.

Dylan Jefferson sat across from them and, when they sat, he came over to talk.

"Good morning Rory, Sam and Mr. Rowe," he said. "I thought I should alert you that Judge Jenkins is sick, and we don't know yet who will replace her."

"Well," Rory said, her face drained of color, "if we don't like the judge we can always ask for a continuance. Thanks for letting us know."

Rory checked her watch, saying "We're already behind by five minutes. I hope that doesn't mean they're having trouble finding a judge."

A few minutes of strained silence ensued.

Then the bailiff came out and announced, "All rise, court is now in session, the Honorable President Judge, Arnold Hall presiding."

Rory caught her breath, astonished that the President Judge would hear the case. They couldn't ask for more. He had a reputation for fairness, but Rory had never gone before him. She would have to be extra skillful. She whispered to Sam, "Wish me luck!"

The judge nodded to Dylan Jefferson. "Mr. Jefferson, would you please outline the State's case?"

"Yes Your Honor," the DA said, as he remained standing. "The defendant, Mason Rowe appears before you today charged with child molestation, a felony of the first degree. The State's case hinges on the fact that the defendant's DNA, found in semen on the victim, a three year old child, was that of Mason Rowe. The police reports and lab results are before you."

"Continue," the judge said, when the silence had stretched out.

"That concludes the State's case." Dylan fidgeted, and then sat down.

The judge appeared confused, and looked through his reports for a moment.

"All right, can we hear from the defense?" He nodded in Rory's direction.

"Your Honor," Rory began. "Mr. Rowe appears to have been charged solely because of the DNA match. He voluntarily gave his DNA before it was requested. The defense would argue that while many consider DNA evidence to be proof positive, it is well known that DNA evidence is easily corrupted. We will show testimony as to how Mr. Rowe's DNA might have been planted on the victim."

Rory continued, "Additionally, there are a number of incidents following the alleged molestation, that point to the so called bogeyman, and could not have been carried out by Mr. Rowe. In the first case, Mr. Rowe was in prison when a co-worker of his, who had previously been interviewed by Mr. Logan, was murdered in the law offices. The murder occurred the day after the victim, Gordon Howe, had left a message asking to meet with Mr. Logan, ASAP, citing new information."

"Following the murder, Mr. Rowe was released on bail, and fitted with an electronic monitor. The point being that Rowe's movements were tracked from that point on, while other victims were attacked by the person who is most probably the bogeyman."

The judge interrupted Rory, saying, "I've read both sex offender evaluations, and I've read the numerous police reports alleging attacks on victims related to the case. To expedite this trial, I would ask that you call your witnesses. Is the State in agreement with that, or do you have witnesses you wish to call?"

"Not at the present time," Jefferson replied.

"Then Ms. Chandler, please proceed."

Rory called Roy Thomas, a Citadel employee, not one of the

original five.

After he was sworn in as a witness, Rory asked, "Mr. Thomas, thank you for appearing today. I realize the information you have to offer may be somewhat sensitive, but it is germane to the case."

Thomas nodded.

"I earlier made the statement that DNA evidenced is easily corrupted. We have ascertained from Mr. Rowe that his form of contraception is the condom. Can you tell the Court if you have any knowledge of how Mr. Rowe has disposed of his used condoms?"

"Well, as I told you before, it was a joke around the office that Mason was seen tossing his used condoms, which were in a lunch bag, into the company dumpster. Someone asked him why he was throwing his lunch away, and Rowe told him what was in the bag. He said that after his fiancée's daughter had found one in the toilet bowl, she'd insisted that he dispose of them elsewhere. I'm not sure that he disposed of them at work after that, but the story was out."

"You say it was common knowledge around the office?"

"Yeah, everyone thought it was funny. He got razzed a lot."

"So, how many people would you say, were aware of this?"

"Well, there are over one-hundred Citadel employees, and probably more than half, except maybe the newer guys, knew it."

"Thank you, Mr. Thomas, I have no further questions."

The DA stood and said, "Just one question, Mr. Thomas. How long do you recall this knowledge being widespread among your co-workers?"

"Couple of years," he answered.

"No further questions," the DA said.

"The witness may step down. Ms. Chandler, do you have more witnesses to call?"

"Yes Your Honor, I would like to call Marilyn Hunter to the stand."

Marilyn walked to the front of the courtroom and stood in the witness box to be sworn in.

"Ms. Hunter, can you please tell the Court where you are employed and how you have knowledge of this case."

"I am a caseworker for Children and Youth Services, and my specialty is placing children in foster homes, and facilitating adoptions. One of my foster children, Carly, who has a history of sexual abuse, was recently removed from a foster home where the foster parents were not, in my opinion, vigilant enough to keep her from a possible predator. During one of my visits, I noticed a necklace she was wearing, and admired it, asking where she'd gotten it. She told me that her friend, 'Charlie', who she'd met at the playground, had given it to her. It became apparent that 'Charlie', was a man, not a boy. The foster parents admitted that Carly had gone unescorted to the playground a few times."

"Consequently, I removed her from the home in question and placed her temporarily in a group home. The very night she was placed there, an attempt to take her was thwarted by vigilant staff. The intruder had slit the screen to her room, but fled before he could be caught."

"Thank you, Ms. Hunter. Can you tell the Court who, if anyone was suspected?"

Jefferson was on his feet, "Defense is leading the witness and asking for a supposition."

"Sustained," the judge ruled. "Ms. Chandler, can you rephrase the question?"

Looking through her notes, Rory said, "Ms. Hunter, can you tell the Court what happened as a result of this allegedly botched abduction?"

"We were fortunate to have a police officer, who'd questioned the girl about the incident, offer to be a temporary foster mother. That was quickly arranged. A few nights after Carly had been placed with Officer Scott, another possible abduction occurred. The officer's dog gave chase to the intruder, and apparently bit him. The dog was stabbed by the intruder, who got away."

"Was Carly ever able to give a description of this person?"

"Let me say it appeared she was *unwilling* to identify the person…"

"Objection! Your Honor, that again is supposition, not fact." Dylan Jefferson said.

"Sustained," the judge ruled. "Ms. Chandler, is it possible we could break for lunch at this point, and return at 1:30?"

"Yes, Your Honor," Rory answered.

"Court is adjourned until 1:30." He banged the gavel and left the courtroom.

Chapter 68

Having packed his things, and not seeing any suspicious cars come down his street, the bogeyman decided it was time to leave.

He'd driven for a few minutes when he noticed, a few cars back, the same car he'd seen on his street earlier. He'd be cool, abide by the traffic laws and find a way to lose them.

The most obvious thing to do, he thought, was to go to the office, and pretend he was going to work. So he drove to work and found a parking spot not too far from the office. After he parked the car, he took his time opening the trunk and taking out his tools. He looked through the box, as if searching for a particular tool. As he was presumably intent on that, he saw in his peripheral vision, the car that had been tailing him drive slowly by. When the car was out of sight, he jumped back in and backed up, making a quick U-turn, and driving in the opposite direction.

Now, what to do, he wondered as he cruised the streets of Media. It was only a matter of time until the undercover cops discovered his ruse. He would just have to go on instinct.

He soon came upon an older black woman, opening her garage door and taking out her trash. There was only one car in the garage. He pulled into her driveway, and offered to help her with the trash.

She looked at him suspiciously and said, "No, I don't need your help, and would you please move your car out of the drive?"

The bogeyman found it necessary to do it the hard way. "Well, I'm helping you whether you like it or not!" He grabbed her from behind and dragged her, with his hand over her mouth as she kicked and struggled, into the garage. Then he slugged her and she fell like a rock.

He ran back to put the trash can in the right place, jumped into his car and drove into the garage, quickly closing the door.

The woman was struggling to get up and he noticed her wig had slipped to the side of her head. Oh God, he thought, she was probably a cancer survivor, and he felt a momentary pang. "You need to do as I tell you," he said.

She was trembling, but didn't want to give in because her granddaughter was inside sleeping. In a show of defiance, she said, "I don't recall inviting you in, this here's Heddie Joneses' house. Now I have to get back in the house and take care of my granddaughter."

"You have a granddaughter?" he asked, trying to control his excitement.

***

Rory was having lunch with her client, Rowe, along with Sam and Sarah. They were discussing the morning's trial.

Rowe asked Rory, "What do you think?"

"Well, I'm surprised by the DA's absence of a case. He's really not putting up a fight."

"It seems they know they don't have a case," Sarah commented.

"Seriously," Sam said. "He offered the only thing they have, and that was DNA evidence. And Rory blew holes through that in short order."

"That's what I thought," Rowe commented. "Do you think he'll just give up at some point?"

"That's up to the judge. When he believes he has enough information to make a ruling, he can call it. I have tons more witnesses, if he wants to hear from all of them."

"Who goes on the stand next?" Rowe asked.

"Sam, who's next?" Rory asked.

"Uh, Hayley Singleton. Are you finished with Marilyn?"

"Hmm, not quite." Looking at her watch, Rory Jumped up. "Time to go back!"

***

The bogeyman followed Heddie upstairs when she heard the baby cry. She gave the man a frown and pursed her lips. "Why you think you have to follow me? You think I'm gonna jump out a window or somethin'?"

He looked at his watch, wondering how much longer he'd have to hide out here. Heddie didn't seem to be remotely cowed by him, and he respected her for that. She was just like his grandma. He was disappointed that her granddaughter was a baby. Some pervs went for that, but not him.

"I won't take too much of your time, but while I'm here, I need to keep track of you."

Once the baby was cleaned up and changed, Heddie carried her downstairs, as the bogeyman followed like a puppy dog.

"This here's Gemma, because she's a real gem!" Heddie said proudly. "Aren't you, Darlin'?" she said, kissing the baby's face.

"Yeah, she's real pretty," the bogeyman admitted. "I'll be leaving soon," he said. "And if you promise not to call the police, I won't have to tie you up."

"I don't have a real cozy relationship with the police, so if you don't do us harm, you don't have to worry about me."

For some reason, the bogeyman believed her. "I'll take you at your word," he said.

***

Herrera's men reported back to him. One of the suspects had made the tail and they'd lost him. When they'd seen him pull up at Rory's office and get his tools out, they moved on. He was a clever one, this bogeyman. At least they could concentrate their efforts, and they'd start setting up roadblocks on major arteries leading out of town.

Before they actually put a BOLO (Be on the lookout) on him, they'd wait for a positive ID by Carly. The girl had agreed to identify him by photo, and Erin would bring her down. It would be at least a few hours before Carly and Erin would arrive. Roadblocks would go up in the meantime.

***

Back in Court, Marilyn was reminded that she was still under oath. She took her seat and Rory began the questioning.

"Ms. Hunter, since you've removed Carly from the last foster home, have you had any other instances…"

"Leading the witness," Jefferson said.

"I'm going to allow that, Mr. Jefferson. There was one serious incident on which she's reported. You may answer the question," the judge addressed Ms. Hunter.

"I was working late at my office one night, and when I left, the security guard was not at the door. It made me uneasy so I hurried to my car. Just as I was getting in, I was pulled from behind by my hair."

"What happened next?" Rory prompted.

"I had pepper spray in my pocket and I directed the spray behind me, even though I couldn't see him. And I guess I hit him because he let go and ran off."

"Has anything else unusual happened to you, related to this case?"

Marilyn went on to describe her abduction and rescue by a "good Samaritan."

She was asked to step down because there were no more questions.

Hayley Singleton was next called to the stand. She relayed the numerous attacks and threatening messages she'd received in the wake of her editorials on the bogeyman in the Daily Times.

When she had finished, the judge said. "I believe I have heard enough testimony to have a good grasp of this case. I will reread the police reports, witness/victim statements and will take the case under advisement. I expect to have a verdict in under a week. In the meantime, Mr. Rowe is to remain on the monitor. That is the order of this Court." He banged the gavel and stood to leave the bench.

"Is that it?" Rowe asked. "I was hoping to have an answer today."

"Me, too," Rory said. "But he's very thorough, and I think he chose to read, rather than hear all the testimony. It could've taken a few more days to hear all of the witnesses. I think it's going in our favor. If he were skeptical, he would've continued with witnesses."

"God, I hope you're right! It would be such a blessing to go back to my life."

"It won't be long now, hang in there!"

Chapter 69

Following the court hearing, Rory went back to her office. She was feeling relieved, and optimistic. She called Marc.

He answered on the first ring. "How'd it go?"

"Well, we didn't get a verdict today; he's taking the case under advisement, and has promised a verdict in under a week. I put on only a fraction of witnesses. He decided to read their statements rather than take up Court time. The State had virtually no case outside of the DNA. Even the judge seemed surprised at that. But I have a good feeling about this."

"That's great Rory! Listen, why don't we celebrate with dinner out? You get to pick, and make reservations. I should be available by 6:30."

"Good idea, Marc. I think I'll get reservations at Spasso, ok?"

"Sure thing, and I'll meet you at 6:30, unless I hear different. Love you, Bye."

"Love you, too." Rory ended the call, a smile on her face.

***

Rory and Sam spent an hour or so discussing the trial.

"Sam, you did a great job as second chair, I couldn't have done it without you. You had it organized to perfection, and that's not my strong suit. Thanks!"

"Thank you, Rory, and I have to return the compliment. I think you were masterful in your presentation."

"I appreciate the vote of confidence. I have a strong feeling this will go our way. And the President Judge is not to be trifled with! I think he'll come to the right decision."

"I sure hope so," Sam said. "Do you mind if I get going now? Sarah and I might go out for dinner."

"You've earned your keep, go on home to Sarah. And if you want to eat at Spasso, Marc and I are meeting there at 6:30. You can add two to our reservation if you want."

"Ok, maybe we will; I'll see what Sarah thinks. Bye now."

After Sam left, Rory stayed later in the office than usual. Of course, there really was no *usual* for her, each day dictated its own limits. She might as well stay until it was time to meet Marc for dinner. She looked forward to their date, and the fact that he'd gone out of his way to give them some time together. She thought she might actually be able to tell him tonight about the baby.

After Sam had left, as far as she knew, Forsythe was the only other person in the office. That made her a bit uncomfortable so she decided to leave early and maybe do some window shopping before dinner.

She went into her bathroom, to check her makeup before she left. Reapplying lipstick, she ruffled her hair, and decided she was ready.

As she opened her office door, she heard loud voices coming from Forsythe's office.

At first she just heard snippets of the conversation, which was evidently about a paycheck.

Then she heard distinctly, "I don't give a fuck about this job, I just want my money!"

Before the door slammed shut, she heard whistling.

Rory had an immediate flashback to the day of the murder. That was the same whistling she'd heard before the door closed. Oh my God! The bogeyman had just left.

Without thinking, she quickly slipped out the front door and ran to her car. She grabbed her cell and speed dialed Roland. It went to voicemail, dammit! But she left a quick message, "Roland, I know who the bogeyman is and he just left my office, I'm following him!"

She watched as he got into a car, one she'd never seen, parked conveniently several cars ahead of her. Rory waited a few moments, until two cars were behind him, to pull out into traffic.

***

Roland had been on the office phone with a lengthy call from another State Trooper when Rory's call came in. He got off quickly and then listened to Rory's message.

Shit! She was going after the bogeyman! He was glad he'd put a bug on her car, so he would be able to follow her on his GPS. He just hoped he wasn't too late. The trooper got into his cruiser; he'd decided it was best to go official, in case he needed to get cars out of the way in a hurry. He got out his phone and activated the GPS. Rory's car was traveling slowly, as it headed out of Media. It looked as if she was going in the direction of Baltimore Pike, but then she turned sharply to the right. There must be a roadblock on the pike, Roland surmised, so they would take back roads. It would take him a while to reach her. He hoped she had Marc's gun.

***

One of Herrera's men discovered the bogeyman's car on Jefferson St., inside someone's open garage. He and his partner got out of their unmarked vehicle and slowly walked towards the house closest to the car, with their hands on their Glocks.

A black woman with a baby in her arms answered the door, looking surprised.

The first officer flashed his badge, "I'm Officer Blake, and this is my partner, Lieutenant Hooper. Do you mind if we come in?"

"Can you tell me what this is about?" she asked.

"That car, parked in your garage. Do you know who owns it?"

"My car is in the garage, that light green Dodge?"

"Ma'am, want to come out ant take a look?"

She walked out onto the porch where she could see the car. Her jaw dropped, "That's not my car!"

"So, I guess you didn't see any strangers hanging around, didn't hear anything?" Officer Blake asked.

"No," she said, "I've been busy with my grandbaby. I didn't notice anyone around, but I thought I heard a car start up a while ago."

"So, that must've been your car?" the officer asked.

"Well, it must've been, because that sure isn't my car! But, how, where could it be?"

"My guess is the man who left his car in the garage, is a man we've been pursuing. Looks like he hotwired your car and left his!"

She went to the kitchen to check for her keys, and showed them to the officers. "I guess he must've done, since my keys are here."

"Can we see your owner's card and can you give a description of the car?"

"Why sure," she said, putting the baby in her high chair. "Now where did I put it?" she muttered to herself, looking through her purse. "I try not to leave it in the car, in case it's stolen, well, I guess it has been. So I'm glad I didn't leave it there. Where else, could I have put it? Oh, here it is, in a special case." She handed it to the officer.

"Ok, this gives us the plate number, and it's a green, '96 Dodge?" Officer Blake asked as he wrote down the information.

"Yes, that's right. Do you think I'll get my car back, Officer?"

"I damn sure hope so, pardon my language. And I hope the bogeyman's still in it," he said.

"Oh my God!" Ms. Jones exclaimed, as the officers thanked her and left.

She closed the door and sank back into it, as the reality hit her. Well, she thought, he sure was nice to us. But she was a bit spooked, thinking of what he might've done.

***

Rory was beginning to think he'd spotted her, and was now leading her on a merry chase. She understood why he'd avoided Baltimore Pike, because it was evident there was a roadblock. So, Herrera must be onto him, or was he just being proactive? She hoped someone was out there to give her backup. And surely Roland had gotten her message by now, she thought worriedly.

She'd just followed him into Ridley Creek State Park, not the bike trail entrance, but a different one, a more remote entrance, with which she wasn't especially familiar. The park office was closed, and she assumed the rangers had gone for the day. She was fighting panic as she stayed farther back from the green car, at the same time noticing that the cramping was back, and hurting more than ever.

As she made the turn onto an even more deserted road, Rory noticed the green car had vanished. Well, fuck it, she thought, this would be a good time to leave. As she prepared to execute a u-turn, her car stuttered and then stopped. Shit! The Prius never ran out of gas, she thought as she tried to remember when she'd last filled it. Then she noticed that the yellow warning light was on: "low fuel" it said. No shit! She grabbed her cell, and saw that she had no service this far into the park. She was fucked, and she was scared. Her one ace was Marc's gun, in the glove box, and the other was the assurance that Roland would not fail her.

Chapter 70

Marc had been sitting at Spasso for the last twenty-minutes. He'd tried Rory's cell, and her office phone, and got only voicemail. He was pissed! But a small part of his brain registered concern. He knew she was working on a difficult case with a dangerous perp, and he'd known her to go after suspects before. His anger turned to fear. What would he do if he lost her? Marc couldn't tolerate the thought. He decided to call Roland, believing if anyone knew where she was and what she was up to, he would.

***

Detective Herrera was pacing when Officer Scott arrived with a sleepy Carly. Both of them looked wonderful, the detective thought. He hugged them. "Looks like that mountain air was good for you!" he said.

"That and a nice clean lake to frolic in. By the way, Carly learned to swim in a few hours. She's a little fish now," Erin praised the girl.

Herrera noticed the pride on Carly's face mirrored the look on Erin's. He was happy for both of them. He hated to bring them down by talking business, but it had to happen.

Erin, who knew him well, said, "Carly has made a decision that should help us find the bogeyman." She looked over at Carly.

The girl straightened her shoulders, and cleared her throat. Then she said to the detective, "I decided that my so-called friend wasn't really my friend, because he poisoned my dog and asked me to lie. He was in the lineup; I just picked the wrong man on purpose." She looked down.

Herrera walked to her and leaned over to tell her something. "You know, it takes a very brave person to tell the truth and admit a lie. Thank you, Carly."

She looked up immediately and smiled at the detective, her face beaming. "That's what my Mama said, too."

"So, can you show me the pictures?" Carly asked.

Herrera wasted no time complying.

***

Trooper Johnson entered the state park, and noticed that his GPS was a little slower. He hadn't expected to lose or have partial service in the park. The trees were dense and cell towers weren't close. His cell rang, but he lost service before he could answer it. Maybe it was from Rory, but would her phone get service in here? He wondered. Looking at the missed calls, he saw the call wasn't from Rory, it was from Marc. He drove until he had 2 bars of service. Then he hit the redial option and soon got Marc.

"Roland, thank God you called! I can't find Rory and she was supposed to meet me for dinner a half hour ago. Do you know anything?"

He hated to have to tell Marc that, yes, he knew even though she hadn't told her husband. "Marc, I'm on it. She thinks she knows who the bogeyman is and went off to follow him. I've got her on GPS, and we're in the State Park."

"Where in the park? That place is thousands of acres!"

"I'm at the stables, still tracking her. I'll let you know when I find her."

"On my way!" Marc answered.

***

Rory's car was stifling with the windows closed and no access to AC. She was able to lower her window on battery power. There wasn't exactly a breeze, but it was cooler outside of her car. Maybe she could get out and look around. She reached over to the glove box to get Marc's gun. Before she could open the box, she heard a crunching sound as if someone was approaching her car on foot.

As she turned towards the window, the bogeyman was staring her in the face.

"Get out of the car!" he demanded. "Now! I'm not playin' here!" He reached in to pull her from the car, because the door was locked.

Without even thinking about it, Rory automatically hit the close button for the window. He got one hand free, but the other one was held tightly. Rory took her finger off the button, fearing that it could cut his arm off, not that he didn't deserve it. He was screaming bloody murder, and somehow got to his weapon with his other hand.

He aimed at her, but she kept moving, and finally managed to get Marc's gun out of the box.

A voice from behind the bogeyman, said, "Rory, let him go, I got him now, and I've been waiting a long time!"

Rory looked and saw Rowe. "He's got a gun, Mason!"

"Let him go," Rowe repeated.

"If you're sure," Rory said, releasing the window lock, and getting out of the car on the other side, gun in hand.

"What, you're going to take my gun from me? Let me wait until you are in position to do so. I want you to look like a hero," said the bogeyman, egging him on.

Rowe knocked the gun from the other man's hand and grabbed him by the throat. "You mother fuckin' son of a bitch, Quinn, it's payback time." He slugged him until Quinn fell, and then he kicked him. "You might have saved my life once, but then you tried to destroy it by hurting my innocent baby!"

Rory watched, spellbound, but horrified. Rowe was slamming Quinn's head into the ground.

"Mason, stop! He's not worth it, just stop! I've got a gun. Let him go!" Rory pleaded. "The troopers will be here soon."

They both heard the siren at the same time, and Rowe let Quinn's head slam to the ground, while Rory trained her gun on him.

She looked up for just a second when she heard the car arrive. In that split second, Quinn got up and took off for the woods.

"I got him!" Roland yelled as he jumped from his cruiser and took off, weapon in hand. He ran in hot pursuit, with Rowe right behind him.

"Stop or I'll shoot!" Roland warned, as the man continued to fight his way through the brambles. Rowe and the trooper were gaining on him as he continued to plod forward.

Rory, losing sight of the men, heard another car arrive. It was the sheriffs. The two burly men got out of the car, asking Rory, "You seen Rowe? He went off the grid. We gotta' take him in."

"Oh, I don't think so, Sheriff, he's with Trooper Johnson, trying to catch the real bogeyman!"

Chapter 71

The sheriffs got lost in the shuffle, as more troopers arrived with two ambulances behind them.

The place was a madhouse, Rory thought as she trained her eyes on the woods, looking for any movement.

As she stood there watching, she noticed a sticky feeling between her legs. She assumed it was sweat, because the car had been so hot. She also chose not to notice that the cramping had increased.

Other troopers followed the trail into the woods to provide backup for Johnson. Within minutes, Roland came out with Quinn, who was cuffed. Rowe emerged behind him, bruised and cut up, but looking satisfied.

The sheriffs came over to Rowe to take him into custody. Trooper Johnson said to them, “Not so fast! This man tracked down the bogeyman and helped me bring him in.”

When Rowe had followed Rory, he’d left the bracelet on intentionally, thinking the sheriffs might come in handy.

“It’s a formality, Trooper. We have to take him in and have the bracelet removed, if the DA agrees. We can’t make that call.”

Trooper Johnson next addressed the other troopers. Referring to Quinn, he said, “This man must be guarded carefully. You can take him to the hospital for treatment, but you both must remain with him at all times. Understood?”

“Yes, sir!” they answered.

“Then, get on with it.”

Roland found Rory standing next to the car. She looked none too steady, and as he walked over to her he noticed her bloodstained pants.

”Rory, have you been shot?” He cried, looking at the blood that had leaked through her pants. He signaled to the ambulance. “Get the EMT’s over here!”

For the first time, she looked down, her legs buckling beneath her. Roland caught her before she hit the ground. "Were you shot?" he asked again.

"No, Roland," she said trembling and tearful, "I think I just lost the baby."

He put his arms around her and held tight until the EMT's arrived, and got her on a stretcher. Roland informed them of her condition. "Take her to Crozier," he said, "and call Dr. Flynn."

He didn't want to be the one to tell Marc. He'd already been in on too many secrets that Marc didn't know.

***

Marc was on his way to the park, going on instinct, but hoping he could find Rory. He heard sirens behind him and pulled over, watching as two ambulances whizzed by him, nearly deafening him. Oh my God! Did something happen to Rory? Was she shot? His worst fears almost immobilized him, but he soon sped up, following the flashing lights.

They entered the State Park, and he was on their bumpers. He kept pace as they blazed through the mostly deserted roads in the park. They were going deep into the interior of the park, places Marc had been unaware of, despite the many times he'd been there.

Making a right turn, the ambulance came to a stop. There were already other ambulances and several troopers at the site, not to mention the news vans, which were just beginning to arrive.

Marc got out of his car and looked for someone he knew. He didn't see Roland, so he went up to one of the troopers. "Excuse me, sir, is Trooper Johnson here?"

"No, he's not. And you are?"

"I'm Marc Chandler, and my wife should be here somewhere."

"Uh, I think they just loaded her into the first ambulance, I'll take you to her."

Marc walked unsteadily behind the trooper until they reached the ambulance. The back doors were still open, and the trooper approached. "Hey guys, this is Mr. Chandler, the woman's husband. Can he see her?"

"Yes, ok, come on in, then we need to leave. We're taking her to Crozier."

Marc had just a moment to assure himself that she'd be ok. He kissed her and told her he loved her. Then he asked the EMT's, "Was she shot?"

"No, she wasn't, but she's losing blood so we gotta' go!"

Marc walked back to his car in a daze, and positioned the car so he could follow the ambulance.

***

Sarah was making dinner and half listening to the news on the TV. She and Sam had decided to dine at home so she could resume studying after dinner.

Suddenly her attention shifted to the TV, there was a breaking news story. The bogeyman had been caught! They showed scenes from the State Park, where he was apparently apprehended. And they showed a woman being lifted into the ambulance. It looked like Rory!

"Sam!" she shouted, "Come here! "

He raced into the room to see if she'd started a fire and saw her transfixed, watching the TV.

"They got the bogeyman, and Rory went to the hospital! I think they took her to Crozier, we've gotta' go!

"Isn't that where Katrina works?" Sam asked. "Let's call Blake, he may know something."

He picked up his cell, but before he could make a call, it buzzed. "It's Blake!" he told Sarah as he answered.

"Hey, Blake, yeah, we just heard it on the news! Do you know if Rory was taken to Crozier? Yeah?" He listened. "So there's no news about what happened to her? OK, we're on our way, see you there!"

Sarah, having heard Sam's conversation, said, "What do they think happened to Rory?"

"Blake said it's all hush-hush, no one really knows. I wonder if Marc knows, he was supposed to meet Rory for dinner in Media tonight. Why don't you call him while I drive?" Sam said as they left the house.

***

Dara got a call from Mason. She hadn't watched the news, because she'd been shopping with Rachel, and had just arrived at her house.

"Dara, are you home?"

"Yes, Mason, we just got in, what's up?"

"If you have to ask, I guess you haven't seen the news, I'm a free man!"

Dara sank into the closest chair, momentarily speechless. "You, you, *what*?"

"We caught the bogeyman, Rory, the trooper and me, we ran him down!"

"Where are you now?'

"I'm at the Sheriff's office; they just took the ankle bracelet off. The DA came over to make sure they did it. He'd called the President Judge, and he okayed it. Can you pick me up at the courthouse? My car's still at the park."

"Sure, I'll be right there! The park?" she asked, confused.

"It's a long story, and I'll tell it all when I see you."

***

Don and Hayley were having dinner and watching the news. They were talking and not really listening, until the breaking news was announced. Then they both turned to the TV, riveted.

"The State Police have confirmed they've taken into custody the alleged pedophile, commonly referred to as 'the bogeyman.'" Hayley shouted.

"Holy shit!" Don said.

"We need to hurry," Hayley said. "I need to get the story!"

"Call your editor, tell her you're on it," Don said.

***

An older model green Dodge was found hidden in the trees in the park. One of the troopers ran the plates and found it had been stolen. They found no keys in the ignition; the car had been hot-wired. They would dust it for prints, as it was probably driven by the suspect. It was no big deal, at least they knew who the owner was, and the car didn't seem to be damaged.

Chapter 72

Marc followed the ambulance as closely as he could, but since he knew the way, he wasn't worried about losing them. He was, however, worried about losing Rory. He'd seen so much blood, but they'd told him she hadn't been shot. He just needed to see her, talk to her, and hold her. Please God, let her be ok. He repeated the phrase over and over again in his head.

When they arrived at Crozier, Rory was whisked into the ER, and Marc hurriedly parked and caught up with the EMT's, tagging along like an uninvited guest. As soon as she was in a cubicle, he was called to the front desk to provide medical information. Fortunately, he could do that. He spent the next twenty minutes signing her life away, not taking the time to read all of the medical jargon, which took up space and said nothing. It was all CYA stuff, and God knew they could be sued anyway, so why bother.

When he'd turned in the last page, he started to go back to the room where he'd left Rory. The nurse at the desk said, "Mr. Chandler, your wife has gone up to surgery. You can go to the waiting room on the third floor."

"Can you tell me what happened to her, why she's in surgery?" he asked, desperate for any news.

"I'm sorry, I'm not authorized to give that information. You'll have to ask her doctor."

"Who happens to be in surgery as we speak!" Marc's voice began to rise. "You mean after all those forms I signed, that doesn't give you authorization to tell me what the hell happened to my wife?"

Just then, Alex and Kate came through the door, and behind them Sam, Sarah, and Blake. They accurately assessed the situation, and went to Marc, circling around him like a protective armada.

"Where's Mom, Dad?" Kate asked.

"She's in surgery, that's all I know," he said, glaring at the nurse. "We have to go to the waiting room on the third floor. Her doctor will come out after surgery."

"Then, let's go up to the third floor!" Sarah suggested. Then she whispered to Marc, "Before security throws us out."

Marc smiled for the first time and said, "Let's go!"

***

Mason and Dara had finished dinner and put Rachel to bed. Mason had the honor of reading three books to the child before she fell asleep. She was so excited to have Mason home that it took some time for her to settle.

They had just sat down in the living room, when the phone rang. Mason went to answer it.

"Do we have to?" Dara asked.

"I think I should," he said. "It's time to set the record straight."

It was Hayley on the phone asking if she could come over for an interview. "Yes, you can. If you'll give us an hour or so to get reacquainted, I'll be happy to spill it."

He turned off the phone before he returned to Dara's side.

"You heard what I said. I bought us an hour. And Hayley's the only one who gets my story."

***

It was quiet at the Scott household. Erin and Carly were exhausted after the trip home, talking to the detective, and unpacking. Carly had fallen asleep before she'd finished reading her Ramona book.

Erin sat with a glass of wine, waiting for Marilyn Hunter to arrive. When Sgt. Pepper barked, Erin went to the door, and looked through the peephole. Seeing Marilyn alone, she opened the door, and then locked it behind her.

"I've become super-conscious of security for some reason," Erin said.

"Well, yeah!" Marilyn said. "Haven't we all? Maybe we can stop being so paranoid now. It's hard to believe they caught him, and Carly was a big part of that."

"Yes, she was, and she's ok with that. It's good to be home, but we had a fabulous time at the cabin in the mountains, Carly loved it! Anyway, I asked you here to talk about adoption. I have no doubts about going through with it. I just wonder how long it might take?"

***

Herrera and his staff were working overtime. But there was a celebratory atmosphere in the office. The bogeyman had been caught, positively identified, and all of the prints and DNA matched. The mountain of paperwork that remained was a pain, but it was important to tie the case up tight. There would be no dismissal of the charges because of sloppy police work, Herrera would see to that.

He answered the phone on the second ring. “Trooper Johnson, thanks for calling. We’ll have to get together, maybe tomorrow and compare notes.”

“Yeah, I don’t mind working on Saturday after a spectacular closing of this case. I just called to tell you that Quinn is at the prison and in seclusion. That’s the safest place for him and the other prisoners. Once he’s found guilty and sentenced, he needs to go to a very secure prison for a long time.”

“I agree with you there, Johnson. We’re working overtime to make sure we dot every i and cross every t. We can’t give him a way out. You know the President Judge who presided over Rowe’s trial has found him ‘Not Guilty’. The verdict came through pretty quick.”

“I know Rory had a feeling he’d rule in their favor. She’ll be pretty happy when she hears.”

“How’s she doing?”

“She should be coming out of surgery right about now,” Johnson said. “I think she’ll be ok.”

***

After an hour of anxious waiting, the door of the operating room opened, and Dr. Flynn walked out. She walked straight to Marc, taking him aside. “I heard you were raising hell in the ER downstairs, so I hurried to you as soon as I could.”

This brought the smile she’d hoped for. “Well, maybe a little. No one would tell me anything. But now you’re here. How’s Rory?”

“Rory will be fine. I would rather she be the one to tell you, but you’ve been waiting a long time. Rory was in her first trimester of pregnancy.” She let him digest that before she went on. His jaw dropped. “I know she never told you and she would be the best person to address that. But before you leap to conclusions, it was not her fault that she lost the baby. The fetus was not viable. I’m assuming she was using the diaphragm, and one of the sperm got through the physical barrier, but not without encountering spermicide. So the sperm, although able to fertilize the egg, was defective, and the fetus wouldn't have made it. It was just a matter of time. I'm sorry, that's a lot to dump on you, but I thought you should know."

Marc stood still, mulling over what he'd just heard, his face drained of color. Then he said, "Thank you, Sally. I appreciate it. And I'm actually relieved; I thought she might've been shot. There was so much blood! And it's hard to think about losing the baby, because I never knew there was one. When do you think I can see Rory?"

"I'll give you her room number, and you can go there and wait. She'll be kept overnight, just to make sure she doesn't lose any more blood and to get her on an IV antibiotic. I would guess she'll be taken to her room within the hour."

Marc walked over to his support team. "Look, why don't you guys go home, since it will be a while before she's taken to her room. They're keeping her overnight for observation. Dr. Flynn assures me she'll be fine. You know how hard she's been working since she got out of the hospital a few weeks ago. She was suffering from exhaustion."

No one seemed eager to leave, so Marc said, "Look, I really appreciate your concern, but I'm assured she'll be fine. I expect to be home later tonight, so she can get her sleep."

Sam was all business, saying, "Ok guys, let's get on the road. I'm glad to hear she'll be all right."

They got up to follow Sam. Kate and Alex stopped to give their dad a kiss, and then they all left.

***

Sam and Sarah were driving Kate and Alex home. Blake had stayed at the hospital to wait until Katrina got off.

It was quiet in the car as Sam drove.

"I don't think Dad told us everything," Kate said, her voice trembling.

"I agree he's keeping something from us," Alex said.

"Maybe he needs to talk to your mom first," Sarah offered, only to have her head bitten off.

"It's not like we're little kids who can't handle things!" Kate said. "We've been through some shit."

Sarah withheld any further comments. Sam, too, was quiet.

"Well," Alex said, "he said he'd be home later, so maybe he'll tell us then."

"I doubt it!" Kate said, her jaw tight.

"Well, we could wait inside the door and ambush him as soon as he walks through the door!" Alex said, trying for some levity.

Kate said, "We've tried that before, maybe when we were ten!"

"Well, if he treats us like kids we get to act like kids!" Kate said, sounding pleased.

Sam and Sarah exchanged a quick look, with eyebrows raised.

***

Marc was nearing the end of his already frayed patience, when finally two nurses rolled the gurney into the room. Rory was awake, but looking pale and drawn. She tried to smile at Marc, but couldn't quite carry it off.

The nurses settled Rory into her bed and left the room, saying, "Hit the call button if you need a nurse."

Marc smiled at Rory and said, "I'm all too familiar with call buttons."

He went to her side, and said, "How are you Rory? I've been worried." He kissed her forehead and looked lovingly at her. "While I was following the ambulance to the park today, I feared the worst, and then no one would tell me anything. Thank God you're all right! I'm still getting used to the idea that you were pregnant. But what happened sure beats a gunshot wound."

Rory smiled through her tears. "And now you know. Can you forgive me for not telling you?" Her eyes searched his.

"I can. After what I was imagining, as I said, this is not a big deal."

"I tried to tell you so many times, but other stuff kept coming up. That's not an excuse, by the way. I thought tonight at dinner would be a good time, but…"

"Did Sally tell you what happened?"

"What do you mean? I lost the baby, surely that's all."

"No, there's more. The fetus was never going to make it. It wasn't your fault you lost the baby."

"She didn't tell me that, at least I don't remember. She was talking to me in the recovery room, but I don't remember any of it. So what did happen?"

Marc did his best to relay what Sally had said.

Rory smiled, and then she started crying. Marc patted whatever he could of her body, which was still wired.

When she could speak, she said, "I was ambivalent about the baby, I just couldn't decide whether or not I wanted it. I thought my carelessness brought this about. It's a relief to know that it was always out of my hands."

"Yes, but it's good to know that my boys are still swimming! And that we can conceive at our age!"

"Our age? Really, Marc, I know some women in their early forties who are just starting their families. We're not in the dark ages!"

"I'm not sure I could go through all that again!" Marc said. "I thank God that we've been lucky with our twins, for the most part," he emphasized for Rory's sake. "I'm kind of looking forward to being what they call 'empty nesters'."

***

The girls were sitting in the nook when Marc got home. It was late, but tomorrow was Saturday. He'd discussed with Rory what to say to the twins, so he was ready for them.

Epilogue

September

Official opening of Chandler and Associates

Attorneys at Law

Rory and her family were getting ready for her big day, the opening of the beautifully completed and expanded office which would accommodate Rory and her three newly-minted attorneys, who had all passed the bar on the first go- round. She was pleased, but not surprised they'd done it; she knew how smart they all were.

As usual in the Chandler household, things were hurried and disorganized. Rory herself didn't know what to wear. She'd already tried and discarded three outfits. It was too late now to go out and buy something. Rory knew her strong suit was not planning ahead. Now she called for Alex. "Alex! I need help!"

Alex took her time heeding her mother's cry for help. Then she came sauntering in like they were getting ready for a day at the beach.

Saying nothing, Alex went to Rory's closet. She looked in and grimaced. "The only problem is that I'm not seeing anything suitable…"

"Great, well, it's a bit late to go out shopping now!" Rory moaned.

"Not my fault," Alex began, "wait, I think I have it! How about this?" she asked bringing out a teal suit, with a purple crepe blouse.

"Oh," Rory said, looking at it carefully. "I do like the color combination, good work! Do I need any jewelry?" she asked.

"A simple strand of pearls would do it," Alex said decisively. "And pearl earrings, if you have them."

"Yes, to both," Rory answered. "Thanks, Honey, I really do depend on your fashion advice!"

"You're welcome!" Alex answered, with a flush of pride on her face. Then she said, "I think I'll wear jeans!"

Rory didn't flinch. She'd given up the need to tell her daughters what to wear. "Fine, Alex," Rory said, meaning it.

"I was kidding, Mom!" Alex said, grinning.

"Oh, but it really is ok with me, if that's what you want to wear," she said.

"I think I can do a bit better for your 'grand opening.' I wouldn't want to embarrass you!"

"You seldom do, Alex, I trust you!"

Kate, passing the open door remarked, "You trust Alex? Is that the outfit she chose for you?" She was clearly looking for an argument.

"Yes, it is, Kate. Do you have another choice?" Rory asked sweetly, as Alex glared at Kate.

"Well, I might, but you never ask me," Kate huffed.

"It's the first I've heard of your interest," Rory said. "I don't have time for another choice today, but any time you want to give me a hand, I'm open to it."

"Ok, good," Kate said, with a hint of sarcasm in her voice. "I'll leave you to finish up."

"I like your outfit, Kate," Rory said.

"This old thing?" Kate shrugged, as she left the room.

Rory and Alex exchanged amused glances. "I'd best dig up something," Alex said as she left the room.

A few minutes later, Marc hurried into their bedroom. "Do I have time for a shower?" he asked.

"A quick one," Rory replied, "but if you're not ready to go by eleven thirty, we can take separate cars."

"Girls ready?" he asked as he peeled off his clothes.

"Readier than you!" Rory laughed, smacking his naked bottom.

Quick to respond, Marc said, "Oh, you want a little action, huh?"

"Sorry, no time," Rory said sweetly. "Better get your buns in the shower!"

"What should I wear?" he asked on the way to the bathroom.

"Oh Jeez, ask Alex!" Rory answered as she zipped up her skirt and straightened her blouse. Then she went in search of her pearls.

***

Rory and family were at the offices just as the caterers pulled up. *Perfect timing*, Rory thought.

She unlocked the office, and directed the servers to the tables that had been set up the day before. They were, of course, set up in the new wing, which Rory believed was perfect. She'd been pleasantly surprised at how well the offices had turned out.

Marc, Alex, and Kate came in behind Rory and began exploring the new offices.

Rory, who was busy directing the caterers, was surprised when her brother Sean, and his visibly pregnant wife, Ginny appeared at the entrance.

"Ginny! Sean! So glad you could make it." Taking Ginny aside, she said, "You look wonderful and I hope you're feeling better."

"Much better," Ginny replied, sounding relieved. "I guess it's true that the first trimester is the roughest, in terms of nausea. It was like it stopped overnight! And the ultrasounds have all been normal, thank God!"

"Do you know the baby's gender yet?" Rory inquired.

"I didn't ask, but if I get curious, I can find out."

Rory's parents were just behind her brother and his wife. "Mom, Dad! So glad you could come," Rory enthused.

"We had to see for ourselves that you are really okay," Rory's father said, tearing up and giving her a hug.

"You know how your father worries," her mother told Rory, but she, too had tears in her eyes, as she reached for her daughter.

Rory knew they were talking about her first hospitalization, since they didn't know about the second.

Marc came over after he'd toured the new space. He greeted his in-laws warmly and said to Ginny and Sean, "Congratulations! Ginny, you look great! So happy for you guys."

Rory took Marc aside as the twins swarmed their grandparents and their aunt and uncle. She whispered, "I think I can be quite happy as an aunt to their baby." She smiled and squeezed his hand.

People began drifting in, and Rory went to greet them. Marc stepped in behind her, listening to their names, so he could welcome them, too.

Rory's former partner Charlie Laws and his wife were some of the first to arrive. Charlie whistled as he looked around, "Wow! Hardly recognize the place, nice job! I see you still have the desk I left you."

"Renovations or no, I'm keeping that desk, Charlie, it's one of my prized possessions!"

Beaming, Charlie said, "I'm happy for you to have it."

"Help yourselves to some food," Rory said as she moved on, greeting newcomers.

Sam and Sarah entered, followed by Sarah's father and his fiancée, Geneva. Rory welcomed them warmly and said, "Congratulations on your engagement!" as she embraced Geneva and shook the judge's hand. They made a stunning couple, Rory thought.

Blake and Katrina came in with Dara and Mason, who seemed to be overflowing with happiness.

She saw Marilyn Hunter enter, with her boyfriend, she figured. Marilyn looked around the room, and made a beeline for Mason.

Mason was standing with Dara, when Marilyn came up and whispered in his ear, "You're my hero!" Then she gave him a hug.

Dara recognized her from the waiting room at the therapist's and nodded, smiling. She whispered, to Mason, "I know you'll tell me all about that."

"You bet," he said, smiling. "There's a lot to talk about!"

Rory had watched the interchange take place and thought she knew what it was about.

Before she knew it, the place was packed and she couldn't possibly welcome everyone. She moved around the room, making sure people were, eating, talking, or exploring.

Rory welcomed Don and Hayley, who definitely appeared to be 'a couple'. She was happy for them.

She found Detective Herrera in one of the new offices, and she stopped to talk with him.

"So," she asked, "Are you happy to have this one off the books?"

"Happy to have it solved, finally. And perhaps Quinn will feel like talking soon. So far he hasn't been 'up to it.' But it doesn't matter; we have enough evidence to convict. By the way, the office looks great!"

Forsythe and his wife, Joie, entered. Rory went up to them and said, "Ah, the man of the hour; you and your team did a wonderful job!"

"Thanks, Rory," Forsythe said, shaking her hand and holding it a moment longer. "I'm going to give it the final inspection," he said, walking off.

Joie took Rory aside and said, "I just wanted to tell you that this may be his last job. You may have noticed his obsessive behavior…anyway, he has early-onset Alzheimer's, and he wants to leave while he can still enjoy his life."

Rory's face fell as she realized why he'd been so annoying. "I'm so sorry," she said to Joie.

"Thank you, Rory. And thanks for putting up with his inconsistent behavior. I'm sure it couldn't have been easy for you."

"It all makes sense now," Rory admitted. "And he led the team that did this wonderful construction."

Rory excused herself to circulate, and urged people to eat. She didn't have time to eat, herself, but she could wait until it was over, and she expected to have plenty of leftovers.

When it appeared as though everyone had eaten at least one plate of food, Rory asked the servers to open the champagne and start passing glasses around.

Rory went to the mike and called Forsythe over. "I'd like everyone to raise your glasses in a toast to Chad Forsythe, the person responsible for pulling off this wonderful renovation! And to the entire Citadel staff! And to my new partners: Sarah Justice, Sam Logan, and Blake Ford, who've passed the bar, and will fill those new offices."

They lifted their glasses and drank, and then gave thunderous applause.

Forsythe asked Rory for the mike. "Thank you all for your well wishes. I have an announcement to make." Everyone looked around in surprise.

"Don't worry, your jobs are safe!" he smiled. "But you will all be getting a raise, which I'll discuss with each of you."

"I'm also happy to announce Mason Rowe, if he accepts the offer, will be promoted to Director of Citadel. I think we are fortunate to have him at Citadel and I look forward to working with him in a different capacity. Please lift your glasses to Mason Rowe!"

Before she lifted her glass, Dara whispered in Mason's ear, "I'm pregnant!"

With a huge grin on his face, Mason said, "I accept with pleasure!" and raised his glass.

THE END

About the Author

Jacquelyn Bishop lives in Media, a charming, small Victorian town within commuting distance of Philadelphia. The Rory Chandler Mysteries, her first three books, are centered in Media.

Though her formal training, both at the bachelor and masters levels, is in the Social Services, her life-long dream has been to be an author.

She writes first thing in the morning, thus her company name, Early Riser Publishing. Jacki finds that writing is a full-time occupation. She does, however, find time to spend with her granddaughter, Lilia, awarded twice as a "Young Author" winner. Hiking, Zumba, travel, and cuddling her cats consume her time when not writing.

www.ingramcontent.com/pod-product-compliance
Lightning Source LLC
Chambersburg PA
CBHW071058250626
47159CB00002B/507
9780990531517